The Orphan's King Copyright 2025 © C.R.R. Hillin

Cover art by Drazenka Kimpel from Creative Dust

Cover Design by Dar Albert at Wicked Smart Designs

Maps by Jeppe Lindrup Mygh

Published by Oliver-Heber Books

0 9 8 7 6 5 4 3 2 1

THE ORPHAN'S KING

C.R.R. HILLIN

I would never have gotten this far without the people who read this book when I was a total nobody and loved and supported the hell out of it. And now people want to spend actual money on it? My book? In this economy? I'm truly honored.

This book was 19 years in the making. It carries a piece of my soul. Maybe all of it. I'm pretty sure if someone stabs my annotated copy with a magic sword I'll become mortal.

It's only fitting that a lot of the book carries my touch as well. So I made a special request to my amazing publishing team to let me design the chapter headings and title page.

So this book is for you, the person reading this right now. You're the reason this is all happening. You're the glue that holds this all together. And no matter who you are, or if you picked up copy #5 or #5 million, I will appreciate you with all my heart.

Go live lives that would make an asshole king burn you at the stake. <3

CONTENT ADVISORY:

This series is about characters who have been through some stuff and live in a very different world and time from ours. It deals with a lot of heavy themes including death, loss and grief, mental illness, suicide, abuse and child abuse, PTSD, and the death and loss of children. These characters also live in a very sexist, homophobic, and bigoted world.

The story may trigger those with a history of abuse or suicidal ideation. Please take care of yourself and don't read anything that will endanger your mental health. I would never wish that on anyone. If you have any specific questions or want page numbers, you are always welcome to contact me. Please visit www.theorphanscode.com for the content warnings for the entire series.

This book contains the following sensitive or graphic content:

Torture
Violence and Gore
Death
Strong Language
Nonconsensual Behavior
Domestic Violence
Consensual Sexuality
Emetophobia

Police Violence
Ableist, bigoted, racist, or offensive language
Alcohol and Drug Use
Discussions of sensitive topics such as slavery, prostitution, war, child abuse, suicide, and self-harm.

The City of
BERMEIA

SEAT
OF THE
CONQUEROR

Sea of Ice

Isles of Myvanwy

Coraln

Anapolno

Courma

Whatelop Mts

Raella
Roni

Kypris

Lyria
Roni

Lyrma

Lakmath
Roni

Cordia

The Great Sea

N
W   E
S

Aradela Ta'wan
Roni

Lithal
Roni

Sarrhana

i

The Deeps
Fiachlan Mts
Ghealach
Ostia
Savilla
Fairwater Strait
Aldaeza
Mirrormere
Yazmin
Antigua
Arrow's Pass
Sivenne
Vazur
Khal' Aleen
White Pier
Seareach

"*They deserved it.*"

It was then that Romero knew he was dealing with a madman.

Oh, there had been signs. Plenty of signs. Who else but a madman could survive days in his dungeons without breaking? He was barely more than a boy, but he'd outlasted every other prisoner Romero had ever put under the knife.

The boy looked up at Romero with dark eyes that burned beneath his matted hair. "They deserved it," he said again. "An' so will *you.*"

And then his head sank back onto his chest, breaking the spell of his burning eyes. Romero stepped back. His heart raced as if he'd just outrun death itself. He struggled to keep his voice smooth.

"You confess, then? To the assassination of—"

"Assassination," the boy cut across him with a scoff.

It galled Romero to allow a peasant to interrupt him—but he bit his tongue. He wanted to see where this would lead.

"Na' an *assassination,*" the boy continued. His voice rasped like a rusted hinge beneath his Courman brogue. If not for the faint scar Romero had noticed on his throat, he might have thought the boy was doing it on purpose, trying to intimidate him. Intentional or not, the effect was unsettling. "They weren't important 'nuff fer that. I slaugh'ered 'em like th' pigs they was."

"And I was next."

The boy made a funny rasping sound. It took Romero a moment

to realize that he was laughing. "N'am bei nan skei, m'leihaan eisbahn cruaidh...," he murmured.

Romero knew the adage. *If wishes were fishes, we'd all have full bellies.*

"Bold of you," he said drily.

He trailed a finger along the row of instruments laid carefully on a table beside him. Blades, pliers, needles. They were sharpened and polished to a shine—those that weren't splattered with gore. It was a collection that would make any man quake in his boots.

He chose a pair of pliers and turned back to the boy. "I'd applaud your cleverness, but you and I both know you didn't do this alone."

"Ah, we do, do we?" A smirk curled the boy's mouth. "Or is tha' jus' what you wanna believe? What, are ya sore that *the Beggar's King* is more royalty than you are?"

Romero backhanded the boy across the face. The boy's head snapped back before he slumped again, spitting out a dribble of blood. Then he snickered.

"Sorry, sorry...sore subject....How's ya neck?"

Romero chose to ignore this, swallowing back his fury. *Only a boy,* he reminded himself. Not even twenty and hanging from the ceiling by meat hooks. Three days ago, Romero had thought this would be easy, that he would cave after a sleepless night and a few beatings and lead him to the mastermind hiding behind the whole plot.

Now, with his entire body bruised and broken, the boy was laughing in his face.

One hand rose unconsciously to the jagged wound on the side of his neck before he jerked it away. "Just a scratch," he said lightly. It was a lie. If someone hadn't pressed a red-hot fire poker to the wound, he would have bled to death. "After all those murders, the infamous Beggar's King failed when it mattered the most. Unless," he added, holding the pliers up to the light to study them, "you were *meant* to fail. You don't really think they'd send a scrawny little nobody to kill me?"

"Why no'?" said the boy, grinning with bloodied teeth. "Ain't that hard, turns out."

"Clearly." Romero raised his eyebrows at the blood streaked down the boy's bare, bony chest, at the ropes on his wrist, at his broken legs. "No, boy—I'm afraid you were tricked. Whoever sent you knew you would never come out alive. And they aren't coming to rescue you. They needed someone disposable to test my defenses. Perhaps..." He raised his eyebrows at the purplish circle branded into the boy's shoulder. "...an orphan?"

The boy coughed. It sounded painful. "Tragic," he rasped.

Romero didn't give up. "So what do you owe these people, really? What's the point of all this pain? I could cut you down right now, you know, and this would all be over. Don't you want a warm bed, a hot meal...?"

"...an' a cold mug o' ale, an' a pretty girl on me knee, an' a song writ about me," the boy mumbled, shaking his head with a bitter laugh. "Righ'?"

"I d—"

"I'm an *orphan,* yeh bloody idiot," the boy cut across him. "I'm na' some soft little lord. I eat rats an' sleep in the gutter. What's next, gold? A title? Ya have *nothin'* that I want."

Romero took another deep breath. *Patience.* "I don't think," he said slowly, "that you quite understand your situation here. If you think your friends are coming to save you—"

"They're no'."

Romero looked up. The boy's head still sagged onto his chest, his body hanging limply from his bonds. But his voice, when he spoke, was clear and strong.

"I have no one," he said. "No one's lookin' for me, no one's comin' for me. No one'll miss me. Ain't nothin' you can offer me." His head rolled, his eyes fixing on Romero's face. "What now?"

"If—"

"Ya want me alive?" He gave a contemptuous chuckle, his chest heaving with the effort. "You'll have t' feed me, let me sleep. Leave me alone. So I can heal. An' then we'll be righ' back where we was...."

Romero sneered. "You want to die? That can be arranged."

The boy chuckled—a cold, scornful sound that sent a chill down Romero's spine. He looked up; their eyes met, and Romero felt a leaden weight drop into his stomach. Those eyes. Cold, calculating, sadistically amused. Eyes that belonged to someone much older.

Someone who had lived the sort of life that turned men into monsters.

He did not doubt that he dealt with a monster now.

"Ya can't hurt me," the boy told him. "No worse 'n anyone else. No worse 'n the soldiers did. No worse 'n me parents did...." He coughed, blood dribbling down his chin. "'S just pain. Worst it can do is kill me...."

Romero watched him for a moment in silence. Then he raised his hand and gestured to his guards. He heard the faint clink of their armor as they saluted.

"Send a message to the captain of the guard," he ordered. "Tell him to send every available squad out to find that other boy. Search *everywhere*. Arrest him as an accomplice to the Beggar's King." He lowered his hand, and behind him, he heard the guard marching away. His eyes met the cold brown gaze of his prisoner.

"If it's so fun and pleasant here," he said softly, "perhaps you'd like your friend to join you."

The boy snorted. "'S been—what? A week?" he said. "Ya won't find him. Ya couldn't find your own arse. Where's this magic group o' *rebels an' anarchists* got ta all o' a sudden? Y' can't go an' find *them?*"

"I don't know where they are," said Romero coldly. "You tell me."

"I told ya everythin' already." The boy lifted his head and stood a little straighter, wincing at the pain it caused him. A fresh wave of blood trickled down the broken scabs of his back where stripes of flesh had been gouged out of his skin with a whip. "I," he said, slowly, deliberately, looking straight into Romero's eyes, "am...the...Beggar's...King. I killed Thomas Salke. I killed Solomon Galen. William Redell. Lucius Carter. Jon Kirke. Me, an' no one but. An' I came here ta kill you. Na' because someone sent me. Because I wanted ta fucking kill you."

He spoke with such force, such strength—such venom—that Romero could summon no response. It was all he could do not to take a step back. He had learned a long time ago how to tell if a man was lying, and this boy....Either every word was true, or he had gone utterly mad. Romero was not sure which prospect was more terrifying.

He started to ask, *why?* Or maybe, *who?* But he caught himself at the last second. Not because there were no answers, but because there were too many. Instead, he asked, "How?"

The boy managed a shrug that sent rivulets of fresh blood spiraling down his arms. "Killin' ain't hard. Stab 'em until they stop movin', then stab 'em some more."

Torture was a sport for Romero, an art form he thought he had perfected. The best negotiators never got their hands dirty. A bit of time, a bit of pressure, and a well-placed threat or two, and most men were more than happy to bare their souls. Only those who resisted went under the knife—or those who had especially irked him. And in the end, without fail, they'd broken.

But not this boy.

It would have been impressive—if it hadn't been so infuriating.

"Tell me who sent you," he said.

The boy's head didn't rise. He was either ignoring Romero deliberately or drifting into unconsciousness. Romero found neither of those options acceptable. He chose a pair of pliers and walked in a slow circle around his prisoner.

"I asked you a question," he said quietly.

The boy still didn't answer.

Romero lifted one of his fingers, closed the pliers delicately around the nail, and yanked.

The boy sucked a breath through his teeth with a hiss. His whole body went rigid, his other fingers clawing uselessly at the empty air. But he didn't scream.

And he didn't answer.

Romero dropped the bloody fingernail onto the floor. The boy hung limp, eyes squeezed shut.

"Tell me who sent you," Romero said again.

The boy looked up, ragged breaths tearing at his throat. He sneered a colorful suggestion as to where Romero could stick his pliers.

Romero took another fingernail. Then, another. The boy tensed and jerked and twisted on the ropes like a fish on a line—but he never made a sound. When Romero finally grabbed a handful of his hair and jerked his head back, the boy coughed, choking on blood. He'd bitten straight into his tongue.

And yet he hadn't screamed.

He certainly knew how to take the fun out of things.

"You," he informed the boy, "are going to tell me who sent you, and where they are. Or you—"

The boy spat a glob of bloody saliva into his face.

Romero released him and stepped back, pulling a lace-edged handkerchief out of his sleeve. He calmly wiped his face and set the stained square of cloth aside. Then he reached for a new tool, a steel contraption faintly resembling a nutcracker.

"That's a shame," he said, and reached for the boy's hand again.

The tool shattered his knuckle with an audible *snap*. The boy bucked and thrashed, arching his back. He groaned between clenched teeth, sucking in a hissing breath, his every muscle tightening against the pain. He tried to wrench free with a grunt, his body twisting with surprising strength. But Romero simply moved to the next knuckle, unperturbed. All his fighting accomplished nothing. It just made the blood flow more thickly down his arms.

"Who are they?" he asked calmly.

No reply. After half a beat, Romero bore down on the next bone with a crack. More struggles, more groans, a stream of foul curses hissed under his breath. But no screams.

And no answers.

Romero drew back, tool in hand, and studied the boy. His face was twisted in pain, his breathing labored. He looked suddenly, disturbingly, young, even younger than he really was. Pain had that effect on people. He had seen grown men break down sobbing, crying for their mothers, saying whatever they thought he wanted to hear— some after only a few minutes.

That was the part that galled him most. He had enemies all over the Peninsula, and all of them could, would, and had sent assassins after him. But this one had gotten closer than any of them—and he was just a boy. An orphan. Nothing but trash that had crawled out of the gutter with all the other rats.

"Why you?" he asked, thinking aloud. "Why you, of all people?"

The boy made a choking sound. It might have been a chuckle.

"I'm sorry I'm na' bigger. Or older. Or is it that I'm an orphan? Ya just seem so *disappointed*, poor thing...."

Romero closed his eyes for a moment, taking a slow, deep breath through his nose. "You aren't the 'Beggar's King'," he sneered, endowing the absurd title with all the contempt it deserved. "Nobody is. It isn't possible. You're merely one of many. The unlucky one given a task he couldn't possibly—"

The boy threw back his head and laughed. It sounded painful. "Just keep tellin' yerself that, alright," he snickered. "Whatever makes ya feel better....I'm the same age's you were when ya murdered yer brother, yeah? You ain't exactly one to talk...."

"Rumors," Romero replied at once. After so many years, the words came to his lips instinctively now. "All rumors."

The boy snorted. "Which bit? That ya killed the king, or that ya weren't his real brother? A bastard, wasn't it? Or a fosterling?"

Romero did not reply. Instead he lifted one of the instruments, a thick pair of clippers, testing the feel of it in his hand.

"Who sent you after me?" he said quietly.

"*Sent* me? Ha! What, ya think some bloody noble threw me a few cuprums to try an' kill a king?"

"Not *a* king," Romero hissed, whirling around. "*The* king, of the largest empire in the world! Alronelin is the largest it's been since the Rebellion! Not even the Conqueror managed to take so much so quickly...."

He trailed away, scowling. The boy's head had slumped forward onto his chest, as if in exhaustion—but Romero had distinctly seen him roll his eyes.

"Righ', righ'," the boy drawled. "*The* king." He glanced up, a ghost of a grin lifting his lips. "Is it 'cause ya wanted his wife? Yer brother's, I mean."

Romero stiffened. "Excuse me?"

"That's gotta sting, huh? She run off to get away from ya? How's it feel that she chose worm food over *you?*"

And the boy laughed—a cold, scornful sound that sent a chill down Romero's spine.

Romero took a deep breath. He dropped the clippers on the table, his eyes skimming the tools. He needed something special. Something that would hurt.

"If you want to die," he mused, his fingers pausing on a knife, "that can be arranged." He lifted the knife and spun it across his knuckles. "But I'm afraid you're persuading me to keep you alive *much* longer."

When he looked up, their eyes met—and a leaden weight dropped into Romero's stomach. Those eyes. Cold, calculating, sadistically amused. And not a trace of fear.

"Oh, ya gonna kill me," the boy said quietly. "And ya gonna do it fast. 'Cause if ya don't, ya know I'll be after ya again."

His neck throbbed. Only then did he notice his fingers pressing to the wound and snatch them away.

"You got lucky, boy," he spat. "That's the only way an untrained boy could even come near a king. *Luck.* You...."

But he trailed away. The boy was watching him, and his bloodied grin was wide and wicked.

Mocking him.

Easy. You won't get anything from him if he dies.

Goddess, but he'd never had to work so hard to keep his temper.

"Am I missing the joke?" he asked, trying to keep his voice steady.

"Ya don' recognize me," the boy said quietly. "Do ya, *Yer Majesty?*"

"Should I?"

The boy's lips spread slowly, his teeth baring into a feral grin.

"Dunno if ya keep up with th' news among us peasants....Ever heard o' the Fishgut Butcher?"

"Yes, of course I—" Romero froze. Then, realizing his own foolishness, he laughed. "You don't expect me to believe that, do you? That was ten years ago."

"Been a busy lad." The smile never flagged, even as he panted and strained against his bonds.

Romero's hand tightened around the handle of the knife. "The Butcher of Fishgut Alley. The man who slaughtered the patrons of a brothel before turning on the owners and burning them in their bed. William Adeney and his wife, if I recall...which makes *you*...?"

"Liam Adeney," the boy said softly. "The Second."

Romero took a step back and appraised the boy. He felt as if he were seeing him—truly seeing him—for the first time.

"I'd heard the rumors, but...your own parents?"

"Monsters," the boy spat, his face twisting in hatred. "They got wha' they deserved. Everyone's gonna get wha' they deserve. I'm gonna make sure of it."

"I'm sure you are." Romero gestured to the dungeons around them. "Once you free yourself, that is."

The boy laughed. "Wha' happened t' them 'others' you were on about? Ain't scared o' them no more?"

"There are no others. You said so yourself."

"No' that you'll ever find." A taunt lingered in his blood-smeared smirk. "Maybe lockin' me up with all them other kids wasn't your brightest idea. I'm a bad influence."

Romero's breath caught. "The *orphans*—where are they? *Where are they?*"

"Maybe I'll tell ya," the boy said. "But first, *you* tell me. An even trade..."

"I'm not playing games with you, boy—"

"You burned it down." And when he looked up, there was no amusement to be found in his face—only rage. Blind, savage rage. "The orphanage. Didn't you? *Admit it.*"

"I swear to the Goddess, boy, if you don't tell me where they—"

"Admit it!" the boy shouted, his voice echoing off the stone walls. "Admit it, ya fuckin' coward! ADMIT IT!"

And despite it all—his tools, his army, his crown, the chains holding the boy back—Romero found himself hiding behind a sneer as a confession tore its way free. "You think I run around the lower city with torches, boy? No. I *ordered* it burned down."

The boy's head hung. His shoulders were shaking. Then his laughter rang out—deranged, hysterical, furious.

"An' you call yourself a man?" he rasped. "You set fire to a building wit' sixty kids inside, an' you didn't even have th' stones to do it yerself!"

"And what choice did you give me?" Romero snarled. "You orphans were out of control, turning against the people in charge, you left me no choice. I exterminated them like the rats they were!"

"Oh, did you?" The boy's eyes burned with sudden malice. "And yet, here I am. Bit of a flaw in yer plan, there...."

"You—"

"How many bodies did yer men pull out of the rubble, d'you think? Did they ever tell you?"

No. They hadn't. He'd been assured that the problem was taken care of. And by the time he found out—

"Pulled 'em out myself," the boy mocked him. "Every fuckin' one of 'em. *Alive.* An' then we were free. We could do whatever we wanted—"

"*Where are they?*" Romero roared.

The boy laughed in his face. "You'll *never* find 'em."

"You little—!"

His hand scrabbled at the tools on the table until it closed around a metal rod. He swung it blindly. It connected with a sickening crack, and the boy swung on his ropes like a loose sail in a storm, his broken legs dragging on the stone. But he only raised his head again, blood staining his sandy hair and dripping down his face, and laughed even harder.

"Where did you hide them?"

"You'll never know."

He swung again. The boy's head snapped to one side, and he coughed and gagged, spitting out a bloodied tooth. But his face turned to Romero again, that relentless grin bloodied and gapped now, but never faltering.

"You'll have ta kill me," he taunted. "An' when I die, it'll die wit' me. You'll *never* find 'em."

"I'll make you *wish* you were dead," Romero hissed. "You think you know pain *now*, boy? Spit it out, or I'll show you what pain is."

The boy spat blood in his face, laughing when he flinched. "Oh, you'll kill me. Ya ain't got a choice. 'Cause if ya don't—"

Another swing; the boy grunted, losing his breath for a moment as the thick bar connected with his ribs. Romero distinctly heard one of them snap.

"Where are they?" he yelled. "I swear to the Goddess herself, I will *rip—*"

Another crack as he swung again. He could feel the bones shattering beneath the flesh.

"—every *bone*—"

Crack.

"—from your *body*—"

Crack.

"And when I *find*—"

Crack.

"Those bloody *kids*—"

Thud.

Romero knew instantly that something had gone horribly wrong.

A stuttering gasp escaped the boy's lips, then a breathless sound of pain, somewhere between whimper and moan. He dangled limp from his bonds, his face bloodless as his eyes stared blankly at the floor. His breaths were suddenly fast, shallow, irregular. Romero, staggering back, saw a bloody mark low on his stomach, rapidly bruising, where the crowbar had hit, and he knew that he had made a terrible mistake. He had struck too hard, and in the wrong place.

The boy was as good as dead.

"No," Romero groaned. "No no *no*—" He gestured frantically for his soldiers. "Damn it, cut him down, *now*—"

They cut through the ropes, and the boy collapsed, the hooks through his wrists clattering against the stones. Romero fell to his knees and grabbed his shoulder, shaking him until his head wagged back and forth.

"No, *no*—someone get a damn healer, *now*, I need to know where he's hiding them! He's got them stowed away somewhere and I—"

A low, gurgling noise made him jump. It grew louder and higher, echoing around the stone walls. It was only when the boy's head rolled on his neck that Romero saw his face and realized that he was laughing.

Laughing.

Still laughing, even now.

"You...lose," he choked. "You...lose...."

"*Damn it!*"

Romero lashed out with his boot, slamming it into the boy's

midriff. The boy's eyes rolled back into his head as he fell back with a grunt.

Romero rose slowly to his feet, looking the boy over in disgust. Then, releasing a slow breath, he turned to the nearest of his soldiers. The man saluted instantly, awaiting orders.

This was a disaster. A failure. But there was still one way to salvage the situation.

"Kill him," he ordered. "I want him burned in the plaza at sundown."

The man hesitated. Even from there, he could hear the boy's rasping breathing. "But—he's still—"

"Then burn him alive!" Romero yelled. "Let that be a warning to those bloody peasants." He nudged the boy with his foot, then spat on the floor by his face. "And let that be the end of it," he said.

Liam was hauled out of the cold shadows and into blinding light, dragged slowly across the ground.

Where was he? And why? There was only a roar of noise, a vicious stab of sunlight, the scrape of stone and the bite of cold air. He could make no sense of it. He was upright, as if they wanted him to walk, but his legs did not respond to his commands. Every time his feet caught the cobblestones, pain tore up his legs, but he couldn't cry out. He couldn't remember how.

Something throbbed within him: a deep, twisting pain, low in his gut. It wiped out everything as it pulsed with the sluggish beat of his heart, every trace of hunger, thirst, and inferior superficial pain. Mere broken bones were forgotten, the memory of them washed away with every wave of agony that broke across him.

And yet....

He had learned long ago, early in childhood, how to block pain, set up barriers through which it could not pass. Pain was invasive, like a line of spearmen pushing in, threatening to encroach upon the fortress of his mind. But it could be stopped. Held back at the walls.

This pain was not something he had the strength to fight. It was crushing, all-consuming. But as it overwhelmed him, it changed him.

Turned him leaden, limp, immobile—but far, far away. Every movement, every tiny jostle, threatened to jerk him back, but he floated above it all like a man floating in still water. Tranquil, silent, still, even as he slowly drowned.

He was going to die. He knew it. The only question was when. It had been days now, he thought, or maybe only minutes; time had no meaning to him anymore. A slow countdown, ticking away until he sank into oblivion—but then, he thought, hadn't that always been true? What was the difference now, really? The longer the hammer beat the nail, the more the hammer itself was chipped away, long after the nail was gone, until all that remained were splinters and filings....

He almost laughed at himself. He wasn't making sense anymore.

They dragged him...up, somehow. His back against something rough. Sticks and logs rattling beneath his bare feet. Pinches at his wrists and ankles. Ropes, he realized, as the roughness scraped against his neck, wrapped so tightly that they lifted his head for him.

He opened his eyes.

The sight before him was one that had haunted him all his life, lurking just out of the bounds of his imagination. A plaza, lit by the dying sun. A platform around him, raising him up, so he could see the hundreds and hundreds of people that spread out before him. A sense of suppression, constraint, as if the air itself were holding its breath, waiting for its chance to erupt into fire and madness.

He had always known it would end this way.

Though the pyre was a surprise.

Still, he had never imagined that quite so many people would come to watch him die. And they were not cheering, taunting, laughing—no. They were watching in silence, their anger bubbling just beneath the surface.

His heart swelled with something like pride. His people. Not the king's—his. And when he was gone, they'd continue the fight. Especially....

His vision swam in and out of focus, struggling, fading—but still, he persisted with his search. Finally, he spotted it: the familiar face in the back of the crowd.

Kayo.

His best friend. His baby brother. Sometimes he still looked at the nearly eighteen-year-old and saw a little kid. Standing on his own pyre, for the first time in his life, Liam truly believed that there might be a Goddess watching over the world—not for his sake, but for Kayo's. Something, somewhere, had brought him home safely, and that was enough. It had cost him everything, but it was worth the price.

His only regret, here at the end of it all, was leaving Kayo behind.

There were people huddled around Kayo. Liam couldn't quite make them out, but he knew by their silhouettes who they were. Their brother, their sisters. The only family they had left, the only family that mattered. They stood around Kayo as if protecting him. Well, they would have to now. Liam had done all that he could.

He closed his eyes.

Be brave, he thought. *Be happy. Be nothing like me.*

The smoke rose around him, the wood crackling as the flames caught. But he never felt the fire touch him. He slipped away, rising far above the earth, leaving his shattered body behind.

⚬⧉⚬

A girl dressed in rags elbowed her way through the crowd. She had only admired a single man in her entire life, and if he was to be executed, she was going to see it. She would never believe that he was dead unless she saw it with her own eyes. And if he happened to escape, all the better; she wanted good seats to that show.

But judging by the crowds, everyone else had had the same idea. Every street from the castle gates to the Gardens was packed to bursting with people. Most of them were taller than her—she'd get around to growing when she came of age, she was sure—and craned their necks to see the gallows until she had no hope of seeing past them.

Vultures, she thought scathingly as she pushed her way through, giving as many nasty looks as she received. Then, when she could force her way no further, she grabbed onto a shuttered window and began to climb. She scaled the building and hauled herself up onto the slanted tiles on the roof.

From atop the roof she had a breathtaking view of the entire city. There was the tangled anthill of stone that was the upper city; there was the strip of grease and dirt along the harbor that marked the lower city. At its far end, she could see the great stone bridge that connected the harbor with the mainland, a faint smudge of green on the horizon. Closer to her, she spotted the delicate rooftops and spreading foliage of the Gardens. Across from it, the castle perched atop the cliffs, towering gracefully above it all. And in every direction, she saw the ocean pulsing, nudging at the cliffs and the sand and the docks in the harbor.

The plaza sat nestled between the Gardens and the Castle, and normally, it sat empty and abandoned. But today it was full to over-flowing with a sea of people, ebbing and flowing and surging like the ocean at the base of the cliffs. She could hear them muttering like a single being in a low, uneasy hum.

In the middle of it all, the gallows sat waiting. But this time, instead of the crossbeam that held the noose, only a single pole jutted up from the planks. And at its base sat a massive pile of wood and kindling.

Her eyes nearly popped out of her head at the sight of it.

They're going to BURN him?!

She had never in her life seen someone burned at the stake. No one had, not in many, many years. They said the ruler of Anapoline was the last, burned alive in front of his palace, then, once roasted, devoured by the citizens he'd starved. But that was on the other side of the Peninsula, and centuries ago, during the Plague. To bring it back now....They threatened it sometimes with Divinæ, if any of them returned and tried to curse or bewitch innocent civilians, but they never found any. It seemed it was not so empty a threat.

Suddenly, she wondered if she should be so eager to watch this after all, or if she should even be present. She hesitated, then shrank against the chimney, hiding in its narrow shadow. In the lower city, with its dirt roads and mud-brick walls, her faded rags, sun-browned skin, and filthy, matted hair would have camouflaged her perfectly in the shadows. The upper city, with its gray stone and black shadows, had proven a much more difficult challenge over the years. And here, near the clean, colorful Gardens, blending in seemed nearly impossible. Yet concealing herself was all the more vital here. Any soldier that spotted her would assume immediately that she didn't belong and throw her into the nearest prison—and he wouldn't necessarily be wrong.

She hugged her knees and hunched down, shivering as the cold air raked across her threadbare clothes. She made herself as small as she could. Then she waited for sundown, watching not the plaza, where nothing was happening, but the castle. It stood still and silent, as it had for hundreds of years. But the pale gray stone almost seemed to glow at this time of day, changing colors with the sky as the sun sank. It was closer than ever, only a few minutes' walk from where she stood —yet somehow, she could see no more of it than she ever had before. It looked the same, just bigger. Still, she memorized the lines of every tower and roof, imagining what might lie behind each crystalline window, wondering if, one day....

Then the bells in the tallest tower began to ring. But there was no joy or celebration in the sound. The tune was a menacing tangle of low deep notes that echoed across the entire city, announcing dire news.

The castle gates creaked open, and she was reminded abruptly of what happened to people like her inside the castle.

The man they led out was barely visible from this height, but she could make out long sand-colored hair, bare feet, tattered breeches— and a sickening amount of blood, smeared across his chest and arms from a dozen different wounds. They had to drag him between two soldiers, and where the crowds parted, they remained divided, for he left a trail of blood behind him thick enough for her to see from her perch that no one seemed to want to cross. When they tied him to the stake, they seemed to need to bind him by not only his wrists, but his ankles, waist, and neck as well, just to keep him upright.

They must be really frightened of him. This she thought with no small amount of pride. They had beaten him to death, yet still they bound him tightly, still they guarded him with a dozen soldiers. It was possible that they had even killed him before dragging him out, as if they were that afraid he'd break loose. And they were burning him, dragging out an age-old punishment in sheer desperation, because killing him wasn't enough. They had to destroy the body completely so that he could never, ever come back. They were terrified of him—as they should be. He was her hero for a reason.

A herald, standing safely to one side, unfurled a scroll and called out in a voice loud enough for all to hear.

"All present, hear this: by the order of Romero Sangor, the Eagle of Rimerock Hills, King of Alronelin, Ruler of Bermeia, Emperor of the Greater Peninsula, Lord Protector of Courma and Lyrma—"

The people were growing restless. Their muttering rose to a clamor of protest, with some even shaking their fists in the air. Some phrases broke free of the general uproar, originating from people who were clearly emboldened by the anonymity of the crowd to say things they would never utter to a soldier's face:

"Fuck the king!"

"Give back Courma!"

"Free the Beggar's King!"

"Bloody Romero, he ain't no king!"

"Get out o' Courma! Get out o' Lyrma!"

"The Beggar King's one of us!"

"Murderer! Usurper!"

"Long live the prince! Long live the prince!"

This last cry spread like fire across the crowd. Dozens of men and women yelled in a discordant tumult, and others joining in, fists raised, creating a chaotic din that made no sense until their shouts seemed, in the same moment, to fall in sync:

"Long live the prince! Long live the prince!"

The girl could not help but cheer, clapping her hands together as she took up the cry. "Long live the prince! Long l—!"

At a shouted command, one soldier lowered his spear, sinking into a fighting stance, and the others surrounding the pyre mimicked him. Others, stationed by the castle gates or at the mouths of the streets leading off the plaza, did the same, and the shouting trailed away into silence almost at once. Nobody needed further reminder of what the soldiers could do.

After a few moments, the herald, who had seemingly grown a bit wiser in the interim, skipped to the point.

"—William Adeney, identified as the leader of the rebel group known as the Beggar's King, wanted for heinous crimes against the Crown, including treason, subterfuge, theft and sabotage of Crown property, incitement of anarchy and rebellion, torture, and murder

—" The resentment of the crowd was nearly palpable at this point; they dared not cause an uproar, but the girl could almost hear their lips curling—"is sentenced to die. On this day, he shall be burned alive until naught remains but ashes." The herald lowered the scroll, which snapped back into a tight cylinder. "And may the Goddess show him mercy," he finished.

This sentiment was sometimes echoed by the spectators of an execution like a prayer—but not today. Today all present stood in grim silence, every face turned toward the man on the pyre. Toward the Beggar's King, who was, depending on who described him, a demigod or a walking nightmare, a blessing or a scourge, a hero or a menace. Champion of the downtrodden: the poor, the hungry, the homeless, the imprisoned, the whores, the orphans. Destroyer of soldiers, nobles, and even—if the rumors were correct—royals.

She wished she could see his face. Artists would put up pictures of him later—probably pictures of him burning, just to make it clear what had happened—but it was not the same. She wanted to meet him face-to-face and tell him how much she admired him, even if he couldn't hear her. Right now, she could barely see him at all.

But she saw the fire when it started.

It spread in an instant, consuming the oil-soaked wood with breathtaking speed. She winced as the flames licked at his legs—but he didn't scream. He didn't even flinch. No matter how high the flames rose, he remained where he was, slumped against his bonds. One of the guards even poked him with the tip of his spear, clearly trying to incite the response that they wanted, but it made no difference. He might not even have survived the herald's speech.

Her chest swelled with pride. No matter what those bastards did, no matter what they tried, they would never have any satisfaction from him.

She could not see the exact moment that he died. There came a point, however, where no merciful Goddess would have left a soul alive in such a body, and that was when the last faint trickle of hope drained from her. She should have known better than to hope he would break free, or that the people around her would rise up and tear him loose. It was strange—such a sudden realization, as if someone had blown out a candle in her mind. A man she barely knew had left the world, and it would never be the same again.

A breeze blew in from the ocean, and she shivered, huddling against the chimney in her torn, threadbare rags. One hand snaked down her shirt, pulling out a long golden chain. At the end of it dangled a shining pendant of gold and iridescent red, delicately crafted into the shape of a blooming rose, which she clutched tightly in her palm. The other hand stretched out, fingers extended, as she counted.

Sank a ship full of cannons and three more full of supplies. Snapped the mast off another. Saved a bunch of whores from soldiers, a bunch of different times. Rained coins down in the square by the markets, after stealing it from somewhere. Started the riots. Freed everyone that got put in jail for the riots. Counting was not her strong suit, but that was, arguably, a lot, and she hadn't even gotten to the good parts. *Killed that fisherman that ratted people out to the soldiers and gave out all his fish. Killed that baker who sold poisoned bread. Killed that merchant that was driving up prices. Killed that man who came in and tried to take homeless people as slaves. Killed that drug lord and all his people. Slaughtered all those soldiers in the night. Crossed into the upper city somehow, broke into the Gardens, scared the hell out of all the rich people who thought no one could touch them. Hung that general from his own bedroom window by the curtain pulls. Left that rich guy, that noble, dead in a fountain somewhere with his head on a pike. Broke into the castle and sliced up the king. Almost killed him, too.*

There would be announcements all over the place tomorrow that she wouldn't be able to read, listing all of those and more. But she'd gotten all the important things.

Almost. She added one more item to her list: *He died a good death.* And in a world where people like them couldn't expect to live long, that was what mattered most. Die a good death, and leave a strong legacy behind. She could only hope to do half as well as the man below.

The fire sank slowly down into its coals, dying along with the sun. But nobody left—not until darkness had fallen and nothing but the faintest of silhouettes could be seen in the light of the embers. They stood together, braced against the early winter chill, and kept a vigil over the body.

No one sang for him. It was blasphemy, heresy, unheard of—but she knew why. They didn't want to break the silence that had fallen over the plaza like a shroud, like a spell, preserving this moment in ice. They didn't *want* to lay the Beggar's King to rest and to send his soul to the Goddess. They didn't want to accept that he was gone.

This was it: the only defiance left to them. The king wanted them to say their farewells, move on, and go away. But they stood unified before the castle, in solidarity, and refused to move. Refused to sing.

Refused to forget.

Kayo heard someone calling him, but he didn't answer. He stood where he was, motionless, and watched his brother die.

They found him eventually, gathering around him. Dominic, Artemis, and Alysia, his brother and sisters. He expected them to talk to him, shout at him, try to pull him away. But they simply stood by him, placing warm, gentle hands on his back, his shoulder, his arm, seeking as much comfort as they gave. Despite their warmth and the cloak he held around his shoulders, he still shivered violently and could not stop.

Together, they watched him burn. Nobody moved, not even as the flames began to die down and darkness began to fall. Nobody spoke—not them, nor the hundreds of people around them. Nobody turned their eyes from what remained of their brother, just visible against a twilit sky hazy with smoke.

Soon it was dark, without a single tongue of flame illuminating the pyre. Kayo stood motionless, his eyes fixed on the last place he had known his brother to be. He couldn't go. He couldn't leave him. Not like this.

Nobody else was leaving, either. Nobody was moving at all. They were just...waiting. The silence was so deep and profound that he imagined he could hear the darkness sinking around him, the smoke rising, the sea crashing against the rocks along the distant cliffs.

Say something, he begged them. *Do something. Please.*

But what was left to do?

Finally, when the moon was high in the sky, they heard movement. The people around them tensed and whispered as the wind carried the sound of rattling armor to their ears, the harsh bark of soldier's voices. They were forcing everyone away.

"Kayo...," Dominic finally said, his voice barely louder than a whisper. "We have to go now. We need to go home."

Silence.

"Kayo...." Alysia took him by the arm, tried to lead him away.

"No...." He pulled his arm free. "Not yet, wh-what...what are they...?" He was shivering so hard that he could barely speak. "They can't just leave him...."

"Kayo, c'mon. The kids 'll be worried."

"Wh-what's going to happen to him? Do-do you think—"

"We need to get back. We need to find something for them to eat."

"What'd they do to him? He...he was...."

"Kayo, *we need to go.*"

"What if he f-felt all that? Could he *feel* all that—that *fire*...?"

"Stop it," Dominic said harshly. "Liam wouldn't have wanted you to watch all this. He wouldn't want you to freeze to death out here. We have to move, now, before those soldiers come our way."

Kayo shook his head, pressed his icy hands to his face. "What are we going to do?" he said numbly. "Wh-what are we supposed to...?"

The three others shared a look, but they didn't answer. They couldn't. They were barely older than he was and knew nothing more than he did.

They tugged at him, but he refused to move. He reached up to scrub the tears from his cheeks with the heel of his hand.

"What are we going to do now?" he kept asking them. "What are we going to do? Wh-what...?"

A gust of wind snaked in from the sea, and he shuddered as he caught a whiff of smoke beneath the stench of salt. On the wind, he heard the soldier's voices coming closer. Fear crushed around his chest like a vice and turned his insides to water. When someone pulled at him again, he let them lead him away.

It didn't matter what he did anymore. What any of them did, ever again.

It was over.

"Kayo. *Kayo.*"

It had been weeks since Liam's execution. Months.

But sometimes, Kayo still smelled the smoke.

"*Kayo!*"

The sharp whisper made him jump. He turned hastily toward Dominic, pasting an innocent expression on the half of his face that wasn't covered by a mask. "What?"

He'd been looking around again, trying to spot the source of the smell, the glow of flame or the first few wisps of gray. And in the lower city, he always started the search in the same place, his eyes pulled there like a compass needle drawn northward. And Dominic had noticed.

"Will you focus, please?" Kayo could barely even see him in the dark, but he could hear Dominic's exasperation. "Before we both get shot?"

"We won't get shot."

"Yeah? You're sure about that?"

He was—though he wasn't sure how. Maybe he just didn't care anymore.

"Just—come on. Should be quiet by now."

He set off without waiting for Dominic's reply, higher up the steep slope of the roof until, at last, the stiff breeze from the harbor sliced through the mask. Even well into the spring, the wind was sharp and cold, but he welcomed it. Anything to erase the stench of the lower city, of stale bodies and old sewage and gutted fish—and smoke. Always, always smoke. He wasn't imagining it. Warm or cold, something was always burning.

From the rooftop, he had a good view of this part of the city—not that it was anything to write home about. A row of padlocked warehouses guarded the water like sentinels, waiting for ships to arrive, to take their cargo and leave more behind. Behind them, it was all ramshackle, termite-ridden houses, pieced together from shipwrecks and old canvas and homemade bricks. Huts, more like—"houses" was a generous term—but who was he to talk? There'd been a time or two when he might literally have killed to curl up somewhere safe from the wind and snow and rain. The whole area was awash with faint, greasy light from torches that belched black smoke, from cookfires and trash fires and the occasional soft glow of a candle behind a shutter, keeping watch over someone else who couldn't sleep.

And—

He didn't want to, but that same spot pulled his eyes again beneath his hood, irresistibly, past the scattered lights and the distant shouting and laughter from the parts of the city he'd always tried to avoid, to a place like a missing tooth—a conspicuous gap in the buildings, a dark void that none of the torches were strong enough to fill.

Even after all this time, they'd never built anything over the ruins. They'd left it all to rot. A warning to the rest of the city, maybe—or maybe they'd just thought it wasn't worth the time and gold to clean up. The ash had been knee-deep like snow, and the reek of smoke had soaked in so deeply he thought he would never escape it.

Why did he keep looking at it? Looking *for* it? He didn't want to be anywhere near it. A thousand leagues would still be too close. Even if he turned his back, he could still feel it there, a looming presence that made the scars on his palms itch.

He turned to find that Dominic hadn't moved, and rolled his eyes. "What happened to staying focused?" he snapped, just loudly enough for Dominic to hear him. "Dom?"

In answer, Dominic pointed out onto the harbor.

It took a moment for Kayo to see what Dominic must have spotted. A dark patch on the water—but it was moving. It was hard to make out the edges of the shape, but from the ripples—not just from the prow, but from a half-dozen oars—it was a ship, and a big one. And it was headed their way.

"Is that what I think it is?" Dominic whispered. Kayo's eyes were much sharper than his.

Kayo slid halfway down the roof, pausing just behind Dominic's shoulder. "It's a ship. Two masts at least. What's it doing this far down?"

"I dunno...."

They sat in silence for a moment, watching. The main docks had plenty of space—they could see it from here, all bright torches and bustling workers even at this time of night—yet the ship veered very pointedly toward the rickety, half-abandoned docks below them. Not a single light showed on the prow or the rails or even in the cabin. And by the sounds of it, or rather the lack of sound, the oars were wrapped in canvas to muffle their splashes in the water.

Whoever they were, they didn't want to be seen.

Kayo tugged on his bootlaces a little tighter and pulled his hood low over his face. "Change of plans. Let's go."

"Go? Go where?"

"Just—follow me."

"Kayo—" Dominic hissed, but Kayo was already swinging off the edge of the roof. After a moment, amid a flood of muttered Lyric cursing, he heard a faint thump as Dominic followed. Just as Kayo had known he would.

Together, they vanished into the shadows.

There were two guards on the dock when the ship finally berthed, leaning on their spears as they watched the goings-on.

"Ain't that a sight, boys," one of them drawled. "Like a crippled bird come in to roost."

"Better off roastin' 'er on a spit, by the looks of 'er," the other said drily.

"Aww, come now, she's still seaworthy, a' least. Give 'er t' me, I'll have 'er shipshape in a shake or two."

"Naw. Pluck 'er dry an' rub 'er in oil, boys, she's a goner. Stick 'er on a spit, prop 'er up both ends, have at 'er...."

"Sounds like a good time, boys, but then what'll you do with the bird?"

The two of them cackled.

On the roof above their heads, Kayo and Dominic crouched, listening for their moment to take a look at the ship. Dominic snickered, and Kayo elbowed him to shut him up. He was trying to focus, and the guards were distracting him.

He risked a peek around the corner. The guards stood near the end of the dock like two pilings that had poked through. Beyond them, Kayo could see the faint outline of the ship against the small waves rolling into the harbor. The shape was unmistakable. Nobody else made ships so slight and graceful. Though the ship flew no colors, Kayo knew her to be a Savillan caravel.

He ducked back undercover with a thousand more unanswered questions. Were the men sailors or soldiers? Why did it fly no colors? Why were they so determined not to be seen?

The two guards seemed to have similar concerns.

"S' what's all this then?"

"Th' *Luminator,* mate."

"It's Savillan, you dunce. *Illuminatori.*"

"Wha's that mean?"

"Fuck if I know. What I meant was what's *on 'er.*"

A man on the deck swung himself down onto the dock. Another tossed him a thick rope.

"'Ey, maybe there's a gal fer you in there, Vilsner, now *that'd* be half a miracle."

"Tchah. Ain't no gal t' be found on a damn boat, it's bad—"

They broke off at the sound of a distant crash. Kayo looked around the corner, Dominic hovering right behind him, following the guards' gaze to the deck of the ship. A scuffle had broken out on deck, several dark figures shouting, their footsteps like drumbeats on the wooden planks. And another voice, muffled, nearly lost in the maelstrom of bass voices—a voice that was, decidedly, female.

Then, under the slack-jawed stare of the two guards, a woman strode down the gangplank. In a dark dress and a thick cloak, it was hard to make out much of her, but when the wind whipped her cloak back, Kayo could see clearly the silhouette of a skirt and a strongly curving figure. She stepped onto the dock with a gracefully pointed foot, then paused, looking back. A trio of men, in plainclothes but heavily armed, followed her off the ship, escorting two more women. One of them was gagged, bound, and struggling fiercely.

Kayo didn't realize he'd moved until Dominic grabbed his shoulder and pushed him back down. "Easy," he muttered under his breath.

He was right—there were too many of them, and if anyone raised the alarm, they'd have every soldier in the lower city on their tails. But every part of him itched to free the woman who was snarling and shouting beneath the gag, elbowing and kicking anything she could reach. And the other woman—pale, with white-gold hair, who was not bound but was clearly just as much a prisoner. When she hesitated at the step down to the dock, one of the guards grabbed her by the elbow and steered her onward at a pace that made her stumble.

The woman in the lead, satisfied that the prisoners were following, swept down the dock. She paused at the sight of the two soldiers standing guard, who were still gaping at her.

"Well?" she demanded of them.

They glanced at one another. "Er—" said one.

"My carriage," the woman snapped at them. "Is it here?"

"*You're* the—?" the larger of the two blurted out, before his companion elbowed him to shut him up.

"Er, yes—Your Highness," he stammered. "Over, uh—"

As soon as he pointed, the woman turned away from him as if he'd never existed. The guards and prisoners followed her as she moved out of sight—but not out of earshot. Kayo, craning his neck to see where she'd gone, heard her voice clearly, giving orders in fluent Savillan. Then she switched to clear, perfect, mildly accented Courman, and he could understand her again.

"No, no—she goes with me. *This* one can walk for all I care."

Kayo risked moving a little further down the roof, leaning as far out as he dared. He caught a glimpse of moving torchlight, the back wheels of a carriage. He could still hear the occasional scuffle as the bound woman fought.

"Who th' hell they got tied up like that?" one of the soldiers muttered to the other. He pitched his voice low so it could not be heard across the dock, but Kayo, right above them, heard it clearly.

"Dunno. They said the ship captain, but—can't be. That's mad, a woman captain."

"Savillans *are* mad, mate. Jus' look at their princess...."

Kayo sucked in a sharp breath, glancing at Dominic. The look on his face confirmed that he'd heard it too. He pulled down his mask and jerked his head toward the carriage, mouthing, *the Savillan princess?!*

"That other one ain't Savillan, though. What's she doin' mixed up in all this?"

"Beats me. Hate t' be in her shoes."

"Why, what're they doin' to her?"

"It's Sangor, mate. I don't wanna know."

A click of a door. The clack of hooves on stone.

The carriage was leaving.

Dominic's hand was on his arm again. He didn't dare speak, but he shook his head firmly, giving Kayo a warning look.

He was right. Of course he was right. Freeing the woman—both women—meant getting past the personal guard of the Savillan princess. Three of the most dangerous men on the Peninsula, thick with muscle and likely wearing armor under their clothes, against two orphans who couldn't remember the last time they'd had full stomachs—they didn't stand a chance. They'd be prisoners themselves in seconds, carted off to the castle to face a grisly execution like Liam's. And they'd likely start a war while they were at it.

Liam could have done it. Liam *would* have done it.

But Liam was dead. And Kayo was just a kid playing dress-up in his clothes. Using the hollow carcass of Liam's legacy as a shield so they could scavenge the city like rats. He wasn't Liam, and he never would be.

Dominic tugged sharply on his sleeve. It was time to go—he was right. But Kayo couldn't make himself turn away. Two women in chains, dragged before the king, just like Liam had been—he had to do *something*—

"Bit young, weren't she? The blonde."

"Older 'n the princess. Not that that's hard."

The guards below were still gossiping, their banter ebbing and flowing as he tried and failed to block them out.

"Good Goddess, I'll wait. I'll wait in a damn line."

"Could let the dough rise a bit there, mate. Maybe they got one that's older 'n a mayfly aboard. Oy! Bardin!"

"What?" yelled a man from the ship's deck.

"Any o' them other prisoners women?"

"Aye, they got another one. Plenty o' men here too, anyone wanna get *them* outta my hair?"

The men below made some retort—but Kayo wasn't listening.

More prisoners. There were more prisoners on board. And the princess and her guards were gone.

Dominic heard them too. He was already tugging at Kayo's sleeve again—but Kayo tugged free.

"Kayo—"

"Watch my back," he whispered.

"Kayo, *no—*"

But Kayo couldn't hear him over the blood pounding in his ears. He slid down the roof before Dominic could stop him, swinging down to land quietly on the street below. The soldiers still stood around the corner, blissfully unaware of his presence.

But not for long. He slipped a knife from his boot and flipped it in his hand as he crept around the corner, as silent as the night and shadows around him. Listening for his moment to strike.

"Think that princess's here to smooth things over, eh?"

"Heh. Prob'ly here to finish Sangor off."

"Sangor never got stabbed. Ain't nobody gets stabbed in the neck an' live t' sing about it."

"My buddy in the castle said it's true."

"Oh yeah?"

"Mhm. Blood everywhere. Almost lost 'im, he said."

"What a shame that would've been. Where's that fuckin' prince gone, eh?"

"Prince's dead, mate."

"No 'e ain't. 'E's comin' with a damn army at his back t' pry Sangor's bloated arse off th' throne, just you wait."

"Yeah? What's 'e waitin' for, then, genius?"

"Gotta be eighteen t' rule. Day he turns eighteen, he'll be back."

"Says who? That's stupid."

"Says history, numbskull."

"There's been child kings."

"Name *one*."

"Soren Oakenheart."

"He ain't real, idiot."

"Is—what was that?"

Behind the soldiers, Kayo froze. He was so close he could smell them—cheap soap, cheap beer, and boot polish—and if they so much as glanced behind them, he would have nowhere to hide.

Both men scanned the docks in front of them, the shorter of the two craning his neck to see farther. Even at this hour, men were hard at work unloading cargo and repairing boats and nets, but only farther down the docks; the shouts and crashes and sounds of tools echoed eerily over the water in the distance. In their part of the docks, all they could hear was the crashing of waves against the pilings.

And—

A crash, a clatter—wood on stone, and something big. This time, it was close enough to make the two soldiers jump. The taller one cursed.

"Stay here—I'll go an' look," he called over his shoulder as he ran off into the night.

The other one sighed, scratching at his scalp as he watched him go.

That was when Kayo grabbed a handful of fingers and hair and jabbed the tip of his knife against the soldier's spine.

"Don't move," Kayo snarled, and added a rasp to his voice for good measure.

The soldier didn't move.

"You gonna call your buddies on the ship?"

The soldier let out a shuddering breath. "N-no."

"Sure you are. Go on, call them. All of them."

Obediently, the soldier filled his lungs. He yelled for help. And he didn't stop yelling until every soldier on the deck of the ship had come running his way.

But by the time they arrived, Kayo was gone.

. . .

The Savillan caravel was smaller than it looked. An open hatch and some rickety steps led down to a musty, mold-crusted cargo hold, where a sparse collection of sacks and barrels had been shoved aside to make room for the prisoners bound to the mast. A solitary lantern swung on a chain from the ceiling, casting a weak orb of light for the two soldiers standing guard. But when it swung away, it left pitch-black shadows behind, and neither of them noticed a black figure slip down the steps and hide among the cargo.

It was the last place Kayo could ever imagine a princess, Savillan or not. Unless the captain's cabin was impossibly luxurious, he couldn't fathom why King Eduardo's only daughter would ever set foot in this place. Fortunately, she was gone, and she'd taken all of the Savillans with her—except for the five prisoners, four men and one woman. The two guards were Alronelinian foot soldiers, and they were hardly on high alert.

One of the guards was drifting about, poking at sacks with his spear. "Not the chow you'd expect for a princess," he commented. "This grain's starting to sprout, look."

"Why don't you go plant 'em, then, farmer?" snapped the other, who was cleaning his nails with his belt knife. Judging from his accent, he had likely never left the lower city of Bermeia, where a puddle of mud was the largest patch of earth to be found.

"Just sayin', I dunno what she was doin' here, they musta had a thousand ships for her to—"

"Shut up an' do your job."

The first guard snorted. He started drumming the butt of his spear against a barrel, listening to the hollow-sounding rhythm it made. "Not much of a job. They's already tied up."

He glanced at the prisoners. One of them, the woman, glared at each of the guards in turn when they spoke. The man next to her scowled at the wall. The man next to him slumped with a head on the woman's shoulder, eyes closed. Kayo might have thought him asleep if not for the dried blood on his face. Kayo couldn't see the other two, but he guessed that they would look the same: brown skin and long black hair like his own, loose shirts and breeches that had seen better days, bare feet despite the cold, black eyes and bleeding lips from the struggle with the guards. And, of course, their wrists tied behind their backs and their ankles lashed to the iron rings on the floor meant for strapping down cargo.

The other guard glanced their way too and scoffed.

"Women on a ship," he muttered. "A woman captain, too. These bruccies ain't right in the head."

He spat on the deck. The woman tensed, turning her burning glare on him.

"Spute ancira sul su punte e te scappo la lingua, curvetza," she snarled.

Kayo understood enough to wince. The guards, however, merely laughed.

"Yeah, okay, sweetheart," one of them said with a grin. "Whatever you say." And he blew a kiss at her, making her face contort with fury.

Kayo's mind was racing, noting every item in the room as he came up with a plan. The crew was alive, and they were clearly fighters. If he could untie them, they might help him overwhelm the guards. But they were injured and unarmed, and Kayo didn't even have his sword.

His boot nudged something that shifted. A sack—and inside was something pale. Sand? No, flour. He frowned. Sand, he could use. But—

One of the guards stiffened and straightened up, looking around.

His eyes paused on Kayo's hiding spot. Kayo ducked, cursing.

"What is it?" the other asked him.

"I thought I saw—"

Kayo didn't stop to think. He grabbed the sack of flour and hurled it at the ceiling.

The air exploded in a burst of white as flour rained down on all of them. The guards shouted and jumped up, but Kayo was already hurling another, grabbing one more as he darted out into the open. He swung the other bag with all his might, and more white powder between him and the guards like a wall of smoke.

"There's someone here!" one of them choked as the other coughed and staggered back. "Get dow—"

Kayo grabbed him first, following the sound of his voice. An arm around his waist hauled him back, sending him crashing to the deck. Kayo snatched his spear out of his hands and slammed the butt of it into the thrashing mass of white-covered cloth and skin, then stepped back, whirling to face the other.

"Where are you?" he was yelling, and his spear hissed as he jabbed it into the powder-clogged air. "Fight us like a man, you coward!"

The spear swung his way, and Kayo ducked it just in time. There was no way past him to the prisoners, and he was a danger to them anyways, swinging wildly like that—Kayo had to disarm him. But—

"The Beggar King!" yelled the other, and Kayo heard him scrambling to his feet. "It's the Beggar King! Go, run and get—"

Kayo ran at him, the butt of the spear raised, and stopped him in his tracks with a jab to something soft—his gut, judging by the strained groan that followed. Another whack connected with his skull, and as the man stumbled, Kayo grabbed him by the collar and heaved with all his might. The guard was bigger than him, but caught off guard, he lost his footing and fell. Kayo grabbed him and locked his arms around his throat, straining as the huge mass of heavy muscle thrashed and kicked and bucked, squeezing even tighter as the guard tried to cry out. It took all his strength just to hold on, but he couldn't let either of them go for help.

The other guard whirled to face the source of the noise, holding his spear in shaking hands. Kayo watched the man's silhouette raise the spear with a yell, stabbing blindly in the whiteness.

The spear caught on the lantern. It shattered—

Kayo ducked—

And with a roar and a flash of light, the air itself exploded.

Kayo woke up choking, coughing as putrid smoke filled his lungs. Somebody was shouting in the distance, panicked and shrill.

"Fire...! Fire...! Fire!"

The words echoed, deafening, until he could not be sure whether the voice rang inside his head or out. His eyes burned as he squinted through the cloud of black smoke obscuring his dormitory, but he couldn't suck in enough air through the gag tied between his teeth. He struggled with his hands for several seconds, desperate to pull it off before it suffocated him, before remembering that they were tied to the bedpost. And, just like it had all night, the rope did not give no matter how much he strained against it. He screamed through the gag, thrashing against his bonds like a landed fish.

"Stoppit, stop—dammit, hurry up, will ya please—!"

He knew that silhouette against the smoke; he knew that voice, though he had never heard it distorted in terror like this. It was Liam, and he had never been so grateful to see him in his life.

Liam clawed at his wrists, tugging frantically on the ropes that bound him. Then they fell away, and Kayo ripped the gag from his mouth, gasping for breath. Liam's arm linked with his, hauling him off the bed and onto his feet.

"C'mon, Kayo—move, dammit, move, we have ta go, now—"

"Liam?" he mumbled. "What's—what's happening—?"

"What th' hell do ya think is happenin'? Just go, GO—"

Kayo took a clumsy step forward, his legs shaking so badly that he nearly fell over. Liam grabbed him by the elbow and hauled him forward, holding him up as he steered him toward the door.

"C'mon, Kayo—move, dammit, move—"

"Wait!" He dug in his heels and turned back. Through the smoke he could see his bunkmates in their beds, lying motionless beneath their blankets. "The others—Dominic—"

"They're already dead!" Liam snapped. "Hurry 'fore we are too! Go, go!"

And Kayo had no choice but to obey. He turned and stumbled after Liam, his brother half-leading, half-dragging him into the corridor.

The doors at either end of the corridor were locked up tight, or had been an hour ago. Now the one at the far end had splintered and fallen half-off its hinges, smoke pouring through the gap. Liam began kicking furiously at the other, driving his boot against the edge of the door like a battering ram, snarling silently as he panted from the exertion. Kayo shrank back against the wall, holding his hand up to his mouth to block the smoke. The fire was chasing them; he could see its faint reddish glow through the broken door, could hear it roaring, cracking, hissing like a living thing. Something fell with a crash in the far corridor, shaking the floor beneath them, and he cried out and sank down the wall, his heartbeat a thundering roar in his ears.

We're gonna die, *a voice screamed inside his head.* We're trapped, we can't get out, we're gonna die—

Somewhere, a little girl was screaming.

A snap—a deafening crash—

And he looked up to see the ceiling crashing down....

Someone else was screaming—not a girl. A woman, in a language he didn't know.

Kayo's eyes snapped open.

The air was thick with smoke, the stench of burning flesh strong in his nose. Something heavy lay on top of him, and he panicked, his whole body recoiling—but the weight slid off at once. A man—the guard he'd been wrestling—limp and still and reeking of charred meat. He'd gotten lucky. The guard had taken the worst of it.

But not that lucky. His whole body throbbed, a searing pain licking down his arms. He sat up, coughing, squinting through a hellish landscape of black smoke and flaming debris.

The explosion had picked him up and hurled him against the wall with the easy contempt of someone flicking away an insect. He could make out nothing through the smoke but the body of the guard—and another body, twitching faintly, just ahead. But somewhere nearby, he could hear the woman screaming—and another voice joining in, a man's. They weren't in his head. They were real—

He dragged himself up, fighting every instinct he had—to rip the mask off his face, to scream for help, to run away. His throat burned like fire, but he sucked in a lungful of the cooler currents of air near the floor and pressed his mask closer to his face as he climbed stiffly to his feet. The ship was rocking as if caught in a storm—or perhaps it was his head spinning. Nausea threatened to send him to his knees again, but a fresh scream surged through his limbs like lightning, and he finally managed to stumble forward. He staggered blindly toward the screams, averting his eyes from the twitching, smoking mass of charred flesh that had once been the other guard.

Luck. Simple luck had saved him. His arms were burned, his sleeves in tatters, but he could still move them—and everything else had been shielded by the unfortunate guard. The prisoners had had no such shield, but they were alive—they were still alive—

He spotted their outlines in the smoke and surged forward, drawing a short kitchen knife from his belt. The woman, still screaming in Savillan, turned to face him as he fell to his knees beside her—and then screamed even louder. He winced, remembering too late what he looked like.

"Amica, esso amica," he rasped in clumsy Savillan, feeling for the ropes that bound her. "Sei—sta—bena?"

"È muerta, Dia mi, è muerta, Antonio è muerta, puertaci furi di qua, piacere—"

He started sawing through the ropes. The man beside her thrashed furiously against his ropes; the man on her other side slumped against his bonds, horribly still.

"Ch'esa?" demanded the conscious man.

"No importi," Kayo snapped, fighting to keep his hand steady as he coughed so hard it hurt his ribs.

The rope finally snapped. The woman ripped free at once and clawed at the ropes that bound her ankles, unknotting them with a swift proficiency that suggested she was merely untying her bootlaces. Kayo handed her the knife, and she slashed through the ropes that bound her companions.

Two of the men slumped to the deck, lifeless. One of them—Kayo couldn't even look at him. His clothes were burned away, his face and chest mottled red and black. But the other—

"Come on," Kayo muttered, shaking his shoulder, patting down his smoldering clothes. "No—no, wake up, please wake up, we have to go—"

He never stirred. But when Kayo pressed a hand to his chest in desperation, he could feel it moving. He was still alive.

"Mueva!" the woman snapped at him as she hauled her companion to his feet. "È muerta! He die! Go!"

"He's still alive!" Kayo shot back. "Mi aieta!"

"Che?" said the woman sharply. She fell to her knees beside him, checking the man's pulse. Then she barked a command at another man, who bent double and, with Kayo and the woman's help, hauled the body over one shoulder.

"Come on," Kayo urged them. "Andiano, let's go, andiano—"

The deck beneath them gave a sickening heave as if to prove his point. He could have sworn that the ship tilted a few degrees in the process.

"Let's go!" he yelled.

The woman nodded and snapped at the other two men, who stumbled through the smoke without hesitation, one of them supporting the other. The last man, burdened with the unconscious sailor, hurried to follow. Kayo ran ahead of them, searching blindly for the stairs in the direction the sailors were moving—they seemed to know the ship so well that they didn't need to see. He tripped over the risers, scrambled up them on all fours and onto the deck above.

The fresh, cool air struck his skin like a thousand sharp blades, but he filled his lungs greedily, coughing as he struggled to keep his balance on the uneven deck. Every step aggravated wounds that he did not yet care to see, wounds that stung like a whip on his back, thighs, and arms. He ignored them as best as he could, his mind a whirl of panic as he tried to remember the layout of the ship and the docks. If he could just get them across the gangplank and out of the open, they'd stand a chance. He just—

The ship shuddered again, bucking beneath his feet. He lunged for the gunwale at the edge of the deck and clung to it, fighting to control his thoughts through the violent undercurrent of desperation pulling at his chest that urged him to leap into the water and flee as far as he could from the black smoke pouring out of the ship.

And that was when he saw the soldiers: a score of them, crowding on the docks. They were running forward, their lanterns bobbing in the night as they poured onto the dock like ants, single-minded and made fearless by their numbers. Shouting, pointing, lifting their bows and aiming arrows—

At him.

Kayo rolled out of the way just in time; with a whistle and a thunk, the first arrow buried itself in the gunwale, and half a dozen more soon followed. They were surrounded. There was no way out. And now that they'd spotted him—

In his head, he suddenly heard Liam's voice—hoarse and grating from a childhood injury, stern and as stubborn and unforgiving as stone. *Focus on what's in front of you*, the voice told him, and he could almost see Liam standing in front of him, his eyes burning with the ferocious intensity of the obsessed. *Focus on what's at stake.*

The Savillans were staggering onto the deck now, stumbling as they fought to keep their balance. They needed him to bring them to safety: they had no weapons, and they were far too weak to fight. He could not battle the soldiers by himself, nor could he outrun them—not with the Savillans in tow. That left only one option.

"Mi aieta!" he called to the Savillans. Two of them rushed forward, and when he grabbed the end of the gangplank and hauled, they quickly followed suit. An arrow slammed into the wood an arm's length from their fingers, and the wood wobbled and bent as a soldier ran onto the other end—but with a final surge, Kayo and the two Savillans managed to shove it off the ship. It tumbled into the water with a massive splash, dragging the soldier with it.

They backed away as more arrows rained down, and Kayo tugged the two men behind the mast. He ripped off his glove, stuck two fingers into his mouth, and whistled three notes, high then low then high, so loudly that the Savillans flinched and cried out in protest. To his relief, a shrill, wavering echo of his notes sounded in the distance, no more than a bowshot away. Turning to find it, Kayo saw a ball of flame flare to light on one of the rooftops, arcing up, up, up, and then back down—

The flaming arrow punched a hole through a tattered sail and buried itself into the mast. It started smoking at once, and the Savillans cried out as fire began to crawl across the canvas.

"It's all right," Kayo yelled. "It's fine, it's my friend, he's on our side—"

But they didn't understand. Neither did he—it wasn't like Dominic to miss. Not until two more flaming arrows followed, burying into the gunwale.

Dominic was burning the ship.

Kayo cursed, turning to the Savillans.

"Go," he ordered them, pointing toward the opposite gunwale, toward the harbor and the docks and the open sea. "Go, now, you have to swim to shore! Go, *go*—"

"But—you—" stammered the woman, her eyes flicking between him and the flames crawling up the ship.

"Tell them to jump into the water!" he shouted, losing patience. "I'm trying to help you, don't you understand?! Go, go *now!*"

"You come," said the woman suddenly, and pain lanced up his arm as she grabbed it. "Come. Sei?"

The words startled Kayo, and it took him a moment to find his tongue. "No," he said. "I'm going to distract them."

"You die," the woman insisted. Kayo was suddenly reminded of Liam, who would never have left him on his own.

But he was gone now—and someone had to take his place. Someone had to take charge.

"I'll be fine," he said firmly, pushing the woman toward the water. "Now go—*go!*"

Kayo nearly had to shove the nearest Savillan over the gunwale and even then, he hesitated, talking rapidly in Savillan to his companions until, at a sharp retort from the woman, he turned and launched himself into the ocean. The woman barked at the other men until they followed. Then, with Kayo's help, she lowered the unconscious man as gently as possible over the edge while the others reached up and caught him.

"You go too," Kayo ordered her, alarmed by the way she watched the men swim toward the distant docks without making a single attempt to follow them. "Ah—sinnora, va, piacere va—"

The woman eyed him calmly as he spoke, almost with a hint of amusement, as if she had completely forgotten where she was and that she was in danger. As she drew closer he realized how young she was —not much older than he.

"Sinnorina—"

She threw her arms around his neck and silenced him with a kiss.

He stood frozen for a moment, stunned and dizzy from her outburst. Then a softer, gentler instinct took over, and he found himself kissing her back, deeply and firmly, one hand at her waist as the other slid up her back.

Her tongue brushed across his lips, sweet despite the bitter smoke clouding their lungs. Then she pulled away, only to press her mouth to his neck and whisper a single word in his ear.

"Grazia."

Then a creak of wood, and a splash—and when he opened his eyes, she was gone.

"*Fire!*"

At a shout from behind, he whirled around just in time to see more arrows pepper the deck in front of him. Another flaming arrow arced across the sky in retort, this time landing on the docks. Dominic was going to burn it all—a wall of fire between him and the soldiers, stalling them so Kayo could escape. But the prisoners were injured. If he followed them, he'd only get them caught again. He'd wait, wait until the last possible second, and then he'd take off in the opposite direction.

That was what he told himself as arrows rained down, as fire crawled across the gunwale and the deck, as the masts lit up like torches until he could feel the heat cooking his face. But he found himself backing up until he hit the gunwale, veins of ice crawling down his skin despite the heat.

He was trapped. The whole place was burning, and he was trapped.

He'd made a horrible mistake.

Sharp taps on the hull, shouts growing nearer. Some of the more courageous soldiers were climbing the ship. The zip of an arrow, a yell, a splash—Dominic had taken one of them down. But an arm rose to loop around the gunwale, followed by a head, a city guard's uniform, and—

The last possible second.

Kayo drew his knife, praying his hand would keep steady.

The soldier called to the others, then rounded on Kayo. Another one started hauling himself over the railing.

That plank—there. When the man stepped on that plank, he would jump.

Fire and smoke tangled overhead, whipped into a hellish storm. It was closing in on him, pressing down.

He could hear children screaming. It was all in his head, he knew it was, but—

The soldier stepped on the plank. Kayo raised his knife—

And the soldier froze, swaying where he stood. One eye stared blankly at Kayo; the other had sprouted an arrow. Kayo recognized the gull feathers of the fletching, the knotwork on the twine—he had made the arrow himself.

The soldier fell to his knees, then slumped forward. And behind him, Kayo saw more—half a dozen more, closing in—and half a hundred more on the docks.

He turned and launched himself over the railing, plunging into the sea.

The smithy had been abandoned long ago, left to rot and crumble, broken windows boarded up by rotting planks. The outdoor workshop was cluttered with piles of rubble and scrap metal, stripped of every scrap of value by scavenging thieves. Inside, dusty sunlight fell from gaps in the sagging roof and touched upon forgotten, rusting tools and equipment.

The citizens of the upper city passed it by without a second glance. Had they bothered to look inside, however, they would have seen a girl sitting inside next to a girl-sized gap in the door, playing with a golden chain around her neck.

The girl had just survived her sixth winter in the upper city—but the years had not been kind to her. The winter following the Beggar King's execution had been especially brutal, and even now, at the advent of spring, a bitter chill bit at her skin whenever the wind snaked through the streets. She had stolen a large man's shirt to become the topmost layer in a hodgepodge of mismatched clothes, breeches underneath shirts underneath two long-sleeved chemises and a summer dress, none of it hers originally, all of it ragged and filthy. The stains told the story of her life in reverse: a dribble of gravy from the last hot meal she'd had, well over a week ago, on the topmost shirt;

a dab of tar from a hiding spot last fall on the dress; ripped knees from a close call with soldiers a year ago on the breeches; food, grease, dirt, lye, blood, halfheartedly scrubbed along with the rest of her on the rare occasion when she scraped off most of her skin and called herself clean. As for the final layer, who even knew what shape it was in? Not her—all she knew was that it itched.

She had made occasional cuts at the neck and armpits and thighs on her clothes to make room for growth, but there hadn't been much of that. Her bony figure and too-small clothes made her look taller than she was, and her snarled mane of hair gave her a bit of much-needed height, but she lamented on a daily basis that she did not have longer arms (for stealing hard-to-reach items) and longer legs (for running faster when she got caught). The wild mud-brown curls hid a thin face set permanently in a bitter grimace and hollow eyes as sharp as a crow's—an ugly one, she would have wagered, judging by a very scant winter spent begging on street corners.

The only thing she liked about her appearance was her necklace, as much a part of her as if it had grown from her skin. She played occasionally with the chain, but touched the pendant only through her clothes, keeping it tucked safely under all the layers and pressed against her skin.

She was waiting patiently for sunrise, ignoring the hunger that shook her entire body, the dizziness, the weakness, the nausea. Every beat of her heart pounded against her chest with such force that she feared it would knock her over. If she moved from that spot without first finding something to eat, she was certain that she would pass out in a dark alley somewhere and never wake again. But she refused to acknowledge it, refused to let it terrify her.

It was her own fault, and she was furious with herself for letting it happen. Once again, like a fool, she had gone searching for a way to slip out of the city—and once again, she had gotten lost. After several days and nights of dodging soldiers, rooting around in piles of rubbish, and trying and failing to catch a few edible rats, she had finally wandered back into familiar territory...and that, she swore to herself, was the last time she would attempt such idiocy. She was nearly eighteen, and would look it soon enough, and she was lucky enough not to have a mark on her shoulder designating her an orphan, a criminal, or any other type of undesirable. After a wash and some new clothes, she could walk through the city gates without attracting notice.

First, however, she had to survive—but she didn't let herself worry about that. Food would come soon enough.

The source of the expected food was the bakery next door, from which emanated the almost unbearably delicious scent of bread and sweet buns. She knew the bakery well. The baker was an absent-minded widower with a penchant for leaving baked goods unattended on the windowsill, and he never seemed to notice when some of them vanished. It was one of the few places where she was guaranteed to find something to eat, as long as she was careful.

From the other side of the wall came a soft rattling—the opening of a window. She held her breath and listened to the clattering of trays beneath the baker's cheerful whistling. She had to press her hand to her mouth to stop herself from whimpering as a fresh wave of mouth-watering smells drifted through the air.

She waited until the whistling receded, until she could hear the baker bustling around at the far end of the kitchen. Then she wriggled through the gap and out into the open, sneaking in a crouch beneath the wide windowsill on which sat dozens of buns, lined up in neat rows. She hid right below the windowsill. Her hand snatched up, and a fat, steaming bun tumbled down and landed neatly into her lap. She grabbed it and scrambled behind a nearby rain barrel, prying open her hands to inspect her prize.

It was just a plain bun, but in that moment, she'd never seen anything so beautiful. Even when she tore the golden crust in half, bathing her face with a soft cloud of steam, she could not quite believe her good fortune. She took an experimental bite. She had learned long ago that eating too fast after long periods of starvation would only make her sick, and her dry mouth struggled with even the smallest bite of soft, fresh bread. But she kept it down. She stuffed the rest of it into her cheeks after that, devouring it so quickly that she couldn't even feel her burned tongue until after the bun was gone.

The nausea passed, and she breathed a sigh of relief, slumping against the wall. Her appetite returning with a vengeance, she looked around, searching for any unwanted onlookers. Seeing none, she crept back out, reaching up to grab another bun....

"STOP!"

The girl shrieked and shot back behind the barrel.

From somewhere to the south rose a sudden violent clamor—screams, shouting, slamming doors and shutters, the thudding of heavy boots—that seemed to be drawing closer. She caught a flurry of movement above her and cringed—but the soldiers running across the bridge above her did not look at her. Their attention was directed further upward still, at something she could not see.

The soldiers stopped in the middle of the bridge, spread out, raised their bows. From their indiscernible shouts came a sharp command, and they pointed them into the air, firing at the rooftops. Something detached itself from the shadows and dashed away just in time to dodge the swarm of flying arrows. It was a man in dark clothes, his face hidden by a hood and a mask.

"The Beggar King!" she heard someone shout, and the call was echoed by voices on every nearby street, raising the alarm. "The Beggar King—it's the Beggar's King!"

The Beggar King—could it be? She shivered as she watched him run, some primal instinct warning her of danger. The Beggar King was dead, she had watched him die, but the way this man moved....It could not be anyone else. Could they have executed the wrong man?

The Beggar King threw himself into the air, and she gasped as he plummeted through space, certain that he would collide with a stone wall and tumble to his death—but there was a deliberation and grace in his flight, a calculated and measured positioning of his limbs, almost as if he had done it on purpose. He latched onto a heavy shutter on the opposite wall, then used his momentum to swing forward, diving feet-first through the window—and vanished.

The soldiers rushed to surround the building, one of them calling frantic, panicked orders to the rest, all of them hurriedly nocking their bows. She looked up, craning her neck to see past the buildings that were in the way, holding her breath, praying that he would somehow escape—

Then someone shouted and pointed, and she saw him: a dark shadow on the windowsill on the other side of the building. A thrill raced through her blood at the sight of him crouched there like a bird of prey, watching the world through the black emptiness beneath his hood. As the soldiers ran toward him, he launched himself into the air again and, with a neat flip, landed in a catlike crouch on a rooftop. She could not help but cheer with the rest, clapping her hands and laughing, heedless of who was watching. The Beggar King ran along the length of the roof and began to climb upward with startling agility, arrows flying around him as he pulled himself upward using hand- and footholds that she could not even see. He hauled himself onto a balcony and began to run.

She jumped suddenly as she came to her senses—the fugitive was getting too close, much too close, and a score of soldiers followed him. Keeping low, she crawled hastily back into the abandoned smithy, scraping her elbows and knees and chin as she wriggled through the tiny gap. She found a far corner and hid in it, hugging her knees as she looked upward, following the sounds.

More running—mostly the unmistakable thuds of soldiers' heavy boots, but she fancied that she could hear the light tap of the Beggar King's quick footsteps. Shouting, coming closer all the while. Clatters against the street outside as arrows rained down.

"Shoot him!" somebody howled. "Ready—aim—"

The reverberating twang of a dozen bows. A tapping on the roof of the smithy like rain. A shout.

"*We got him!*"

A crash.

With a sickening crack and crunch of splitting wood the roof collapsed, sending splinters and stones and tiles and dirt raining down. Something dark and solid tumbled downward and collapsed with a sound like a sack of meat hitting a wall. Peering around a barrel, coughing, the girl saw the black-clad fugitive lying face down in the center of the floor in a pool of dusty sunlight, the shaft of an arrow jutting out from his shoulder blade. His sleeves were in tatters, the skin raw and red.

She stayed where she was, holding her breath, her eyes searching the remnants of the roof. She could hear soldiers calling to each other, their voices drifting down through the hole like the last few sprinkles of dust.

"Do you see him?"

"Is he in there?"

"Someone go look!"

"No—wait a minute, you idiots! The roof ain't gonna hold you either! Get down to the street and surround the place, keep your bows out, he's not gonna go down without a fight—c'mon, move it, move!"

They were coming for him. And if they found him, they would find her—

She would never be able to explain to anyone, especially herself, exactly why she did what she did then. It was easily the bravest and most reckless thing she had ever done, and, she thought as she left her hiding place and ran toward the black figure crumpled on the floor, the stupidest. Yet still she did it. Still hurried over to kneel by his side, confirming that he still breathed. Still grabbed him by the bootlaces and dragged him into the shadows.

He was not large—she had expected the Beggar's King to be much bigger—but he was heavy, so heavy that the effort of pulling him dragged her vision into blackness and made her head start spinning again. But the sound of soldiers' boots on the street goaded her onward, and desperation gave her the strength to finally pull him behind a cracked counter piled high with rusted metal, shielding them further behind a small, overturned wheelbarrow. She fell back against the counter and held him close, clutching his chest to hers, afraid to break the silence within the smithy with even the smallest breath as the soldiers gathered outside. Every heartbeat she felt against her skin was a relief, especially the ones that were not her own.

"In there—"

"Can you see him?"

"—don't see anything—"

"—some rubble, some old metal scraps—"

"He's got to be in there somewhere!"

"You two, get this door open, go on—"

Amongst the thuds of boots on the street and the voices shouting back and forth she heard the rusted iron-bound doors scraping in protest as the soldiers obeyed the command. Then came heavy foot-falls on the smithy floor, slowly approaching the open space in the center where the man, by some magnificent stroke of luck, had fallen

—instead of on one of the tangled nests of abandoned metal, the anvils of multiple sizes scattered about, or the ancient, rusting furnace that dominated the back corner.

The girl held her breath as the soldier inspected the wreckage, not even daring to look. Her entire being was focused completely upon listening to his footsteps and determining, by the sound, where he was...and where he was going to be.

After a long silence, in which her heart threw itself with painful rapidity against her ribs, the captain finally shouted up to his companions: "All of you, search the streets, half in each direction—hurry!"

"What?"

"He's escaped, Captain?"

"He must've crawled through this gap here and run off—get after him, what are you waiting for?"

"Yessir!"

A loud clamor on the street signaled the departure of more of the soldiers. The footsteps scattered in different directions, then faded into the distance. The captain followed his men, and as the sound of his boots against the cobblestones faded, utter silence reigned once more over the street.

The girl let out an audible sigh, releasing a shaky breath. The Beggar King sagged in her arms, and, exhausted by his weight, she allowed him to slump to the floor. The fletching on the arrow stuck in his back brushed against her as he slid out of her arms.

It had been a long time since she'd interacted with anyone at all, and she had never had much of a moral compass. Should she...help? She should help. It was the *Beggar King*. She'd heard a thousand stories about him and his heroic adventures, some even taking place after his supposed death. She couldn't just leave him there to die or get arrested, especially after a spectacle like that. She had never seen anything like it—until he had gotten himself shot, at least, like any idiot could do.

Helping was the least she could do. She had no idea how, but that seemed only a minor detail. She could at least start with the arrow still stuck in his back. Surely it couldn't hurt to do the nice thing and pull it out—or at least, it couldn't hurt *her*.

With a calm fortitude born from the knowledge that she would not feel anything that she did, she grabbed the arrow and jerked it free. To her surprise it came away easily, with very little blood, leaving a wound no more serious than a bite from a small dog. The arrow seemed to have struck at a high angle, and his leather armor had blocked the worst of it. What she wouldn't give to have this man's luck....

She hurled the arrow away, where it fell with a clatter amid one of the piles of scrap, and rolled the fugitive onto his back.

She was surprised to find that nothing he wore was black, though it was so dark it was difficult to tell. It was all deep blue, deep brown, deep green. Not even his boots were black; they'd clearly been lighter once until a crude hand had rubbed them down with deep brown polish. Dark breeches, dark gloves, dark hood, and a dark scarf tied around his mouth and nose like a mask. A dark shirt, too, but in tatters now—judging by the charred fabric and the shiny red burns on his arms, his luck had saved him more than once this day.

After a moment's thought, she pushed the hood carefully back and pulled the mask away. She would not have dared to do so if he were conscious, but this was *the Beggar King*—she *had* to see who he really was, if for no other reason than to say that she had.

Above where the mask had been, his eyes and forehead were smudged with what looked like paint—once black and red, now eroded to smears of ash-gray and watery crimson. She studied his face with fascination. Fierce brows, full lips, a strong jaw. Dark hair and golden-brown skin, like a Savillan, the long hair tied behind his head in a tail of rippling silk. A deep scar across his temple, another smaller scar just below his ear, where a small hoop earring shone faintly in the light. High cheekbones, long lashes—she couldn't see much else behind the paint.

But something was wrong with his face, and it took her a minute to realize what it was. The man was not a man, at least not in her opinion. He was just a boy, a few months older than her at best. She leaned back on her heels and scowled at him. He was not the Beggar King after all—only a pretender. Certainly not worth the effort it would take to help him further. Time to abandon him to his own fate and flee the scene before the soldiers returned—*after* she picked his pockets.

With a deftness born of practice, she frisked him, searching his pockets and shirt for anything worth stealing. She took his knife, but other than that, he had nothing. She couldn't deny her annoyance. She had expected the Beggar King to have sleek black armor, beautiful custom-made weapons, silk and velvet clothes, or at least enough in his pockets to buy a hot meal, but she was disappointed. Even his boots were too worn and dilapidated to steal. In his pockets she could only find two cuprums and a little pink seashell, of all things. He wore a few bracelets on one arm, but they were crafted of string and yarn and beads and looked like a child had made them—several years and one or two fires ago. She doubted they were worth anything, but she cut them loose and took them anyway. The *real* Beggar King would know as well as anyone that there was no honor among thieves—and this pretender had it coming for deceiving her.

She could at least steal his earring. If it was real silver, it could be worth—

The boy's eyes snapped open. His fist shot out and slammed into her jaw.

"*Ow!*" She reeled back and clutched her cheek, lashing out indiscriminately with her other hand at his face and chest. She hadn't spoken in months, maybe years, and the words tore at her throat like broken glass as they left her, but that did not stop him from hurling every curse she knew at him. "Dammit, that *hurt,* ya stupid mud-brained sunova *whore*—"

The boy rolled over and ducked out of her reach, lifting his hand in supplication. "No—I'm sorry, shit, I'm really sorry, I didn't mean—"

He froze, his words dying in his throat. His hands rose to his face; his eyes fell to his mask on the floor. For a few seconds he merely blinked at it, as if he could not remember where he had seen it before. Then he sat bolt upright with a startled shout, making the girl shriek and raise the stolen knife.

"Please," he said, raising both hands in front of himself. "It's all right. Please don't be frightened, I'm not going to hurt you—"

The girl laughed aloud at that. "Hurt *me?*" she repeated scathingly. "I've got yer knife, idiot, how 'bout I hurt *you?*"

The boy swallowed and nodded, taking a deep, steadying breath.

Then, slowly, he reached into his boot and drew a dagger from a hidden sheath. She stared at it as he dropped it on the floor and slid it over to her. She snatched it up without thinking. This was a proper dagger, belonging to a high-ranking soldier or a paranoid nobleman—but how had she missed it? She was beginning to lose her touch.

"*Now* you've got my knife," he said quietly, his eyes studying hers. "Go on and take it. Just—*please* don't yell. If anyone finds out who I am—"

"I don't *know* who ya are," she snapped. "You're crazy. Who *does* that, flyin' around dressed like *him,* doin' backflips out o' windows—screw you, you're on yer own—"

She rose to her feet—but the boy stood and grabbed her wrist, pulling her back.

"Wait—who are you?" he asked her. He watched her in confusion, his expression blank.

She twisted free, her lips curling in a snarl. "Get off o' me!"

"What's your name?"

"What d'you care? I *said* don't touch me!"

He withdrew, but his eyes never left her. They were bright and long-lashed, with irises the color of honey in the light—and completely empty, even as he swept them over her. She flinched away from his scrutiny.

"What's your problem?" she demanded.

He blinked, then lifted his eyes slowly to meet hers. "You're my age," he said.

"S-so what?" She took a step back, putting some distance between them; she was beginning to wonder if he'd lost his mind.

"Well...I don't know you."

"An' I don't know *you,* it's a big city, who gives a—?"

"Where do you live?" His brow furrowed; this simple question seemed to be taking all his concentration.

"None o' yer business," she fired back.

"Do you live *anywhere?* With your parents—?"

"Do I *look* like I got parents?" she said irritably. "Wouldn't tell ya where it was if I did have a home, ya bloody lunatic....Ugh." She massaged her jaw with her fingers. "Ya punch like a baby...shoulda just let the soldiers have ya."

He stiffened. "*Soldiers?*"

"Well, I *assumed* so," she sniffed. "What with th' armor an' all."

"What soldiers? Where?"

"The soldiers that were just chasin' you five minutes ago. How d'you not—?"

"They're after me?" he breathed, his face paling in sudden terror.

"Yeah...what's wrong wit' you, don't ya remember?"

"Oh no—no, no, no—" He shot up so quickly that it made her jump. "C'mon!"

"I said let go o' me!"

"C'mon, we've gotta go, we gotta get out of here, you have to hide—"

"Get *off!*"

"*Please,*" he begged her. "Please, come on. I don't want you to get hurt because of me—just come with me, please, don't you want to get out of here?"

"Outta—?" She looked up at him in sudden excitement. "You mean outta the *city?* You know how t' get out?"

"Of course I do," he said confidently. "Yeah, c'mon, I'll show you."

This time, when he reached for her hand, she let him take it. He smiled faintly; she had a strange feeling that he had, somehow, mistaken her for somebody else—somebody that actually mattered to him. But she didn't care. She could handle a single skinny madman and his frail punches. If he could really get her out of here, help her escape....She could live a whole new life. Find work, buy a home, create a brand-new identity and be whoever, whatever, she wanted....

"What's your name?" he asked again.

She rolled her eyes. "Shut up."

The boy beamed at her. "Perfect," he said happily. He led the way back into the street, grinning like a fool all the way.

He managed to get them lost within minutes.

"It's...it has to be...this way?" he muttered to himself, making a hesitant step toward the left fork in the path. "No...."

The girl groaned, burying her face in her hands. "Goddess *above*, where're y' even tryna go?"

"Just...down," he said, gesturing vaguely toward the lower levels. "I'll find it from there."

"You couldn't find yer own ass," she snapped. "It's this way. I swear, if y' just take me to the damn gate, I'm gonna *kill* you—"

"We're not going to the gate," he promised her. But his certainty faded almost immediately. "Where...where are we?"

"What, you wanna map? I'm tryna take us lower, like y' said."

"Yeah, but...I've never been here...."

That, she thought, was probably for the best—but she would never admit it to him. They were descending deep into the bowels of the upper city now, into the maze of ancient buildings erected a thousand years ago. Now these buildings were reinforced—or, just as often, pierced through—by columns of stone sometimes as big around as a small house, which had been added throughout the years to reinforce the layers of architecture that climbed higher and higher over their heads.

These relics of Bermeia's past were little more than overly elaborate infrastructure for drainage now: all the trash and refuse of the roads and homes above eventually washed down here. During the rainy months, the whole place flooded with watery sewage that reached the rooftops. And just like any sewer, the old city was inhabited by pests—including the human ones. Here, where even the faintest sunlight could only be seen in quick glimpses at high noon, only the lowest types of people and industry thrived, having been driven out or banished from the world of hardworking and morally upright citizens above. Among the ruins thrived hundreds of shifty-looking shops, like the "apothecary" that sold only poisons, the "smithy" that fenced stolen and illegal weapons, the "inn" filled with naked women, a "general store" that bought slaves and shipped them to Riazli in the south, a "tavern" where men gambled on cards, dice, and dog fights, and a tavern that was actually just a tavern, but every man inside could be hired to kill another man for a handful of coins.

Whether the trash consisted of wastewater, eggshells, or human beings, the old city was the receptacle for all the city's unwanted refuse, the entire network of streets serving as one enormous trash heap for the civilized city that towered above it. But the girl had never dreamed that there was an even lower and filthier layer—a place that repulsed even the old city, where even fouler waste could collect and ferment.

And yet, there she found herself after following the boy: standing on the filth-splattered, debris-littered, slimy-cobblestoned dead-end alley that served as a funnel for the grate in the wall at her feet. A grate that, judging by the smell, led to the city sewers.

"You must be jokin'," she said flatly. "There is no way in *hell*."

"No, I...it's this way," he insisted. "This is the only way to get there."

He had only become more muddled, if that were possible, as their journey into the old city had progressed. Judging by his now-permanent grimace, his slight stagger, and the way he had leaned against the walls for support over the past few minutes, the girl could only assume that his injuries were paining him and clouding his mind. Despite herself, she felt bad for him—but not enough to take one step further.

"Come on," he pleaded when she would not move. "You have to hurry, they're coming for us."

"I'm not goin' down there with *you!*"

"But you...they're after you," stammered the boy, blankly, as if he could not understand her reluctance. "The soldiers...you can't let them find you, don't you know what they'd do to you?"

"Of course I know!" she shouted at him. "But I don't got a choice, what else 'm I s'posed to do? Where else is there t' go?"

He recoiled slightly, startled by her outburst—but he stood his ground. "With me," he said firmly. "The sewers run all over the place, under the whole city—there's an exit at the bridge, and another one by the harbor. I'll show you."

She eyed the grate, considering the prospect. She had never been further down than this, had never wanted to be—but had she known there was a network of tunnels buried below the ground, she might have changed her mind. It was certainly worth exploring, especially if it linked one part of the city to the other. She glanced at the boy, who was leaning against the wall, watching her with half-closed, half-focused eyes. She had his knives, after all—what could he possibly do to her?

"Please," he said, with an expression like a dog begging for scraps. "I just—I don't want you to get hurt because of me."

She glared at him. He blinked back at her, milking those long eyelashes for all that they were worth.

In the end, it was not his words that convinced her, or his innocent eyes. It was not what she stood to gain. It was the realization that she did not have anything to lose.

She shoved at the grate with her heel, pushing it back from the small square hole.

The boy gave her a faint smile. "That's my girl," he murmured, making her flinch. Then, with a visible effort, he pushed himself away from the wall and swung himself into the hole. She held her breath as she eased herself into the darkness in his wake.

She landed with a splash in fetid, ankle-deep mud—at least, she hoped that it was mud. It splattered all over what was left of her skirts and soaked instantly through the rags wrapped around her feet, and she wrinkled her nose at the foul smell of it as she looked around. They stood in a tunnel carved into the bare stone, so low that the boy's head nearly touched the ceiling. The tunnel sloped sharply downward, allowing the oily brown sludge to trickle slowly away. Another grate punctured the ceiling not too far away, within bowshot, providing just enough light to navigate.

She looked to the boy, expecting him to lead the way—but instead, to her revulsion, he doubled over and retched into the water at his feet. She stumbled back with a startled exclamation, edging over to the tunnel wall as he heaved again and again.

"What's th' matter with you?" she demanded. But the boy just shook his head, panting and clutching his stomach, waiting for more to come. After a minute or so, when it didn't, he spat and stood, wiping his mouth on his sleeve.

"Sorry," he mumbled. "The smell...."

The smell made her want to vomit, too—but somehow, she doubted that that was all. He had been weakening the entire way here, and now he seemed alarmingly pale beneath the vestiges of paint, shivering faintly despite the fine sheen of sweat coating his forehead. She looked up at the grate and cursed—there was no way she could climb back out on her own.

"You sick?" she asked him. "Is it catchin'?"

He blinked at the sound of her voice. Then his eyes drifted away, bleary and unfocused. His hand rose and clutched his head, his face twisting in pain. "I...I need to go home," he stammered.

The sound of his voice frightened her worse than the vomiting. He sounded nothing like he had mere minutes before, bold and confident. Now, his voice whined like a tired child's.

"D'you...d'you know which way t' go?" she asked him.

He looked around, frowned, looked again. Then he pointed. "That way," he said quietly. "Then right. A thousand paces, maybe."

"Good...okay...." She cast one last longing look at the grate before turning away and following the tunnel downward. The boy trailed behind her, his eyes half-closed, his feet stumbling as if his boots were too big.

The tunnel curved left, then swung back to the right, then curved sharply again. A thousand paces, he had said. That wasn't far, even with bare feet. She lifted her chin, wading confidently through the sludge. If that was the price to leave the city, she would happily pay it.

They walked onward in silence. More than once, she nearly asked him a question, then closed her mouth with an annoyed huff. She was furious with him, and told him so with every pointed glare she threw his way, cursing her own annoying attack of weakness that had led her to care about a crazy fool who'd fallen through a roof. This stupid kid, dragging her around a reeking sewer tunnel, wandering into parts of the city that sane people usually avoided, threatening to collapse from some unknown illness that he had probably spread to her.... And what would she do, she wondered, if he did collapse? She'd already robbed him, and she wasn't about to touch him or stay anywhere near him. Her only options were to go back to where she'd been or continue on ahead. And dark and damp though they may have been, the sewers, at least, didn't have soldiers. It might be useful later to know the way through.

She glanced over her shoulder as she rounded another corner and saw the boy falling behind. "Hurry up," she called back to him. "I need ya t' show me—oh. Ugh...."

As she turned the corner she was immediately assailed by another hot wave of stale, foul-smelling air, strong enough to make her pull the collar of her shirt up to her watering eyes. Behind her, the boy bent over and retched again. She stepped out of the way, watching in mild fascination as he gagged and heaved without producing anything more than spit. At last he stood, shakier than ever, and plunged blindly past her along the path.

The source of the horrible stench spread out before her, but even as she clutched her shirt to her face, she couldn't help but be amazed. They stood on the bank of a large underground river, lit by small grates placed sporadically in the stone ceiling. If she squinted, she could just barely make out the other side—where, incredibly, she saw houses. Little windows and doors in a wall of stone brick stretching up past the ceiling, all of them crammed together. They were not inhabited—they looked as if they were filled to overflowing with broken stone—but they strongly resembled the buildings of the old city nonetheless. They stretched on infinitely, breaking only to allow more water to flow into the main river, and she realized: this *was* the old city. They had flooded the streets with water and built up all the houses so that a new city could be constructed on top of it, using the buried neighborhoods to funnel their waste and detritus to the sea.

The river reminded her a little of the main street in the lower city when it flooded in the summer. Some of the original road remained on their side: a narrow, slimy walkway carved out of the stone, eroded and slippery from centuries of constant wear. She winced as she edged along it in the boy's wake, keeping her back pressed against the wall.

"Don't worry." He had paused and looked back at her, or at least in her general direction. "It isn't deep." He waved a hand vaguely at the level of his upper thigh, indicating the depth of the river.

Her lip curled in revulsion. "That's *not* what I'm worried 'bout." But she straightened up and pulled away from the wall all the same. If he wasn't afraid, why should she be? She followed him with stubborn determination down the path, silently thanking him for his sluggish pace. It made her small, cautious steps seem a little more natural.

Their side, too, was lined with those little stone houses, crammed together. She got a close look at one as she passed it: the doorframe still had hinges, and she saw fat rusted nails dotting the mortar between the stones around the windows. But there were no doors, no shutters. Not even any boards, the way they shut up a house in the lower city when it was empty. There was just a solid wall of—she touched it, shaking her head at its coarseness—gravel? Solid mortar? It seemed to be a bit of both.

"Wha's this?" she demanded of the boy.

"Mm?" He looked around, blinking vaguely. She tapped the wall behind the doorway for emphasis. "Oh...'s liquid stone."

"Wh—*really?* I saw 'em use it once t' fix the seawall, 's like magic, 's jus' sand 'n water but when it dries—"

"Lime."

"It—what?"

"Not just sand. Lime."

"What's that?"

He didn't answer. She shrugged and grabbed one of the rusted hinges, trying to pry it loose.

"Where'd th' door go?"

"Rotted," he muttered. "Wood...rots away down here...."

He had started wobbling, and now he reached up, clutching at his head with one hand. She watched him closely as he walked, frowning at his odd behavior. He kept tilting his head and moving it oddly, as if he had water trapped in his ears. Occasionally he would stop, looking around in confusion. When this happened, she would give him a firm shove to set him into motion again—though she was careful not to touch his bare skin. Crazy or not, he was definitely ill. She was certain that he was going to die of it; the only question was when.

"Which way next?" she asked him, but what she meant was, *Will we get there before or after you pass out?*

"Huh?"

She sighed, nursing a headache of her own—a headache that she could trace directly back to the moment they had met. "Which way d'we go?"

"Up here...it's a right."

"Oh. Good." A left turn meant crossing the disgusting underground river. "Is it that tunnel, up ahead?"

"Hmm? Mm-mm. There's a sign...."

"A sign? What sign?"

He didn't answer; he just passed the opening by without a second glance. It was another tunnel, narrower, but lined with more rows of houses filled with liquid stone. She inspected it all over to make sure there was no "sign", pausing just inside and craning her neck to see farther down. The walls were far from clean, but there were no marks that seemed to be made on purpose. But the next tunnel wasn't far....

He passed that one too—and as she crossed behind him, she saw another very wide tunnel, identical to the one they traveled now. She groaned. They were almost certain to get lost, if they weren't already. There were probably dozens of different intersections like this one, they could wander around for years and never find a way out.

Yet the boy turned to the right without a moment's hesitation— and by the time she turned the corner too, he had vanished. She heard him splashing up ahead, down a slender earthen tunnel, and slipped in behind him. There was no walkway here, only an alleyway flooded with ankle-deep water. As she turned the corner, something on the wall caught her attention: a little mark scratched into the grime, something that looked vaguely like an arrow, pointed in the same direction as they traveled.

"Is this it? Where d'we go from here?"

He gave no response, nor did she expect one. The water splashed beneath her feet as she ran to his side, watching him closely as she matched his pace. One look at him told her that he was nearly at his limit.

Water. It was water beneath her feet, not sewage. She bent to scoop some into her hand, inspecting it. Clear as glass, nothing like the brownish water of the lower city. She took an experimental sip. It was so cold that it made her teeth ache—but beautifully sweet, sweeter even than goat's milk.

"This is...where is this comin' from? Are we still in the upper city...?"

The boy didn't answer her—but he didn't have to. The houses had given way to walls of bare rock, rough and uneven, and from one of the ragged gaps in the stone poured a tiny crystalline stream of pure water. There were more beyond that, shimmering every few feet. There were grates here too, through which sewage should have drained from up above and sullied the water, yet it was clean.

"Can y' believe—?"

The boy had stopped completely. He had both hands planted

against the wall, his head hanging down, loose strands of damp hair hiding his eyes. She approached him cautiously, fearing that he might vomit again—but his eyes weren't even open. As she watched him, he slumped forward, his forehead pressing against the stone.

"No—no, no, don't—" She lunged forward and grabbed his shoulders, steadying him on his feet. "We're so close, don't pass out on me, we're almos' there—c'mon—"

His eyelids flickered. His head shook wearily back and forth. "Almost there," he repeated, mumbling like a drunk.

"Yeah...yeah, we are," she promised him, though she could guarantee no such thing. An unfamiliar emotion writhed uncomfortably inside her guts like a wriggling snake. Whatever it was, it drove her to take his wrist and lead him forward, though with poor grace, all the while cursing her own weakness and reminding herself that she would come to regret it.

"C'mon. 'S not far. Come on...."

He moved sluggishly, at a frustratingly slow pace, like a sleepwalker—but at least he moved. His boots splashed heavily in the shallow water as he followed her. She was so focused on making sure that he kept moving that she didn't even notice the glow up ahead, not at first. Daylight, she thought. Perhaps the tunnel led outside—perhaps, she thought excitedly, they were even on the other side of the wall—

They turned a corner, ducked under a low-hanging precipice—and hit a dead end. Or at least, that's what she thought at first. Then, hauling the boy forward with a none-too-gentle jerk, she saw that the wall ahead was not solid stone, but comprised of many stones stacked loosely together, like bricks. And to one side there was a small gap, water flowing merrily through, bright sunlight on the other side.

She ducked into the gap, hauling the boy along behind her—then let him go, looking around in open-mouthed amazement.

She stood in a pool of flowing water bathed in sunlight from a small, crumbling hole in the stone far overhead, as if part of the ceiling had collapsed. A slender tongue of water lapped over the edge of the hole and cascaded down, forming a wall of clear water in front of her like a rippling pane of thick, uneven glass. She looked up, squinting in the unexpected light—and saw a splash of blue sky. She hadn't seen the sky in so long, not since....

She frowned. The hole in the ceiling was not small; the longer she looked, the more she realized that she could have dropped an ox through it without dislodging a single stone. It was simply very, very high up. She looked around, but the walls were smooth, and there was no way out that she could see. They were stuck.

"Well," she huffed, whirling around to face the boy, "this's just—"

Her words cut off with a curse and a violent start. She dove forward and fell on her knees. But she was too late to catch the boy, who had collapsed into the water. His face was bloodless, his eyes glazed beneath half-closed lids, his body heavy and limp. She shook him, splashing everywhere—then screamed at the sight of a faint red tendril of blood in the water.

"*H-Help!*" she shrieked, looking wildly around for something, anything, that could assist her. "Somebody, we need help, *help us!*"

She was still shouting as a soft noise behind her caught her attention. She was still shaking the boy, her fingers digging into his shoulders, as she turned to face it. But she had no time for a fresh cry before a huge figure in dark clothes, dangling from the end of a rope, wrapped her in a bone-crushing embrace and swept her off her feet.

S he screamed and struggled, but the man crushing her against his body didn't even seem to notice. Then, at last, he let her go. She stumbled back, wincing and throwing up a hand against the sudden, blinding sunlight.

She was—

Where was she?

The courtyard was long and curved and narrow, lined by columned arcades. A fountain sprang from a worn bas-relief and into a shattered basin, filling the air with the sound of falling water. A massive statue of the Goddess towered overhead, arms outstretched. The walls soared high overhead, but above them—

Nothing.

Just blue, clear sky.

She stared at it blankly, mentally calculating. How far had they gone? How high up?

"Kayo!"

She flinched—but the shout wasn't aimed at her. Two women were running across the courtyard toward them, one blonde and one dark-haired, and in an instant the blonde had the unconscious boy in her arms. The girl backed away as the dark-haired one joined her, as the big man knelt and helped them lower the boy to the ground. They all clustered around him, murmuring anxiously to one another.

"What happened to him?"

"—found him passed out in the water—"

"—looks like he hit his head—"

"Kayo? Baby? C'mon, wake up, talk to me—"

The two women could not have been more different. The blonde one, her hair falling over her shoulder in a disheveled braid, looked a little older—though that might have just been the exhaustion written plainly on her face. Her clothes were plain and worn, her apron covered in stains. In contrast, the other woman looked like a princess. She was beautiful, with features that could have been painted by an artist and a curving figure accentuated by a dress fit for a noblewoman.

The man was something else altogether. He'd seemed as massive as a bear when standing, and even kneeling and hunched over, he was formidable. He'd cut his hair close to his scalp, and shaved his face, but his clothes were little better than rags. The worn edges of his breeches stopped high above his bare, dirty feet, and his shirt....

She sucked in a breath. Just below the torn-off sleeve of his shirt, a purplish welt of scar tissue bubbled from brown skin, shaped like a circle.

An orphan.

She backed away until she hit the wall, looking wildly around. *Escape.* She had to escape. The way she'd come was a dark hole where water from the broken fountain spilled in—that way was no good, the drop was too far. But there had to be another way out—

There was a door at the end of the courtyard, recessed deep into the stone. Yes—there—if she could just reach it—

But as soon as she edged a step in that direction, the big man turned toward her. She froze as he stood up. He towered over her, casting her in shadow.

"And who are *you?*" he asked. He sounded, inexplicably, as if he were trying not to laugh.

She stood rooted to the spot, not even daring to glance toward the door.

"You all right?" he said.

The man took a step closer—and she found her voice at last.

"*Get away from me!*" she screamed.

He reeled back. "Whoa. Take it easy—"

She bolted. The sodden wraps around her feet slipped and caught on the rough stone, but she pushed harder, ran faster—

Halfway there, a strong hand closed around her arm.

"Hold on a minute—"

"Get off me!" she shrieked. "Don't *touch* me!"

"Just calm down—"

But she thrashed and struggled with all her strength, clawing at the iron hand with her fingernails, kicking at every bit of him she could reach.

"Lemme go! Let *go!*"

"Stop yelling!" one of the women shouted. "Someone will *hear* you—"

The voice was coming closer—they were surrounding her. In desperation, she shoved a hand into her skirts and scrambled for a weapon. Her fingers closed around a knife—the one she'd taken from the boy. She gripped it hard and swung it up and out and down—

A smaller, softer hand grabbed her wrist. The dark-haired woman yanked her close, twisting her hand at an odd angle until it started to throb. She yelled and fought, but the knife fell from her fingers.

The dark-haired woman held it up to the light. Her expression darkened, blue eyes narrowing to slits.

"This is *Kayo's*." Her grip tightened until it hurt. "Where did you get this?"

"No it ain't, I didn't—"

But the woman wasn't listening. "Hold her, Dom," she instructed the man, and then she started patting the girl down. The girl shrieked and fought, but the woman managed to find her pocket under her skirt and dig around inside. She finally extracted the contents, holding them out in her palm: two cuprums, a little pink shell, and a handful of yarn and beads.

The woman looked up, her pretty face taut with anger. "You *robbed* him?"

"I did *not*—"

"Did *you* hurt him?"

"No! No, I never, let *go*—"

"He's awake!"

They all turned to the blonde woman, who still knelt beside the boy. He was stirring, his eyelids fluttering.

"Let's settle this," the man said, and he steered her firmly toward the boy. She had no choice but to stumble forward, and when he shoved her, she fell to her knees. His firm hand on her shoulder kept her pinned down.

"Kayo," the man said loudly. "Do you know this girl? Who is she?"

She held her breath as the boy's eyes slowly opened, drifting across the sky before finally landing on her face.

She could practically feel the man's breath on the back of her neck. He was too big, and there were too many of them. Without a knife, they could do anything they wanted to her, and she wasn't strong enough to stop them.

Please, she prayed as the boy with the strange name blinked at her. *Please say something, tell them I didn't hurt you, tell them to let me go, please....*

A lazy, dreamy smile drifted across the boy's face. One hand drifted upward, the fingers resting on her cheek with surprising tenderness.

"Rose," he slurred with a vacant smile. She looked down and jumped at the sight of her necklace swinging freely against her chest. "It's a pretty name," said the boy. "You're so pretty, Rose...."

His hand slid down to her neck, tangled in the chain of her necklace. Then he dragged himself up and pulled her down in one quick jerk, stifling her cry by pressing his lips to hers. She gagged in shock as his mouth moved against hers, tasting vomit and blood, and tried to jerk loose. But he wouldn't let go. The chain was biting into her neck, and she couldn't breathe—

Her hand balled into a fist and lashed out.

The women screamed as her fist slammed into his eye. With a groan of pain, he released her, the chain still trapped in his fingers. Her necklace bit into her skin as he flopped back onto the paving stones, his eyes rolling back into his head. She felt the chain snap, then jerk free as his hand fell to the ground.

"That's enough," the man growled, and he dragged her up and away. She staggered and tripped, trying vainly to plant her heels into the stone.

"No! Let *go!*"

She glanced back and saw a golden glint in the boy's hand. She screamed and clawed at the man's hand, at his arm, at anything she could reach.

"No! No no *no!* Lemme go lemme go lemme *go* lemme—"

Darkness and shade. Indoors—stone and echoes. Dirt and stone. And then—

"*Ow!*"

He dropped her without warning, and she crashed to the stone floor so hard that black spots erupted before her eyes. She scrambled onto her hands and knees, diving blindly toward the light—just in time to see a door slam in her face.

The light snuffed out like a candle. On the other side, she heard metal scraping as a latch fell into place.

"You can stay in there until you calm down," said the man's voice on the other side.

She leapt up, lunging for the handle of the door. It wouldn't budge.

"Ya rat-faced *bastard!*" she yelled at the door. "Get *back* here! Ya can't just leave me here! Come back an' fight me like a man! Come *back!*"

But he was gone, his footsteps already retreating.

She shrieked in wordless fury, hurling herself against the solid wood until the effort made her dizzy. But even when she threw her entire weight against it, again and again until her shoulder throbbed, it did not budge. She sank to the floor with a scream of frustration.

Once she'd caught her breath, she looked around. There wasn't much to see. Feeling around, she could find only stone floors and stone walls. The ceiling slanted, sinking so low on one side that she banged her head on it. The whole space was only a couple of paces across, and so narrow that she could touch both walls with her arms outstretched.

Despite the warmth of the fresh spring day outside, it was freezing cold, and she shivered as she slumped against the wall and wrapped her arms around her knees. If not for a crack of grayish light under the door, it would have been completely black. That was also, she imagined with a grim twist of her mouth, her only source of fresh air.

She let her head fall into her arms, taking deep breaths as she tried to think.

That man was an orphan. The boy might be, too. She'd followed an *orphan* through the sewers and into a strange place—and even saved his life! She'd hidden him from the soldiers! The very thought made her sick. They were criminals, cutthroats, thieves, everybody knew that. They'd burned down their own orphanage, for the Goddess's sake! The city guard had a bounty on their heads!

And she'd *helped one*. That was almost as bad as *being* one. How could she have been so reckless? Why didn't she check for a mark before helping him?

She no longer wondered why he was impersonating the Beggar King. The orphans in the city were probably behind every rumor she'd heard of someone dressed like the Beggar King while engaging in petty theft and vandalism. The real Beggar King would never have bothered to steal an armful of bread from an unattended cart, but she wouldn't put it past an orphan.

This place, then, must be their nest. The soldiers had been looking for it for ages, with no luck. Of course not—no one would ever have thought to look for them in the upper city, let alone this high up. What was this place? A rich man's house? A closed-off section of the city? Had they wandered all the way into the Gardens?

It was useless to speculate. Only one thing was certain: she was doomed. The orphans would come back for her soon enough, and then—

She didn't know. But she'd heard plenty of rumors of what they were capable of doing.

No. She couldn't let that happen. She got up and paced back and forth until she got dizzy again, then sat back down, only to get up and pace once more. There had to be a way out of here—or a way past the orphans—or a way to signal for help....

There had to be a way.

After what seemed like hours, a distant sound made her pause. There it was again—footsteps. She froze as they came nearer, grew louder. There was nothing in her cell to use as a weapon, so she backed up against the wall, balled her fists, and prepared to fight.

The latch turned, and the door swung open. She hurled herself at the blinding light—

—and skidded to a halt, staggering back, as she stared down the end of an arrow.

The dark-haired woman stood beside the man. She held a bow, half-drawn, the arrow pointed right at the girl's heart. Everything about her, from her posture to the expression twisting her face, said she was prepared to fire.

"Don't move," the woman barked. "Don't make me shoot you."

"Artemis," the man warned her. But the woman—Artemis?—didn't seem to hear him.

"What happened to Kayo?" she demanded.

"*Who?*"

"*Kayo,*" repeated the man, as if she were being deliberately dense. "Our *brother.*"

She stared at him. "Your *brother?* Orphans ain't got *brothers.*"

Artemis made a scathing sound deep in her throat. The man rolled his eyes. "That kid you *punched,* then. *What happened?*"

"I didn't do *nothin'* to him, I didn't *touch* 'im—"

"How did you find this place?" Artemis demanded.

"Wh—he *brought* me—"

"And why the hell would he do that?" the man snapped, venom dripping from every word.

"*I* dunno, I don't *wanna* be here, jus' lemme go!"

"Not until we figure out what happened," Artemis cut across her.

"I *tol'* ya what happened! He *fell,* he hit 'is head, an' when he came to, he said come with 'im. I didn't know it would be *here.*"

"Kayo wouldn't *do* that," the man argued. "He wouldn't be that reckless."

"He might have been," Artemis muttered to him, lowering her bow just a little.

"*No,* he *wouldn't.* Not after last time."

"We'll just have to ask him."

"He's *knocked out.*"

"Well, we can't just—"

"*Let me outta here!*" she roared.

They jumped, and the point of the arrow snapped back up to aim at her chest.

"Just tell us what happened," said the man, holding up his hands in a calming gesture. "And we will. All right?"

"*No*, we will *not*," Artemis said with a warning glare.

"Arty, we can't *keep* her here!"

"Well, we can't let her *go*, she'll go right to the soldiers!"

"No, she won't. Look," said the man, turning back to the girl, who tensed. "Let's all calm down here. I'm Dominic, this is Artemis. And we're *not* going to hurt you. All right? We'll let you out of here, and you can go home. No harm done. So there won't be any need to tell anyone about this place, right?"

His smile was winning, his voice low and soothing. He almost had her convinced.

Almost.

But the orphan's mark was still branded into his skin—a warning that he couldn't be trusted.

She opened her mouth and hissed at them like a cat. And as they recoiled in shock, she looked them in the eyes and told them in the coarsest terms she could think of where they could stick that bow.

The two stared at her, then glanced at each other. Artemis slowly lowered the bow, easing the tension on the string.

"Forget it," she said, disdain practically dripping from every word. "She's not going to talk."

But the man was watching her with an odd, flat look—a look that chilled her to the bone. "Give me the bow," he said.

"Dom—"

In the time it took her to blink, the bow was in his hands— nocked, drawn, and aimed. The bow bent under the strain, but his arm never wavered. He pointed the arrow between her eyes, and her stomach dropped. Artemis was not the archer, she realized—*he* was.

She stiffened and pressed her back against the wall, her eyes locked on the tip of the arrow. It was just sharpened wood—but at this range, with his strength, it would punch right through her.

"Now," he said calmly, but there was a rippling undertone of fury behind his words that twisted her stomach into knots, "you listen to me. I don't care who brought you here—*nobody* threatens my family.

So if I were you, I'd start talking. Because the *second* you step out of line, you give any *hint* that you'll sell us out, I will put an arrow in your neck. You got that?"

She looked from him to Artemis, her heart pounding in her ears. His dark eyes were icy; he clearly meant every word. And Artemis, though wide-eyed and anxious-looking, made no move to stop him.

She swallowed and lifted her chin.

"I never touched 'im," she told them both. "If you don't believe me, go ahead an' shoot. I don't gotta answer to a bunch o' *orphans.*"

Artemis winced—but Dominic didn't. He kept the bow drawn, ready to fire; she scowled back at him, silently daring him to do his worst.

After a long moment, Dominic scoffed and lowered the bow.

"C'mon, Arty," he said, throwing a last contemptuous glare her way. "Let's go."

"What? Dom—"

"She'd sell us out for pocket lint," Dominic snapped. "Let her rot."

"Wait, you can't—" She scrambled to the door, but it shut so hard it whacked her in the face. She yelled in pain and hurled herself against the solid wood, pounding it with her fists. "Wait! You get back here! GET BACK HERE, YOU COWARDS!"

But after pounding until her hands stung, after screaming herself hoarse, she could hear only silence on the other side of the door. With a shriek of rage, she gave up and started to pace. Back and forth, back and forth....

If he doesn't die, I'll kill him myself, she fumed. *That lying orphan bastard, he was never going to get me out of the city!*

She should never have believed such an audacious claim. Orphans weren't allowed out of the city, everyone knew that. They'd made it nearly impossible for everyone else, too. There was no chance that someone like her could ever pass through the gates without being harassed by soldiers, mark or no mark. And she simply couldn't take that risk.

He better come back here and let me out, she thought, working herself into a fury. *He better tell them it was his stupid idea, he better be sorry for getting me into this, he'd better beg on his hands and knees, then I'm gonna rob 'em blind and get the hell out—I* should *rat 'em out, they got it comin', every last one—*

But this fantasy seemed feebler with every passing hour. She grew dizzy again, her body heavy and her head foggy, and she decided she should conserve her energy. Huddled in the corner of her cell, the icy stone digging into her spine, she tried to force her sluggish brain to think. But all she could manage was a growing anxiety that gnawed in her gut as ferociously as her hunger.

What if the boy *wasn't* coming back? What if he'd died? Or worse—what if he turned on her? He'd escaped, so he'd gotten what he wanted. It would be nothing to him to let his so-called "family" do whatever they liked to her. The thought infuriated her. It wasn't right, it wasn't fair, but she knew that the law of the land didn't apply on the streets. The orphans could do whatever they liked to her without being caught—and what was one more crime on top of all their others? What was it to the soldiers, either? The orphans could only die once.

She had to make a plan. If someone came back, she could fight them—she had to—but it would be better to escape before then. She devoted herself to memorizing every inch of her cell. For hours and hours, she ran her fingertips along the walls and floors and door, squinted in the darkness to look at the door latch from every angle, felt the hinges and the bolts and the tiny gap at the bottom of the door. She spent another hour shredding her fingernails as she tried to pry the metal bits from the wooden door, to remove the hinges or pull a loose bolt free or break the latch somehow. She gave up only when her fingers were too slick with blood to grip the metal, and sat against the wall again, pulling splinters out of her hands with her teeth.

Exhaustion crept up on her bit by bit. At first, she tried to fight it, but then, realizing that her escape would take longer than she'd hoped, she decided to get some rest. She curled up on the ground and tried to make herself comfortable. The cold soon had her shivering so hard that her head knocked against the floor, but she wrapped her arms around her knees and tried to ignore it.

When she woke, she could hardly tell that she had slept at all. She was so sore and bruised that the simple act of sitting up brought tears to her eyes. But her head was a little clearer, her body a little more energetic, and her temper back in full force.

She would find a way out if it killed her.

Time passed. She didn't know how much. There was nothing to do but explore her prison over and over again. She paced and shouted and pounded on the door, but more out of boredom than anything. It was a waste of energy, and she knew it.

Her only clue to the passage of time was her hunger. It had been gnawing on her stomach already, more an irritation than anything else. But then it started to hurt. Her gut felt as if it were devouring itself whole, gnawing her apart with the ferocity of a wolf. She was so dizzy she could barely stand, and so hungry she was tempted to lick the dust and grime right off the floor.

Worse was the thirst. The discomfort quickly snowballed into misery, her mouth bone dry and her throat aching. A headache snuck up on her and refused to let up. That made concentrating on her escape, already a difficult enough task, nearly impossible.

What worried her most, though, was when the pain in her gut stopped. She felt weaker than ever, and the dizziness made her feel seasick on dry land, but her stomach simply...gave up.

That meant days had passed in the world outside the door. Two or three days without food or water. And while she was no stranger to hunger, the thirst was agony. The upper city had no shortage of fountains, and even in the lower city, water was plentiful enough for those who weren't picky about the taste or the color.

Orphans or not, these people wouldn't just leave her here, would they? They couldn't just lock her up and leave her to starve. Hunger alone wouldn't kill her for a while, but she suspected the thirst would get her much more quickly. Did these people know that? If they wanted her dead, why didn't they just shoot her?

No. They didn't want her dead. They wanted her to *suffer*. But to what end? When they finally came for her, what would they do with her? Her imagination conjured many possibilities, but none of them were pleasant.

It took everything she had—every ounce of stubbornness and strength and fury—not to fall into despair. To push from her mind the ways that this could end. To convince herself that the orphans hadn't forgotten her there—that they would come soon enough. Maybe the boy would show up. Maybe he would help her escape. He owed her that much. Surely he'd had time to tell them that she'd helped him....

Unless he was dead.

That thought gave her chills. If he died, they'd blame her. And then....

She found herself sitting against the wall and staring blankly into the air in front of her, oblivious to the cold, to the hard stone, to her cramping muscles—to all of it. Time would pass, and eventually something would happen. All she could do was wait.

And then....

She thought she imagined the voices at first—but then they grew louder. She turned her head listlessly toward the door, unable to move any other part of her body. A voice was shouting; it sounded like the man who had pointed an arrow at her face.

"—don't lecture *me* about putting everyone in danger! *Why* would you *bring her here?* What were you *thinking?*"

"I *told* you, I don't remember!"

Her heart leapt into her throat. That was the boy's voice. He was alive.

"You still *did it!* And now all the rest of us have to clean up *your* mess—"

"I never asked you to!"

"Well, *you're* sure as hell not gonna do it!"

"You haven't even given me a chance! If you'd just—"

"Then *deal with it.* Whatever you're gonna do, do it. *Now.* Before someone comes *looking* for her!"

A horrible silence fell. She held her breath, waiting. Then, finally:

"Fine. I will."

The other one didn't respond. Instead, she heard footsteps. Drawing nearer, and nearer, and....

She pulled herself to her feet. Whoever opened the door, she'd wait for an opening, then rush past them. Whatever was coming, she'd be ready.

The latch rattled, and the door swung open.

It was the boy. His head and arms were bandaged, his face was bruised from her fist, but he was alive, awake, alert.

"Thank the Goddess," she croaked, her weariness weighing her down like armor. "You gotta get me out of here, they think I—"

A sword whipped through the air. The boy held it, and his eyes were hard and cold.

"Get back," he snapped.

She stepped back until her shoulders pressed against the wall. "What're you—?"

"Shut up," he said. The tip of the sword didn't waver. "You're going to tell me who you are and how you got here. And don't even think about lying."

"How I—don't you recognize me?" she demanded, struggling to keep her voice steady. Her throat burned like fire with every word. "You brought me here! I saved your life!"

"That's what you told my brother and sisters," he retorted. "But I've never seen you before. Who are you?"

"I...I was...you don't remember?" Her voice rose uncontrollably, sharp-edged and spiteful in her frustration. "I was right there next to ya. I helped y' through th' stupid sewers when y' couldn't even walk by yerself—for the love of th' Goddess, you *kissed* me, you *idiot!*"

"Enough!" he snarled, and something in his voice silenced her at once—something angry, something deadly. She shrank back, sucking in a sharp breath. He was glaring at her with such loathing that she felt a lump rise in her throat.

The tip of the sword moved close enough to snag her shirt.

"I could kill you," he said softly. "I could run you through right now, and no one would care. No one would even know that you were gone. Would they?"

She stared at him in mute horror, unable to believe her ears. How could she have been so wrong about him?

"Or," he continued, relentless, remorseless, "you can leave. *If* you tell the truth. And you can have this back."

And he slipped his hand into his pocket and withdrew her necklace. He held it up, the rose glimmering faintly in the half-light.

"Hey—give that back!" She tried to push forward, but the tip of the sword jabbed at her, stopping her.

"Where'd you even get something like this?" He held it up and inspected it with wonder in his eyes.

"Give it *back!*"

"Is it real?"

"That's mine. Ya can't just *take* that!"

"Yeah?" His lip curled. "Whose pocket did you pick it from?"

"I said it's mine! Now give it back!"

"You want it back? Then tell me how you found us."

She took a deep breath, fighting a surge of anger rising in her chest, hot and bitter and powerful. "I already said ya *told me* t' follow you," she said, matching his contemptuous snarl with one of her own. "If you don't believe me, that's *your* problem."

"Why?" he shot back. "My pockets were so full you thought I must've had more at home?"

"*No,* I—Goddess, you *gave* me your knives, I didn't even want your stupid rubbish *bracelets*—"

"Thanks so much for taking them, then." His voice practically dripped with rage. "Goddess forbid you leave anything behind. How did you follow me all this way?"

"I didn't—you *brought* me here!"

He scoffed. "And why would I do that?"

"Well, *I* don't know, do I? You told me you knew a way outta the city—"

"What? You do?"

"No, ya said *you* did! But *obviously* you were just lyin' so I'd follow you—"

"Why?"

"I don't *know,* you horse's ass! There are all these soldiers ev'rywhere—"

"Why? What did you do?"

"Nothin'. They were chasing *you!* I was just tryin' to hide—"

"Why were they chasing me?"

She stared at him. But he seemed sincere—torn between confusion and alarm, as anyone might be in discovering soldiers on their tail. How could he not remember any of this?

"Oh, I dunno," she said sarcastically. "Maybe dressin' up like th' Beggar's King wasn't yer best idea. What th' hell were you *doin'*?"

"I don't know." He blinked, his eyes wide and blank.

"I don't get it, how could ya not *remember?* Ya fell through the damn *roof.* I pulled an arrow out o' ya, then the *soldiers* came after ya —" She waved her hands for emphasis, and the boy flinched and jumped back. It only irritated her more. "—an' then ya dragged me halfway 'cross th' city, into th' *sewers,* and then I get thrown in *here* by a bunch o' stupid orphans! What is *wrong* with all o' you?!"

"Shut *up!*" The sword rose again, close enough to brush against one of her curls. "Just *shut up—*"

"Go ahead an' kill me then!" she yelled, flinging her arms to either side. "Go right ahead, if ya got the guts! I'm *sick* o' this, I had it with *all* o' you, I'm not sayin' another word t'one more filthy, lyin' *orphan!*"

He recoiled. She stood her ground. Her arms ached with the effort it took to keep them outstretched, but she didn't lower them. He didn't lower his sword, either. They glared at one another for a long moment, the air between them aflame with mutual rage.

Then, at last, the sword fell away.

She would have laughed in his face if she weren't so exhausted. Spineless rat—she'd known he wouldn't have the guts. She could see in his eyes that he wouldn't have the nerve to so much as scratch her with his rusted pigsticker of a sword.

He stepped back, his lip curling with contempt as he looked her over.

"I don't have to kill you," he said. "And I don't have to let you out. I don't have to do anything." He tucked her necklace back into his pocket. "Problem solved—one way or another."

It took her a moment to realize what he was saying—and that moment cost her dearly. "*No.*" she yelled, lunging forward. She staggered toward the light—

And he slammed the door in her face.

Sheer desperation hurled her against the door, shoving the latch and hammering the thick wood with her fists. "Wait!" she howled. "Ya can't jus' *leave me here!* Come back! Let me *go!* Get back here! GET BACK HERE, ya rat-faced—lousy—soft-spined—son of a *whore—!*"

She threw everything she had at the door, summoning the worst curses and insults that she could imagine as loud as her rasping voice would allow. But the boy didn't take the bait.

He was gone. And with him, her last chance.

Exhaustion crashed into her like a tidal wave, dragging her down to her knees. She let it pull her under. Let it drown her. The crushing weight of the silence outside made the last flicker of hope, of anger, of defiance flicker and die inside her chest.

It was over. There was nothing left to do but wait to die.

Romero woke with a strangled gasp like a shipwrecked sailor clawing his mouth free of the waves. He shouted and flailed, fighting against the covers. Dark eyes narrowed in malice swam above him. He heard a rustling, saw a shadow pass along the wall.

The assassin was here, he was *here*—

He scrambled for the knife hidden under his pillow. He found it, slashed—

"Your Majesty!"

"Guards!" Romero yelled. "*Guards!*"

"Your Majesty, *please*—"

"Amore?"

That voice threw him—girlish, as high as a flute. He sat up, shoving his hair out of the way and squinting in the early morning light.

A woman stood next to his bed—alarmed, but quickly recovering. It took him a moment to recognize her.

"*Auna?*"

"Good morning, my love," she trilled in Savillan, smiling at him as she extended her hand. "Did I surprise you?"

"I—no. I mean—" He felt as if he'd been plunged into the sea, tumbling head-over-heels with no way of knowing up from down. Auna, the daughter of King Eduardo Allesino, the princess of Savilla, was here—not in her palace on the other side of the continent, but here, in his room, by his bed, still wearing her traveling clothes. "I was expecting another, uh...letter...." His mind was racing as he bent to kiss her hand, but by the time he sat up again, he had pasted on a smile. "What have I done to earn such a pleasant surprise?"

Auna giggled, her fingers closing around his so he couldn't pull away. "I just couldn't help myself. I had to see my betrothed again—I couldn't wait another minute."

Betrothed. He'd almost forgotten.

Shit.

"But how did you get here so quickly?" He slid out of bed, still shaking the cobwebs out of his skull from the nightmare he'd been trapped in. "Weren't you in Aldaeza—?"

"Three weeks ago! I commandeered a caravel, and you would not believe how quickly one can travel in such a small ship, my darling—"

"One caravel? Your father let you travel in a merchant ship?"

"Don't be silly, Romero." Auna gave him a playful shove. "I'm a grown woman now, I hardly need his permission."

"But he does *know* you're here?"

Auna flashed a wicked grin. "It's a surprise for him too."

"Oh. Oh—" Romero caught himself before the curse could leave his lips. But Auna's face fell.

"You aren't upset with me, are you, my love? I thought you'd be happy to see me."

"Of course I am," said Romero smoothly. "I only wish I'd had a bit of warning to put my castle in a proper state—and myself," he added, gesturing to his rumpled night clothes. Auna laughed again.

"Never mind that—it hardly matters what clothes you're wearing, does it?" Her grin returned in full force. "But first—I brought a gift. Two, in fact."

"Gifts? My darling, you shouldn't have—"

"Oh, but I did. And they are very good gifts." She lifted her hand to touch his cheek. Her almond-shaped eyes gazed up at him with a besotted expression that caught him off guard, and all he could think was, *Goddess, she's young.* "Consider them my wedding gift."

Distracted as he was, he wasn't sure he heard correctly. "Wedding...gift?"

"Why, of course. You said we'd marry when we could be together. What's to stop us now?"

"Ah...." He let her fold herself into his arms, his hands resting on her waist. "Well, my darling, of course we will, but you're too young—"

"It's Alronelin, silly, girls younger than me marry all the time! Oh, I'm so excited, Romero, I don't want to wait a single day. Say we can start to plan the wedding, won't you?"

His stomach sank, but he kept his smile firmly in place. "Certainly. Right away."

She smiled and hummed contentedly. Her fingers slid under the neck of his shirt, and her smile faded. "Oh, that hideous scar—tesoro mio, you poor thing—"

He brushed her hand away from his neck. "It's fine. Auna—"

"If you hadn't taken care of that wretched peasant, *I* would have for what he did to you—"

"You'd have to wait in line," Romero said drily. "Auna," he added, tensing as her hands were inching their way slowly down his back, "if you'll allow me a moment to make myself decent...."

"Darling, I'm sorry. Of course. And once you have, I'll introduce you to your gifts! You'll be so excited—"

"Introduce me?" He laughed, lifting her chin with a finger. "Did you get me a pet, darling?"

"In a manner of speaking—I found a Divinata," Auna blurted, unable to contain her excitement any longer.

"A—*Divina?*" he said sharply, switching abruptly to Courman. The kingsguard at his door stiffened at the word, raising their weapons. "Where?"

"In the next room, my love. And I—"

He didn't wait to hear the rest. As soon as she gestured toward the door, he sidestepped her and burst into his sitting room, almost afraid of what he might find.

A woman sat primly in a chair by the window, watching the sunrise through the thick glass. But for four more of his kingsguard stationed around the room, keeping their hands on their weapons and their bodies carefully out of arm's reach, she might have looked right at home. Plump, travel-worn, and young—twenty or twenty-one at the oldest—she cut an imposing figure nonetheless. Long, pale hair flowed loose around the shoulders of hooded robes the color of ash. The robes were cut square across her shoulders, baring her collarbones, where swirling silver-and-gold arabesques glimmered on her pale skin.

Only the Divinæ knew how to make those tattoos.

Romero stared at her. Then he turned to stare at Auna, who stood at his shoulder, looking very smug. "You brought a Divina from Savilla?"

"Oh, no—I captured her trying to *enter* Savilla," said Auna. "At Arrow's Pass."

"She was in Alronelin?"

"Indeed she was. I thought you might like to speak with her."

Romero turned, eyes raking over the Divina.

"Indeed I would," he muttered. "Auna—give us a moment?"

And before Auna could reply, he shut the door in her face and turned to the Divina. She was watching the proceedings with utter serenity; it was impossible to say how much she had understood. Her eyes met his, and he tensed—but she smiled.

"Please, Your Majesty," she said in Courman, gesturing to the chair across from her. "Have a seat."

Romero, stunned, felt almost compelled to obey. He found himself walking across the room almost without meaning to. But he took control of himself and straightened his back, resting his hand on the back of the chair she'd indicated. It rankled him to be ordered about in his own castle, but he bit it back.

"You seem to have my men well trained," he said dryly, shooting a brief glare at the nearest kingsguard, Archer, who had the gall to look unabashed.

"I told them not to touch me," she said. "They were all too happy to oblige."

Romero almost snorted. He bet they had been. Their eyes followed her every movement, and he saw one of them tense as she waved a careless hand. His kingsguard were a superstitious lot.

"Strange, isn't it? How quickly men forget about us. The Divinæ have existed for over a thousand years but were banished for only fifteen, and only from Alronelin. Twenty years ago, no man would have dared lay a hand on me."

"Twenty years ago, you weren't even born," Romero snapped.

The girl smiled. "Divinæ are not bound by the present," she informed him.

Romero did not bother asking what this meant. He frowned at her, analyzing every move she made, her demeanor, her tone, trying to read her. She sat there unafraid, back straight and face smooth, looking him straight in the eyes with the authority of a queen.

No...a goddess.

He turned to gesture at his kingsguard, ordering them out. They didn't hesitate. Within seconds, he and the Divina were alone.

Romero walked around to the lounge and sank slowly down onto the soft pillows, legs and arms spread, decorum forgotten. He was aware of how he looked: barefoot and bareheaded, clad only in the breeches and the wrinkled undershirt he'd fallen asleep in, his dirty hair unbound and wild around his shoulders. But this was his castle, his city, his kingdom. He had no need to impress upon this girl exactly who he was. The ring on his finger could do that well enough.

"Listen to me, girl," he said. "You can—"

"Lucy."

"What?" he snapped. He was not used to people interrupting him.

"Lucy," the girl repeated. "That is what you may call me."

"*May?*" His lip curled. "Girl, I don't know who you think you are, but you are one wrong word away from the worst mistake of your life."

The girl watched him without a trace of fear. "Is this how you always speak to your guests?"

Romero laughed aloud at that. "Guest? You are my *prisoner.*"

She looked around, one pale eyebrow rising delicately as she took in the open door and her own unbound limbs. "Am I? No chains bind me. No walls confine me. No one has forced me to do anything other than what I wish. Even your soldiers have obeyed me." She folded her hands in her lap, smiling. "There is no need to fight for the upper hand, Your Majesty. We can discuss these matters with civility."

A sudden urge to slap her nearly drove Romero to his feet. He forced it back with difficulty, reminding himself that it was a waste of effort. He could hurt her in a thousand better ways.

Romero reached for the wine someone had left on the table and filled a silver cup for himself. It was from last night, stale and warm now. He drained it in one go before filling it again. The wine was a bit sweet for his taste, and he suspected they had watered it down, but it was enough to smooth the frayed edges of his nerves. He turned back to the girl, drawing his composure around himself like a cloak.

"Who are you?" he demanded of her.

The girl merely frowned at him, tugging pointedly at her robes. "I would have thought that was obvious," she said.

Romero set his cup carefully back onto the tray and walked around the chair, stopping in front of the girl. He leaned forward, planting one hand against the back of the chair, right beside her neck. She recoiled from him at once. But even shrinking back as far as she could, he was still close enough to see every speck of color in her wide blue eyes.

"I was thinking," he said softly, "that I might throw you to the dogs. Then I thought it might be a bit more entertaining to throw you to my men instead." He smirked as he saw the color drain from her face. "That won't kill you, oh no—it will just teach you a lesson. I might just do it, if you insist on showing no respect. I *might* just do it for fun." He straightened up again, though his eyes did not leave hers. "We shall have to see, won't we?"

The girl seemed to wilt as he withdrew. He could see her hands shaking as she folded her arms protectively across her chest. "You wouldn't," she breathed. "You wouldn't dare."

Romero shrugged, pouring himself a bit more wine. "Gods and goddesses don't scare me," he said. "I am a king. An emperor. As close to a god as this world will ever see."

"I-I would lose my powers—they come from chastity and—"

"No, you wouldn't. Those are just rumors. Old wives' tales. I have seen Divinæ touch men a thousand times without losing their powers."

"Have you, now?" the girl replied. She rose to her feet and slowly offered him her hand. "How sure are you, exactly?"

Romero's eyes flicked from her hand to her face, trying to read an expression that was not there. Then, carefully, he made as if to greet her like a lady. She did not move, even when his fingers were so close to her own that he could feel the warmth of her skin.

In one sharp movement, he grabbed her wrist and twisted hard. The girl gasped in pain, staggering, crying out when he twisted further. He hauled her toward him, pulling her close.

"I know all about your kind, girl," he hissed into her ear. "I know all the games you play. And I know that your Goddess won't stop me from doing whatever I want."

"You're hurting me—"

"Good," he snarled, and shoved her back into her chair. She landed so hard he heard the air escape her lungs as she smacked against the wooden back. He felt no small satisfaction at seeing her emotionless facade crack beneath a wince of pain.

"I have *years* of frustration with your kind to carve out of your hide," he told her. "So if I were you, I'd start talking."

She glared at him as she massaged her wrist. "I thought you were meant to be *charming.*"

Romero almost laughed. She was trying to be brave, but he could see the terror in her eyes.

"Not this early in the morning. Now. Who are you?"

"I'm—a Divina. Lucy. I don't—"

"What were you doing in Alronelin, *Lucy?*"

"Trying to leave." She took a deep breath and sat a little straighter, all expression slipping from her face once again. It didn't matter; Romero knew that she was still shaken. "I assure you, however much you want me to be gone, I want it even more."

"But why would I want you to leave? You're an honored guest." And he lifted his cup in a silent toast, smirking at the look on her face. "So," he said, when she offered nothing further. "Arrow's Pass. The Divinæ sent you there?"

"No. I...." The girl looked away, tucking her loose hair behind one ear. "I ran away."

"You *ran away?* Can a Divina *do that?*"

"No." She shrugged. "I assumed they'd catch me. But your *betrothed* caught me first."

Romero tried not to wince at that. "Why would you run away?"

"Because—because I—" The girl hesitated, and Romero leaned forward, sensing that she was struggling to answer without revealing something important. "I just wanted—*out,*" she blurted at last, the words bursting free like water from a ruptured dam. "And they wouldn't *let* me. I hate it all, I'm not even *good* at it, maybe that's why they let me escape, maybe they just don't *care,* but then why wouldn't they just *let me go?*" She waved her hands in a frustrated gesture, demanding answers of Romero, who watched with fascination. "They said once you're marked, you can't leave! But I didn't *ask* to be marked, I didn't *ask* to be taken from my family, nobody asked what I wanted at *all—*"

"Your family?" Romero cut across her, leaning forward. "Divinæ don't *have* families. They're not allowed them."

"Well, *I* do." She hesitated, biting her lip. "I mean...I did. Before they took me away."

"The Divinæ...*kidnapped* you?"

"Yes, they did." She cleared her throat and busied herself with straightening her robes, adjusting the shoulders until it hung just right. These Divinæ must not have been accustomed to men at all. A lady of the court would never dream of adjusting her clothing with a man in the room, let alone the king. But Lucy hardly seemed to care. "When I was fourteen. Usually they take younger girls, but they made an exception for me. They gave my father a bag of gold, they said I *belonged* to them. And then they took me. And he *let* them. Nobody bothered to check if *I* had any opinions on the matter—"

Romero tried to cut her off with a wave of his hand. He had no interest in hearing her complain like a spoiled noble girl protesting her arranged marriage. She did not see it, or perhaps she was unaccustomed to following commands, so he spoke over her.

"Where did they take you? Where are they hiding?"

"I *don't know.* I was *kidnapped*—blindfolded, bound—I have no idea where the shrine is. Far, far away."

"But you *escaped* from it."

"Not from there—from some village in Saltreach. We went to heal a sick child. Before that—our shrine was—I don't know. It didn't have windows. Somewhere cold."

Romero sighed. Of course he would get a Divina that was utterly useless. "And this family of yours—where are they?"

Lucy stiffened. "I-I don't want—the Divinæ left them no choice, it wasn't their fault—"

She was scared for them—scared of what he would do with them. Which meant—

"They're in Alronelin?" he demanded.

Lucy took a deep breath. Then, in a tiny voice, she said, "They're in Bermeia."

"But you said you were taken when you were fourteen. That can't have been long ago—"

"Seven years," she whispered.

Romero slammed his cup on the sideboard, slopping wine everywhere. "The Divinæ are recruiting in *my* country?" he hissed. "In *my* city?"

Lucy looked away, her hands gripping her knees above her skirt. "I...doubt they ever stopped."

Romero shook the wine from his hand as he stood. "Who else have they taken?" he barked.

"I—I don't know."

"Names?"

"I don't know any names, I don't know where anyone was from—"

"Any boys? Were *any* boys taken?"

"I—no," stammered Lucy, looking up at him at last. "There aren't male Divinæ, there wasn't a man within ten leagues of our shrine...."

Romero took a deep breath, fighting to regain his composure. At some point along the way, he had forgotten her age, but now it showed through—twenty-one, if he'd heard correctly, and she looked it. A young woman, weak, friendless, face-to-face with one of the most powerful men in the world. Even half-dressed and rumpled from sleep, he towered over her. She seemed very small in her chair, her wide eyes staring up at him in fear, waiting for more questions.

And he had more. Far, far too many. He walked over to the window, collecting his thoughts.

"Do they know you're here?" he said at last.

"The Divinæ? I expect they knew where I was going before I did."

"And?"

"And...what?"

"Are you still a member of their Order?"

A long silence. Then, finally, in a small voice, she said, "I don't know."

He turned to face her. She averted her eyes, hugging herself around her middle.

"Can you see the future?"

Her every muscle seemed as tense as a violin string, but she sat up and looked at him then, straightening her spine. Pride, he thought— or defiance. "Better than some," she said. "Not as well as others."

"Prove it."

The simple statement made her jump, staring at him as if he had gone mad. "I beg your pardon?"

"What did you expect, girl? That I'd take your word for it? Just because you look like a witch doesn't mean you are one."

"We are not *witches,* nor are we a-a group of—roadside vendors! We do not tell fortunes for a handful of coins! We are scholars, priestesses, healers. We fix broken bones, and—and punctured lungs—"

"Go on." He gestured vaguely to the room at large. "Tell the future. Prove that you can be of some use to me."

"I-I can't just—"

"Otherwise," he cut across her, "I see no point in keeping you around."

That seemed to render her speechless. Romero thought he saw her face grow a shade or two paler. She brushed her hair over her shoulder, making no attempt to hide her distaste as she looked up at him.

"A server is on his way to this room," she said. "He has a tray of meats and cheeses for you. He brought enough for several people, including me. No one is sure who I am or if I am to be treated as a guest. He is about fifteen years old, dark-haired, the child of a noble. It is considered an honor to serve you, so many of the noble families have offered a young person or two—but not someone so valuable as to be missed, of course."

Romero shook his head, already looking for his wine. *Useless,* he thought sourly. *Lying witches, I knew they couldn't tell the future, I knew it was all just for show....*

"But he's wasting his time. You won't eat it."

Romero froze with his cup halfway to his lips.

"They are good servants, you know, very loyal to you. They try to keep food around you at all times in the hopes that you'll eat more. Fruit, cheese, bread—simple things like that. They give you watered-down wine when they know you prefer something, anything, that is stronger. They cook a wide variety of foods in order to tempt you. But you still haven't eaten properly in months. The head cook cries some-times out of fear. He thinks you don't like his food, he thinks he'll lose his position or that you'll have him killed. He doesn't know that you're afraid it's all been poisoned."

Romero watched her rise slowly to her feet, her ghostly image reflected in the window glass.

"The stress and fear ties your stomach into knots and steals your appetite. You woke up screaming this morning from another night-mare about the Beggar's King. You thought he was in your room again. You can't sleep soundly because you've heard rumors that he's back from the dead. You know it's foolish—no one can return from the dead, and you *watched* him die—but you worry all the same. Did you kill the right person? Was he working alone, or as a member of a larger group? Is this new Beggar's King coming to kill you too? Or has he joined with your other, more dangerous enemies?"

"I...." Romero turned to the girl, clenching his hand around his cup to stop it shaking. "You...." His mouth was dry and ashen. He could not get the words out.

"You try to bury the fear under women and wine," the girl contin-ued. She stood up, straight and tall with her chin raised, her eyes like sapphires coated in ice. "And you've abandoned most of your respon-sibilities. Not just your fencing, you've ignored that for years, you real-ized *that* mistake when the Beggar's King attacked you—but your duties as king have fallen to your inferiors. It's not that you don't have the time. You don't sleep, so you have nothing *but* time. You've simply lost your motivation. You tell yourself that it doesn't matter, the kingdom will still be there once you've found it again. Still, you *would* sleep...if you fully trusted your kingsguard after their failure last time. And you *would* eat...if instead of these strange, complicated dishes, they would bring you a lamb pie just like the ones your mother used to make. Back when you weren't King Romero Sangor, Emperor of the Greater Peninsula. When you were just...Vil."

His entire being seemed to shudder at the sound of that name.

Something deep within his chest was crushed, flailing, gasping for breath. His knuckles were white against the half-filled cup in his hand.

"H-How...?" he rasped. "Where...where did you hear that name?"

The girl took a step closer, her dirty, cracked feet gliding soundlessly across the rug.

"Vilhelm Romero," she said softly. "That *is* your name, isn't it? Your real name? You told Trentin that—the king, I mean, King Trentin the Third, when you were brought before him. But it's your father's name too, and he wanted yours. He confused you, and instead of a name, you gave him a surname. And it stuck."

"I don't want to hear this," Romero whispered. But he could not even hear himself. He felt like a fish on the docks, chest heaving, mouth moving uselessly, making no sound. "I don't want to hear it...."

But the girl continued, stubbornly, pitilessly. "Trentin had sent them looking for traitors, not a little boy. His last surviving child, Rafael, was there, learning how to be king. He was six years old—only a little younger than you. Trentin was horrified by the mistake, and, to set an example for his son, he chose to take you in. Foster you with a servant family in the castle, give his son a playmate. But no one ever called you by your proper name again. You didn't want them to. You wanted to hear your mother saying it, or no one at all...."

Romero's cup crumpled in his hand.

He gasped and cursed, snapping out of his trance at once, shaking wine and blood off of his hand as the twisted mass of silver tumbled to the rug. The wine burned like liquid fire as it seeped into the punctures in his palm. A serving woman scurried forward out of thin air, kneeling down to mop up the mess on the rug. Romero grabbed the cloth from her hands and wrapped it hastily around his palm, glaring at the Divina girl through watering eyes.

"How did you know that?" he gasped, wincing as he cradled his stinging hand. He panted as if he had just run miles, sucking in sharp breaths between his teeth. "How did you...?"

He trailed away, his jaw clenching shut. The girl said nothing. She merely watched him, her gaze level and steady, standing in the middle of the room like a statue. He saw no pity in her eyes, no anger, no fear. Nothing at all.

"How...?" he asked again, but he could not finish. He knew how. He stared at her chest, watching the light sparkle off her gold-and-silver tattoos, the swirling arabesques dotted with tiny diamonds embedded into the skin. No one but the Divinæ knew how to make those marks—and now he knew that she had earned them.

"That is the past, of course," she said. "Do you want to know your future? I see a thousand of them stretched before your feet, each one shifting with each decision you make and each decision anyone makes that affects you. Your future is foggy, unclear, but what is clear is this: all three of the people you seek will cross your path by summer's end. Every single one."

"They—?" The words left him breathless.

Seventeen years. For seventeen long years, he had searched the entire Peninsula for Serena and her son. He'd wanted to give up a thousand times, but he couldn't; even now, in the back of his mind, he was plotting how to invade this Divina shrine and search the women there for someone fitting Serena's description. And now—

"Wait—*three*? What do you mean, *three*?"

"And the first," she cut across him, "is already here."

His heart sank. She must have meant Auna. But he'd hardly been looking for her—which meant that Lucy was just bluffing. He took a slow step forward, breathing hard. His hand burned as it clenched around the cloth. With his other hand, he reached for his knife—only to realize that he had left it under his pillow. "You lying, witch," he snarled. "If you're trying to scare me—"

"You asked for your future," she said calmly. "I told you. Do not blame me for the results."

"I should have known," he hissed. "I should have known not to trust any of you bloody snakes, I should've wiped all of you out when I had the chance—"

"You never did." The girl eyed him coldly as she stood up a little straighter. "And you never will. Do not blame all of us for the sins of one, Romero. We are not all weak-minded poison peddlers, betraying trust and faith for mere gold."

Romero stopped short, his nasty reply dying on his lips. "You... know about that?"

"About the Divina who sold you poisons? Of course we do." Her face twisted into a sneer of pure loathing. "She was one of our best alchemists, extraordinarily talented, but we never dreamed her capable of creating such horrible concoctions. We would have killed her for that, and for peddling Divinæ secrets like a common fishmonger, had you not killed her first. You couldn't have anyone *else* using those poisons or telling anyone about them. You needed to blame our order for what you did and convince the world that we were demons."

"No," Romero corrected her, "that was why I would have *executed* her. I *killed* her because she spouted off some crazy nonsense about how a flower is going to kill *me*."

The girl tensed. Turned to him, met his eyes, her face a pale, stiff mask. "What did you say?" she demanded. "Did you say a *flower?*"

"A rose," he scoffed. "She must've been mad. She kept insisting that roses were going to kill me. And a load of nonsense, some skipping rhyme about fathoms and lies and bones."

"'Full fathoms five...,'" the girl whispered.

Romero stiffened at the words. The girl shook her head slightly, as if shaking herself out of a dream, then continued in a voice so soft he could barely hear. But he did not need to hear. Those words had been burned into his memory, every letter carved into his heart.

> *Full fathoms five lies the father of lies*
> *Of his bones are moral code*
> *Those are thorns that pierce his eyes*
> *Swords of flame and rose*
> *Nothing of his shall fade*
> *Yet nothing of him shall remain*

The words sucked the breath out of him, tossed him into freezing water.

"Yes," he said softly. "That's the one." He paused, swallowing hard, squeezing his eyes shut so he could think. "But what does it *mean?*"

The girl shook her head. Her eyes drifted toward him, slipping back into focus; she seemed as if she were waking from a dream. "Nothing," she said softly. "Nothing at all. Just a skipping rhyme...."

But the look in her eyes revealed the lie.

Romero stood in silence for a long moment, staring at her. Then, at last, he snapped out of his daze.

The first is already here.

Was she lying? There was only one way to find out.

"*Max!*" he yelled. "Get in here!"

Maximilian appeared in the doorway before he had even finished speaking. Romero gestured angrily at the girl as he swept past, shoving his steward aside, still clutching his injured hand against his chest.

"Have her put in a room somewhere," he snapped. "Or in a cell, I don't care. Just get her out of my sight. Auna? Auna!"

"Your Majesty, she's in—"

But he knew where she'd be.

He stepped into his bedroom to find that someone had opened the windows, stoked the fire, and made the bed. Auna had made herself right at home. She sat curled up on the chair by the window with a cup of tea, wearing a fresh dress. Romero blinked at her, still a little dazed by her presence and surprised, frankly, not to find her in his bed.

She set her cup aside at the sight of him, twisting around in her chair. "Well?" she said, beaming. "Did you enjoy your gift?"

"Where's the other one?"

Her smile faded. He couldn't even imagine the expression on his own face, but it must have been far from the exuberant joy she'd expected. "Well, she's a bit more—ah—*unruly*, my love, so your kingsguard put her in the study and locked her in. I'll—"

"Who is it?"

But he knew the answer before Auna spoke. He had known as soon as the Divina had mentioned it. *The first is already here.*

The name still struck his heart like a dagger.

"Serena. Serena Sangor."

Time continued to pass in the orphan's pitch-black cell—slowly, cruelly, relentlessly onward.

Even if the girl had wanted to move, she couldn't. She was weak, frighteningly weak, and even trying to lift her head sapped all of her energy. She barely had the strength to catch herself as she slumped to her side on the floor, shifting a tiny bit to find relief from the hard stone. After that, she did not move again.

But she kept breathing—whether she wanted to or not. She stared at the grime-coated stones in front of her eyes, at the tiny sliver of grayish light under the door, somehow both resigned and shocked. Some part of her floated at a safe distance, watching in utter disbelief, whispering, *I can't believe it. I'm going to die. I can't believe this is how I'm going to die.*

Shut up, screamed the rest of her—her weak body, her aching muscles, her ice-cold flesh. *Just shut up and let it end.* Life was not worth clinging to if this was all that was left.

But had it ever been worth clinging to at all? Her memories took root and siphoned her strength until they possessed her completely, until she was reliving them over and over again. And it was an empty life. An endless, monotonous chain of days spent scavenging and stealing, nights spent huddling for warmth. Violence, fear, hunting, running, hiding. And what was the purpose of it all? All she'd ever aspired to was finding the next scrap of food or sheltered corner.

No one would care. No one would even know that you had gone.

He was right. When he finally got rid of her body, it would be as if she had never existed at all.

She began to hallucinate people and things long forgotten. A ghostly echo of the parents she'd dreamed up when she was little sat across from her, and a little house came to life around them: warm and smelling of bread, with jars of flowers and bright quilts on every surface.

We loved you, their voices said, as soft and ephemeral as spider-silk. *We never wanted to leave you. We would have been proud of you.*

She turned around and saw a fire burning in an old rain barrel, a gaggle of scruffy, ragged men huddled around it. They turned and welcomed her among them with open arms.

We're sorry. We never should have left you. It was all our fault.

But their hands never touched her. Instead, two soft, frail, wrinkled hands rested on her shoulders and pulled her into a familiar embrace. A stocky body pressed her close with surprising strength, enveloping her in an apron that smelled of lavender and rosemary.

It was a dream. She knew it was a dream. But she didn't want it to end. And she couldn't make it end, even when it changed. When men in soldier's garb tore the arms away, overturned the brazier and scattered the coals as her parents turned their backs and ran, as the crackle of flames and the reek of liquor drowned her. *We don't want you anymore. You're terrible. You're rotten. You're ruined. You're nothing.* Waves of cold washed over her like floodwaters as the boy appeared again, bringing an army of soldiers as he dragged her into the ocean, and his echoing voice said *Rose, Rose—*

"Rose? Hello?"

She was in the cell again, in the dark and the cold, alone—but now it was spinning and tumbling as it sank through dark water, dragging her with it.

"I *know* you can hear me."

Goddess, she was so tired. Her whole body throbbed and ached so badly that not even the most pleasant dreams could distract her. The hard stone dug into her ribs as she floated somewhere between consciousness and unconsciousness, eyes closed, with that voice leaking in under the door.

"You know what? Fine. Keep shutting up. *That'll* help."

Footsteps. It sounded like someone was pacing outside the door. Her parents, the men, and the soldiers stood silently in the dark, turning their heads toward the sound.

"You know, you aren't acting very innocent, *Rose*. All you've done since you got here is insult us and threaten us. How the hell am I supposed to convince Dominic and Artemis to let you go when you're being like this?"

Her mouth was so dry she could feel the skin on the roof of her mouth cracking. Every breath was deafening in her ears. And her pulse—it felt like every thump of her heart was strong enough to make her whole body shudder.

"You could *try* being nice, for once. You could tell me what *really* happened. *Without* all the yelling and insults. And where do you get off insulting orphans, anyways? You think you're better than us? You're *exactly* like us. Whatever put you on the street, if it had happened before the orphanage burned down, you would've been right in there with us. And it's not like we *asked* to be in there. It was *hell*. And we didn't *do* anything. I wish we *had* done something, then at least it would've made *sense*. We only—"

The voice stopped abruptly, and so did the footsteps. There was a long silence before it spoke again.

"Maybe you're...*kind* of right. Liam was like that. But we're not—we're not all...."

The voice exhaled in a loud huff, and the footsteps started up again.

"You're lucky we're not all like Liam. He would have killed you already. No hesitation. But he's gone. So now I—now I have to—"

Did he *never* stop talking? He'd won. Why didn't he just *go?*

"If you're not going to talk, fine. I'll just assume the worst. So, you saw someone dressed like the Beggar's King being chased by soldiers, and, I don't know, just *followed* him? And what, did you whack me in the head so you could rob me? I *like* that knife, you know—and why would you take my shell? And my *bracelets?* What the hell is wrong with you? My—one of the—someone *gave* those to me, they're my good luck charms. I guess it didn't *work*, but—whatever. So then—I guess you decided to follow me home? Maybe you thought you could get some kind of reward if you found the hideout for the Beggar's King?"

More silence. More footsteps.

"The *problem* is...if I was so out of it I didn't even know you were following me...I don't know how I even got home. And the soldiers wouldn't have just given up looking for me. Your story is the only one that makes any sense. And I...I mean, I...I guess I can't blame you. None of this is really your fault. It certainly doesn't deserve a death sentence. I don't know why I let you in here, but I did, and—and that's on me. Right?"

Another pause. By the time it occurred to her that he wanted a response, he was already talking again, pacing more feverishly than ever.

"I just—have to *think*. I can finally fucking focus for the first time since I woke up, I just—okay. So. It's not about what you *did*, none of *that* means you deserve to die. It's about what you *will* do. If I don't kill you, I have to let you go. And you'll tell the soldiers all about this place...and we'll all be killed. Even the kids. I can't let that happen. They didn't do anything wrong. Of *course* I'd kill a stranger to save them. But it's just—so *unfair*. People can't be put to death for crimes they didn't commit yet. If they could, if that was how it worked, all of us would've been killed already.

"But...maybe you won't sell us out. Right? I know you're mad at us, you have every right to be, but I—I'll make it up to you. However I can. Whatever it takes so you don't bring soldiers here. They're not going to reward you, you know. They'll probably turn on you. But if it's gold you want, I'll—I'll make it happen. I swear. Okay?"

She heard the question in his voice, but his words were blurring together, swimming around in her head like fish through murky water. It didn't matter anyways. She just wanted to go back to sleep.

"What's the matter with you? Are you seriously just going to ignore me? I'm trying to *fix* all this." The footsteps were coming closer now. "Look—here's what we're going to do. I'm coming in. I'm going to blindfold you, and we're going to walk out, and then—then we'll talk terms. And if you want to give anyone up, you can give me up. Just not—anyone else. Okay?...Rose?"

Silence. And then the latch on the door clicked.

"Rose...?"

Light leaked into her cell, then poured, then flooded, chasing the ghosts away. It seared her eyes beneath the shelter of her eyelashes, but she didn't have the strength to close them.

He sucked in a breath.

"Rose! Oh, *shit—"*

A rustle of fabric, a shadow between her and the door. A creak of leather by her ear. It sounded as if he were kneeling over her.

"Wake up, damn it, *wake up—"*

He was shaking her. Her whole body wanted to recoil from his touch, flinch away, push him off, but all it could do was throb in agonizing pain. She made a little sound, involuntarily. The hard stone scratched against her cheek, dug into her side.

"No—no, no, *no*—don't die, you *can't* die, you *can't* be dead, oh Goddess...."

Something touched her cheek. She didn't have the strength to flinch, let alone pull away or fight back. A hand, with long slender fingers, callused but gentle. It touched her neck, then her lips.

"No, no, I don't understand, it was just a couple of days—just a couple of days—Lis! *Lis!* Anybody?!"

Goddess above. Even after killing her he wouldn't shut up.

"Damn it—okay, okay, it'll be all right, just—just let me—"

Then strong, warm arms scooped under her arms and knees, and suddenly she was rising from the floor. The muscles strained like cords against her skin as she was jostled around, as her weight shifted. Her head sank onto something solid but warm, covered in scratchy fabric.

This was real. Wasn't it?

"It's okay. It's okay, Rose. I've got you...."

She could feel the rumble in her ear as he spoke, feel the rise and fall of her makeshift pillow. A smell filled her nose, sweet and spicy and rich—like leather, like burning cedar, like the sea after a storm. She wanted to breathe it in deep, drink it like spiced wine.

"It's all right...you're all right...."

His voice was a low, constant murmur of reassurance in her ear. She was so tired—and Goddess, so dizzy—when he moved it made her head spin.

"You're gonna be okay. Just hang on...hang on...."

Light and shadows moved across her eyelids. His hands were warm. She could feel his skin against her cheek. How long had it been since someone had touched her with tenderness and not violence? Surely someone had, once.

There had to have been someone who loved her.

Surely....

A brief pause—and then a few more steps—and then she sank gently onto a soft, warm surface. Her head settled onto a stiff pillow. Rough fabric tickled her nose, but she couldn't find the strength to move.

The warm arms slid away. But something warm brushed her hair from her cheek—a callused finger, whisper-soft against her skin.

"It'll be okay. Just—just stay here. I'll be right back. You'll be okay...."

Footsteps—slow, at first, then rapid and loud, receding fast. Running away.

She was asleep again before their echo faded.

S*erena Sangor.* Here now. It couldn't be—

"Get out," Romero said numbly.

Auna stiffened. "I beg your—?"

"I—need a moment. Please," he added, attempting to smooth the affronted look on her face. "I must get ready for the day. I have other audiences."

"Well, all right. If you *insist.*" She stood and strode out, her nose in the air.

He was going to pay for that later, he was certain. But he didn't care. The moment the door closed, he stripped naked and ran to the washbasin, scrubbing vigorously at his face for a few seconds before turning and hunting for clothes. A servant took over, handing him a cloth for his face, then helped him dress in clothes of velvet and silk covered with gold embroidery. He scrambled to throw on his best boots, polished to a high shine, combed his hair, and even attempted to shave, until the razor in his shaking hand nicked his skin and he had to yell for the servant to finish for him. He twisted his ring over and over around his finger, the same ring worn by Rafael all those years ago, made from heavy gold and a large and flawless ruby with the eagle of the Sangor family etched upon it. As the servant arranged a stray lock of hair, Romero gave a skittish laugh that made him jump.

"How do I look?" Romero asked him, but he was too impatient to wait for a response. He jumped up and fled the room, donning his sword and a crimson cloak while hurrying down the corridor.

He hated himself for doing it, but he hesitated outside the door to his study. His courage had failed him, and he could not bring himself to walk into the room. He felt like a teenager again, as young and nervous as he had been the night he had met Serena. It felt as if an age had passed since that night, yet his heart still trembled the same way. It was with Serena's face in his mind that he managed to steel himself at last, and walk in.

His heart leapt to his throat at the first glimpse of dark curls and brown skin. She looked up—almond-shaped eyes wide with terror, shapely lips curling into a snarl. Simple men's clothes, old and worn and dirty. Bare feet, and hands scraped raw from struggling against the ropes that bound her to the chair. Hair in a wild tangle, a cut on her cheek. Fearless, fiery, and defiant—just as he remembered.

It wasn't her.

The disappointment crushed him like physical pain—like being slammed to the ground by an armored man, like being pinned between the hard earth and a large horse. It took him a moment to catch his breath; he had to turn away. He cursed the witch, his hand tightening around the grip of his sword, but without much passion. He was too drained, too empty, to feel anything at all.

Serena was not here. She was a thousand miles away, if she still lived at all.

But this woman....He turned and inspected her more closely. This woman was not a queen. Romero had seen enough kings and queens to know what parts of their nature they could not hide even when they tried. Nor, by any stretch of the imagination, could this twenty-five-year-old sailor be the thirty-five-year-old noblewoman that he knew Serena would be now. And this woman was nothing like her. He could tell by the way she held herself, the way she glared at him, the way she twisted her mouth.

Yet—incredibly—she looked like Serena. So much so that the sight of her took his breath away for an instant before he remembered that she was a stranger. She had the same dark eyes, the same full lips, the same curves to her figure. Her hair even curled the same way. He had seen sisters who did not resemble each other as closely.

He bowed low to her, his head spinning with a hundred half-formed thoughts that scrambled to coalesce into a coherent idea. "My lady," he said, graciously offering his hand. "Can you understand Cour—? Ugh!"

He recoiled in disgust as the woman spat in his face, hurling foul curses at him in Savillan that he, unfortunately, understood perfectly. Her harsh voice, her twisted face, left him shaken, unnerved. He had imagined this so differently....The bitterness rose in his throat until he could no longer bear it, and he lashed out, striking her hard across the face.

"Basti," he spat in Savillan as she gasped for breath, the mark of his hand darkening her cheek. Serena had cursed at him that way once, in a voice that was far too similar, and he could not bear to relive that moment now. "Enough of your impertinence. I am the king of this land, woman, and I *will* be treated with respect."

She was bound and unarmed. He towered over her, surrounded by his guards, his sword ready to draw at his side. He could easily over-power her...yet when she looked up at him, he saw only blazing fury in her eyes. "Do what you will with me," she snarled, "but I am a free woman of Savilla, and I will bow to no man! You will have no respect from me, you disgusting man, until you lie dead by your own hand."

Her words shocked him—infuriated him—but he stopped himself from hitting her again. It would accomplish nothing; it would only bruise Serena's face. He sank to one knee instead and lowered himself until their eyes were level. She watched him with narrowed eyes, neither spitting nor cursing, waiting for him to speak with an expression that made it plain that he could say nothing to appease her.

"Why do you hate me?" he asked her. "We've never met."

"You bring soldiers into my country and refuse to take them out," she informed him coldly, her head held high. Perhaps she was not a queen, but she would have made a good one. Such pride and compo-sure in a situation like this was impressive. "Your men *tied me* to a *chair*. You drove a daughter of Savilla into exile, you *murdered* a child of Savilla! You are a monster, and you will—"

"Wait—*who?*" He had assumed that the "daughter of Savilla" was a reference to herself, but talk of a child threw him off. "What daugh-ter? What child?"

"You do not know?" The scorn in her voice was clear. "Your king married a Savillan woman, you did not know this?"

He scowled. *His* king? "I know whom he married. What of it?"

"She was not a princess, she was—ours. A daughter of Savilla." She repeated this as if it should have some sort of meaning to him. "And their son, he was—" and here she said something that he could not understand, listening hard though he was; it sounded like *il regalo de fiore.* But he had no time to puzzle it out before her leg swung toward him, her heel flying at his face.

"But *you—!*"

He recoiled, but not quickly enough, and her heel smashed into the side of his nose. He lost his balance and fell back with a grunt of pain, his hand flying to his face. She lashed out again, snarling, but she was too far away this time. Still, she strained against the ropes that bound her, her eyes blazing in fury.

"He would have brought us peace!" she yelled at him. "He would have freed us from Allesino, but you—you *murdered* him!"

Romero gingerly felt his nose. *Il regalo de fiore.* By *regalo,* he supposed she meant the prince, Rafael's son, but *fiore....*The word was only vaguely familiar. He recalled it from a poem about the sacking of Aldaeza during the plague, used to describe the way a fire spread. Blossoming? Burning? The word was a puzzle of its own.

"You *monster,*" the woman snarled at him. "Only a coward murders a child, you do not *deserve* to be king! And we see you prowl around Savilla, looking to take us as you did Courma and Lyrma. You think yourself the new Conqueror? You are *nothing,* you have—"

"What is your name?" he interrupted.

The woman paused, clearly analyzing the question for any hint of a trap. Finally, she hurled the word at him as if it were a missile that might hurt him, every syllable insulting him without subtlety. "Angela." She pronounced it the Savillan way, *Ánghela,* with a soft noise in her throat somewhere in the middle of the word that he doubted he could replicate. "What have you done with my crew?"

"Your crew?"

"That traitorous little *brat* captured them," she spat. "Your *betrothed.* They have done nothing wrong! I demand you free them at once!"

He hadn't the faintest idea what had happened to her crew, and he didn't care. "I would worry about yourself, Angela." He didn't bother trying to pronounce her name the way she did. "Once your king finds out who kidnapped his daughter, he will demand that I bring you to justice. If I were you, I would appeal to my merciful side."

Her furious expression melted into utter shock. "*Kidnapped?!* I *never*—I did not even—she did not tell me who she was! She paid for a cabin, how was I to know who she was?"

Romero let her rant. He settled in a chair across from her as if it were a throne—for, as Rafael's instructors had taught him, when one was king, every chair one blessed with one's presence was a throne.

"—overpowered by *two men,* we never guessed they were—whatever they are, the princess's guard—and only *then* did she—"

"That's enough," he cut across her, and his tone silenced her at once. He looked straight into her dark eyes—eyes that were not Serena's. Something in his stomach twisted painfully. "Now, Angela. I'm sure this has all been a great misunderstanding. When I discuss with King Eduardo how his only daughter appeared at my docks, I'm sure I could convince him of your innocence."

Relief flickered across her face. "I *am* innocent, I—"

"If," he continued, speaking over her, "I felt so inclined." He shrugged, as if his hands were tied through no fault of his own, and rose to his feet. "Perhaps I will. I do so love being shouted at. Or perhaps my *traitorous brat* of a betrothed will want me to find some room in the dungeons. I suppose we'll see."

She flinched as if his voice was a whip cracking through the air. "Wait—"

Her voice broke. Romero took that as his cue to leave. He could not bear the crying, not now, not from someone who looked like that. He shut the door, but he made the mistake of looking back. In the instant before it closed, he saw Serena's face crumple, saw Serena's shoulders hitch.

Serena rarely broke down, not where anyone could see. He'd only seen her look like that once in all the years he'd known her. She'd sunk onto a chair in a corner after Rafael's funeral, when everyone else had gone, and started sobbing.

Guilt twisted low in his gut. He shoved it away, took a deep breath, and turned around. Maximilian was waiting nearby as always, his hands clasped behind his back.

"Max," he said. "Where is Princess Auna?"

"In the sunroom, Your Majesty. She said she will wait there for you to—erm—'find time' for her."

Romero pressed his lips in a thin line. If only he could leave her to her tantrums instead of bending over backward to appease her. "This woman—her crew—do you know where they are?"

Maximilian hesitated. Romero knew that look. He sighed but gestured for his attendant to deliver the bad news.

"Her ship exploded early this morning, Your Majesty. Her crew escaped."

"*Exploded?*"

Maximilian winced. "It seems...the Beggar's King was responsible."

Romero despised how the ridiculous title made him feel—the wave of nausea and chills, the crushing pressure on his ribs. The wound on his neck, long since healed, seemed to throb.

Worse was the fear. He remembered the red-rimmed eyes from his dream, the shadow looming over him as he lay, paralyzed and helpless, in his bed. At the same moment that the Beggar's King was destroying the ship, Romero had dreamed about him. And that meant—

Don't be ridiculous. The Divina girl must have messed with his head. He shook himself and fought to remember the question he'd been about to ask.

"Was Auna the target?"

"No one's certain, Your Majesty. He seemed to wait until she left before boarding. Our soldiers gave chase, but he escaped."

"Damn it," Romero growled. He strode off with nowhere to go, burning off his anxious energy. "And he was alone?"

"No, Your Majesty. He had accomplices covering him as he escaped—three or four, I'm told."

He shoved a vase as he stormed past it, but the satisfyingly violent crash and the way the servants jumped did little to soothe him. His hand found the hilt of his sword and gripped it tightly.

"The ship's remains are being dragged from the harbor now. Captain Ainsley is waiting to speak with you."

"Who?"

"The harbormaster, Your Majesty."

"Does he know anything about the Beggar's King?"

"I don't believe so, Your Majesty."

"Then I have no time for him. Tell him to do his job next time."

"Your Majesty, if you can coordinate a—"

"And that woman. The captain." He had to admit, she was... intriguing. It wasn't often that someone had the nerve to speak to him like that. "Keep her under close watch, but treat her well. Find a room for her. And don't let Auna go near her. She's *mine*."

"Yes, Your Majesty. I have taken the liberty of ordering Commander Bachellier to gather intelligence relating to the Beggar's King in the hopes that he discovers something that can identify the imposter. He promises to make a full report tomorrow. He believed the previous imposters to be mere petty thieves in disguise before, but as this is far more egregious...."

Maximilian continued to babble on nervously, but Romero was no longer listening. The boy, the Beggar's King, was dead—he had seen to that himself. But what did it matter if another one immediately stepped in to take his place? These rebels and traitors were like mice. If you caught one, the only thing you knew for certain was that there were a hundred more that you couldn't see.

And there had to be a mastermind behind it all. He thought he knew who—but he had yet to puzzle out *how*.

"Enough," he finally said, holding up a hand to silence his steward. He could not handle all of this, not now, not all at once. "Summon the commander now—I don't want him having time to make up any excuses. Tell the captain of the castle guard I'll speak to him next. And," he sighed, pinching the bridge of his nose, "have someone prepare a suite in the Queen's Tower for Princess Auna and arrange for chambermaids."

"Yes, Your Majesty." Maximilian hesitated. "And...if she should mention something about a wedding...?"

Romero groaned. There was no way to let her down gently. He'd have to find some way to keep her happy until he could send her back home.

Unless....

On a sudden whim, he turned left instead of right, heading for the sunroom.

"Fetch the commander," he ordered Maximilian, who bowed and vanished. He'd fetch the man swiftly—but Romero intended to make him wait.

He had a wedding to plan.

S omeone was singing.

She knew the voice, but she couldn't remember when or where she had heard it before. And the song—she knew it too. She knew every rise and fall of the melody. She couldn't make out the words, only the shape of them, but she could almost remember....

Then something burned in her mouth, making her cough.

"Rose?"

Reality came crashing back down, like a wall of icy water after a weightless dive. Light and sound and walls and an open door. Someone was in her cell with her. Leaning over her. Resting warm hands on her shoulder and head.

She tried to jump up, lash out—but all she managed to do was push herself up a few inches on shaking arms. A pair of warm hands reached out to help her, steadying her when she was struck by a wave of dizziness.

"Easy, now...it's all right...."

She looked up, blinking, but her savior's face was out of focus. All she could make out was a thick blonde braid and hazel eyes. She turned her head and pushed the intruder weakly away.

"Leave me 'lone...."

That was what she meant to say. But her voice sounded distant in her own ears, garbled, slurring. A rasp of air that burned and stabbed on the way out.

"It's all right," the blonde woman repeated. "It's okay, Rose, just let me help you up."

"Why're you...why...?"

"Here. Sit up, have another sip of this."

A bottle touched her lips, tilted. Something trickled into her mouth, something that burned. She choked and spat it out, but her head was already clearing.

"It's okay, Rose. You're okay. Just take it easy."

The dark, the cold—the boy, the shouting orphans—it was one of *them*. She had to get up now, get out of this cell, away from these people—

She lurched and slipped, tumbling to the ground. Her landing was soft, but it still rattled her teeth in her skull and made her ache right down to her bones. She stared blankly at a messy stack of cheap paper in front of her nose, shoved deep underneath some furniture. The topmost piece showed a detailed sketch of a tree.

"Careful!" A hand closed over her arm. "Here, let me help—"

"I'm not stayin' in here."

"You need to slow down, you're not—"

"I don't wanna be in here."

"Okay, you don't have to be, just let me—"

She found the door and latched onto it. Hauled herself up onto shaking legs. Shoved away the hands that tried to hold her back.

"Gotta—get outta this—stupid—"

"Aren't you thirsty?"

She stopped, looked around and down. The woman's hands held a cup of water.

Goddess, she *was* thirsty.

She made sure that she was solidly outside of the cell before dropping to her knees on the floor. Panting, struggling to catch her breath, she reached blindly for the water.

"Here, drink. Just relax, it's all right."

She drank. The cup seemed unbearably heavy, enough to make her arms shake from the effort of lifting it—but the water was so pure and sweet that it nearly brought tears to her eyes. She drained it without thinking, then let the cup fall, cursing herself for letting a single drop of it spill.

"Here." The woman pressed the cup into her hands again—once more filled to the brim.

The more she drank, the more the fog inside her head seemed to dissipate, until she could look around with fresh eyes once more. Her eyes flickered between the blonde woman and the open gate of her cell —only it wasn't her cell. She was in a different room entirely, a grand hall, with a high ceiling above her and an ornate balustrade at her back, like something out of a castle. The door across from her hung open, showing the room she'd come out of—and the bed she'd fallen off of. It was a proper room, with a little colored-glass window and everything.

She looked down at her arms and legs, scuffed but otherwise unharmed. She didn't know what had happened, but somehow, she was...free.

"Rose? Are you feeling better?"

She stared blankly at the woman who knelt in front of her, studying her face. She was twenty or so, certainly older than the boy— far too old to be an orphan. She wasn't pretty like the other one, but she had a sweet, kind face and warm eyes. She finally remembered where she recognized her from: the woman had been leaning over the boy, trying to help him, while the other two had been busy grabbing her and shouting at her and locking her up.

"What...did y' call me?" she rasped.

"What?"

She coughed, wincing at the pain in her throat, and tried again. "Why're you—c-callin' me that?"

"Rose? Isn't it your name? It's what Kayo called you, and I thought, with the necklace—"

A flash of gold and red. She snatched at it so fast that her head spun.

"That's mine!"

"Go on and take it. It's—"

She spilled water all over her front as her hands lunged for her own neck, struggling with her hair as she slipped the chain over her head. The pendant slid back under her shirt, heavy and cool, right where it was meant to be. Her left hand lifted automatically to wrap around it.

"You...brought it back." She eyed the blonde woman in fuzzy suspicion. "Why...?" She looked around, frowning. "Where...?"

"These are our rooms," the woman said, gesturing to the doors in the wall behind her. "Mine's down near the end."

"Oh...."

It still hurt to talk—it hurt to think, to breathe, to sit up straight —but not as much as it had before. But the sunlight—and she could feel the breeze—and—

Her drifting eyes found the ceiling—and the gaping hole where it had collapsed. For a moment, she thought herself back in the smithy, but through this hole, she couldn't see stone or bridges or people. Just blue. An unmistakable shade of blue.

The sky.

She sat up slowly, soaking it all in—and that was when she noticed the sea of green. Down below the balustrade, nestled in the stone, she could see vines—shrubs—trees—

A *garden.*

She'd never seen a garden before.

What *was* this place? Was this heaven? If not for the orphan and the cramps in her stomach, she would have almost believed it.

"Can you drink some more?"

She turned to the woman, who was pouring something else into the cup from a little saucepan, something warm and fragrant with green and yellow bits floating in it. The smell of garlic and onion made her mouth water.

She nodded, and then the cup was in her hands, and her teeth latched onto the edge as she drank as if every bit of her wanted to stop it being torn away. And Goddess, it was incredible, sweet and salty and flavorful and....

"Slow down," the woman warned her.

She ignored her, draining the last dregs of the cup. It filled the clawing, aching void in her gut faster than she would have thought.

"More?" she panted, out of breath from the effort.

The woman shook her head. "Give it a minute. If you eat too much all at once, it could make you sick. Are you feeling all right? Are you hurt?"

"Hurt?" She pushed herself up, her hands curling into fists. The effort made her head spin. "Of course I'm—fuckin'—"

"I know," the woman said quickly. "And I'm so, so sorry, I really am, I swear we didn't mean to hurt you—"

"You *locked me up!*"

"I know, I know, and if I'd known you didn't even have any water—"

"For a—a—a *week!*"

"What? No—it wasn't even two days." The woman looked at her with an expression that made her uncomfortable—something sad and concerned and more suited for a sick baby than a furious nearly-grown adult. "When was the last time you ate anything?"

"I—what? It was—" She had to stop and think. "I had a sticky bun right before that *boy* showed up."

"And before that?"

"I—I don't know."

The woman gave her a look that made her want to knock her teeth out.

"But it's all because of that stupid boy!" she said. "If he hadn't *dragged me here* and *locked me up*—"

"It's not his fault. We're sorry," the woman said quickly. "Really, we are, we never meant for that to happen—"

She sat up to tell the stupid, simpering woman that she'd rip her pitying eyeballs out of her head and shove her apologies up her ass before she'd listen to their damn excuses—but then she thought better of it. *You aren't acting very innocent*—that's what the boy had said to her. Yelling and threatening had been what had gotten her locked up in the first place. But if she played along, and pretended to accept their stupid apologies, perhaps she could catch them off guard later.

She decided it was best to do the thing properly. She slumped back against the wall, letting her head loll. "'M dizzy," she mumbled. "And hungry."

"Here. You can have a little more." The woman poured more broth into the cup. "And then you need some rest. We can sort all this out later."

She looked around as she drank, trying to slow herself down. This place was like something out of a dream—the ornate arches, the slanting shafts of sunlight, the salty breeze snaking through the delicate balustrade. It seemed impossible for something so huge and empty to hide in the Bermeia she knew. And the garden—she didn't know of anywhere in the upper or lower city that had that much empty space to sacrifice for flowers.

"Where...?"

"This is our home," the woman said, gesturing around. "Mine and—well, you met the others."

"But, who—?"

"Oh, I'm Alysia," said the woman, though she must have known that wasn't what she'd meant. "And you're Rose, right? Or...?"

She opened her mouth to deny it, but then thought better of it. She nodded, and Alysia smiled.

"Well, Rose, it's nice to meet you."

She considered glaring at Alysia, but didn't have the strength. She looked around. "But this place, is it—?"

"Later. For now let's get you to bed. I'll sit with you until you fall asleep."

"No—no, that's okay," she said quickly. "I'm not tired. Just hungry."

"Oh. Well, in that case, let's go to the kitchen," Alysia said. "I can make you something—if you're feeling up to it, I mean."

"Yeah," she said firmly, and dragged herself to her feet to prove it. It took all her strength, and the effort made her head spin, but she forced her legs to hold steady.

Alysia grinned. "Then follow me."

Rose.

Rose.

Rose.

That was her name now. Letting Alysia assume that her name was Rose was far easier than explaining that she didn't have one and probably never had, but it was going to take some getting used to.

"So are you from around here?" Alysia asked her as she led the way through a dark corridor. Then light washed over them, bright and blinding. They were in the narrow courtyard again, the sunlight slanting in at steep angles.

She squinted, holding up a hand to shield her eyes. "Huh?"

"Where are you from?"

"Uh. Here?"

"The upper city?"

"No. Lower."

"Oh." Alysia dragged a stack of wooden tubs out of the shadows and started lining them up on the ground next to the fountain and filling them with water. "You can sit if you like."

Rose eyed the fountain, then sank to the ground a good distance away from it, watching Alysia work. She vanished through the little door, then reappeared, hauling a heavy, steaming cookpot. Rose was curious to find out what the rest of this place looked like, and perhaps get a better idea of where exactly she was, but the room inside looked cramped and dark. The thought of going in and potentially getting cornered by the other orphans was not appealing in the slightest.

Alysia dumped the hot water right into the first tub, which had an odd metal construct attached to it. Then from her apron she drew out a handful of little pouches, adding a pinch to one tub, a dash to another. She disappeared one more time, emerging with an armful of clothes, which she started to sort. Underclothes, mostly, undyed linen with the occasional stripe of blue or red. Some of them seemed very small.

"So, Rose," she said as she worked. "How long have you been on your own?"

Rose stared at her. "What's it matter?"

"Just making conversation." Alysia shrugged. "This is really boring."

It certainly seemed so. Rose couldn't imagine what all of the buckets were for—especially the one filled with blue water.

"What *is* this place?" she asked, looking around at the high walls, the colored-glass windows, a handful of them shattered.

"It's...a shrine," Alysia said. She dumped some fabric into the bucket of hot water and tossed in some creamy soap that she scooped out of a bowl.

"A what?"

"A shrine. It's, um...the Divinæ used to live here."

"The *what?*" Rose stiffened and looked around again. "But they're—"

"I know. That's why it was empty."

Rose stared at her. "So what, y' just *moved in?* And made it yer... what, yer *nest?*"

Alysia snorted. "We're orphans, not *rats.*"

"What's th' difference?" Rose snapped.

Alysia sighed and wiped her hands on her apron, brushing her hair out of her eyes. But the look she gave Rose wasn't angry. She just looked sad again. "I don't know how long you've been on the streets," she said, "and I don't know why. But if it had happened before the orphanage burned down, you would've been right there with us."

"No, I wouldn't," Rose retorted. "I didn't do nothin' wrong."

"Nor did we." She cast a wistful look around the courtyard. "Just...bad luck."

Rose scoffed. "I been on my own for *years,* lady. *Ages.* Y' didn't see me there 'cause I didn't wanna fuckin' be there."

Alysia frowned. "You mean they didn't *catch you?* But how—?"

"Lis? Alysia?"

Alysia's head whipped around, her eyes finding the door she'd left open. "Oh, damn," she hissed under her breath. She cast a final, panicked look at Rose before another woman walked out—the pretty woman who'd menaced her with the bow.

The pretty woman's mouth fell open at the sight of her. Rose jumped to her feet, fists at the ready. But the woman turned immediately to Alysia.

"*Lis!*" she hissed. "What are you *doing?* She can't be *out here!*"

"Well, where else was I supposed to keep her?" Alysia snapped back. She kept her voice low, glancing anxiously at the windows that lined the courtyard.

"Kayo said not to let her out!"

"That was yesterday. Things change."

"That was *this morning.*"

"Whatever. I can't keep an eye on her if she's locked up."

"If Kayo sees her—"

Alysia snorted. "What, am I meant to be scared of Kayo now? Anyway—Rose, this is Artemis," she said, gesturing. "Artemis, Rose."

She announced Rose's name so proudly, as if she were the one who'd been named after a lifetime of only "girl" and "hey, you" and various unrepeatable curses.

Artemis glanced uneasily between them. "Right," she said at last, slowly. "Well, good luck to you and...um, Rose. I—"

"Arty," Alysia cut across her. "Rose and I were going to do the washing. Would you...like to help?"

Artemis stared at Alysia as if she'd announced her sudden wish to sprout horns and disappear into the forest.

"You want *my* help?"

"Yeah," said Alysia. "You know—if you're not too busy."

Artemis raised her eyebrows at Alysia. Rose looked from one woman to the other, frowning. There was clearly something going on between them, but she could not read their expressions. They seemed to be having some sort of silent conversation.

Artemis, Rose noticed, had a much nicer dress than Alysia. It was sky-blue and clearly new, still spotless and full of color, and it had layers like rich women wore with a lot of extra skirts underneath. The top skirt was a little short and hitched up at the front so the one underneath, dyed a slightly darker shade of blue, could show. It was embroidered all over with swirling patterns, too. Her fancy little heeled slippers alone were worth more than everything Rose had seen put together; the dress, on top of that, was simply ridiculous. It had to be worth a small fortune. What was a girl like that doing *here?*

Finally, Alysia seemed to win. Artemis sighed. "Sure, if you need me," she said, and started taking off her dress. "I can hang them up."

Alysia beamed. "Thanks," she said, and grabbed the odd metal device affixed to the tub.

The horrible slosh and creak and scrape of metal that followed made Rose wince and cover her ears. "What *is* that?" she yelled over the noise.

Alysia just shrugged, her arms straining with clear exertion as she turned the thing in the opposite direction. The grayish-white soup within wavered, then started spinning around again, widdershins this time.

Artemis, meanwhile, had removed her dress and was inspecting the laundry in just her chemise. Several other snowy-white chemises went into the bucket of blue water as Rose watched in amusement, imagining the look on the prissy woman's face when her underclothes turned blue.

After a few minutes, Alysia finally stopped. She sank down, panting, and started sifting through the soapy mess. She handed a sopping-wet lump of a shirt to Artemis, who inspected it, dunked it into the fountain, and then shoved it into Rose's arms.

"*Hey!*"

"Squeeze the water out of this, will you?"

"Huh?"

"What, have you never washed anything before?"

"Yes," Rose lied, scrunching her nose at Artemis when her back was turned. She took the wet lump and squeezed it between her hands, twisting out of the way as water dribbled between her fingers. Artemis sighed.

"You have to get more out. Like *this.*" She took the shirt and folded it in on itself, then pressed her hands down on it. "Like kneading dough."

"I dunno how to—"

"Just—keep doing that. Okay?"

Rose huffed and took the shirt back, mimicking what Artemis had done. At last Artemis snatched the shirt away from her and draped it over the edge of the fountain in the sunlight. Rose took this to mean that she was done with all that, but Alysia immediately handed her something else.

"Rinse that, will you?"

"Why'm I puttin' more water in just so I can get it out again?"

"That's how things get clean," Artemis told her.

"I didn't sign up to do your damn *laundry.*"

"Well, thank you. It's a big help." Alysia was busy rubbing soap onto a different shirt, using her fingers to scrub it deep into the fibers around a reddish splotch in the fabric.

Rose scoffed. "No point. Need a helluva lot more hot water an' soap for this lot."

"Mm-hmm."

"'Cause you orphans *stink.*"

"So do you," said Artemis, reaching out a hand. "Do you mind?"

Rose shoved the piece of fabric at her, only for Alysia to hand her two more. She shoved them into the fountain and left them there. "I *told* you, I ain't doin' your *chores.*"

"We all help out around here," Alysia said mildly, barely even looking up.

"Wh—you got a *lotta* nerve askin' for my help after her an' that big guy *locked me up!*"

"Dominic," Artemis corrected her in a lofty voice. "My affianced, thank you *very* much."

"Your—? Oh," said Rose with a snort. "Y' mean you two 're screwin'?"

"*Rose!*" Alysia scolded, but Artemis burst out laughing. Even her *laugh* was pretty. Rose was really starting to hate her.

"Don't yell at me, she an' her *lover* nearly *killed* me!"

"Oh, please," Artemis scoffed. "You seem like you're right back to normal."

Rose bristled. "Y'know—"

"You don't have to help," Alysia interjected. "I just thought you'd like to sit out in the sun, maybe wash up."

"No," Rose snapped.

"If you're going to stick around, you need a bath," Artemis said sternly. "There are *rules.*"

"Arty—"

"Who says I wanna stick around? Show me the damn door an' I'm *gone.* There a way out that ain't flooded?"

Artemis gave her one of those looks that mothers gave their misbehaving children. Rose decided immediately that she didn't like it—or her.

"Rose," Alysia interrupted. "Do you know what's in the kitchen?"

"Who cares?" Rose was already heading for the door at the other end of the courtyard. "This the way out?"

"A huge bowl of porridge. All yours."

Rose paused, her hand hovering over the door's latch.

"It's even warm."

She would have stabbed someone for a hot meal. She *had* stabbed someone for much less.

"Also, that isn't the way out."

Rose tested the latch, just in case. It lifted, but nothing happened. She pushed, but it didn't budge.

"It's a good deal," Artemis commented. "Twenty minutes of laundry for a nice hot meal? Bet you won't find a deal like that in the city."

Rose turned around. At the crafty look in Artemis's eyes, she seriously considered stabbing someone again. Goddess, she needed a weapon.

"Can't I do something else?"

Alysia shrugged. "You can scrub dishes."

Rose groaned, clawing her hair impatiently out of her eyes.

"It's *just* washing, you baby," said Artemis, and Rose heard something in her voice that sounded very much like laughter. "Come on."

Rose was supposed to be someone different. Someone new. And Rose, Rose decided, was certainly no coward. So she stomped grudgingly across the courtyard, shoving up her various sleeves, mentally resigning herself to loathing every second of it.

There was no mistaking it; Artemis definitely laughed as Rose knelt on the edge of the fountain beside her. Rose glared at her, but she had already turned away.

Some of the clothes they handed her were very small. Children's clothing, she thought, must surely be easier—but they weren't. By the third or fourth item of clothing, she was out of breath. But she refused to let Alysia see, and refused to complain.

"What *is* all this stuff?" she asked Alysia, who was humming to herself as she worked and didn't seem to be straining at all.

"Clothes," said Alysia, raising her eyebrows.

"What's it look like?" Artemis added.

Rose decided it best not to talk to them after that.

She'd been disappointed in that boy for his choices in clothing when impersonating the Beggar King. Was it really so hard to dye a shirt or two black? But now she saw that any color at all was asking too much of these people. The tiny clothes were made of old yellowish linen and undyed wool that had to be rolled up and pressed to release the excess water—and all of them were falling apart at the seams. She could pick out the larger clothes by color: the chemises for the two women were also linen, but violently white in comparison to the rest, and the clothes for the two men twisted through it all in various shades of dark gray and dark blue and dark green. All of it looked very faded in the daytime, too, and full of holes, with every edge frayed—except for the chemises floating in the blue water. To her disappointment, they came out whiter than ever. They *had* to be Artemis's, judging by the pristine condition and the careful way she laid them out to dry.

Their ridiculous clothes infuriated her. First this stupid *boy,* and probably his stupid friend, had had the brilliant idea to impersonate the Beggar King after his death. It was so disrespectful that she made a vow to punch him again for it before she left; once was not enough. But they'd done it so *lazily.* The boy had had one decent weapon on him, and that was all. Everything else had been old, faded, frayed, and cheap. Even his vest had been cheap, flimsy leather. They'd probably stolen the knife. Why couldn't they have stolen some decent clothing, too? The *real* Beggar King would never have been so sloppy. But then, he also wouldn't have gotten himself *shot*, or fallen through a *roof*, or asked someone for help and then taken her *prisoner*—

It happened while she was distracted, lost in her angry thoughts while leaning over the water to grab a stray item of clothing: a firm hand pressed against her hip and pushed.

She barely had time to scream before the water rushed up to swallow her.

The water was deep enough to bury her. Rose flailed wildly, but neither her feet nor her hands could find the surface. Just the bottom—the falling water pushing down and down and down, filling her ears with noise. Her fingers clawed along the rough stone at the bottom, searching for something, anything—

Something grabbed her, dragging her back. No—up. Her head broke the surface, and she sucked in a huge breath, then started coughing.

An odd sound made her look up and around, shoving her dripping hair out of her eyes.

Artemis was laughing.

Laughing.

Rose was coughing so hard she couldn't breathe, but she struggled out of the water anyways, onto and over the edge of the fountain, collapsing in a heap onto the sun-drenched paving stones. Every breath she sucked in was laced with water, tickling her throat and triggering another fit of coughing. She bent double and choked it all up, her abdomen cramping so hard she had to fight not to retch.

"Don't be so *dramatic*, Rose," Artemis's voice snickered above her. "It's just a little water, you can—"

"*I can't swim!*" Rose screamed at her. Burning-hot rage was clawing inside her, fighting the chill of the water, threatening to burn her to cinders—but by the Goddess, she was going to take the woman with her. "I coulda *drowned*, you *idiot*, you can drown in a fuckin' *bucket—*"

Alysia held up her hands. "Whoa, Rose, it's okay."

"—and—*fuck,* ya got me *wet,* this is *all my clothes,* I'm gonna fuckin' freeze to death! Are you insane?"

"It's not even winter—"

"It still gets cold at night! People fuckin' die when it rains! An' my *necklace,* it's not s'posed to get wet, it'll *rust—*"

"Gold doesn't—"

"Fuck, I'm gonna get *sick,* people get *sick* if they're soakin' wet all night. Ya think I can afford a fuckin' healer? You *bitch!*"

"Hey, now—"

But the anger was twisting, hardening, giving way to something that hurt—something that burned in her throat. And, to her horror, her eyes.

"Rose, I-I was just messing around, I didn't mean to scare you."

"*I'm not scared!*" she yelled.

And then she started to sob.

It was horrible, humiliating, weak—but she couldn't stop. She knelt in this strange new place and shivered and coughed and sobbed so hard she thought her ribs would crack.

"Hey—hey, now," Alysia stammered, and Rose heard her step onto the pavement, saw her shadow block the sun as she knelt across from her. "Hey, it's all right, don't cry—"

"I'm *not* cryin'!"

But she was. Goddess damn them all, she was *crying.* What was *wrong* with her?

"Is this just because you got wet?"

"*No,*" she sobbed. "I mean—*yes—*"

But it wasn't. It was—*everything.* The water and the cell and being trapped with orphans and the long night alone and talking to people for the first time in years and not even realizing that, Goddess, she hadn't talked or sung in *years,* and nobody had cared, nobody had even wanted to talk to her. It was the terror of being surrounded by soldiers after an exhausting week of no food and no safe place to stay and worrying she might never wake up when she went to sleep and the Beggar King was gone, really gone, and she'd been stupid enough to let some imposter lie to her about leaving the city so he could drag her through some hellish underground *nightmare* and then into another, even worse nightmare after that—

It was strangers and back-breaking work that they'd mock her for if she didn't do right and wishing so hard that she could stop but knowing that they'd turn her away if she did, and she hated this place, but she couldn't make herself leave, because where else was she supposed to go? Here there were people who hated her and had threatened to kill her but at least there was food, so she *had* to stay, she had no choice—

It was the little voice in her head that kept stomping its foot like a toddler, shrieking *I want to go home, I want to go home*—but neither it nor she knew where *home* was—

It was *let her rot* and *liar* and *you robbed him?* and *Goddess forbid you leave anything behind* and *one way or another, our problem's solved* and *no one would care. Nobody would even know that you were gone.*

It was everything.

"I-I'm so sorry, Rose," Artemis said after a long silence. "I didn't know you—I didn't think you'd get so upset, I just—you just needed a wash, and you weren't—"

"Well, I'm fuckin' clean now! Are you happy?" Rose shouted at her.

Artemis threw up her hands in surrender. "No! I-I'm sorry, all right? I'm really sorry—"

She wasn't helping. For some reason, the words *I'm sorry* triggered a fresh flood of tears every time. "Jus' go away! Jus' leave me *alone....*"

Artemis said nothing. She just got up and walked away.

And somehow, that felt even worse. Alone again—as she'd always been, as she always would be—

But Alysia hadn't left. She knelt beside Rose, blocking the sunlight.

"Rose?" she said gently.

Rose sniffled and wiped her eyes, glancing at Alysia from behind a curtain of hair. She held a wooden comb.

"Rose," Alysia said again. Rose marveled briefly at the strangeness of having a name, just one simple word that somehow encapsulated her entire identity, and wondered if she would ever get used to it.

Rose. It sounded so final, like a lock clicking into place—but she didn't hate it. It matched her necklace, for a start. But *Rose* sounded like somebody...else. She could hear the boy's voice echoing in her head, calling her name in her dreams. He'd sounded as if he'd actually cared about her.

Rose. That could be someone that someone cared about. Someone who mattered. If Rose spoke, people might listen. If Rose died, people might notice.

"Can I brush your hair? You don't have to move. I don't need water, I swear."

Rose stared at her blankly, looking straight into her hazel eyes.

"I know it's been a rough couple of days," Alysia said quietly. "And I know she just made it worse. And I'm sorry. *She's* sorry. None of this is your fault. We shouldn't have pushed you so hard. Or—*actually* pushed you." She stopped for a moment, clearly struggling for words. Then she gave up and said again, "We're sorry. Really. You don't have to help anymore, and Artemis is going to get you some dry clothes. We'll wash and dry yours so they're good as new. All right?"

"I don't want to stay here." Rose meant it to sound scathing, but the words had no heat behind them.

Alysia nodded. "I know. I—well—in a little while, someone can walk you home."

Rose stared at her. "Walk me *home?*"

"Yes, of course—to make sure you get there safely. And apologize to...who did you say it was?"

Rose considered lying—but what was the point? She was wet and shivering and utterly defeated. She hugged her knees and muttered her reply into them. "Nobody."

"What?"

"I said *nobody,* okay? I ain't got—I ain't got a—" She took a deep, shuddering breath, fighting back a fresh wave of tears. "I don't got anywhere to go. Okay? So jus' let me *out,* I jus' want *out*—"

She had to stop; she couldn't stand for Alysia to see her break down.

After a long pause, Alysia lifted the comb. "So, can I...?"

Rose didn't answer. She just curled up, hiding her face against her knees. Alysia seemed to take that as assent. Rose felt a soft tug on her hair as Alysia began combing the tangles out of it.

The silence was both welcome and peaceful. Just the warmth of the sunlight, the trickle of water. She couldn't hear the city noises at all—the horses and footsteps and carriage wheels and neighbors calling to one another and happy children shrieking and grouchy men yelling for all of them to get out of the way and shut up. That was a losing battle, though. Bermeia never slept, never stopped, never fell still or silent.

Those sounds had been a firm constant in her life. The lack of them was...unsettling. It made her feel somehow naked.

"Rose?" Alysia said softly.

Rose sniffled, wiping at her nose with her sleeve.

"That ain't my name," she said.

"It's not? I'm sorry, I thought—then what is?"

"I don't know," Rose said quietly.

Another long silence. Then, softly, Alysia said, "Oh."

Rose's eyes started to burn again. In that soft *oh*, she could hear as much emotion and understanding as an hour-long play. And she hated it—and the silence that followed.

But when Alysia finally spoke, she didn't say any of the things Rose had expected.

"Well," she said, "'Rose' is as good a name as any, don't you think?"

Rose touched the spot where her necklace hid, feeling the familiar ridges of its petals. She nodded.

"You know," Alysia told her, quite casually, "I don't know what my real name is either."

Rose swiveled around to face her. "Huh? Why not?"

Alysia shrugged. "Apparently I got trampled by a horse. Look." She pushed her braid aside and lifted the hair off the back of her neck. Rose could see a tendril of scar tissue snaking up out of sight, a patch of white ropy skin where the hair could not grow. "Whatever it was, it got me pretty good. I woke up in the orphanage days and days later with no memories at all."

"Really? *Nothin'?*"

"Nothing. And I mean *nothing*. I couldn't even remember how to walk or eat. I had to learn how to speak all over again." Alysia shrugged again, as if that sort of thing happened to her every season or so. "But I remembered Kayo. We were brought to the orphanage together. I'm the one who named him, but I could never get it to sound quite right...my name either. It's like remembering a song you heard in a dream."

Rose winced as the comb found a snag, but the pressure vanished before she could complain. "Where were you 'fore the orphanage?"

"I don't know. The horse kicked all that out of my head, too, and Kayo was too little to remember anything. I guess we were out in the streets—but I don't know why. There was a storm," she added thoughtfully. "A bad one. I think I remember laying in the street in a puddle, and rain was falling on me, and when the thunder struck it made the whole world shake...."

Rose shuddered. "How old were you?"

"Six or so." Alysia used her fingers to ease a snarl of hair apart. "You know," she added, dropping her voice to a conspiratorial whisper, "the orphanage thought we were rich."

"They what?" A laugh snaked out of Rose's throat—not at the words, so much, but at the eyebrow-wagging mischief on Alysia's face as she said it. "Why?"

"We had on nice clothes," Alysia told her. "Even Kayo, and people who can afford nice clothes for a baby—they must be crazy rich. The orphanage treated us a little better at first because they thought someone might come for us. But no one ever did." A wistful sigh ruffled Rose's hair. "It was nice while it lasted."

Rose hesitated. It seemed almost profane to speak about such things on such a beautiful day, while Alysia still held a pleasant note in her voice. But she'd always wanted to know. The question left her in a whisper. "Was it really that bad there?"

Alysia's hand hesitated for just a moment. Then the comb resumed its work. "Yes," she said simply. "However bad you think it was, it was worse."

Rose couldn't help but shudder, a cold weight dropping into the pit of her stomach. "But then—why'd you do it?"

"Do what?"

"Whatever ya did t' get *sent* there. Weren't you scared?"

"We didn't do anything."

Rose snorted. "I ain't *stupid*. I heard all 'bout it. It was like a prison for kids. I know you all got branded like prisoners do, an' you had t'work. They wouldn't 'a put ya there if ya didn't do *somethin'*."

The comb paused. "Rose...do you know what an orphan *is?*"

"Well—yeah. Jus' like I said, whoever got sent t' the orphanage is an orphan."

"No, Rose. An orphan is just someone who lost their parents."

Rose opened her mouth, then closed it again. "No, it ain't."

"That's the definition of the word. We didn't get sent there because we did something. We got sent there because there was nowhere else for us to go."

"But...no, that can't be right," Rose protested. "I heard you was all criminals, I heard one a' you even burned the place down."

"None of us would have done that," Alysia said quietly. "I think it's more likely that everything you've heard is a lie."

"But—but I heard—"

"Kayo was just a baby when he was brought there. How could a baby do anything wrong?"

Rose had seen plenty of babies do things that had made her want to lock them up, but Alysia had a point. Even she knew that babies and small children couldn't be held accountable for their actions. Not in such a powerful way, taken from their families, branded and locked away, made to work day and night.

But the soldiers didn't care. They were cruel enough to take any child for any tiny offense. Except—

Except she'd heard of kids being taken by mistake. Their parents had had to come get them. Some of them had had some trouble, but they'd gotten their kids back in the end.

Which meant that the only thing that had kept Alysia and the others there was a lack of parents.

"So everyone there—they didn't do nothin'?"

"Well, there was one," Alysia muttered, admitting this with extreme reluctance. "Did you hear about the Fishgut Butcher?"

"Yeah. So what?"

"He ended up there."

"What? That was really a *kid?*"

"Mhm. Nine years old."

Rose swore quietly, both alarmed and impressed. "Who was it? What was he like?"

"Um—well—"

But fortunately for Alysia, who clearly didn't want to talk about it, Artemis came bursting out of the open door. She held a pile of fabric in her arms.

"I'm *so* sorry, Rose," she blurted out at once—and she almost looked as if she meant it. "I didn't mean to—I was just—"

"Go *away*," Rose growled.

"I got it," Alysia told her. "Can you grab shears, please? And some oil?"

Artemis looked between them, chewing on her lip, and then set the fabric down and flounced back into the kitchen.

"Bitch," Rose muttered under her breath.

"She was just messing around," Alysia said.

"Just *messing around?* She coulda *killed* me—"

"She was playing a joke on you, that's all. It's what she would've done to me."

"*You?* No way she woulda pushed you in."

"If I needed a bath, she would have, yeah. It's what sisters *do*. And you *did* need a bath."

As much as she wanted to deny that, she couldn't. "She still—"

Artemis returned, holding her apron together to form a pouch. She set the items within on the edge of the fountain. She opened her mouth, perhaps to offer her help—but then her eyes met Rose's, and she decided, wisely, to leave.

"What're those for?" Rose asked, pointing to the shiny silver shears and the glass vial of yellowish liquid that Artemis had left behind.

"Your hair," Alysia said. "It'll help get the tangles out." And she went to work with her new tools. The soft *shiiick* of the shears so close to her ear made Rose a bit nervous, but she kept quiet. Perhaps, when Alysia put them down, she could steal them. Without a weapon, she felt more helpless than she had in years, and she didn't like it at all.

"It's such a lovely color," Alysia commented.

"What is?"

"Your hair. Look—it's red."

Rose looked up. Alysia held a strand of her hair up to the sunlight. Even damp, it was a deep orange red that faded into brassy gold.

"Huh," was all she said.

"Didn't you know that?"

"I don't spend all day lookin' at my own hair," Rose snapped.

"*I* would, if it was this color. Now, doesn't it feel better to have it clean and brushed?"

"No," said Rose sourly. "If I get sick, I'm gonna *kill* her—*an'* that boy—"

"Kayo."

"Huh?"

"That's his name. Kayo. And please don't. It would be a waste of all the work you did to save him."

"Wait. You believe me now?"

"I never doubted you. It didn't seem like you were lying."

"I *wasn't*."

"I know." The comb paused. "If what you said is true, you saved Kayo's life."

"Oh, good," Rose said witheringly. "So 's all worth it, then."

Alysia chose to ignore this. "If you hadn't helped him, the soldiers would have taken him. And then he—well." She sighed, her breath ruffling Rose's hair. "We...lost our brother recently, like that. If we lost Kayo too...." She gave herself a little shake. "Anyway. We should really be thanking you."

Rose snorted. "Some thanks."

"I know—and I'm sorry. I really am."

"Make *him* say sorry."

"I'm sure he will. Just—keep away from him. All right?"

"Why do I gotta keep away from 'im?" said Rose indignantly. She should have realized that someone would find some way to make all of this *her* fault. "I didn't *do* anythin'—"

"I never said you did. He should keep away from you too. He's just—he's—have you ever lost anyone? A parent, a sibling?"

The question took Rose by surprise. "No." She'd never had anybody to lose. Maybe a long time ago, but now....

"So you don't understand. Look—he's not himself. He's hurting. You don't know him. He's never like this."

"Right." Of course his friends would make excuses for him. It wasn't his fault, he was acting out of character—and he would continue to do so, right up until the day someone killed him for it. She could only hope she was the one who held the knife.

"I mean it. Just...you two stay away from each other, and everything will be fine."

"Suits me. I'll get 's far away 's I can get once you people *let me out*."

"I know. Listen, Rose, I know you want to leave, but—"

"But I can't," Rose said, scowling. "Because you're not gonna let me."

"That's not it at all. Look, if you want, I'll convince Kayo to let you leave. He's just worried that you'll tell the soldiers about this place, but I know you won't."

Don't be so sure, Rose thought, but kept that thought firmly to herself.

"It's just...why would you *want* to?"

"Huh? 'Re you crazy?" Rose almost laughed in her face. "Like I *wanna* be locked up here all my life—"

"Not locked up," Alysia said quietly. "That was a mistake. We shouldn't have been treating you like an outsider—because you're not. You belong here with us."

Rose stared at her. Against all logic, she looked as if she meant every word. "Y' can't be serious."

"Well," Alysia said, very gently, "it's not like you have anywhere else to go. Why not stay here? It's warm and dry and safe, you'd have your own bed, there's a hot meal every night...."

Rose frowned down at the disintegrating rags wrapped around her feet. "Now I know you're lyin'. That boy said there wasn't enough food."

"We'll make do." The comb wove its way through her hair again. "We always have. But everyone here—"

The door swung open again, cutting Alysia off. Rose jumped, but it was only Artemis. "Need help with the dress?" she said cheerfully.

Rose said "No," at the same time Alysia said, "Yes." Artemis seemed to hear only Alysia's voice. She was kneeling at Alysia's side before Rose could blink, tugging at the back of her shirt.

"Good goddess, this is a mess. How did you get these knots so tight?"

"I dunno. It was botherin' me so I reached back and—hey!" she yelled as she heard the clean *shiiick* of the shears and felt her shirt loosen.

"Relax," Artemis said briskly. "I'm a dressmaker by trade, I can fix it."

"Don't *cut* my *shirt*—"

"I'll untie them," Alysia said, and Rose felt their hands jostling at her back. She tried to turn around, but someone had her shirt in a tight grip.

"Let *go* a' me, I don't *want* 'em off—"

"We'll wash them for you," Alysia promised her again. "Arty, Rose was saying she might like to stay."

"I was *not*—"

"Oh, for—Lis, we *can't*," Artemis hissed, lowering her voice as if to prevent Rose from overhearing, though she was practically speaking right into her ear. "We're barely making ends meet as it is—"

"*Liam* would've let her stay. Otherwise what else is the point?"

"*Liam* would have *killed her.*"

"Well. Yes. But—"

"Kayo's not going to let her."

"Really? C'mon, Arty. It's *Kayo.*"

"Yeah, but you saw him. He'll want her gone."

"Wanna bet?"

"Oh, please. You haven't got two cuprums to rub together."

"I'll do your washing for a month."

A pause. Then: "Deal," said Artemis. Rose felt their hands smack together behind her back.

"Okay, *forget* it," Rose grumbled. "I ain't sittin' here listenin' to—"

But as she climbed to her feet, half of her clothes stayed behind. She whirled around and saw them in a pile on the floor, cut loose by the shears Artemis quickly hid behind her back.

"You *ruined 'em!*" she yelled. "Those're my *only clothes!*"

"I told you I could fix them," Artemis said, unfazed. "If they're even *worth* fixing. They look like they're about to fall apart."

"What do *you* care? Give 'em back! I'm gonna freeze to death!" She was already shivering as the breeze snaked through her final sodden layers of clothing.

"I got you a dry dress," Artemis pointed out, pointing to the pile of fabric she'd brought. "Yours need washing anyways."

And she and Alysia tugged her wet clothes over her head. It was a mark of how weak she was, how dizzy and confused, that they managed at all. She tried to fight them off, but it didn't seem to work. In what felt like an instant, she was completely naked in the courtyard, shaking like a leaf.

But before she could scream, or cry, or start hitting them—she honestly did not know which—Alysia slid a clean chemise over her head. It was simple linen, with short sleeves, and it reached past her knees.

"Here. This goes underneath," Alysia told her, handing her a thin pair of what looked to be drawers.

"These are for *men,*" Rose protested.

"No, they're not," Artemis said, and lifted her own skirt with a smirk. Rose, blinking in stunned silence, saw a similar pair of drawers topping Artemis's bare, shapely thigh. "Or maybe they are. Who cares? They're comfortable."

Rose gave a nervous laugh as Artemis's skirt fell again. It was all the convincing she needed to pull on the undergarment and tie it in place. No sooner had she finished than Artemis dropped the dress over her head.

"Hey!"

"Put your arms up."

"Gimme a *second—*" Her voice was somewhat muffled as she fought her way out of the dress. Artemis tugged it down to her shoulders and yanked it into place while Alysia started tightening ribbons. Rose looked down. The dress was olive-green and simple, with tie-on sleeves striped blue and white. After seeing what most of their clothing looked like, she was surprised they had anything this colorful lying about.

"It'll do," said Artemis with grim satisfaction. "But try and put on some weight, huh?"

Rose snorted, throwing Artemis a glare. She shoved her hair back from her face; it was already drying, and when it was clean, it liked to rebel. She was about to tell the orphans so, but then Alysia's gentle fingers combed her hair back and tied it with a ribbon.

She felt at it, frowning. Only the top had been tied up; the rest of it was a damp, wavy curtain down her back. The knot seemed tight enough to hold, at least.

"There," said Artemis, putting her hands on her hips with the same look of exhausted satisfaction with which a shipwright might view his final creation. "Now, was that so bad?"

"Horrible," said Rose flatly. She turned to Alysia. "Where's th' food?"

"I'm so embarrassed, *amore*," Auna said for the dozenth time. "I really thought that was Serena Sangor!" She reached across the table for Romero's hand, which he slid quietly away on the pretense of raising his teacup.

They were taking tea in the sunroom, bathed in light from the windows that arced along the walls and stretched up to the center of the ceiling. Somewhere, Romero imagined, the commander was waiting for him to arrive, but he'd be waiting for some time longer. For the first time in a long time, he wasn't desperate for a pitcher of wine or signaling covertly to Maximilian to interrupt so he could escape back to his rooms. A plan was forming in his mind even as he made small talk with Auna, and he was itching to put it in motion.

In light of that, the whole situation seemed almost humorous. "I really don't understand how. There's no mistaking that woman for any sort of queen. Did I tell you she spat in my face?"

"*Dia mi!*" Auna's hands flew up to her mouth. "A peasant, spitting on a king! I should have her whipped!"

Romero silently thanked the Goddess that he'd had the sense to warn Maximilian about Auna. She could give all the orders she liked, but that didn't mean his servants or guards had to listen. And hopefully, she would never be the wiser. Maximilian had a true gift for keeping all the women in his life away from each other.

"So you spotted a woman on the docks in Aldaeza and assumed she was Serena in disguise? And then—what, you asked her for a ride to the other side of the Peninsula?" He laughed aloud as he imagined it.

"Well, when you say it like *that,* it sounds so silly!" But Auna was laughing, too. "It seemed such a perfect coincidence! I needed a ship to Alronelin, and I knew you were looking for her, so—"

"I thought you'd met Serena?" Romero chuckled.

"I have! Well—it was years ago. But even you admitted it's a likeness!"

"They do look similar," he admitted. "Except that Serena is my age."

"She looked quite old to *me.* Quite haggard. It must be all that sea air."

Romero pressed the back of his hand to his mouth to suppress a chuckle he couldn't stop. "You thought Serena was in hiding, in her *own* homeland, as a *sailor?*"

"You must admit she's the type," insisted Auna. "I've heard all the rumors about her, I think that's *exactly* the sort of thing she would do."

Romero thought he knew what sort of rumors she meant. Serena had scandalized the nobles and the royal court and anyone else born into this life. The royal families of the Peninsula were so homogenous inside and out—especially after centuries of intermarriage—that he was certain Auna's upbringing had been the same. But Serena hadn't been royalty at all. And while she'd gotten on wonderfully with the royal court with her flawless manners and effortless charm, she'd taken after the other sort of Savillan women, the sort that spoke their minds and wore their hair loose, and had earned herself a reputation for unapologetic boldness.

"She would," he admitted, and looked out over the garden as he sipped his tea.

Serena could have easily disguised herself as a commoner. Perhaps she had; perhaps that was why he'd struggled to find her for so long. And she was certainly fierce enough to spit in the face of any king.

He wondered if he should tell Auna that Serena was missing a finger. But then she might ask how she had lost it. He had no desire to relive that night.

"Well, that's one more dead end," he said, toying with one of the little cakes that had been served with tea. "So you have no idea at all where she might be?"

"I don't, my love," said Auna apologetically. "She hasn't been to court since I was young. Surely my father could tell you where she is?"

Romero grimaced. "He's been...uncooperative."

"Ay, you don't have to tell me." Auna's tea erupted into a fragrant cloud of steam as she sighed into it. "Stubborn man. I don't understand why he objects to you bringing her home." She took a sip, frowning. "Why doesn't *she* want to come home?"

"I don't know." Or more accurately, he didn't know which of a dozen reasons she had chosen. But something Angela had said gave him an idea of why King Eduardo didn't want Serena—or her son—in Romero's hands. *He would have brought us peace. He would have freed us from Allesino.* He'd thought it odd that someone would say they needed freeing from their own king, but the woman was Savillan. Savillans had a history of losing patience with their rulers. Perhaps Eduardo was feeling the pressure and thought that the prince taking the throne in Alronelin would only make matters worse.

He decided it was time to broach the subject most prominent on his mind. "Speaking of your father, my dear," he said to Auna, "he'll be wondering where you are. Perhaps you should send him a letter?"

"Well, I—yes." Auna had turned to look out over the garden. "I will. Only...what shall I tell him?" She risked a glance at him, her eyes wide and worried. "You won't send me back home so soon, will you, my love?"

Romero pasted on a smile. "Why would I send you back home?" he asked her. "You don't want to leave already, do you, *tesora*?"

His flattery worked. She smiled, her entire posture shifting in relief. "Oh, not at all," she fawned, looking up at him from under her eyelashes. "I had thought, once I arrived, you and I...I had hoped we'd spend some time together."

Good Goddess. She really wasn't subtle. "Of course," he promised her. "Why don't you write your father, then? Tell him you'll be here awhile."

"Oh, of course I will," Auna promised him. "I'd hate for this to cause you trouble. I'll make sure he doesn't send his entire army after me!" She laughed at her little joke, and he faked a laugh too, even though he knew it was a real possibility.

"Perfect," he said. And he slid his chair a little closer, turning to face her. She looked up with wide eyes as he reached out and tucked a stray lock of hair behind her ear. "I'll write him too—and ask for his blessing. If you like."

Auna lunged forward and threw her arms around him. "Truly? Oh, Romero! That would make me so happy! I could plan the wedding right away!" She gasped, her hands flying to her mouth. "Oh, my love, why wait? We could get married now, tonight—"

"Easy, my darling," he cut across her. He rested a hand on her shoulder, his voice low and soothing. "What good is it to ask your father's blessing if we give him no time to respond?"

"Oh—right." She gave a nervous, fluttering laugh. "Of course. How silly of me! But then that gives us time to do the thing properly. Oh, it will be lovely, Romero. Don't worry about a thing, I'll plan it all, of course."

He smiled and nodded and played along as she told him her ideas for flowers, feasts, balls, invitations, tiaras. Was this what princesses grew up learning? It sounded like a nightmare—but he made no effort to rein her in. If he played this little game well enough, that particular wedding would never take place.

Hours later, after a grueling day of tedium and frustration, Romero finally found the time to sit in his study and plot. With a pen in one hand and a glass of wine in the other, he read the letter that Maximilian had just given to him, penned by Auna and addressed to her father. The tone of the letter seemed a bit cold to him, though admittedly, Savillan wasn't his native tongue. Her girlish handwriting explained that she was visiting Bermeia as his guest—neglecting to mention whose idea that was—and that she had accepted his proposal and planned to wed him. He'd made no such proposal, but the details hardly mattered. The letter was merely proof of life. He'd send it to her father, of course—along with a letter of his own.

He scratched a few notes, then paused with his pen on the page, thinking. Then he took out a wooden box from the sideboard and selected a few wooden figurines from within, elaborately carved to look like kings and queens from the past. A king in red, representing himself; a queen in white for Auna; a blue-clad king for her father. He positioned them just so, imagining a bird's eye view of a battlefield with their armies gathered on both sides. He'd learned early in his tutelage that this was how most battles were fought: gathering information like ammunition, selecting just the right bits to hurl at the enemy, riposting when they retaliated to push them in the right direction. And the key to winning, he knew, was to have an army hiding in the woods: leverage, as King Tristin had put it. He'd once joked that leverage and a woman's breasts affected men in much the same way: a small hint that it was there was enough to get what you wanted. Rafael had blushed cherry-red when he'd heard that. He'd been an excellent swordsman, but manipulation had never been his style. And look where that had gotten him.

He had leverage aplenty on Eduardo—his daughter, for a start, and his superior army. Not to mention several nasty, damning secrets. But how best to use them? He'd have to start with a light touch, then prepare for all the possibilities of what he might do next....

His ear caught a faint tapping sound. He looked up—but he saw nothing but a cat, wandering in from the corridor in search of mice. He clicked his tongue, and it wandered over, purring, to jump up on the desk and rub against his hand. Then he spoke to the empty air.

"Corrine. To what do I owe the pleasure?"

He could not see her behind him, and for a moment, he wondered if he had been wrong—but then a hand rested on his shoulder, another combing through his hair. "You've learned so much since we first met," a low voice laughed in his ear. "A bit too late, though, I'm afraid."

"I'm not dead yet," he pointed out, jerking his head out of her grip.

She reached for the cat—whether to pet it or shove it, he didn't know, but the cat bolted before she had the chance to do either. "How did you know?"

"You left the door open."

"Hmm. Well spotted."

With a soft rustle of silk against silk, Corrine perched on the edge of his desk, right where the cat had been. She crossed her ankles and straightened her back, looking every inch the queen in her silk gown and jewels, as if the desk were a throne. She cast an appreciative eye over the figures as she helped herself, uninvited, to his wine.

"What are you plotting now?" she asked him.

"None of your concern," he snapped.

"Of course it is." One hand traced idly down his arm, then slid under the sleeve, raking the nails lightly over his skin in a way that gave him goosebumps. "I heard you've acquired some new pets."

"What, the cat? They're everywhere. Who even knows where they—?"

Her hand tightened, the nails biting into his skin. "Don't play stupid with me, Romero. I know all about them both. The Divina *and* the princess."

"Oh? And how did you hear about that?"

She sniffed. "Why else do you keep me around? Not that I could have missed the gossip flying about. You can't *possibly* be considering marrying the girl."

"Is there a reason I shouldn't?"

"Well, for a start, you *have* a wife. *Two*," she added with a hint of scorn.

"And yet, no heirs," Romero snapped. "So I suppose I have every right to find another. The only question is what I do with the old ones."

"Old," Corrine scoffed. She had a point. Marisa, his first wife, was a couple of years older than he was, but there was no way of knowing how old Corrine might be. She hadn't aged much over the past few years, either. "I'm happy to see you're plotting something, at least. Otherwise, I'd question your sanity. She's practically a child."

"She's of age." He flipped a page aside, feigning boredom. "I'm sure all the gossips are convinced that it was my idea."

"Shouldn't they be? What is it, then? Did she tell you that she's pregnant?"

"I won't fall for that again," Romero said, throwing a sour look in her direction. "Can you even *get* pregnant?" he added, raising his eyebrows pointedly at her stomach.

She just shrugged. "So, then—what's your plan?"

He knew he should dismiss her. He knew that she couldn't be trusted. But if anyone would know what to do, it was her.

"I've been exchanging letters with her since the last time I was at court. Eduardo hasn't been quite as forthcoming with certain information as I would like. So—"

"You turned the charm on his daughter," Corrine said, nodding. "And it worked a bit too well, I suppose?"

"Too well? Hardly. Now I have a hostage."

"Hmm." She tapped a fingernail against her lips, considering the possibilities. "And the wedding?"

"A ruse. To keep her happy."

"Does it have to be?"

He looked up at her. Her expression was carefully neutral, but something cold and wicked gleamed in her eyes. Like a cat watching the panicked struggles of a mouse trapped under its paw.

"You've married for less," she pointed out. "And marrying the princess of Savilla puts you in line for the Savillan throne right behind her brothers."

"Savilla doesn't work like that."

"It does now."

He couldn't help but smirk. "I like the way you think."

"Hmm...." Her eyes roved over Auna's letter and his notes. "Then what, pray tell, do we need with all these missives? Is it a polite warning before you make your move? Do you want to see him beg first?"

He shook his head. "If he gives me what I want, he can keep his bloody throne. *And* his daughter, if he even wants her back...."

"This is about Serena, isn't it?"

He froze, the tip of the pen digging into the page. He didn't dare look up. "Why would it be?"

"You think he knows where she is. You're going to suggest a hostage exchange. Serena for his daughter. Aren't you?"

He took his time answering, tracing the same word over again with fresh ink. "It's not likely to work. Auna's hardly his favorite child. He won't care if I send her back."

Corrine sighed. "Not with *that* turn of phrase," she said. She plucked the pen out of his hand and scratched a few notes. "Maybe he doesn't care who marries the girl, or if he ever sees her again. But things happen. The Beggar's King is on the loose, and you have your share of other enemies. He doesn't want her *dead*."

Romero barked out a laugh. "You think I can convince him I'll have her assassinated?"

"Why not? You wouldn't lose much sleep over it if you did." She set the pen down and showed him her work. "And with a subtle hint at the power you stand to gain if you marry her."

"He'll claim the marriage isn't legitimate."

"Will he? Who else is going to want to marry her after this? And if he doesn't give an answer to your satisfaction—well, the girl's already here."

Romero leaned back, looking up at the ceiling. "I assume you heard about the ship captain?"

"I did. But I'm guessing the rumors that she kidnapped Auna aren't quite true."

"Oh, quite the opposite. But when I went to speak with her, she started shouting at me. And something she said....She thought I killed Serena's son. And she said she was a daughter of Savilla, whatever that means, and so was Serena—"

"Oh, is she? Hmm. That explains some things."

Romero's head snapped around to face Corrine. "You know what that means?"

"Sure. Sons and daughters of Savilla—that's what they call people with indigenous blood. When the Conqueror took over, his people interbred with the indigenous, so there aren't really many left, but some of their practices are still around."

"Practices? Like what?"

"Oh, who knows? Blood sacrifices and summoning gods and nonsense like that."

"Serena never spoke about that—she never did any of that—"

"Oh, really?" Corrine raised an eyebrow. "Didn't you watch her cut off her own finger?"

"That was a—a Savillan tradition. Not some barbaric savage ritual—"

"Well, Savilla's not like here. Some of that old stuff stuck around." Corrine let her gaze drift to the dark windows, thinking. "I thought they'd all died out. They're not organized, are they? If there's a group out there that thinks you killed one of them...."

"I don't know." He brushed back his hair, grimacing down at the papers on his desk. "She seemed to think that the boy would 'free them from Allesino.' That's the phrase she used. But he's the heir to *this* throne. *My* throne. Not his."

"Hmm...." Corrine's nails tapped against the top of the desk in a staccato rhythm as her fingers crawled across the desk like a spider. They crept onto his arm, tapping the buttons at his sleeves. "Sounds to me like there are more than a few threats to the Savillan throne."

A smirk curved his lips as he realized what she was thinking. "I wonder if Eduardo has been informed of these threats?"

"If not, he should be. For his own good." A glint of teeth showed as Corrine smiled. "And I can think of a few others who would like to know as well."

Something low in his gut seemed to stir, plummeting and rising again. That sly look on her face sent waves of heat crawling across his skin. He leaned in, one hand bracing against the desk just beside her thigh. "So if he's not cooperative, we'll give his enemies a little nudge, and see if that throne can be vacated. Shall we?"

She slid a finger under his chin, tilting his head until their eyes met. "Why even ask?" she said softly, her eyes glinting like obsidian in a raging storm. "A king takes what he wants."

He stood slowly, and as he rose, he brought his body closer. His hips slid between her thighs, easing her legs open beneath her skirt. One hand rose to tuck a curl behind her ear, delicately touching her diamond earring.

"You know I love seeing you done up so nicely," he told her. "So I can watch you come undone."

His other hand rested on her thigh.

He expected resistance, but Corrine's sly smile never wavered. "Oh?" she said. "By whom, exactly?"

His fingers tangled in her skirt, sliding it up her legs. The other drifted down to the neck of her gown. "How fond are you of this dress?" he whispered in her ear.

She didn't answer. He didn't need her to. He leaned in to kiss her, his fingers drifting up her leg beneath her skirt....

A hair's breadth from her lips, he froze.

Something sharp was digging into his navel.

"Don't move," she advised him.

He didn't move. He hardly even dared to speak. "You can't—you can't have a—"

"Can't I?" The knife traced its way down his stomach. "You need to learn how to ask for permission, Your Majesty."

He winced as the knife found somewhere far more delicate than his gut. But he held her gaze. "A king takes what he wants."

For the space of a heartbeat, he worried he'd made a grave mistake. The knife didn't shift, and her expression didn't change.

She could do it. She would. If the notion struck her, she'd run him through and leave him there to bleed out, and no one would ever know she'd done it. Corrine was ruthless. She was the only woman he'd ever feared. Her, and—

"On your knees."

The words were so unexpected that he couldn't process them. "What?"

A sting of pain made him suck a breath through his teeth. He pulled away, but Corrine's hand snatched a handful of his hair and pulled him back. She yanked him so close that he felt her lips move when she whispered to him.

"I *said*—"

Her knife dragged its way up his shirt, snagging at the fabric, until it paused at his throat.

"On your knees, *Your Majesty.*"

And she pushed him down—he let her push him down. The chair got in his way, but he kicked it aside as he knelt obediently at Corrine's feet. He looked up at her, and tangled in his fear was a reluctant admiration of her power—and a hunger, so raw and burning that it took all his self-control to ignore.

The knife was at the back of his neck now, the tip hovering just behind his ear.

"Do you remember how we met, my husband?" Her voice was as soft and playful as a purr, but the grip on his hair was like iron.

"Vividly." It had happened much like this, in fact.

"And what was it that I told you then?"

Looking up into her eyes, he thought he knew what a mouse felt when it was caught in the grip of a cat.

"You told me...." He swallowed. "To convince you that I was worth keeping alive."

Her laugh sent shivers down his spine. "Then I suppose you know what to do now."

Oh, but he did, and she didn't need the knife to persuade him. He slid his hands up her skirt, shoved the fabric aside, and kissed his way slowly up her thigh. She wasn't wearing anything to slow him down—she must have planned this all along, the crafty little minx.

The knife stung the back of his ear. Her hand in his hair pressed him closer. "Faster," she ordered him.

It must have amused her to bring a king to his knees, to order him about like her own personal slave. But something about it was driving him mad. He was rock hard, already aching to feel her close around him. But he'd have to earn it.

For once, he didn't mind the challenge.

The first brush of his tongue made her shudder and sigh. He felt her thighs relax, spreading open, inviting him in.

He didn't need to be asked twice.

Corrine knew exactly what she was doing. She clouded his head like strong liquor, muddied his judgment so he fell victim all too easily to her persuasion. And the idea was certainly tempting: Savilla under his control instead of a constant thorn in his side, a peninsula unified under his name, an empire so strong its enemies would buckle before it.

A king takes what he wants.

But he did write the letter, in the end. Instead of dictating to Maximilian, he decided to pen it himself.

He sealed it up with Auna's letter rolled inside and pressed his ring into the wax. An eagle with a crown above its head was left stamped onto the wax, the sigil of the Sangor family.

Without Corrine over his shoulder, the letter made it clear what he truly wanted. A little bribery, a little flattery—and the slightest hint of a threat. He knew Eduardo would read his true message as plain as day.

Find me Serena. Find me her son. Or you'll never see your daughter again.

B eing clean wasn't so bad. Not that Rose would ever admit it, to Alysia or anyone else, but she couldn't help feeling a little smug. She felt shiny and new, with clean pink fingernails, clothes that didn't itch, and hair that bounced with new life. As she sat in the orphans' kitchen and ate the bowl of porridge she'd been promised—or rather, inhaled it—she thought that nothing could ruin her good mood.

Nothing except—

"Where did you get that necklace?"

Rose's hand shot up to the necklace, which had slipped free of her dress. "Don't touch it," she snapped, narrowing her eyes to slits as she turned to glare at Artemis. "It's *mine*."

Artemis, sitting across from her at the table, laughed and held up her hands. "Easy—I'm not going to take it. I just thought it was pretty. Where'd you even find something like that?"

"I was born with it."

Artemis shot her a quizzical look. Rose couldn't understand what was so difficult to grasp. She'd always had the necklace—might as well ask her where her fingernails came from.

"Is it real gold?"

"No."

"Oh. So—that's just glass?"

"Sure."

Artemis didn't press the subject, and Rose breathed a sigh of relief. *One minute,* she prayed. *Just one minute without everyone asking questions....*

It certainly wasn't the first question Artemis had asked. What did she remember about her parents, or her family, or her escape into the upper city? Nothing. At least nothing Rose cared to divulge to her. Could she read—write—knit—sew—spin—cook? No, but she could outrun all the local boys and squeeze into even the tiniest holes. Did she know her numbers? No, but she could catch rats with nothing more than a stick, a bit of string, and a few crumbs. Somehow, Artemis didn't seem very impressed with her skills, but Rose was unfazed. If the woman ever found herself starving in the streets, she would quickly realize which abilities she should value more.

The orphans' kitchen was not what she'd expected for such an old, grand sort of building. Sure, the rounded walls had plenty of windows with patterns of frosted glass, but shouldn't the kitchen of a shrine—whatever that was supposed to be—have a big kitchen like a noble's house? She'd heard that the castle kitchens had two giant ovens big enough for a grown man to stand up in, and ceilings so high servants had fallen and broken their backs while trying to dust the beams, and enough food preserved in the buttery to feed the whole city for a week. The cellar, she'd heard, had enough beer and wine to flood every street in Bermeia. Did this place even *have* a cellar?

Still—it was a nice big room, larger than some houses that she'd seen. There was enough room for a cold hearth with two huge cauldrons hanging over it, some narrow tables shoved against the walls that held bowls and bottles and all sorts of odds and ends, and one large table lined with benches that filled the middle of the room.

The shears were right in front of her on the table. Rose had to force her eyes away from it, unwilling to let Artemis see her interest. Her moment, she knew, would come—if she could be quick.

Artemis had spread herself out across the table, slowly stitching a sea of dark yellow fabric. Another dress, Rose thought, but she didn't care enough to ask. They both turned every once in a while to glance out the open door to Alysia, who was spreading out the wet clothes and emptying half of the tubs. Two of them were left behind, shoved into the corner of the courtyard; these, Artemis said, needed to soak overnight.

"What's your surname?" Artemis asked her.

Rose gave her a withering look. "My wha'?"

Artemis gave up with a sigh.

A set of steps on one end of the room wound upward; a door, blocked by a table and a pile of junk, sat at the other end. There were windows, too—in this room, sure, but a dozen more looking down onto the courtyard. Now that she wasn't so starving she could barely think, Rose was itching to see where all the doors and windows in this place might lead. It was difficult for her to articulate the idea, but she knew that knowledge was a sort of power—and knowledge over the terrain doubly so. The fights she couldn't win, she fled, and her intimate knowledge of every alley and balcony and unlocked door in the upper city had saved her hide more times than she could count.

But first, she would have to give these two the slip. And judging by the way Artemis's sharp eyes kept fixing on her, that was going to be tricky.

Alysia finally returned, wiping her hands on her apron. She smiled at Rose. "Was the porridge any good?"

It had been flavorless and as thick as liquid stone, but Rose, who had once scooped up rotting berries that someone had trodden on and eaten them right then and there, wasn't about to complain. "There more?" she asked hopefully.

"Not until tonight," said Alysia. "Be careful, will you? I feel like you're eating too much as is."

Rose scoffed. As if there could be any such thing.

"Great," said Artemis with a bright, fake enthusiasm. "She's fed. Now let's get her out of here before Kayo spots her."

"And then what? Hide her for the rest of her life? We can't avoid him forever."

Rose tried to interject, but Artemis wasn't listening.

"We told him to fix it, so he fixed it. You can't just swoop in and rescue him like you always do—"

"Always? I don't do it enough! Look at the state of him, he didn't know what he was doing, he barely knew where he was. Ask Rose, she'll tell you herself."

"I—" Rose tried to say, but after barely glancing at her, they went back to bickering.

"We already told him we can't take in anyone else when he asked us about what's-her-name—"

"This is different, that girl didn't *want* to come."

"Oh, and this one did? She said Kayo *kidnapped* her."

"He—"

"That girl had a family that would miss her, she had a job, a whole life—" Alysia gestured to Rose without looking around. "Just *look* at her. She actually *needs* us."

"Hey!" Rose said hotly. "Doesn't anyone—?"

"So you think we should just shrug this off as—as temporary insanity—and *adopt her,* and just—move on?"

"That's exactly what I think."

"*Doesn't anyone care what I wanna do?*" Rose exploded.

Alysia and Artemis stopped dead, blinking at her as if finally remembering she existed.

In the ensuing silence, she could have easily told them what it was, exactly, that she wanted. But as she opened her mouth, she realized that she didn't know.

It should have been simple: stay, or go? But she was torn. If half of them didn't want her here, she wouldn't inflict herself upon them— or perhaps she should, just out of spite. This place wasn't meant for people like her, but there was food, and she had nowhere else to go. She didn't want to be kicked out, but that didn't mean she wanted to stay.

She had to work out a strategy, which she couldn't do without more information. And get a weapon—but one thing at a time.

"I got questions," she told them.

Artemis raised her eyebrows. Alysia, however, seemed to expect this. "Okay."

"What's goin' on with what's-'is-name?" she asked them.

Alysia and Artemis exchanged yet another look that she didn't understand. "He's doing much better," Alysia finally answered, though her shoulders hunched a little as she busied herself with tidying up the kitchen. "He was in a bad way that first night, but it passed, thank the G—"

"Yeah, I don't care," Rose cut across her. This earned her an affronted look from both women that she chose to ignore. "I meant why w's he *like* that? He's the one who *brought* me here, he *made* me come along, I didn't *wanna,* but then he didn't even *want* me here!"

"He doesn't remember why," Alysia said, but in a very gentle voice that made Rose want to throttle her. "You said he hit his head. He must've gotten a little...confused."

"Confused," Rose repeated. She meant it scathingly, but Alysia merely nodded. "So he's all better now, then?"

Again, she endowed every word with contempt—and again, Alysia ignored it. "He seems to be. So if the two of you just keep away from each other for a little while—"

"I don't wanna hide."

Artemis raised her eyebrows. "You *want* to talk to him?"

"Talk, sure, yeah," said Rose savagely. "We can talk all he wants after I punch 'is teeth in."

Artemis gave Alysia a withering look that quite clearly said, *What did I tell you?* Alysia sighed, brushing her hair back.

"Rose, *please* don't do that."

"He tried t' *kill me!*"

"No, he didn't. He just—we just didn't know what to do with you. If you hadn't been so hostile from the start—"

"Don't you blame me for this! I didn't want any part of this!" Alysia tried to talk over her, but Rose wasn't having it. She had already exploded, and they could just sit there and watch it all burn. "For fuckin' *once* I did somethin' nice 'cause I *thought* that fuckin' idiot was th' fuckin' Beggar's King, 'cause 'e *said 'e was,* an' 'e dragged me through fuckin' *hell* an' then *locked me up,* an' now you people are actin' like it's all *my* fault when I didn't even ask to—!"

"Lis? Lis!"

Someone was outside, calling Alysia's name. A man's voice. Rose could hear footsteps running closer.

"Fuck," said Artemis.

There wasn't time to curse. Rose backed into the nearest table and reached behind her, grabbing for the shears, scrabbling with her other hand for something to throw. Just as her fingers found something, the door burst open and the boy tumbled in, out of breath.

"Are you okay? I heard—"

And then he spotted her.

For a moment, the two of them froze, sizing each other up. He could not hide his shock and confusion as his eyes looked her up and down, her clean skin and her dress and her boots. He didn't look how she remembered, either, but more like the dream she'd had when he'd appeared, where he'd been dressed in paler clothes and bandaged up his arms and around his head. He seemed a bit shaky still, and limped a little too. She noted with no small satisfaction that her fist had left a bruise around his eye—and she noticed, also, that he was unarmed.

Then the shock twisted into rage, and he stepped forward.

She grabbed a pincushion and hurled it right at his face. It did absolutely nothing, but it was enough to make him flinch. She dove in while he was distracted and brought the shears down with all her strength—Alysia and Artemis screamed, but he caught her wrist in midair, his fingers like an iron cuff, and she couldn't wrench free—

"Kayo, stop!" someone was shouting. "*Stop it!*"

Rose tried to kick him, but it did no good; he yanked on her arm, and her snarl turned into a shriek of pain as he twisted her arm and slammed her fist into the table, forcing her to release the shears. She clawed at his face with her free hand, stomping and kicking and trying to shove her knee into his gut.

His fist snapped back and slammed into her cheek.

Her spine smacked into the table as her vision exploded into darkness and stars and angry red flares of pain. Dimly, over the scuffle of her blind struggles, she heard shouting, felt something tugging on her—

"What the fuck are you doing? Have you lost your damn mind?"

"What are *you* doing?! Get *off* me!"

"Kayo, stop it, you don't—"

"She attacked Lis! She had a weapon!"

"No, it wasn't—"

"You'll kill her, she's half your size, *stop it!*"

Something forced his hand off of her arm. She straightened up, gasping for air, to find the giant bear of a man filling every spare bit of space in the kitchen as he wrestled with the boy. With a swift, neat movement, he pinned the boy's arms back. Alysia and Artemis had run around the tables to join the fray, but they didn't seem to be helping much. They were both trying to explain, talking over one another in their haste.

The boy wasn't listening.

"*Let go of me!*" he yelled.

"Yeah, let 'im go!" Rose snarled. "Let 'im face me like a man 'stead of lockin' me up like a *coward!*"

He turned his burning glare on her. "And what do you call going after my *sisters?*"

"Kayo, *no,*" Alysia said quickly. "It's not like that, she's not going to turn on us, she won't do anything to hurt us—right, Rose?"

Rose gave a wild laugh, pressing her hand to her throbbing cheek. "You better fuckin' believe it! *First* thing I'm doin' is goin' *right* to the soldiers an' tellin' them *'xactly* where to find you, you sonuva—"

With a roar of fury, he lunged at her again. The man only just managed to hold him back.

"Kayo, for fuck's *sake*—"

"Let me *go!* Get the fuck off me, Dominic, I swear to—"

Rose darted forward, more than happy to help him get free so she could hit him until he cried, but someone grabbed a handful of her dress and yanked her back. She snarled and struggled, but could only watch as Dominic dragged Kayo back out the door and into the courtyard with the fountain. Kayo struggled free, but Dominic kept a firm grip on his arm.

Alysia ran out to help, keeping one hand on the door. Artemis didn't move, and neither did the firm hand on the back of Rose's dress.

"Kayo, *enough,* just calm down for a—"

"You're taking *her* side? Are you fucking *kidding* me?! She had a *weapon!*"

"I'm not taking sides, I'm trying to stop you from—"

"How is this *my* fault? *She* attacked *me!*"

"It won't solve anything if we go straight to killing each other."

"She's just scared," Alysia interjected. "And she has a right to be."

"I ain't *scared!*" Rose protested, but nobody was listening.

"I can't *believe* you! She could have *killed* you, I was just trying to—"

"She wasn't doing anything, I swear—"

"She *attacked* me!"

"I mean, you *did* lock her up, she's not exactly—"

"*Will you stop it?!*" Kayo exploded, his voice rising to a shout.

"*This isn't my fault!* You said handle it, so I handled it, you can't shout at me for every fucking thing and then go behind my back and make it worse and then *blame me for that too!* I told her to leave, and you just let her make herself at home. You gave her a *weapon.* Can't you see that she's dangerous?"

"She's *not,* Kayo. It's just a—"

Kayo's fist swung out again, connecting with a thud that made Rose wince and Artemis scream. Dominic reeled back, Kayo grabbed him by the shirt and then it was an all-out brawl, both of them tangled up together, yelling and snarling.

Artemis ran outside to join Alysia, but they couldn't get close. They both shouted for the boys to stop, and Dominic struggled to lock his arm around Kayo's neck. Rose ran out too, but she had no intention of helping. She just wanted to get a better view.

Quick as lightning, Kayo ducked free of Dominic's arm. And then, somehow, Dominic was on his back, and Kayo was pinning him down and punching him again and again.

"Kayo, *stop!*" Alysia finally managed to grab Kayo's arm and haul him back. He struggled, but it was enough for Dominic to shove himself free and sit up, panting and pressing one hand to his face. Artemis helped him up as Kayo scrambled to his own feet, and if not for Alysia holding his arm, he might have leapt at Dominic again.

"Are you insane?" Dominic yelled at him. "Have you lost your damn mind?"

"I'm the only one who *hasn't!*" Kayo roared back. "You can protect *her,* but it's on *your* heads, next time I won't fucking bother!"

And he wrenched his arm free and stormed off, vanishing through the columns of the arcade. Rose heard a distant door slam shut.

The remaining orphans stood there a little longer, as still as statues. They didn't move until Rose hawked and spat a mouthful of bloody saliva onto the floor.

"What?" she said as they all turned to look at her, wiping her mouth with the back of her hand.

The others exchanged a look. Alysia opened her mouth, then closed it again and shook her head. Dominic dabbed at his lip, which was bleeding down his chin, and turned to Artemis.

"Arty, what the *fuck,*" he demanded.

"Don't look at *me*. Lis is the one who showed up with her."

"I couldn't just leave her in that room," Alysia protested, her hand stiffening around Rose's dress. "She wasn't well. She couldn't even stand—"

"Lis wants her to *live here*," Artemis told Dominic, who groaned.

"Lis, she *can't* stay. Kayo's not wrong about this one, if she's just gonna sell us out—"

"Hey!" Rose protested. "I ain't—"

But no one was listening to her.

"She doesn't mean it. She's just trying to get a rise out of him."

"Am not!"

"If the soldiers find out what Liam was up to...."

The three of them exchanged dark looks. "Who's Liam?" Rose asked, and their dark looks fixed on her. No one answered.

"Rose," Alysia said at last, "why don't you go upstairs with Artemis?"

"So you can talk about me behind my back?" Rose snapped back, and she knew from Alysia's wince that she was right. She twisted free of Alysia's grasp. "You think I don't know what's goin' on here?"

Dominic snorted, clearly amused. "No," he said, "I don't think you do."

Rose folded her arms, perching at the edge of the fountain. "Oh, really," she said, raising her eyebrows. "So the Beggar's King *weren't* here, then."

They froze. Stared at her.

"I may've been born at night, but it wasn't last night," Rose said, a trifle smugly. "That stupid boy w's dressed like the Beggar's King, he w's just shit at it—an' *Liam*—that's *gotta* be William Adeney, huh? I knew—"

Dominic crossed the courtyard so quickly that she barely had time to flinch before he'd grabbed her arm. He leaned in close, his nose almost touching hers. His face was bruising and smeared with blood, and his eyes were hard and cold.

"I thought I warned you," he said softly. "I don't know what you think you know, but I am not letting *anything* happen to my family. If you rat us out to the soldiers, I'll turn you into a pincushion before you can say a word. Do you understand me?"

"Let go o' me!"

"Do—you—*get—it?*"

"Dominic, *stop—*"

Rose kicked him repeatedly, but he barely seemed to feel it. Then abruptly he backed away. Artemis had him by the arm, hauling him back.

"Don't *threaten* her," she warned him. "Goddess, that's *enough* for one day, isn't it?"

Dominic turned his wrath on Alysia instead. "What the hell did you *tell* her?"

"*Nothing!* I didn't tell her *anything!*"

"Then *how did she know?*"

"I don't *know,* maybe Kayo—"

"I know because I ain't *stupid,*" Rose said with a scathing look at Dominic. But she could feel something swelling in her chest—an excitement and joy that she hadn't felt since seeing Kayo fly through the air. She glanced up at the windows, half-wondering if she'd see his face peeking out of one. "Liam Adeney's the Beggar's King. They said so at the execution, but I heard he w's the Fishgut Butcher too—who w's an orphan. Like all o' you. It ain't that hard to figure out. All o' you keep sayin' *brother,* but that obviously don't—anyway, so it's true? This was his hideout?"

"We don't know what you're—"

"Yes," Alysia said. "It was."

"*Lis!*" Artemis yelled, and Dominic hissed a curse.

"It's no use lying to her! She knows too much, we're already cooked. But you don't understand," she added, turning desperately back to Rose. "It's not what you think."

"So you knew him?" Rose's heart leapt into her throat. "He was your—your—?"

Alysia nodded. "Our brother." Dominic snorted, but Artemis slapped his arm to shut him up. "Well—sort of," Alysia corrected herself. "We knew him for a-a long time. Kayo and I. Kayo wears his old clothes sometimes when he goes out—like a disguise."

Rose frowned. "So *he's* your—your leader?"

Dominic burst out laughing.

"Hey!" Rose snapped at him.

"Sorry—sorry," he choked. "It's just—no, no—Kayo our *leader,* fuck me—"

Alysia shot a glare at Dominic, who sobered in an instant, clearing his throat. "People made up that name for Liam," she said firmly. "Kayo's just...playing the part. But only out there. No one's in charge here."

"'Specially not *Kayo,*" Dominic sniggered. "Liam mighta thought so, but *Kayo*—"

Artemis pinched his arm. He yelped and clapped a hand over the spot, giving her a mournful look.

"So they *did* fake the execution!" Rose said eagerly. "I thought they must've, it was just for show, nobody's been burned alive in ages—"

"No," said Dominic, and for once, his voice was small. The women on either side of him grimaced. "It wasn't fake. They...wanted to make an example of him."

"Oh." Rose couldn't speak. It was like watching him burn all over again. "Oh. So—he's just—that boy's just—"

"It helps, sometimes," said Dominic. "When we dress up like Liam. They're still—scared of him."

We. So Kayo wasn't even the only imposter. He and Dominic had just been dressing up like the Beggar's King while they picked pockets and stole candies, just like every other troublesome boy in the city. Just for fun.

"Oh," she said again. It was all she could think to say. She sat at the edge of the fountain and looked up at the windows again, but this time, she knew there would be nothing there. Not now, not ever again.

Still—he *was here.* He drank water from this fountain, walked across this courtyard, ate at the same table where she'd eaten. She couldn't picture him doing such mundane things, couldn't even imagine what his face had looked like when it wasn't all banged up— but at the thought of it, a happy thrill climbed up her arms. She had to know more, had to see it all.

"So...?" Alysia said quietly.

She turned back to them. They were all staring at her, standing together in a little cluster, waiting.

"So...what?" she said.

Dominic and Artemis simply looked suspicious, wary—but Alysia could not hide her terror. "Are you...going to rat us out?" she asked.

Rose could have held it over their heads forever, she thought, and enjoyed every second. The other ones certainly would have deserved it. But Alysia had been kind to her—kinder than anyone had been in a long time. And the look on her face was making her stomach squirm.

So instead, she simply said, "Don't think so."

"You don't *think* so?"

"Nuh-uh." Rose was enjoying herself enormously, watching their eyes pop and their mouths hang open. She sat up primly and crossed her ankles, hands folding in her lap, the picture of ladylike innocence. Or, at least, the best impression she could muster.

They were staring at her, waiting for an explanation. But she just shrugged.

"I liked the Beggar's King."

The three of them looked at her, then at each other, then at her again. Then Dominic burst out laughing.

"Dominic!" Artemis scolded him.

"Sorry," he choked, his shoulders still shaking. "Sorry, I just—she had me for a second, she really did." He was still chuckling, grinning like a fool.

"This *isn't funny!*"

"Are you kidding me? Didn't you see her punch Kayo? It's hilarious." He eyed Rose up and down again, but this time with an appreciative eye. "You stickin' around, then?"

"Uh—"

"Maybe," said Alysia, with a faint smile in Rose's direction.

Dominic grinned. "Good. It was gettin' boring 'round here."

"*Dominic—*"

"Aw, ease off, Arty. She *said* she wouldn't rat us out."

"She said *maybe,* so don't *push her.*"

"All right, all right. Goddess, you're so *mean* to me, I thought you *liked* me—"

"Yeah, well, I'm reevaluating that at the moment. Go scrub some dishes."

Dominic groaned, and kept groaning, more and more loudly, as Artemis shoved him back into the kitchen. But Rose saw Artemis lean in and kiss him, and saw him smiling as he disappeared. Alysia watched them go, then turned back to Rose. Her little smirk widened into a wide, bright smile—not pretty like Artemis's, but warm and sunny and real.

It wasn't until she tried to smile back that Rose realized she already was. For the first time in years—maybe ever—she was grinning ear to ear. Her jaw was already beginning to ache from the strain. But for some reason, she couldn't stop.

The sun was setting, a welcome relief for Rose. It was stiflingly hot in the sunshine out in her little corner of the courtyard, but she wasn't about to let the orphans drag her inside. Not with that boy on the loose and out for blood.

The shadows had nearly consumed the courtyard by the time Alysia dried her hands and put the last of the washing away. "Come on," she said to Rose. "Let me show you the place."

Rose hesitated, glancing toward the fountain. Dominic was sitting beside Artemis on its ledge, making little knotted missiles out of the discarded fabric he was meant to be collecting. Every once in a while, he'd flick one at her. One was still caught in her hair. She'd thrown a spool of thread at him in retaliation, but that had only encouraged him.

"You said there'd be dinner."

"It needs to be cooked," Alysia said patiently. "And we can't start until after dark. Someone might see the smoke."

"Oh."

"And we eat upstairs anyway. So we might as well head that way."

Rose needed no further convincing. She trailed along behind Alysia, following her back into the kitchen. Her eyes didn't quite adjust to the semi-darkness until they were halfway up the spiraling steps. If she *did* mean to stay here, she thought, she'd need to cover one eye like a sailor.

The stairs continued upward, but Alysia veered deeper into the building after one flight, leading Rose through an empty hall and down an empty corridor. At the end of the corridor was another empty hall, nearly identical to the first, only this one was a little more brightly lit. The ceiling was high, supported by beams that looked thicker than the length of her arm, and their footsteps echoed in the silence.

It was beautiful in its own way, this place—in an ancient way, in a broken way. The colored-glass windows seemed to glow as they collected the dying light from the west, too weak to cast the colored sunbeams she had seen earlier. Dust motes drifted lazily overhead. Above an archway leading to another, much shabbier staircase, a massive hole in the wall further up showed a yawning darkness. Yet neither the hole nor the rubble from it strewn across the floor seemed out of place, nor the dirt and the dust. It all simply *was*—a ruin frozen in time.

"If only we could fix this place up," Alysia sighed, as if she could read Rose's thoughts. "I would give anything to see it how it used to be. But I suppose there are advantages to living in ruins—"

"Ow!"

Rose had trodden on something sharp. She lifted her foot to find a large splinter jutting out of her heel. Alysia made a noise of alarm.

"Are you all right? We'll have to get you some shoes."

Luckily, the thick calluses on Rose's feet had shielded her from any real harm. But she did sense an opportunity in the horrified expression on Alysia's face.

"I need a knife t' get it out," she said in what she hoped was a casual voice. "You got one?"

"I think tweezers would work better." Alysia seemed to know exactly what she was trying to do. "They're upstairs. C'mon. It's not far now."

Rose glanced at the splintery-looking stairs that spiraled up out of sight. "I *ain't* goin' up those stairs."

"Oh, they're broken," said Alysia.

"They're *what?*"

"Yes, don't go anywhere near them. But don't worry about it. We'll climb up *that*."

And she pointed. Rose turned to follow her gaze, then looked higher, and higher....

"Hope you're not scared of heights."

A knotted rope, so frayed and dirty that she hadn't even noticed it against the graying walls, dangled at knee height by the stairs. In the time it took to follow its path upward, Rose prayed at least a dozen times that the rope didn't lead where she thought it would—but her luck didn't hold out. The rope trailed up the wall, into the ragged hole near the ceiling, and into the darkness out of sight.

She looked back at Alysia, whose eyebrows were raised.

"After you," she said.

Alysia shrugged and started climbing the rope. She made it seem so easy, bracing her shoes against the wall as she went, looking for all the world as if she were taking a leisurely stroll up the wall. Soon she was so far up that the fall back down would snap her spine.

There was nothing else for it. Grimacing, Rose grabbed the rope and swung herself on. At least if she broke her neck, Alysia would too.

It wasn't as if she hated climbing. Anyone who lived in the upper city quickly grew comfortable with heights. But she never did it for *fun.* Still—if these orphans could do it every day, she could certainly do it just this once.

Don't look down, she reminded herself. *Don't look down.*

The rope swayed a little in a way that she had not caused. She stiffened and clung to one of the knots. But it was just Alysia, who had reached the top.

She was getting dizzy. Was that normal? She had to stop—but there was nowhere to stop. She kept going until she couldn't find the strength to climb any higher, then clung to the rope, head spinning, shoulder braced against the wall. She couldn't keep climbing, but what other choice was there? The only other option was to let go.

"Rose? Are you all right?"

Rose didn't have the energy to sigh, nor to say all the irritated comments that flew to her tongue. In the end, she merely rolled her eyes—and started climbing again.

"Almost there," Alysia encouraged her. "Um, don't—don't let go, all right? If you're stuck—"

Shut up, Rose would have groaned if she could breathe. *Shut up, shut up, shut—*

And then she reached up and found not rope, but solid wood. She scrambled onto the blessed wooden ledge and gripped its splintered edge, gasping for breath. It was only then that she realized that Alysia had held out a hand to help her up; Rose couldn't bring her face into focus, but she seemed concerned.

"Are you all right? You scared me, I didn't realize—"

"I'm fine," Rose rasped.

"I'm so sorry, I know you've had a rough few days...."

"Don't make fun o' me," Rose snapped at her, and hauled herself to her feet. Alysia had the good sense not to reply.

When Rose finally looked up, she saw that they stood not on a ledge, but on a landing. The hole in the wall seemed to have pierced through the stone and into the narrow stairwell. Rickety-looking steps led down into the darkness like broken teeth in the mouth of some huge beast, and Rose needed no encouragement to stay away from them.

Across from them, the stairs ended in a door. With her hand on the latch, Alysia tossed her braid over one shoulder and looked back at Rose. "Are you coming?"

This was, thought Rose, the strangest day of her life by far. She was almost afraid to find out what lay on the other side of that door. But the fall from the landing was very steep, and she was eager to be far away from the edge.

The door swung open, and Rose walked in.

A roar of sound assailed her like a physical beast: shrieks and shouts and cries, all of it echoing in a horrible grating clamor. She winced from that as much as the sudden brightness, her hands half-rising to cover her eyes or her ears, she didn't know which.

She stood at the far end of an enormous hall crafted from graceful arches of stone, a half-cylinder vault that stretched out to an impossible length ahead of her. The walls were broken at intervals by elegant windows of colored glass that extended from the floor into graceful teardrop points high overhead. At the far end, light poured in from a vast window facing south, a huge circle like a stylized sun filled with shards of thick glass of every color arranged in intricate patterns, glowing white-gold. Dusty sunlight washed across the rough boards of the floor, and darting between them—

"There's *more o' you?*" she hissed to Alysia, who just rolled her eyes.

The room was full of children—laughing, shrieking, wailing children. They jumped and ran and tumbled and climbed and fell all over the place, dozens of them, none older than twelve and few older than six or seven. The tallest boy was still a head shorter than her. Two of them ran past her, yelling incomprehensibly, and she yelped and leapt back.

"Relax," Alysia said, smirking. "They don't bite."

"What are they *doing?*"

"They're just playing."

"Playing *what?*"

"Who knows. Just ignore them. Come on, I'll find those tweezers."

She set off across the room. Rose inched along the wall in her direction, staring.

In every single part of this so-called shrine, she realized, there had been something *off* about the place. She didn't quite have the vocabulary to describe it, but she knew the way it made her feel: like missing a step while walking downstairs, like seeing a building with slanting walls or a drawing of a person with incorrect proportions. This place seemed like two buildings mashed together. No, not just buildings. Two sections of the city; two cultures; two eras in time; two entirely different worlds. The garden growing indoors. The graceful rooms full of nothing but rubble.

And now this room.

The walls were as thick as her arm at least, but the ceiling seemed weightless, delicate arches and swirls growing upward like a tree. The windows were works of art, every single one of them—and the big one was breathtaking.

The rest of the place—including the children—looked like a nest of rats burrowed into a wall. Stacks of crates, baskets, and sacks lay in clusters all over the place, piled in every corner and around every vertical beam. Rough planks nailed in clumsy rows stretched across the space, full of many cracks and gaps that the orphans had attempted to bridge with braided rush mats. Judging by the thick layer of dirt on the ground, the rush mats, also filthy, weren't quite doing their jobs. But the children didn't seem to notice. They were, every one of them—and there was roughly a score of them by her count—as sweaty, grimy, and ragged-looking as the beggar children of the lower city. Many of them ran about in a state of undress. One little boy wore an oversized shirt that reached down to his knees and nothing else. Several others, of indeterminate gender, were bare-chested. The little girls wore either a chemise or a dress, but never both. None of them seemed to have shoes.

And stranger still, belonging to another world entirely, were what the kids had created to make the place their own. The crates had been painted in bright colors with flowers and animals. Little hands held little toys made of wood and metal and fabric, some of them sweet, some of them battered and unrecognizable monstrosities. Wire and thread and fishing line crisscrossed above her head, and dangling from them were odd little ornaments: a little painted bird in flight, a cascade of colored glass like a waterfall, a trio of hollow metal tubes, a collection of tiny metal bits attached to a ring. She reached up to touch the ring, and it spun on its axis, throwing strange, faint shadows onto the wall and floor. The metal tubes tapped together, tinkling a little tune.

The Divinæ had lived here, Alysia had said. How much of this had been theirs? How much belonged to the orphans?

And how were there so *many* of them?

Alysia paused at a stack of crates, reaching for a basket stacked on top. Rose joined her, favoring her injured foot, careful to give a wide berth to the children. She had never seen so many in one place.

"These are all *your kids?*" she hissed to Alysia.

"Oh, Goddess no."

"Then whose? That other girl's?"

"Artemis? They—are you joking?" Alysia looked around and frowned at her before returning to her search. "It would take one woman a lifetime to make this many kids. At *least.*"

"But then, how—?"

"We're just taking care of them," Alysia said briskly. "You don't have to worry about it." She finally extracted a pair of tweezers from the basket. "Come sit down, I'll fix your foot."

"I'll do it," Rose said, and snatched the tweezers out of her hand.

She sank down onto the nearest crate, lifted her foot, and set about finding the splinter.

"You lied to me," she accused Alysia, who insisted on sitting nearby and looming over her.

"I did?"

"*You* said you orphans weren't recruitin'."

"Oh, for—we didn't *recruit* them. It's not like we *kidnapped* them—"

"Naw, you'd never do *that*."

"They *want* to be here," Alysia insisted, ignoring her sarcasm. "For the same reason you do. For a safe roof over their heads and steady meals."

"I never said I wanted t' be here," Rose pointed out. She'd found the splinter, and with one sharp movement, she grabbed it and plucked it free. She let it fall, but Alysia quickly bent to pick it up. Rose massaged her foot carefully, searching for the stabbing pain that meant she had left something behind. "But I don't wanna be an orphan neither."

Alysia sighed. "I never said—"

"Hi!"

Rose whirled around. One of the little terrors had run right up to her, looking directly at Rose as her face split into an enormous grin— minus a couple of teeth.

"You're Rose, right?" she said brightly. "I'm Sara!"

Rose glared at the little girl, wondering if this snake had venom in its fangs. "How'd you know my name?" she demanded. An hour ago, she hadn't even *had* one.

"Uh—don't ask her that," Alysia said hastily. "Sara, *not now*."

"But I'm just being nice," the girl complained, turning her huge, pleading eyes to Alysia instead. "I don't want her to be scared of us!"

"I'm not scared," Rose snapped. Which wasn't *strictly* true. The little girl looked much like the rest of them, with a face that needed scrubbing, hair that needed brushing, and a dress that didn't fit properly. She wore a little embroidered animal on the front of her dress—a white-and-brown rabbit—as proudly as a medal. But something about her unnerved Rose.

"You're not?" The girl tilted her head, giving her a puzzled look.

Then she shook her head. "Yes you are. 'Cause you're not used to other people, right? That's why Kayo wanted you to come here. He felt sorry for you."

"*Sara—*"

"He *what?*" Rose snarled.

"He was sad for you. 'Cause him and everyone else, you know, they always had each other. And you were *supposed* to be with them too, but instead you were all alone. He thought—"

"Sara, *enough!*" Alysia said sharply. "Go play."

"Hmph," said Sara, pouting. But then she turned and fled.

Rose could barely speak. "How—why—how did she—?"

"She's guessing, she doesn't know what she's talking about," Alysia said hastily. "I'm so sorry about her, I swear she doesn't mean anything by it—"

"She wasn't guessing! She *knew my name!*"

"She's just nosy. Please don't let her upset you, she's not—"

"He *said* that about me?" She wasn't upset. She was *furious.* "He said he felt *sorry* for me? That son of a whore, I'll show him *sorry,* I'll *kill 'im.*"

"*Rose,*" Alysia cut across her, raising her hands when Rose glared at her. "Nobody said any of that. She made it up. All right? Just *ignore her.* Can you put this over there for me?"

She shoved a basket in Rose's arms. Rose grabbed it from her, seething, and shoved it onto a different crate. There was hardly room. As poor as these people seemed to be, from their clothes alone, every crate and basket was overflowing with clutter.

She poked through, curious. The basket held fabric scraps, most small enough to fit into her palm. Another held nails and screws and odd little tools and a small hammer. Another was full of broken glass. The crate was stuffed with fabric, arm-length rolls and folded squares and hand-sized scraps, and there was another just like it. She poked around, investigating. Bottles and jars of strange substances, tiny shirts and dresses, thread, yarn, buttons, little pieces of cork. One basket was full of other, smaller baskets. There was a pile of old buckets and pails in the corner, most in need of mending, and a dozen sacks stood propped against another stack of crates. Some of it she couldn't even recognize. Most of it looked like trash. It seemed like these orphans never threw anything away.

She palmed a pair of shears as she passed and was about to stuff them down the front of her dress before she realized that she didn't have anywhere to hide them. Without a half-dozen layers of fabric to protect her skin, they'd slice her to ribbons. Still, they had so much stuff, piles and piles, surely they didn't need it all. Maybe they wouldn't even notice. She would have to come back before she slipped away. She'd need a weapon, surely—those other orphans had taken hers—and a blanket, and some extra clothes, and....

"Here," Alysia said behind her, and Rose jumped, shoving the shears hastily back into their basket. Alysia held up a pair of boots in one hand, two wool socks in the other. "Try these on."

Rose just stared at her. Stared at the boots. After a moment, Alysia brandished them again, shaking them a little. Rose held out her arms, and Alysia dumped the boots into them, placing the socks in Rose's open hand.

"Go on," she said. "I don't have all day."

"For me?" Rose finally managed to stammer.

"If they'll fit you. They seem about your size. Give them a try."

And she turned away, looking for something else.

Rose stared at the boots in her hand, turning one of them over, inspecting it closely. Then she hiked up her skirt and brushed the dirt off her feet. She couldn't find the heel on the socks, so she just shoved her feet into them. But she took a bit more care with the boots, sliding her feet in carefully before lacing them tight along her shins.

She stood up gingerly, then looked down. Her skirts were a bit short, stopping just around her ankle, so the boots poked through. They were old and brown and faded, the paint chipped off the wooden heel, the flimsy leather held up only by the tight knots she tied—and they were too big for her. Even the knots couldn't fix that.

She loved them.

"Do they fit?" Alysia asked her. "Are they too big?"

"No," Rose lied. She would have said anything it took to keep them. "They're perfect."

"Oh, good." Alysia smiled. "I'm glad someone will get some use out of them."

"You're—" Rose swallowed. Her mouth was suddenly dry. "I can
—keep them?"

"Sure. For as long as you're here. I need your help. Are you
coming?"

She handed Rose a basket, and Rose took it, trotting behind her
in silence. With every step, she willed herself not to slip or fall or stumble, no matter how much her foot slid inside her shoe. She'd never had
shoes before. She hadn't realized how much work it took just keeping
them on.

Alysia was chattering away as she led Rose back through the maze
of children. Rose dodged sticky fingers and screaming mouths as best
as she could, following Alysia out, barely listening.

For as long as you're here.

They could say what they wanted. She was never, ever going to
take them off.

The children, Rose decided, weren't street children. Street children, as
seen often in the lower city, were children who had nowhere to go but
the streets or the docks. Some of them didn't have homes; some did,
but they were so horrible, or even dangerous, that the children spent
as little time in them as possible. Most of these children roamed the
streets even at night, sleeping in any sheltered or secluded spot they
could find. During the day, they didn't beg. That was for the blind or
deaf or sick, for people missing arms or legs. For everyone else, it was
far more lucrative to pick pockets, steal, or scavenge what they could.

Street children started out frightened and only a little dirty, but
within a few days, they turned filthy and feral and cruel—if they
survived that long. But these children were noisy and lively, smiling
and laughing and screaming as if they had not a care in the world.
And while they weren't exactly *clean*—she could smell their pungent
little bodies whenever they got too close—they'd clearly washed
recently. They looked more like the other children in the lower city,
the ones who played and explored and ran about just for fun. The
ones who went home at night and stayed there. The ones who had
dinners to eat and families who'd miss them.

They seemed so alien to her. Children like that always had. She'd been a street child all her life, and she'd never gotten along with *this* sort. Sometimes, rarely, they'd invite her to play a game, but she'd never known the rules—and a parent had always come around to shoo her away. But usually, they ignored her. Or made fun of her. Or threw things at her. She wasn't sure which was worse. At least when they threw things, she got to keep whatever they hurled her way.

And to see so many up here, in this bizarre place...her mind couldn't quite wrap around it.

"Why aren't they outside?" she asked Alysia, who was mending a small shirt with a needle and thread. It took her a long time, because she kept looking up to check on the children and losing her place.

"Hmm?" Alysia glanced up yet again, as if she didn't know who Rose was talking about. "Oh—you mean to play? They're too noisy, unfortunately. When they play in the courtyard, people in the city might hear them and get suspicious. We'll move them downstairs when it gets too hot."

"People in the—wait. Where are we?"

"The upper city. But sort of on the edge." Alysia shrugged. "I guess the Divinæ wanted privacy. Works fine for us."

Rose frowned up at the vaulted ceiling, at the central beam that she could have strolled across like an empty street. "How'd you *find* this place?"

"Same way you did." Alysia knotted the thread and snapped it loose with her teeth. "Through the sewers. We followed the clean water and climbed up."

Rose glanced at Alysia, watching her sift through the other clothes and silently wondered if she was playing some sort of joke. But Alysia didn't even glance at her.

"But if *you* could find it, how come no one else could?"

"Like the soldiers? I don't know. Maybe because we've been careful. Or maybe it's been abandoned so long, nobody even thinks about it anymore."

Rose frowned. "But how—I mean, this many kids in the sewers—"

"Oh, that was years ago. There weren't so many of us then. Just the ones who made it out of the fire."

"Like the Beggar's King."

"Who, Liam? Yeah, like him."

"Did he find this place?"

"He and Kayo did, I think. But all us older ones helped fix it up. Down below it's all boarded up, you know, but people had gotten in before—to steal things, I guess. So we had to look through the whole place, find the safest rooms, and get everything useful that we could find where we needed it. And clean. Good Goddess, it took ages to clean...."

"The Divinæ left stuff behind?"

"Mm-hmm. They must've left in a hurry when the king banished them. There was food in the cellars, clothes in the chests. Some of the beds even looked slept in."

Rose tried to picture it, but she couldn't. The Divinæ were before her time. And from the rumors, they could do everything from blessing a child to dragging a man out of the jaws of death. And read minds, tell the future—but that was probably just in the stories.

Alysia didn't offer any additional details, nor elaborate on any of the holes in her tale. Rose suspected that Alysia might be upset with her for attacking Kayo. Well, good. She wasn't about to waste time apologizing. She wanted these people to be a little afraid of her. It was the only thing keeping them from locking her back in her cage.

But the sun was setting. The big window faced west, she thought; the yellow glow was slowly reddening. And she was growing restless. Being indoors, that was the problem—she had never spent this long cooped up in one place. She didn't even like sleeping on the same doorstep twice in a row. And with the sun setting, she had only a few minutes of daylight left to find a safe place.

Whatever was going on here, with all these children, this room wasn't it. Just being in it made her head throb and her muscles tense until she wanted to climb up the walls just to escape. The still air was making her skin itch, though that might have been due to the protective layer of dirt that had been scrubbed off.

She drifted around the room, looking around, trying out her new boots. She was careful to avoid the kids; they seemed just as eager to avoid her. She tried to look out of the colored-glass windows, but could make out nothing useful. Nor could she steal anything from the piles—not without somewhere to stuff it. With so many beady little eyes watching her, she didn't think she could get away with it anyways.

Finally, she ended up back at the door. She looked around, but the kids were paying no attention, and Alysia was focused on her sewing. No one seemed to care when she slipped out onto the landing. Once out there, she immediately realized why: there was nowhere to go.

Except—

The way up didn't dead-end at the landing and the door. Metal rungs jutted from in between the stones, forming a ladder—and at the top of it, ringed in orange light, was a trapdoor.

This was it—the secret to this place. In all the stories, everything good was kept at the top of a tower. Princesses, treasure, dragons, tomes full of forbidden knowledge. The only people who bothered climbing that high were determined enough—or desperate enough— to find something *really* good.

And she was feeling quite desperate indeed.

Rose climbed the ladder without waiting around for some orphan to find her and stop her. When her head brushed the trapdoor, she climbed a little higher, gaining some leverage, then pressed her head and her arm against the wood and pushed. It shifted, slowly, and sunlight dazzled her as she squeezed under the trapdoor and emerged onto solid ground. She stood up, looking around.

She found herself at the very top of the tower, where a flat stone space was open to the air, but for a waist-high battlement and columns like slender stone ribs meeting to form a halo overhead. She clutched at the battlement in alarm as she looked around. It felt as if the fickle wind could give one strong gust and send her flying over the edge.

But the view was worth it.

In the upper city, the sky was always out of reach. Looking upward through the never-ending levels of the city, she had never been able to see more than a sprinkle of stars across the tiny ink-blue patches of sky. If not for her time in the lower city, she might not have remembered the stars or the moon at all. But in the lower city, they could only be glimpsed through clouds of greasy smoke from all the chimneys and torches and trash fires, and only on streets where the floors of the houses didn't stack outward, each level larger than the last, until the buildings cast the entire street in shade like an a very leaky roof.

But now the entire sky stretched above her and around her and below her. This was the highest point in the shrine, and there were few buildings in the upper city that even came close. On her level she saw the tops of a mansion or two, the gold-plated dome of some grand building, a watchtower, and a half-dozen aqueducts crisscrossing through the maze and down into the depths. Beyond them, she could see the cliffs, and the wastes, and the endless, endless sky.

And the sea.

Alysia had said the shrine was close to the edge of the upper city, but she'd been lying. It *was* at the edge. To the east, the shrine's roof sloped in every direction, then dropped off suddenly—and then the water began. She'd never seen such a view of the sea, like a huge, endless sheet of greenish glass. It almost made her hate it a bit less.

The sun was setting. The few clouds she could find were stained pink and orange with undersides of purple; the sky beyond them was a storm of color. She could even see the sun as it set in the distant west. Below her it was already dark, candles lit and windows shut as the sun sank behind the city walls and the other buildings. But this high, she had the sun all to herself. She leaned over the balustrade, staring at it hungrily, wishing she could devour it whole and make it a part of herself forever.

As the sky grew darker, more and more lights flared to life, spreading across the upper city and what little she could see of the lower city. Looking down into the upper city made her dizzy; it just went down and down and down forever, until the lights in the windows looked like little golden pinpricks. But the Gardens to the north glowed like a cluster of stars. The noble's mansions scattered across the crest of the hill, facing away from the lower city and looking out over the trees and the grasslands, every window glowing with the warm amber light of expensive lanterns. And at their end, beyond the plaza where the Beggar's King had died, across a bridge set black against the empty land it crossed—

The castle.

It glowed like a fallen star in the deepening night. Its pale stone walls seemed to glow from within, every window sparkling with lantern light until the whole place shone like a beacon. She had caught glimpses of it before, and had seen porcelain facsimiles in china shops that glowed in this way when illuminated from within by a candle. But nothing could compare to the lovely sight that she saw now. She leaned against the battlement, her chin resting on her elbows, and drank in the sight of it, breathing in the familiar smells of salt and fish and wood smoke drifting in with the cool, fresh breeze.

When the sun finally set, she tore her eyes from the castle and found a sky full of stars. Countless millions of them, each one bright white against the velvety black night. So tiny, so distant, but so clear she could have counted them—if she could even count that high. She didn't even try. She just perched at the edge of the balustrade, looked up, and drank it all in with a heart thirsty for something beautiful. The castle, the sky, the glowing lights, the familiar smells of salt and fish and wood smoke drifting in with the breeze from the ocean....

"Lis!"

Rose jumped so badly that she nearly tumbled over the railing. She looked around, but she was alone on the top of the tower.

"Lis! Are you up there?"

This time, she recognized the voice as Kayo's. She slid off the balustrade and set her feet firmly on the floor, tense and ready for a fight. Even his own family had thought he was unhinged. The last thing she wanted was to run into him again, unarmed.

"She's here," someone else called—the man, Dominic.

Footsteps. Then:

"Lis—where's that girl?"

She leaned over the battlements as far as she dared, straining to catch every word. It was a long, long way down. She dug her fingertips into the stone and focused on her boots, planted firmly on the ground.

"What girl?"

"You know what girl. Where is she? I thought she was with you!"

"Not for a while, no."

"Lis!" Artemis's voice this time. "You can't just let her run around!"

"I'm sure she's fine."

The voices seemed to be floating upward from somewhere below.

She crept to the trapdoor, which was open just a crack. They must have been standing right below it.

"Well, I locked all the doors," Dominic said. "If she breaks out, we'll know."

"I don't want her breaking out at *all!* It's too late then! Not to mention the kids—"

"Kayo, relax," said Alysia. "She's not going to go anywhere near the kids."

"Damn it, we can't *risk* that!"

"Well, what's your plan, then, Kayo?" Artemis said, exasperated. "If you want her to stay here, we'll have to trust her eventually."

"I *don't*. I mean—not for long, just—until she promises she won't—"

"It's called *lying*, mate," Dominic pointed out.

"More like *extortion*," Artemis added dryly. "She *wants* us to think she'll rat us out. That way we'll give her whatever she wants. And if we say no to her, off she goes."

"Good," Kayo said savagely. "Let her show her true colors. Then we can take her out and be done with it."

"We're going to have to do that anyway," Dominic said. His voice was quiet. She had to lean in to hear him. "You realize that, right?"

"I *said* I'd handle it—"

"The only way she's not a risk for us is if she's dead. I'm just saying it like it is."

There was a long, horrible silence.

"Where was she last?" Kayo finally said.

"Kayo, just leave her—"

"Lis, this is important. She was with you last, right?"

"I'd assume so, but that was hours ago. Did you check the kitchen?"

"Yeah."

"Then go check everywhere else."

"Fine," Kayo snapped. "I'll go ask Sara."

"Kayo, don't. You can't keep encouraging her—"

But the footsteps retreated again. Kayo had gone.

Rose stayed where she was, listening closely. Alysia had to have known where she was. Why didn't she say anything to the others? Was this a trick, somehow?

After a moment's silence, one of the orphans sighed.

"What a nightmare," Dominic grumbled. "Kayo sure can pick 'em...."

"Oh, come on. She's not so bad," Alysia protested. "It was a rough start, she's just scared—"

"Scared. Yeah, right. She's having the time of her life, holding this over our heads. You saw how much she hates orphans. She's got to be *dying* to see this place burned to the ground."

"She isn't stupid enough to mess with the soldiers."

"Why not? She looks just like anyone else now. Ain't got a mark. They won't bother her, not with the *Beggar's King* on the line...."

"I thought you two liked her!"

"Doesn't matter if I like her or not. If she's dangerous, then that's it. There's too much on the line."

"I'm sure she'll be reasonable. We could talk to her—"

"Are you joking? She hissed at me like a cat. Nearly wet myself. She's like a wild animal."

"Well, what else can we do? We can't just *kill* her."

"I think that's exactly what we'll have to do."

"*Dominic!*" both women protested at once.

"I mean, I don't *want* to. But Kayo sure as hell won't. And if it's her or us—"

"She hasn't *done* anything!"

"Hey, I'm not sayin' I won't give her a chance. All I'm sayin' is, if she walks out that door, I'm shooting."

"*Dominic....*"

"I'm not giving her a chance to rat us out. What do you wanna do, try to run with twenty kids? Barricade the doors? They'll turn us into mincemeat."

"We've brought all these kids in here, what difference does one more make?"

"She's not a *kid*," Artemis pointed out. "She's just about grown. And Dominic's right—she's dangerous."

"She's only *threatening* us because we threatened her first. If we're just *nice* to her—"

"We'll be nice," Dominic promised. "Just—Kayo's right. We shouldn't leave her alone with the kids. Or anyone else."

"Think we should help look for her?"

"She'll turn up for dinner, I bet. C'mon, Arty. I'll help you bring it up."

And they left.

Rose's hands were numb from gripping the ring of the trapdoor. She let go and stepped back, wrapping her arms around her ribs as she stared down at the rotting wood. Then, slowly, she looked up and around, searching the vast, empty sky.

The moon rose above the buildings of the upper city, casting a shimmering silver ribbon over the waves in the harbor. The faint smell of smoke and cooking food drifted up from somewhere below. Dinnertime—but Rose didn't move. She stood where she was, looking out over the buildings and the castle and the ocean and the greenery beyond the city walls, and wondered how, with all this space, she'd still managed to get herself trapped.

And the worst part was, it shouldn't have hurt. She shouldn't have let these people trick her into thinking she might belong here—or anywhere. She shouldn't have trusted them. She shouldn't have believed that a bunch of orphans could be anything other than the backstabbing, cutthroat sneaks that everyone said they were.

But it hurt all the same.

She couldn't even hate them for it. They were just doing what she should have known they'd do. No—it was herself she hated the most.

You idiot. When will you learn? Stupid, stupid, stupid—

"What are you doing?"

She started so badly that she nearly fell off the wall. She whirled around, heart in her throat, and reached for a weapon that wasn't there.

Kayo stood by the trapdoor. Somehow, he'd climbed up the ladder and through the trapdoor without a sound. His glare was as hard as stone as he gave the trapdoor a kick, slamming it shut. It was a pointed gesture. A warning. She could not escape without fighting past him, and no one would hear her if she screamed.

She couldn't breathe. She kept searching her skirts behind her back, scrabbling for a knife she knew wasn't there. But she straightened her spine all the same, eyes narrowing.

"What're *you* doin'?" she spat back. "Was nice an' quiet until *you* showed up. An' smelled better," she added with a sneer.

He fixed her with a look that made her sick to her stomach with fear. Grown men made her nervous, but teenage boys were something else altogether. They *terrified* her. She tried never to linger around them, never to catch their attention. They were as loud and lustful and violent as any grown man, but with twice the temper and half the self-control.

"I'm protecting my family," he said. "Whatever it takes."

He had a knife in his belt. He was armed. Somehow, she had to get it from him—or get *him* before he could use it.

"You're an orphan," she scoffed. "You don't *have* a family."

She shifted her weight to one foot, preparing to sidestep if he lunged. He was much taller than she was—she could use that. If she pushed him hard enough, he might fall over the edge of the battlement. It was a long way down. He couldn't hurt her after that. And then, if she ran fast enough—

"Nor do you," he retorted. "But at least I have people that would notice if I fell off this tower and splattered all over the street."

A wave of ice pulsed through her blood, and her stomach sank. She steeled herself, fighting it as hard as she could. She refused to be afraid. Men like him couldn't hurt her—not anymore.

"If ya came up here t' kill me, then kill me," she challenged him. "Or are you scared?"

"*Scared?*" His voice distorted with rage, mirroring his twisting face. "You think I'm too *scared* to hurt you? You think it's *brave* to kill people if you don't have to, that *fear* is the only thing stopping anyone? No one's a *coward* for sparing someone's life, for—for having some *semblance* of a moral code—"

She snorted. "Sounds like what a coward would say."

"You just wait," he snapped. "If you're ever in a position to kill someone, you won't find it so easy. You have no idea—"

"I was," she cut across him. "An' I did. An' I ain't lost a bit o' sleep over it."

Kayo recoiled, revulsion twisting his face. "And you call *us* criminals," he snarled. "You're a *monster.*"

The words hurt, but she didn't let him see how much. She just raised her chin a little higher. "Least I killed 'em in a fair fight," she shot back at him. "I didn't lock 'em up an' leave 'em to starve."

Kayo paled at this, the dark circles beneath his widening eyes suddenly prominent. His nostrils flared as if he were struggling to breathe. Rose could not help but feel a stab of vengeful satisfaction at the look on his face.

"Who'd you kill?" he demanded.

"None o' your business," she snapped.

"That's where you're wrong." She saw his hand rest subtly on the hilt of his knife. "Why are you still here?"

"Oh, you want me to leave?" she said with mock surprise. "Oh *no.* I'll jus' miss it *so* much here. Let me jus' say goodbye to the ten thousand kids."

"You're not going anywhere," he cut across her with a glare that could have cut stone. "The second we let you go, you'll run to the soldiers. You'll tell them that you found the hideaway of the Beggar's King, crawling with rebels and outlaws and orphans and kidnapped children, packed with weapons and enough provisions for a siege. Won't you, *Rose?*"

Her lip curled. "Is any o' that wrong?"

Kayo's arm swung in the air, and Rose flinched—but his fist came nowhere near her. It slammed into one of the columns instead, so hard that she winced at the sound of the impact.

"*All* of it is!" His voice rose to a shout that echoed across the rooftops. He shook his hand violently at his side; Rose saw beads of blood welling up near his wrist. "You don't know what you're *doing!* This is our *home,* don't you understand that? This is my *family!* And the soldiers will kill them all! Every single one of them!"

Rose snorted. "No they won't."

"They're *soldiers!* Don't you know *anything?* There's no orphanage anymore, there's nowhere to put them, and people like *you* think orphans are all criminals and—and monsters! They can do anything they want to us, no one's going to stop them! They'll slaughter all of us and call it *justice!*"

"*You're* the one who kidnapped them, maybe you shoulda *thought* o' that."

"We didn't *kidnap* them, we *saved* them! You don't understand. You don't know what their lives were like—Sara met you, remember her? Her parents *beat* her, she had to jump out a *window* to escape, just because she's a little *different*—and Andrew and Carolyn, she can't even *talk* anymore, her father's the one that *did* that to her, they'd be *killed* if they went back to him—you have *no idea* what they've been through, what we're *protecting* them from. They're *happy* here, they have a family and a home. They don't deserve to have all that taken away!"

"So turn yourself in if you're that worried," she sneered. "I don't give a fuck about them, *they're* not the ones who locked me up."

"I *can't*." He ran a hand distractedly through his hair—he almost looked as if he were considering it. "They need me. They'd die without me. They need *all* of us."

"Oh, so you're doing it for them, then? Runnin' around pretendin' to be the Beggar's King? What good's that doin' *anyone?*"

"Everything I do, I do for them! You wouldn't understand—"

"You're just a dumb kid playing dress-up!" She was shouting too, but she couldn't bring herself to stop—or care. "You're *ruinin'* him. You're messin' up *everything* he did. It's not some stupid *game!*"

"You think I'm playing games?" he said furiously. "Go on and tell the soldiers then. You think they'll just let you go? You think you're so much better than us? They won't see a difference."

"I'm *not* an orphan!"

"Then your parents can show up to stop them killing you for fun," he spat. "Do you think they actually *care* about you? Do you think *anyone* in that castle gives a damn about you?" He flung out an arm toward the glowing castle on the cliffs. "You'll be lucky if you make it to a cell with the rest of us—and Goddess help you if you do," he added with a snarl. "I swear, I will hunt you down and make you wish you were dead."

I'm not afraid, she told herself—but it didn't stop another pulse of cold through her limbs. She could see in his eyes that he meant every word.

"I didn't ask for this!" she yelled at him. "I ain't done *anythin'* to you people, not even after you dragged me here an' locked me up! I wish I never saved your life, I wish I never bothered, I shoulda just let 'em take you! I wish I had! I wish I'd never come here!"

"Well, nobody wants you here either, *princess*," he shot back, lip curling. "So why are you still around?"

"Let me fuckin' leave then, you sonuva *whore*, I don't want *anythin'* to do with you dirty orphans an' your million kids an' your stupid fake *family*."

"Like you'd know what a real one looks like! If the soldiers get you, no one'll even notice you're gone—except your regulars down by the docks, I guess," he added savagely.

"You—!"

With a scream of rage, Rose dove at him, swinging her fist at his face. He stumbled back, startled, and his hand snapped up. His fingers closed around her wrist, but he was too slow to stop her knee slamming into his gut.

"Ow, *fuck*—"

"Let go a'me!" she shrieked. She kicked at his shin as hard as she could, stomped viciously on his foot over and over again, wriggling like a fish on a line to twist free of his grip.

"Get *off* me—"

"*Hey!*"

A sharp whistle made them both wince. Kayo let go, and Rose stumbled back, smacking hard into the battlements. She looked around, chest heaving, to see Dominic climbing the ladder—and he looked furious.

"Have you two lost it?" he demanded. "We can hear you yelling through the fucking windows! The whole damn city can probably hear you!"

Kayo protested at once, his voice overlapping with Rose's as she tried to argue over him.

"She *attacked* me—"

"He has a knife, he was gonna *kill* me!"

"She was threatening us again—"

"He tried to push me off—"

"No, I *didn't*—"

Dominic stuck his fingers in his mouth and whistled again, a high shrill sound that pierced through Rose's ears like a needle. "Both of you shut the fuck up," he growled. "Kayo, get down from here and leave her alone."

"But I—"

"*Get lost.*"

Kayo's shoulders stiffened. For a moment, Rose thought he would fight back—but he didn't. With a final parting glare for both of them, he climbed down the ladder, slamming the trapdoor shut behind him.

Rose was left behind with Dominic, her stomach sinking. She couldn't fight someone his size. Even with a weapon, she'd be lucky to get one good hit in before he picked her up and threw her off the roof.

But she wasn't going to go out easy. In her right hand, hidden by her skirt, she gripped the knife she'd snatched from Kayo's belt.

Dominic sighed, his fingers raking through his hair. Then, to her surprise, he bent down and opened the trapdoor again.

"C'mon," he said with ill grace.

"Huh?"

He paused halfway down the ladder, raising his eyebrows at her as if *she* were the one who'd gone insane. "It's nearly midnight. I'll show you where we sleep."

"No."

He just stared at her. Her temper, on edge since Kayo had shown up, threatened to burst forth again.

"What?" she snapped. "I ain't goin' anywhere with *you*. All o' you just *leave me alone.*"

He sighed again with the bone-weary exhaustion of a dying old man. It was, in her opinion, a bit much. "You can't sleep up here."

"Watch me."

He just kept staring at her. What did he want her to say? She was tempted to kick him—his face was right at knee height. But finally, with yet another sigh, he shrugged and descended the ladder. The trapdoor, balanced on his head, fell into place with a soft thump, and then she was alone. Just as she'd wanted.

She fell to her knees at once, leaning over to study the trapdoor and find some sort of mechanism to lock it. But all she had was the knife—a small, pathetic kitchen knife, barely even worth the steel it was made from. Its chipped blade clearly hadn't been sharpened in a while. She nearly flung it down in a fit of pique, but stopped herself at the last moment. Maddened by the rage pulsing through her veins, she believed wholeheartedly that he had done it on purpose—that he had armed himself with this ridiculous knife knowing that she would try and steal it from him.

But it was better than nothing.

"*He'll* see," she muttered, pacing back and forth in a futile effort to burn away some of her fury. "I'mma gut 'im with this stupid little knife, he'll wish he fuckin' sharpened it then. Pathetic, stupid, spineless *idiot*...."

But the night was still, the room below quiet. Even the wind had quieted. There was nothing to fan the flames inside her. And as they flickered and died, she felt her anger bleed out of her, leaving her empty.

There was nothing to block the trapdoor—except for her. So she sank down on top of it, hugging her knees, and fought as hard as she could against a sudden urge to sob.

They were going to kill her. They were never going to let her go—and they were never going to trust her to stay. The second she climbed down that ladder, she'd find a knife in her ribs. Kayo hadn't had a chance to attack before she did, and he was a coward. She could handle him, maybe. Although remembering how he'd run along those rooftops, climbing up walls and swinging through the air like he was born to it....Well. It wasn't a fight she was eager to have.

Dominic was another puzzle altogether. He was twice Kayo's size, and she knew he was strong. When he'd said he would kill her, he'd meant it, too. There was no heat to it, no emotion at all, just a man talking about killing her with the same bored, detached air as he might talk about killing a rat. That was all she was to him, in the end. But he'd had her alone up there, with a steep drop on every side and nothing to stop him but a tiny knife that he probably hadn't even seen. So why hadn't he done anything?

Alysia had been nothing but kind to her. But the others walked all over her. Even Artemis—who'd held those weapons far too comfortably to be ignored, who'd talked about her with suspicion and disgust.

Rose didn't think she was capable of murder, or anything that might get her dress dirty, but she wouldn't stop the others.

She had no allies here—or out there, in the city. No one on her side. Kayo was right: if they killed her, no one would notice, or care.

Only her anger kept her from bursting into tears. Maybe she *would* rat them out to the soldiers. It would serve them right—they didn't fight fair. Kayo had tricked her here, and the rest of them had ganged up on her, hit her and locked her up, robbed her—and then they'd threatened to kill her. She hadn't even done anything to them —not yet. They thought a few comments and a punch or two in self-defense were bad? They couldn't even dream of all the damage she could do.

Something tapped against the bottom of the trapdoor; she thought she felt it shift. She stiffened in alarm, grabbing the stone wall —but she didn't hear anything, and whatever it was, it didn't happen again. She settled back down, but she couldn't relax. So she kept her eyes open, watching the stars and plotting and trying very hard to ignore the chill in the air, and her gnawing hunger, and the aches and bruises all over her body.

It was close to dawn before her exhaustion finally caught up to her. She curled up on top of the trapdoor, covered herself up with her skirt, and fell asleep to thoughts of slitting their throats in their beds. Then she would comb every inch of the place, stuff everything of value into a sack, and stroll out with full pockets and a light heart.

Kayo thought no one would notice if she was gone? Then she'd make sure they noticed that she was here. If they didn't have the guts to kill her, she'd make them wish she'd never been born.

Kayo wandered into the kitchen later than usual the next morning, arriving just as Artemis was preparing to leave. Dominic, who was clumsily mending a shirt at the table, twisted around.

"You look like hell," he said by way of greeting.

"You're not my type either, prick," Kayo snarled back.

"*Kayo!*" Alysia scolded him as Dominic gave him a wounded look.

"What? Nobody asked him."

Alysia frowned at him, but she didn't have the heart to press him further. He did look rough, his hair loose and tangled, dark circles under his eyes. By the looks of it, he'd slept in his clothes—or hadn't slept at all. She reached out and brushed back his hair.

"Couldn't sleep?"

He let her fuss over him for a moment or two, then ducked free of her hand. "I'm fine, Lis." But he didn't look at her when he said it, and she heard a note of guilt in his voice as he gestured to the paper she was scribbling on. "Want help with that?"

"I'm all right."

"Help Dominic," Artemis chimed in, "he's the one who needs it."

Dominic saw an opportunity to abandon his work and took it, tossing the shirt onto the table. "Yes, please. I don't know how all of you do those tiny little stitches."

"It's called 'patience,'" Alysia said.

"And not being blinder than a damn bat," Kayo added, setting to work on the shirt. "Who let you near a needle anyways? I'm going to have to rip all these out first."

"I didn't exactly volunteer, mate. *Somebody* was sound asleep."

"You're a butcher," Kayo muttered, picking loose thread from the torn fabric. "Are you heading out, Artemis?"

"Just about," said Artemis. "I might have tomorrow off, but I'll have to bring some things home with me."

"Then you don't have the day off, do you?" Kayo snapped.

Artemis just rolled her eyes, but Alysia could see the effort it took Dominic not to say something nasty. He turned to Alysia instead and asked, "So. How are we doing?"

"Not great," she said dully.

"So...?"

She shrugged. "A week, maybe? More if we cut back—"

"No," Kayo said firmly. "The kids aren't getting enough as it is."

"But that will buy us a little time—"

"We can't do that. Liam would've said so too. It'll mess with their growth."

"We can't do things the way we did with Liam," Alysia said bluntly. "Not anymore."

Kayo just stared at her, as shocked as if she'd slapped him. Dominic and Artemis looked away. Alysia wished she could snatch the words back. Artemis's voice had been echoing in her head too much, accusing her of babying him, coddling him, but she hadn't meant to sound so harsh. But nothing she could say now could erase what she'd said then—because it was the stark truth.

After an awkward silence, Alysia cleared her throat and stood up.

"I'll try to find work today. Can I walk with you, Arty?"

"Of course." Artemis stood and dusted off her skirt, then paused, glancing at Dominic. "Are you two planning to, um—go out again?"

"No," said Dominic.

Kayo threw him a sharp look. "We're not?"

"No," said Dominic again, more firmly. "I'll look for work today too. We'll be fine if I can find something."

"I'll go too."

"No," Alysia said. If she was going to make him hate her, she thought with resignation, she might as well do the thing properly. "I need you to watch the kids."

"Oh." Kayo sank back again, letting his eyes fall back to the embroidery. "Okay."

Alysia bit her lip, but didn't speak. Neither did anyone else. Artemis just stood there, turned halfway to the door.

The tip of her charcoal stick rapped against the paper, a nervous tick she couldn't seem to stop. There was no need to bring up the numbers on the paper. They all knew what they said. But the silence was unbearable. She had to say something.

"Rose didn't show up for dinner last night," she finally blurted out.

Kayo just scowled at his work. Dominic exchanged a glance with Artemis, then shrugged. "So?"

"You gave her a huge bowl of porridge at midday," Artemis added. "Maybe she wasn't hungry."

"You *did?*" Kayo said sharply.

"Don't start," Alysia warned him. "I had to, she looked like a good wind would blow her away."

"*Good.* Then she'd be *gone.*"

"Kayo...."

"Still," Artemis commented, tucking a strand of hair back into her braided twist, "I thought she was only here in the first place to eat our food."

"That's what worries me."

Dominic snorted. "She's fine. She's probably still on the roof."

"She spent the night on the *roof?*"

"Not like it's snowing," Dominic scoffed. "I left her a blanket. She'll come down when she's ready."

"Will she?" Alysia countered. "She's probably hiding up there because she's scared of us."

"Why would she be *scared* of us?" said Artemis.

Dominic didn't answer; he simply cleared his throat and cast a pointed look at Kayo, who scowled at him.

"Oh, for—she's not *scared,*" he snapped. "She probably just knows no one *wants* her here."

"*I* want her here!" Alysia protested.

"What the hell *for?*"

"You're the one who brought her here," Dominic chimed in. "Against her will, for some reason. Which—*why?* Even you're not *that* desperate, are you?"

"It wasn't—I *didn't!*" Kayo said indignantly. "I don't want her here, I don't want anything to do with her!"

"And yet, here she is."

"Look, I don't *know,* okay? I don't *remember.*"

"Sara said you felt sorry for her," Alysia told him.

"What? No I didn't, why would I? She'd slit all our throats for a couple of coins—"

"Oh, come off it," said Dominic.

"What?"

"You're full of it. Admit it, you *did* feel sorry for her."

"I *told* you, I don't *remember.* I—" Kayo made a frustrated noise, throwing down the needle. "Okay, *fine.* I did a *little,* when I first saw her. But she was already *here.*"

"So you musta felt sorry for her when you first met her, too," Dominic reasoned. "Makes sense. She looked rough. But we can't adopt every stray we find."

"I *know* that. Look, I don't know what I was thinking, obviously I was *wrong.*"

"No, you weren't," said Alysia.

Kayo and Dominic both turned to blink at her. "Huh?"

Alysia shrugged. "I think I get it. You felt for her."

"I don't feel *anything* for that—"

"I did, too. Anyone with a heart would." This she said with a glare in Dominic's direction. He managed to make himself look innocent. "Just *look* at her. It's not like you stole her from a castle. She's had it rough for a *while.* Probably for her whole life, by the sounds of it. I would've thought she belonged here, too."

"Well, don't tell *her* that," Dominic snorted. "Apparently living here's a fate worse than death."

"Just be nice to her, okay?" Alysia said. "She doesn't know what she's doing."

"Come off it, she's nearly grown."

Artemis scoffed. "Dom, how many times have your cats bitten me and you told me it was my fault?"

"Well, they—oh, c'mon, Arty, you too?"

"Lis is right," said Artemis firmly. "It's not like we *should* take her in. We can't really afford to, but—I mean—"

"We should," said Alysia. Artemis hesitated, then nodded. "Yes. We should."

"*Artemis!*"

"What? I don't feel right about how we treated her. She doesn't know what to do any more than we do."

"Are you kidding me? She knows *exactly* what she's doing."

"If we're nicer to her, she might come around," said Alysia. She shoved the paper aside and stood up. "Just try," she begged Kayo. "Please?"

"Don't look at *me*. I've been trying to stay *away* from her."

"That works, too." She swooped down and kissed his cheek before she departed. "See you later."

"Bye," he muttered. She half expected him to scrub at his cheek where she'd kissed him, as if to erase the mark of it, but he just turned back to his sewing. The last thing she saw before she left was the delicate pattern he was embroidering, the outline of a little yellow sun.

"I can't tell if he's doing better or worse," Artemis commented as they crossed the courtyard, pitching her voice so the roar of the waterfall would drown out her words to everyone but Alysia.

"We really are too hard on him," Alysia insisted. She unlocked the door at the far end of the courtyard and let Artemis pass through ahead of her. "You know he's hurting."

"I *know,* but—maybe you're just being too *soft* on him," Artemis pointed out as they followed the stairs spiraling down into darkness. "It's been months."

"You know how close they were. And the way Liam died—"

Alysia saw Artemis wince in the fading light. "Still. I don't know if it's just about Liam. He was pretty bad before."

"Don't say that, Arty. He's just had a rough time."

"Yeah, for the past—what, four years? Five?"

"You *know* him. You know he's not really like this. He's sweet and generous and—"

"I know who he used to be. Maybe he's just...changed."

"No." The image of the embroidered yellow sun burned bright in her head, the care and love poured into each stitch. Did he know how happy it would make the little boy who wore it next? The kids wore those bright little patterns like badges of honor. He had to know—and that was why he did it. That was why he'd brought Rose to the shrine. That was why he was hurting so much now. Not because he didn't care—because he cared too much. "No, he hasn't."

They knew their way by feel now, and Alysia found the door at the base of the steps without pausing. When she wrenched it open, she saw the look on Artemis's face. She didn't look convinced. But all she said, before she and Alysia parted ways in the street, was, "I hope you're right."

Dominic watched Kayo seethe in silence, pouring all his frustrations into the little embroidered sun. He was filling in the center now, tugging the thread and stabbing the needle perhaps a bit too hard, but still working with a smooth, swift grace that Dominic could never have managed.

"You gonna be okay on your own?"

"I'll be fine."

"Right...."

Dominic knew what he had to say, but he didn't want to say it. Kayo was already bristling like a hedgehog, ready to lash out at any moment. But Kayo seemed to sense what he was thinking. He looked up, glaring.

"What? You don't think I can handle them? You're worried I'll burn the place down?"

Dominic winced. "No, I didn't—"

But Kayo's eyes darkened at the look on his face. He stood up, throwing the shirt down and kicking the bench roughly back into place. "Thanks for the confidence," he snapped, his voice dripping with sarcasm. "I'll try not to get us all killed."

"Kayo, come on." Dominic hastened to follow him upstairs. "I just—are you gonna be okay? You know, with Rose around?"

"What, like any of you care what I think?"

"*Yes.* We do. It's just—"

"What?"

Kayo whirled around at the top of the stairs, his expression thunderous. Dominic was far from scared of him, but he fought the urge to move back a step or two. Instead, he took a deep breath.

"Look," he said. "We fucked up with her. Not just you. All of us. You've gotta see that."

"It won't matter once she's *out* of here."

"Yeah. It will. She's on our conscience. And I know she's on yours, too."

His face twisted a little, the angry mask cracking. "I—I didn't—I never meant—"

"I know. And I know she's not the easiest to get on with. But we kind of owe it to her. And how you've been treating her—"

"So what do you want me to say?" Kayo burst out. "She threatens all of us and I, what, let her walk all over me? What the hell do you want me to *do?*"

"That depends," said Dominic.

"On what?"

Dominic shrugged. "On what kinda man you wanna be."

At that, Kayo stopped short. He struggled, clearly wanting to protest, but unable to find the words. Finally, he shook his head.

"She's going to fucking stab me," he muttered as he turned away. Dominic trotted behind him.

"Well, you had a good run."

Kayo snorted. "Did you forget how to count?"

"I said a good run, not a long run."

"*Me?* Now I *know* you've lost your mind."

But he was, Dominic was relieved to see, smiling a little as he left.

Rose woke up cramped and cold on the stone floor. For one horrible moment, she thought she was back in the cell—until she shifted, and the sun shone right into her eyes. She uncurled and stretched her stiff muscles with a grimace, looking around. Nothing had changed except the position of the sun, which had reappeared with a vengeance to blind her.

It was hard not to be surprised that no one had appeared to bother her, even this late in the morning. But for some reason, she was disappointed too. And why should she be? All these people ever did was harass her.

Maybe she wasn't disappointed. Maybe she was just hungry.

There was certainly no food up here. She stood and shook herself loose, looking out over the city, at the sun high overhead and the infinite, gleaming ocean. She still had the knife she'd stolen from Kayo—but where could she stash it? After a bit of feeling around, she finally discovered that both the dress and chemise had handy little slits in the skirt where her hands could plunge right through to her bare skin. She had no pockets, but she was able to slip the knife carefully into the string of the drawers beneath. There, it would remain undetected...as long as she was careful how she sat.

She hauled the trapdoor open and peeked inside. No one was there—but somebody had been. There was a wool blanket draped over the top rung of the ladder. Was that for *her*? Was that why someone had tried to open the trapdoor, to give her a *blanket*? It wasn't *snowing*, it wasn't freezing, she wouldn't have died. Did the orphans just think she'd...like it?

She shoved the thought aside. She couldn't let her guard down. That was just what they wanted.

The room was empty, but she could hear the children's distant voices. Was there ever any escaping them? She'd have to pass them to leave, but hopefully she could escape notice. She crept down the last few stairs, approaching the door carefully and peeking in.

The kids were swarming around like they always seemed to be, but Alysia was nowhere to be found. Kayo was with them instead, running around as if trying to catch one. He snatched up a small one and made a big show of turning him upside down and shaking him. The child screamed and thrashed, but he was cackling madly the whole time. The others were laughing too as they turned on Kayo and started climbing him like sailors scaling a mast. He sank down to the ground, but he made no attempts to free himself at all, even when one of them climbed onto his shoulders. His was the only deeper laughter in a storm of high-pitched giggling.

She stared at him, dumbstruck. It occurred to her that she'd only seen him smile once before—right before she'd made the decision to follow him.

And then he spotted her. The smile disappeared, his eyes narrowing to a glare.

Rose flinched and whipped her head back out of sight. Her hand scrabbled for the slit in her skirts, closing around the hilt of her knife, as she pressed her back to the wall. She listened for his footsteps, waiting.

But nothing happened. Even after a full minute of waiting, he didn't come. When she finally heard his voice, she flinched, but it was far away.

"One, two, three—go!"

She dared a peek around the doorframe again and saw him standing in the middle of a knot of excited children. At his signal all of them scattered across the room. She blinked at them, trying to find some semblance of reason to their running around. It must be some sort of game.

She took a chance and darted past the open door, then paused again to see if he'd turn up. But she could still hear him talking to the children, as if nothing had happened. He wasn't coming after her—yet.

He must have locked the place down, put the other orphans at the doors. That was why he didn't care if she tried to escape. Or—

He felt sorry for you.

Rage pulsed through her blood like fire. So that was it, then. He didn't think she'd even *bother* trying to escape. He thought she'd be so grateful for porridge and ruins and shoes that she'd be tripping over herself to keep them happy.

Rose had learned long ago, in bits and pieces over the years, that being underestimated and overlooked worked to her advantage. Her stature, sex, and physical appearance had kept her safe in ways her actions never could have, even if they endangered her at the same time. She should have been glad that Kayo didn't consider her a threat. But that didn't quench her fury. It only gave it a slight sweetness to soften the edges of the fire, a bit of smugness for her malice. If he didn't think she was a threat, she was going to make sure he regretted it.

She walked tall and straight to the rope at the end of the landing, flipped her hair over her shoulder as she swung herself down. She didn't care if he saw her anymore. Let him come after her if he dared.

It wasn't difficult to retrace her steps back to the kitchen. But once there, she could find nothing of interest. Not only were Alysia and the others absent, but there wasn't anything to eat. The cookpot hung empty over a cold hearth, and aside from a few dried herbs hanging upside-down from the top of one window, there was nothing edible in the place. She even checked a few of the jars and bottles. But the only substance that looked appetizing was, upon tasting it, decidedly not. Gagging and scrubbing at her tongue, she gave up and stomped out into the courtyard.

She'd half-expected to find someone here, too, washing clothes or dishes or whatever else. But the courtyard was still and quiet. She looked around, but she could see no faces in the windows that had been left open, and those that remained closed were colored glass and tiny and, she guessed, difficult to see through.

But not impossible.

Was one of the orphans waiting at the window with a bow nocked, prepared to take her out if she leapt down the gaping hole in the fountain? If they were, she decided, after scrutinizing the fountain and the hole from a safe distance, perhaps it wasn't necessary. She couldn't see a rope or a ladder nearby that the orphans might use to get in or out, and she remembered the drop being quite high, and the water being very shallow. Plus—it was *water*. And it only led into the sewers, which—while eventually leading her back to the upper city— would leave her there slathered in filth and soaking wet.

With this new dress, she had even less protection from the cold and damp than she had before. It had only one advantage: with it, and with her clean skin and hair, she could blend in a bit more easily. But if she came out covered head to toe in sewage, that sole advantage was lost.

No—that way out wasn't worth dying for. If she was going to find a way out, she'd need another one. One that the orphans didn't know she knew about.

It was time, she decided, to find out what was hiding behind the blocked door in the kitchen.

It wasn't difficult to get to the door. All she had to do was slide the table just far enough so she could wriggle behind it. It wasn't even difficult to get the door open: the latch was stiff, but a firm yank finally pushed it loose.

The difficult bit, she realized as soon as she pushed it, was that it was blocked on the *other* side. Something large and heavy stopped the door from opening more than a hand's breadth. Whatever it was, it didn't want to budge.

But there was *light* on the other side of the door. And light meant a way out—possibly. For all she knew, a door stood on the other side, wide open, leading right onto an upper city street. With new motiva- tion, she shoved the table back a little more, got a new angle, and shoved again.

This time, the *thing,* whatever it was, moved a little.

Encouraged, she shoved a bit more, and a bit more. Once she could squeeze her knee through the gap, she used her thigh as a lever and pushed even harder, forcing first her leg, then her hips, and then her entire body through the gap. With one final shove, she kicked the door half-open, then stood, panting, to gaze upon her triumph.

The door had been blocked by, of all things, a chest of drawers, which had fallen against it. It had been so heavy that when she opened each drawer, she expected to find cannonballs, or horseshoes, or perhaps an interior entirely filled with lead—but except for cobwebs and rat droppings, it was empty. The narrow room was cluttered with other furniture—a table with a missing leg, a few thatched chairs without their thatching—and lit by a tiny window that did not open. A door, left cracked, led somewhere dim and grayish.

She was halfway to that door before she remembered the orphans that might or might not be on her tail. After a moment's thought, she went back into the kitchen and pulled the table back from the other side, nudging it carefully back into place. Then she shut the door again, and, for good measure, shoved the chest of drawers against it. There—let them sit there scratching their heads as they wondered where she'd gone. Snickering, she dipped out of that room and into the next.

The room opened out onto a corridor, lit by big windows at the far end. She dashed down the long stretch right away, grabbing for the latches on the windows—but if they could open before, they couldn't now. After prying and wrenching on them as hard as she could, even until she thought they might break, they still didn't budge. Annoyed, she shook the numbness from her hands and looked around. There were plenty of doors, plenty of rooms—surely one of them had a way out. And if none of these did, she spotted another spiraling staircase at the opposite end.

She backtracked until she found the narrow room with the chest of drawers blocking the exit. But there, she paused. The orphan's hideout was massive, and she'd clearly only seen a fraction of it. If she meant to keep exploring, she'd need a plan.

A brief meditation on the subject led her to a strategy. She'd used others like it while navigating the city—though this, she hoped, would be a bit simpler. Most of the doors were cracked or hanging fully open, so once she'd explored a dead end, she'd simply shut the door. She'd start at the end of the corridor, by the window, and head right—and at every fork, she'd choose the path to the right. And— down, she decided, glancing at the staircase. She'd head to the right, and down. If there was going to be an exit into the city, she felt confi- dent that it would be on one of the lower floors. That way, all she had to do if she got lost was head left and up, ignore the dead ends, and keep going until she made it back to the one door she had left open. She propped it open with the broken table leg, just in case, and set off.

Her strategy would have worked perfectly—if not for the traps.

She had been right about the shrine. It *was* massive, and she *did* need a strategy to avoid getting lost. She found herself wishing quickly for a spool of thread, half-remembering some old children's tale about a monster's labyrinth. She'd never liked it, she recalled. Why did a monster need a labyrinth, anyway? From what she could tell, it was something like this place: long curving corridors, enough twists and turns to have you going around in circles, lots of dead ends. But wouldn't a locked door be a much better way of keeping people out? And wouldn't the monster want people to come *in*, so it could eat them? If *she* were a monster, she decided, she'd have a den that was easy to get into—impossible to miss, even—and let anyone and everyone in. Perhaps she'd even use a lure, like the scent of fresh bread, or a beckoning salacious girl. The sort of men who fell for that, in her opinion, deserved exactly what they got.

But as she went on, the shrine reminded her more and more of a different story: Vheldalam. The Sleeping City. Rumor had it, one day everyone simply vanished. Fires were left burning, beds were unmade, carts sat abandoned in the street. There were no signs of people leaving en masse, no more than the usual footprints at the gates. It was as if someone had cast a spell and made them all disappear. And anyone who set foot inside the gates—to investigate, to loot, to look for loved ones—disappeared too. There was only one person left in the whole city: a princess, hiding at the top of the tallest tower in the castle. From there, she could see the whole city, just in case someone actually made it through.

Rose wasn't quite sure if the princess bit had been part of the original tale, or an addition that she'd tacked on herself long ago. But if she *had* made it up, it must have been when she was very young, skulking around windows and in the shadows to eavesdrop on people telling stories. A story, she'd learned quickly, could be anything: an old woman reciting a tale to her grandchildren while she sat and knit was wonderful, but a couple arguing with the windows open, or a drunk man telling his woes to an apathetic bargirl, were still good alternatives to the crippling boredom of having nothing to do and nowhere to go.

Even so, she could certainly do better now. A twist, she decided—that was what it needed. The people who went into the city never came out because the princess stood on her tower with a longbow and shot them all. Perhaps *she* had cast the spell that had made everyone disappear. Maybe she'd meant for it to do something else, like cure an illness, or maybe she'd only been trying to make *one* person disappear. Or maybe she'd just wanted some peace and quiet. A small part of Rose's mind mulled over these options, trying to puzzle out which one would lead to a better story, as she wandered through the shrine.

She sang a little as she went. At first, she simply hummed, but it felt too good to stop. And why *shouldn't* she sing? Goddess, how long had it been? And what could she possibly be afraid of now? The orphans? Let them find her. Let them hear. Her anger fueled her reckless courage, and she sang full-voice, stretching her rusted vocal cords with an old sea shanty.

> *Come all ye young sailors an' list now to me*
> *I'll tell you a tale of a port at sea*
> *Where the wine and ale flow fast and free*
> *And the women ain't bad neither*
> *(After a drink or two)*

> *Good wind, bad wind, gale wind, no wind,*
> *All together 'til the end, heave ho!*

> *We followed the stars to the port of Alberth*

We fought with the wind for all we was worth
For we knew what was waiting, a night full of mirth
And the feel of solid land and
a pocket of coin to spend

Good wind, bad wind, gale wind, no wind,
All together 'til the end, heave ho!

Sea shanties were good practice, as it happened. Sailors didn't have to carry a tune. She sang a few more, just because she wanted to, just because it felt good to sing. Maybe, she thought happily, she'd even work her way up to a ballad—if she felt like it. Who was there to stop her?

Down and through she went, slowly finding answers to all of her questions. It was not only the large windows in the corridor that could not be opened; *none* of them did, at least none that faced the exterior. Every time she felt a latch turn, her heart leapt to her throat, and she held her breath as she wrenched it open. But every time, she found herself looking at a courtyard. She was certain that this had been done on purpose, to keep people out—or in, maybe—but by the orphans, or the Divinæ? She wouldn't have put it past the orphans to go through and break every window latch. Breaking something didn't require any skill.

There were at least three courtyards—four, if she counted the garden she vaguely remembered with the giant hole in the ceiling. At least one door, too, seemed to lead outside; or she assumed it did, because it was sealed shut. Not just locked, but shut so firmly that it didn't even rattle in its housing, and she couldn't see light coming from the edges or the bottom.

The window beside it was colored glass, but through a cracked pane, she thought she could see a sort of balcony. She hesitated, then gave the glass a sharp poke. The cracked pane broke along the fault line, the top piece sliding down to join the other. She eased the glass out carefully and looked through the hole.

The upper city was there, all right—far, far below. She couldn't see any people, any movement—and she doubted that anyone would hear her even if she shouted.

She'd have to go even farther down, then. How far down did this place *go?*

So farther she went, finding room after empty room along the way. If the Divinæ had lived here before it was vacant, they had certainly left a lot behind. She'd expected empty rooms, but most of them had a few bits of furniture, even if it was broken or damaged. Some of it even looked as good as new. Most of the drawers, cabinets, and wardrobes were empty, and any fabric left behind had been repurposed as rat bedding, but it wasn't all bad. If she'd stumbled across this place, she would have made it home, too.

Which begged a question: why *hadn't* the orphans made this place home? Not just the one tower, but all of it? She decided eventually that they had—that there was a wing she hadn't discovered yet, full of bedrooms just like the ones she was currently exploring, and that was where they kept the little children at night. She couldn't even be sure that they *didn't* come into this part of the shrine— although she was. Something about the silence, the stillness, the layers of dust made her certain that she was the only visitor in a long time.

Perhaps the place was simply too big, and this part wasn't needed. Perhaps the only way through was the door she'd found, which they'd been unable or unwilling to open. Or—

Or it was the traps.

It happened when she had descended a flight of stairs and paused on the last step, waiting for her eyes to adjust to the darkness. The room below was large and windowless. She could barely make out something up ahead, dangling from the ceiling. It was, she thought, a row of pots and pans—which meant the room was a kitchen. That long table underneath had to be a chopping-block, and there, at the back, would be the ovens.

She'd been eager to raid the place for forgotten knives, but she had no luck in that regard. After poking around in all the cabinets and feeling around in the ovens and hearths, all she'd earned herself was a sneezing fit and a nasty cut on one arm from the jagged edge of an oven. The pots and pans didn't seem too bad, but what was she meant to do with a pot? Beat someone to death? No—she had to do better than that.

She'd shaken herself off and ventured into the next room, squinting to see in the darkness—

And hurled herself to the ground as something whistled through the air.

She'd moved on pure instinct, and for a moment, even as she was falling, she scolded herself for overreacting—but then she heard the crash. She hit the ground hard, but rolled over at once, struggling to free her legs and arms from the tangles of her dress.

A thick beam swung from a rope harness over the doorway— wildly at first, but quickly settling into a slow, almost soothing rhythm.

She stared at it blankly, chest heaving, until it stopped moving, and even longer after that. Then, for some reason, she started to laugh. She kept laughing as she picked herself up, the laughter somehow both weak and hysterical.

Traps.

They'd set *traps.*

No wonder they weren't worried about her escaping.

Her mind whirred like bug wings, so fast she could barely follow her own thoughts. If they'd set traps in certain areas, that meant they wanted her out of those places. Which meant either they were hiding something good, or that was the way out. That meant she was going the right way—but there would be more, she was certain of that. This one must have been triggered somehow, but she hadn't felt a trip wire, and it was too dark to see clearly. If there were more, she'd have to work out—

Her arm felt sticky. She pressed her hand to it, unconsciously, and felt wetness. She recoiled, sucking in a breath. Her hand and the sleeve of her chemise were both painted dark with blood.

She burst out laughing again. And then she thought, *Shit.*

The darkness, the traps, and now the blood. That was more than enough for one day. She edged her way around the beam—*Goddess,* she thought, *this thing would've whacked off my head*—and took off at a run.

She had the layout of the place in her head, more or less, and could have found her way back—only she didn't want to go back. The narrow courtyard where the orphans spent their time was the last place she wanted to be. And if she emerged from the secret door, it wouldn't be a secret for much longer.

So instead, she aimed for what she thought must be another courtyard—the last one to find. If the place was structured how she thought it would be, she'd run into it just up ahead. She paused before she emerged, utilizing the renewed light to inspect her arm. It really was bleeding a lot. After a moment's thought, she untied the sleeves from the rest of the dress, then took her little knife and sawed at the elbow-length sleeve of her chemise. She'd meant at first to cut off the bloody part, but at a second thought she sawed it off at the shoulder, then did the other one to match. The sleeves had been bothering her all day.

With those out of the way, she had two ruined sleeves to tie around the wound. She wrapped the bloody sleeve around her forearm, then tied it in place with the other sleeve, pulling it snug. All it had to do was last the night. After that....

Goddess, she was tired. After that—who knew? She might have to fight the boy again, or all of the orphans, or survive another few traps.

But first, she had to find her way out.

She forgot to check the latch on the door before she pushed it down with all her strength—but miraculously, it gave way. Light and fresh sea air poured over her in a blissful wave, warmth and coolness all at once. She blinked, dazzled, keeping herself half-shielded by the door until her eyes adjusted. It didn't take long. The sun was setting, and the light was fading orange and red.

At first, despite the breeze and the sunlight, she wasn't certain that she had actually found the courtyard. There was still a roof over her head and a wall to one side. But on the other side of the balustrade that ringed the room, it opened and dropped off to reveal—was it a courtyard? No, it was too green for that. It was—

The garden.

Now she remembered seeing the greenery after stumbling out of the cell, bathed in sunlight from the hole in the ceiling while Alysia had chattered in her ear. She'd forgotten all about it, dismissed it as a dream. Yet here it was. A garden, a massive garden, planted right in the middle of this—what was it? A courtyard? A hall? She didn't know; her vocabulary had hit its limit.

She leaned over the balustrade, staring hungrily at the garden down below. The room had three levels, and she was on the third— but how could she get down? It seemed too much to hope that there was a similar door two floors down that wasn't locked or blocked. There had to be another set of stairs around here somewhere, one that she could use to—

"Rose?"

She ducked behind the balustrade. She heard footsteps and hoped that the owner of the voice—Dominic?—would retreat...but no such luck. When he spoke again, his voice echoed around the entire garden.

"Rose? That you? What're you doing up there?"

There was nothing for it. She stood up, leaning casually against the balustrade, as if she'd merely dropped something and bent to pick it up. Dominic stood across from her on the floor below, frowning up at her.

"Nothin'," she said.

Dominic raised his eyebrows. "You scared me half to death," he complained. "I thought we had a rat. Are you looking for your room?"

"My room?" she said, anger rising up her throat like fire. "You mean my *cell?*"

But to her surprise, Dominic snorted. "A cell? The damn door don't even lock. *Cell*," he scoffed, shaking his head. "An' here I was thinkin' you was there all day. Don't tell me you slept upstairs?"

She opened her mouth to give a retort—but she was distracted. If he didn't mean her cell, then—"*My* room?" she asked again.

"Yeah...you're a bit too high," he said, and eyed her for a lingering moment as if worrying she'd lost her mind. Then he pointed. "Down here. Last door down. Stairs are down that way too."

"Oh," she said, because she couldn't think of anything else. Then she blurted out, "What d'you mean, *my room?*"

"I mean, yours. As in, possessive," Dominic said drily. "Where *you* sleep, and keep your stuff, and nobody else is allowed in. Want me to say it again in Lyric?"

She *had* a retort to that, a well-rehearsed one—but she couldn't quite spit it out. She had too many questions. "Why?" she asked, because that was the biggest one—and then, suspiciously, "What's it cost?"

"What, you got money we don't know about? Please," Dominic scoffed.

"But then—"

"Fuck, it's empty. Just take it. Who cares?"

Clearly, he didn't. He was walking away again. Rose stood there, frozen, still processing what he'd said. He paused as he rounded the corner, looking back.

"You're gonna show up to dinner, right?" he called up to her.

If he hadn't been practically shouting, she would have wondered who the hell he was talking to. "Um...yeah?"

"Good," he said, and flashed that bright, crooked grin up at her. "Don't be late. Those kids 'll eat your share in a heartbeat."

And then he was gone.

Rose waited until the sound of his footsteps had faded, and then a few seconds longer, before she set off in the direction he had pointed. Sure enough, yet another slender tower with yet another spiraling staircase wound its way down from there. She picked her way carefully down the steps—there was more than a little rubble here, and she'd learned her lesson by now—and emerged onto the floor below. There, at the end, was the door he'd indicated.

The door was open—and so was the window inside. This one didn't open onto a courtyard, either. It opened onto the sea, onto a wide sky of pink and orange broken only by the long tendril of the far side of the bay in the distance. The breeze was like a cool finger wrapping around her, caressing the sweaty skin behind her neck and down her chest, beckoning her closer.

The room within wasn't large. There was just enough room for a narrow bed, a bedside table with a washbasin, and a wooden chest. The bed looked as if it had a real mattress, and it even had a pillow: a canvas sack of something tied tightly and placed at the top of the wool blanket spread over the bed. A small, faded rug sat just by the door.

It looked—*familiar.* She'd woken up in this room—no, not this exactly. The bed was on the opposite wall. She cocked her head, trying to remember.

Was it a different one? The other doors were open, too. Not the one next to hers, but all three of the ones beyond it. She gave the door next to hers a tentative pull, but the mechanism didn't budge. She snorted. *Of course the damn lyin' orphan would say the doors don't lock. But obviously—*

But then she crept to the next door, and the room within distracted her completely.

It looked just like the one that was, supposedly, hers, only mirrored. But this one was clearly inhabited. Clothes lay scattered around, spilling out of the open chest. On the windowsill perched a number of tiny items: shells, colorful stones, something shiny and metallic. The washbasin had been set aside on the floor, next to a stack of papers hiding under the bedside table, the topmost bearing a sketch of a vaguely familiar tree. A few sticks of charcoal lay on top of the bedside table, alongside a bit of crumpled-up paper and—

A book.

Before she knew what she was doing, she was already reaching out, closing her hands on the book, sinking onto the bed to look at it. It was leather-bound and heavier than it looked, the paper yellowed and curling on the edges. She turned it over and traced the words etched into the front. A *book,* here, of all places. If she—

"Well, *that* ain't yours."

Rose jumped up, clutching the book, and found Dominic leaning against the balustrade in front of the door. "Where'd *you* come from?" she demanded.

"*My* room," he said, pointing. She bit back a curse; he'd been hiding in the ones she hadn't inspected yet, only pretending to leave. She shouldn't have fallen for such a basic trick. "We've all got one, 'cept Arty an' me share. Not that you *asked*. Too busy snooping?"

"I wasn't—"

"Yes, you were," he said, smirking. "It's fine, just put the book back."

She did so, reluctantly. She thought she could see the shape of another one buried in the tangled blankets. "But it's a *book,*" she protested. "D'you know how much it's *worth?* I barely even *seen* one. You could get gobs of gold for it. Why's it in *here?*" she added, looking around. She would have expected it to be in the middle of its own room, on display on a stand, or in a library like in the stories. Perhaps if a Divina lived here, Rose could understand it. That would be where they kept all their spells and things, but—

"For reading," said Dominic, and his eyes twinkled as he laughed at her in a way that almost—*almost*—made her forget to be annoyed. "What else?"

"*Reading?*" She looked around again. The room seemed rather small and messy for that sort of business. "Whose room is this?"

"Kayo's."

Rose backed hastily out of the room. Dominic laughed so hard that it echoed off the walls.

"Don't worry," he told her, and gave an ostentatious wink. "When I tell 'im there was finally a girl in 'is bed, I won't tell 'im who."

Rose stared at him as he kept laughing, chuckling to himself at his own joke. She glanced back into the room—*Kayo's* room—and then at her own. The one in between caught her eye. "You liar," she accused him. "You said the doors didn't lock. *That* one's locked."

"It ain't locked," said Dominic, rolling his eyes. "It's *broken*. Liam locked it up somehow before he died. We can't get it open. You wanna shut yourself in, go ahead. We got some boards an' nails for ya, have at it."

"Liam—you mean—that was *his* room?" Rose said excitedly. "The Beggar King's?"

"Yeah, sure, his," said Dominic carelessly. "Break in if you like. Kayo won't like it, but ain't nothin' in there. Looks just like yours."

"But his stuff, at least—"

"What stuff? We're orphans," Dominic said dismissively. "We don't have *stuff*. Well, Kayo does," he added, raising his eyebrows at the mess in the room. "But hell, even our room's half-empty. What the hell happened to your arm?"

Her hand rose to hide the makeshift bandage. "Nothin'."

He shook his head. "Arty's gonna be furious. Oh well. You comin'?"

Rose, who had been staring at the sketch of the tree and trying to remember where she'd seen it before, looked around. "Huh?"

"Dinner. I'm headed that way. You comin'?"

She bristled. "I ain't goin' nowhere with *you*."

"Why not?" he said with a careless wave of his hand. "Tà sinn uihe arahn aité. It's Lyric," he added when she scowled at him. "Means, we're all headed to the same place."

"No, we're not. There's *two* places." She pointed up, then down. Dominic chuckled.

"Y'think? My mum used t' say it. She probably meant the ground, or somethin'—I dunno, maybe she *did* mean hell. She was a—what d'you call 'em? Sal-whatever girls? An' she wasn't very optimistic, y'know?"

"Your mother was a *salacious girl?*"

"Sure was. 'Course, that ain't what she called it."

"Oh. So—you were, what, an accident?"

She'd meant to sound scathing, but Dominic just laughed again as he wandered back down the corridor. "You bet. But she—don't just stand there, we ain't got all night—she wasn't too—"

"I told you, I ain't goin' *nowhere* with you!"

He stopped and turned around. He seemed genuinely surprised by this. "Seriously? What's it matter?"

"You wanted to *kill me!*"

He scoffed. "That was, what, two days ago? Get over it."

"Wh—you—"

"Well, *I'm* headed to dinner." He waved over his shoulder as he left. "You can do whatever you want, I'll just eat your share. Bye!"

Rose stared after him for ten full seconds—long after he'd vanished around the corner—before cursing and stomping after him.

If she'd thought that the children were chaos incarnate before, it was nothing compared to how they behaved at dinnertime. She felt as if she were wading through a shoulder-high tide of hot, sweaty bodies with only her elbows to protect her. Some of them tried to duck past her—without success. It was all she could do to keep the shallow bowl of porridge in her hand from spilling.

Once free of the throng, she backed away, clutching her bowl close and watching the clamor in the light of a single hanging lantern. Little hands grabbed a bowl from the mismatched stack on the floor and crowded in close to the cookpot that Dominic had hauled all the way up. But Alysia refused to be rushed. She measured one precisely measured scoop of porridge into each bowl presented to her, careful not to spill a single drop. The child in question would then elbow their way free and sit with the others to devour the porridge in the messiest, most graceless way possible, then give themselves the human equivalent of a tongue bath.

Rose wrinkled her nose as she perched as far away from them as she could get: on the curved sill of the enormous window. It was dark now, but she could still see a few of the city lights through glass stained in blues and purples by the night. It was a much more appetizing view than the one in front of her—or the porridge. Alysia had given her two scoops, not just one, but it didn't taste any better than it had the day before.

Still, she had to admit—the children were *interesting*. She would have preferred the peace and quiet without them, but from a distance, they were fascinating to watch. She'd noticed before that they played different games than the ones she knew, and even sang different songs and skipping rhymes. Now she was intrigued to see that they had their own little groups. She scooped up her porridge with her fingertips—the children weren't wrong; it was impossible to eat the tarlike paste with any dignity—and watched the scene unfold as she would have watched a play in the square. There was one big group made up of lots of little ones. Each child fought hard to sit next to one or two friends in particular, and the larger circle broke into several smaller ones like moons orbiting missing planets.

Then there were smaller groups that splintered off. An older girl chased two toddlers around with astounding patience, trying to cajole them into eating a bite before the rest of the room distracted them again. Three girls sat in a little group all to themselves. Judging by their age and demeanor, she guessed they thought themselves too good for the main crowd. And then there was the last cluster, who'd retreated as far away as they could get—which meant they were the closest to her. The rejects, she guessed. Kids that even other unwanted kids didn't want.

"Who the hell are you?"

Rose jumped and swore as a boy appeared around a nearby beam. He was ten or eleven years old, with blonde hair—and he had a little girl who looked just like him clinging to his shirt. She was staring blankly off into space—but he was scowling at Rose.

"Huh?" she said.

"I asked who the hell you are," the boy snapped. "And what you're *doing* here." He folded his arms, looking her up and down with an expression that made it clear he didn't like what he saw. "Well?"

Rose shoved her bowl aside. "'Scuse the *fuck* outta me?" she retorted, rising to her feet. "You've got a *lotta* nerve—"

"Hello!"

The girl from before popped up near her elbow, the one with the rabbit on her dress. The one who had known her name.

"This is Andrew and Carolyn," the girl said, answering a question Rose certainly hadn't asked. "An' this is Rose," she added to the kids.

"So?" Andrew snapped. "What are you *doin'* here?"

"You think I *wanna* be here?" she shot back at him. "If you think I'mma let some snot-nosed—"

The little girl, Carolyn, let out a wail. Andrew turned immediately and wrapped her in his arms. "You *scared* her," he accused Rose, as if it was somehow *her* fault.

"So go away then!"

Andrew glared at her—and to her surprise, she found herself taking a step back. Something about the kid made her skin crawl. But then Carolyn wailed again, an oddly babyish noise for a child her age.

He put an arm around her shoulders and, with one final nasty look at Rose, walked away.

The other girl turned to Rose as if nothing had happened. Sara, Alysia had called her—a suspiciously innocent sort of name.

"I was looking for you last night!" she said. "How come you didn't come eat?"

"I—I didn't—Go *away*," Rose snarled at her, rattled—by her, by Andrew, by *all* of this.

The little girl just shrugged and sat on the windowsill by Rose's feet. "I see," she said, with the same air of grave sympathy that a woman might use to comfort a friend who'd caught her husband cheating. "It's probably scary, with all of us. And Kayo and them. They got real mad at you, but they're not bad, I swear!"

Rose stiffened. "What did they tell you?"

"Nothing," said Sara matter-of-factly. "I just know things. Only— I'm not supposed to talk about them," she added with a rueful wince. "Oops."

But Rose was not going to let it slide so easily. "Know *what* things?"

"I dunno. *Things.* Stuff other people miss, I guess. D'you wanna come play?" she added brightly.

"No," Rose snapped. "What *kinda* stuff? What were they sayin' about me?" The girl must have overheard them talking about her— had they been planning to get rid of her?

"Oh, I mean—no one *said* anything. I just meant, don't worry!" And her gap-toothed grin hitched right back. "They aren't going to hurt you, they wouldn't do that! No one wants to get rid of you! When Andrew got here, he thought they would too, but he's okay. See?"

She pointed, but Rose wasn't listening. Her eyes snapped to Sara's face, narrowing. How had the girl known what she was thinking? She'd even used the same words....

And then several things clicked into place.

"You're a *Divina!*" she hissed.

"What—no!" Sara squeaked. "No I'm not!"

Rose thought as hard as she could about smacking her across the face—and Sara flinched.

"I *knew* it!" she snarled. "You can *read minds!*"

"No, I *can't!*"

"Then how'd you know? Huh? Goddess, what're they doin' with a *Divina* here? Are they *crazy?* And—"

It occurred to her, suddenly, that she was complicit in this. If anyone came—not just soldiers, *anyone,* there were lots of people who hated the Divinæ —then they'd see her talking to the girl and wouldn't know the difference. The thought made her stomach clench.

"I gotta go," she said, and climbed hastily to her feet. She was eager to get as far away from this little girl and her huge, wounded eyes as she could. "I—*shit.*"

Kayo had just walked in. Rose sank to the floor below the windowsill at once, making herself small. He hadn't seemed to notice her. He dove right into the bigger group to stop a little girl who was smacking her porridge happily with a pudgy fist.

Sara slid off the windowsill and crouched beside her. She was practically close enough for Rose to smell her breath, but Rose didn't dare move. At least the little girl wasn't touching her—and even as she thought that, Sara shifted her leg, careful to leave a gap of space between them.

It was eerie, watching someone respond to her thoughts in real time. She decided immediately that she did not like it.

"Go away," she hissed. "And *stop reading my mind.*"

"Stop *thinking so loud,* then," Sara said, and had the gall to look offended. "Why're you hiding from Kayo? He's not gonna do anything."

Rose wanted to argue—but the girl had a point. Kayo wouldn't fight her in front of his precious kidnapped kids. He'd want to shield their delicate eyes from the harsh realities of a knife fight and a slashed throat. But it wouldn't be hers, she thought savagely, thinking of the knife hidden under her dress—and then she quickly stopped thinking about that.

"Alysia said she'd find you some pockets," Sara whispered. "An' Kayo's not gonna fight you, silly."

Rose bit back a groan. But she did stand up again and take her seat next to her abandoned bowl.

Sara sat happily beside her, swinging her legs. "What would *you* do if you could read minds?" she asked Rose.

Rose, who had her eyes on Kayo, barely gave the question any thought. "Go crazy," she replied. "You gotta kill everyone just to get some quiet. And it ruins all the drama. Half the fun is the lying."

"Drama? Oh—like people arguing," said Sara, nodding sagely.

"Not just *arguing,* it's—you don't get it," Rose said irritably. The girl was distracting her. "People have these whole lives that join together, and nobody knows, not even you, but then you find out in little bits and pieces just listenin' to them talkin' at the water fountains or in line or whatever, an' they all act so nice but every one of 'em's probably got somethin' hidin' in there—"

"They do," Sara assured her. She was watching Kayo too, but only, it seemed, because Rose was. "*Everybody's* interesting, if you listen. I don't like the bad things, though. I like the *good* things."

"Like what?" said Rose, making no effort to hide her scorn. She had no reason to believe there *were* any "good things." People were nice to the people they liked just as they were careful of the objects they liked, but outside of that, they didn't care.

"Yeah," said Sara, and she suddenly sounded much older than she looked. "That's what I hate the most. When they don't care. Some people are just tired. They *can't* care, you know? But other people just...don't want to."

Rose sighed, massaging her temples with one hand. "You *gotta* stop doin' that."

"Sorry."

Alysia had set aside a bowl for herself and given Dominic and Artemis the same two scoops that Rose had gotten. Now she was scraping everything left into a final bowl, until it nearly overflowed. Sara and Rose watched as she brought it to Kayo. *Oh, great,* Rose thought sourly. *The big fake hero gets the biggest bowl because he's* so *important.*

But Kayo barely even glanced at the bowl before turning away. Alysia persisted, crouching next to him as she spoke to him. She was clearly trying to convince him to eat. But he very gently pushed the bowl away, shaking his head. This happened twice more before Alysia finally gave up. She gave Kayo a pointed look, half worry and half irritation, and then set the bowl down right in the middle of the group. Several of the children cheered before practically diving headfirst into the lukewarm porridge.

"What the hell is he *doin'?*" Rose muttered. "Why didn't he want it?"

She'd barely even realized that she'd spoken out loud until Sara replied; perhaps she hadn't. "He *always* does this," she informed Rose, in a tone that seemed to be mimicking someone else. "He wants *us* to have it—well, them. The other kids. Alysia *hates* it."

"So then what's *he* eating?" She swore to the Goddess right then and there that if he was somehow eating better than she was, she was going to march right over there and wring his—

"Nothing, I guess," Sara said, shrugging. "He's hungry. I can tell. I don't *get* it." She was frowning at Kayo as if trying to figure out a puzzle. "He gets so upset about it. But it's just *food.*"

Rose didn't understand either. *Good,* she thought. *Let him be hungry for once.* But the thought brought her no satisfaction. She just wanted to know *why.* It made no sense. Why would—?

Kayo looked up. Rose stiffened as their eyes met—but he simply turned away, as he'd turned away from the food. His smile hitched right back as he leaned in and tickled a little boy who shrieked with laughter.

He'd *dismissed* her. As easily as he'd dismissed a bowl of unappetizing mush.

Rose shoved her empty bowl aside and stood up.

"Hey, wait—you're s'posed to put your bowl up," Sara called desperately after her. "That's the rules! Rose!"

But Rose was already marching right past Kayo with her eyes on the door and her head held high. *Fuck you,* she thought as she left. *Fuck all o' you. I'm outta here.*

S he stepped into a world made of mist, bright but out of focus, like a mote of dust floating in a beam of sunlight. As she walked forward, it formed slowly around her and bloomed into existence. A floor tiled in massive slabs of marble painted with detailed landscapes sprawled before her. Walls of white stone stretched high overhead, ending in a pointed tower so far above that she could barely make out the glittering brass of the bells. Huge windows glowed with blinding sunlight. And there were books—resting in alcoves in the wall, stacked high on wooden shelves, piled in corners like treasure in a dragon's lair. Voices whispered like fluttering pages all around her, drifting through air that smelled faintly of sunlight and glue and ink.

The library of Anapoline—or at least, what Lucy imagined it to look like. It had been destroyed long ago in the fires, but here, in her imagination, it lived on in perfect beauty.

She had always loved this library. It made sense to her: a bright, safe, comfortable space where all the knowledge of the world was at her fingertips, stored in books with messages that would unravel any mystery, if only she could find the right one....

"Lucy!"

She opened her eyes.

Back in the mundane world, one of her sisters was approaching, her worn shoes peeking out from beneath ash-gray robes just like the ones Lucy herself wore. Lucy stood as Prudence beckoned her forward.

"The Highest will see you now."

Lucy followed her in silence down the damp stone corridor; she did not think she could speak if she tried. A lump of nerves was crawling up her throat, a wriggling mass of worms through which no words could pass. Her anxiety heightened sharply as they approached a door set into the far wall. The door was iron-bound wood, just like any other, but Pru shied away from it as if it contained a snarling beast.

"Just through there," she told Lucy. Lucy nodded and reached for the handle, pulling with all her strength against the weight of the door. As she slipped into the room, she heard Pru skittering away down the hall like a frightened mouse.

As the door closed behind Lucy, she stepped into the room. Stone seats curved around the walls, rising up to form a small amphitheater that stretched up to the pointed windows. And at the very front, in the place of honor—

She froze at the sight of the Highest in their black robes.

But they were not alone. The three elderly women were surrounded by others dressed like Lucy: old women, young women, women in their middle years, all of them dressed in varying shades of gray. In the sunlight shining down from the windows, she could see the tattoos sparkling beneath all of their collarbones, swirls of gold and silver inlaid with tiny gems.

"Come forward, Daughter," called one of the Highest in a reedy voice, and Lucy nearly swooned. It was not often that someone of her station was summoned directly by Highest Evanwyn, and even rarer that it ended well for Evanwyn's victim.

Lucy stepped into the middle of the amphitheater, trembling from head to foot. She focused on the floor, inlaid with stone to form a picture of green land spilling across a deep blue sea. She stepped past emerald islands scattered across the blue like a broken string of pearls, past a harsh, rocky coast of pebble beaches and towering cliffs, finally stopping before a castle with smooth, pale walls, backed up to the cliffside, perched atop a city like a tangle of ropes piled high. Bermeia, the city of her birth, though she had not seen it in years.

"Highest," she said, curtsying. "Mothers...Sisters."

"Stand, Lucy," said Evanwyn gently, waving a hand. "You owe no homage to us today."

Lucy stood, but kept her head lowered respectfully, her thick straw-colored hair spilling over her shoulders to hide her face.

"I expect you know why we called you here?"

Lucy looked up, puzzled. Was that humor, at a time like this? From Evanwyn? And indeed, the old woman in the middle was smiling.

"Yes, Highest," she said respectfully. "As you suggested, I have taken a day and a night to think about my choice."

"And...?"

Lucy held her head high, hoping desperately that her fear did not show. "I have not changed my mind," she said firmly. "I volunteer for this task, Highest."

The other women turned to each other, a faint murmur rippling through their ranks. But when the Highest beside Evanwyn straightened her hunched old shoulders and spoke, the entire room fell silent to listen.

"What we ask of you is vital, Daughter," said Callista, speaking slowly and deliberately, her ink-dark eyes boring into Lucy's. "Critical to the future of our Order, and indeed, the future of all the Goddess's children. We would not ask it of anyone unless we had no other choice. But we are running out of time and options, and so we must rely on you to perform a near-impossible task. We must ask you to risk your life, the sanctity of your being, the health of your flesh, the strength of your mind and will, and the innocence of your young soul, alone, without our guidance and support. We must implore you to outwit and outmaneuver a man whose ruthless intellect has engineered countless atrocities. And all for a trifling bit of information."

Lucy shook her head. "It is no trifle, Highest," she protested. "As you said, this information is vital. Not only what we can gain, but what we can keep out of the wrong hands."

The other women murmured amongst themselves again, but Lucy saw smiles and nods of approval and felt heartened. These women were not here to chastise her, she realized. They were here to support her. They were her mothers and sisters not just in name, but in spirit.

"You know what you must do?" asked Evanwyn.

"Yes, Highest," said Lucy.

"Are you confident in your ability to gain his trust?"

"Yes, Highest."

"And your ability to decipher what information he must be told, and what secrets he must never know?"

"Yes, Highest."

"And your ability to convince him that your lies are true?"

"Yes, Highest."

"And your ability to withstand scrutiny, questioning, and torture?"

Lucy swallowed, feeling an icy chill creep in from the thick stone walls. "Yes, Highest," she said, and she was grateful that her voice did not tremble.

Evanwyn nodded, but she still did not seem satisfied. "You have been trained well, Daughter," she said slowly, turning to her fellow Highest in supplication. "You have memorized our teachings and our prophecies. You have a wide arsenal of skills at your disposal. But still, I worry that you do not have the experience necessary for this undertaking. He may be just a man, but I would fear for the safety of any of us at his mercy, even myself and my sisters. I have strong doubts about our decision," she said bluntly. "And none of us would blame you if you felt the same."

Despite Evanwyn's reputation, Lucy was still shocked that she would express her discontent in such a manner. The other women glanced at her, some angry, others nervous, but she could tell that they, too, had their concerns. As did she—but in the end, it had to be done.

"Highest, I am not the most skilled of our Order," she said, allowing her voice to ring clearly around the room. All of the women fell silent, listening closely. "I have never proved myself exemplary among us. And I have only a small fraction of the experience of any of the women in this room. I am well aware of my limitations. However, it was the decision of all the Highest that this undertaking would be best accomplished by someone young and inexperienced like myself. My age is a disguise for my true intentions, and my ignorance is a tool that I can use to conceal the truth. And besides...." She hesitated, then shrugged, eyes downcast. "None of the rest of you can be spared," she said. "But I can."

Some of the women spoke softly among themselves again, but Lucy stood quietly, waiting for the three Highest to speak. For a long, painful moment, the three women regarded her in silence, and her stomach began to twist again as the seconds dragged by.

Finally, Callista leaned forward, reaching out to close one hand around the banister between them. The once-polished ebony of her hand was now dusted with ashen grey, the skin paper-thin with wrinkles like crumpled satin, the arthritic fingers spiderwebbed with delicate veins, but the grip of her callused pink palm was as strong as it had ever been.

"Lucy," she said softly, "my dear child, if all you want is your reward, you may have it. There is no need to risk your life...."

Lucy hesitated, taken aback; she opened her mouth to stammer something, hardly even knowing what that might be. But before she could think of something to say, Vivienne, seated on Evanwyn's other side, brushed her long silver curls carefully over one shoulder and leaned forward, watching Lucy with her piercing green eyes.

"Make no mistake," she said, and though she spoke quietly, her voice rang out like a bell around the room. "This is no simple task, my dear. But I have faith in you." And then she smiled, and the ghost of her old self shone briefly through, the beautiful young woman that she had once been. Age had weighed her down until she could no longer dance, nor run, nor climb a tree, let alone do half the things she had in the stories Lucy had heard, but it had not taken the bright, fervent sweetness from her eyes. She could still be found in the garden most mornings, limping as her old war wounds tried to stymy her, whistling to the flowers as she watered them and chatting cheerfully with the birds and squirrels as she fed them crumbs from her breakfast. "You were chosen not for your abilities, but for your courage and ingenuity. Those are the talents you will need to outwit this wretched man and find the answers we need."

"But, Highest," Lucy protested, flustered, "I was not chosen for this —I volunteered."

Vivienne smiled. "The Goddess has her own ways of doing things," she reminded Lucy. "We can no more understand her mind than a man could understand ours. But I believe that she chose you, Daughter. And that she chose well." She held out her arms, gesturing to the women gathered around them. "All of us are here because we have faith in you. You are never alone, Daughter. We are with you, now and always. You have our strength, our knowledge, and our love to help you."

Lucy, overwhelmed, could not speak. She bowed instead, her heart swelling in her chest.

"Thank you," she finally managed to say. She stood up and looked

at each woman in turn, silently meeting her eyes. "Pray for me, Sisters,"
she said softly. "I will need it."

The women around her nodded solemnly, some of them pressing
their fists to their hearts in a gesture of honor and strength. The three
Highest glanced at one another, and in their eyes, she saw that they were
confirming something with one another, making some sort of decision—
though what that could be, she could not guess.

Then, slowly, creakily, Evanwyn stood. She walked up to Lucy and
took her hands, pressing them firmly between her own.

"Go now, Daughter, and know that our hearts go with you," she
said. And then she bared the stumps of her teeth in a wicked grin. "And
give my regards to the king...."

"My lady?"

She opened her eyes, and her room in the castle swam into focus.

A maidservant was staring at her. Lucy's stomach twisted with
guilt and dread for a split second before she realized that she'd said
nothing aloud. The memory and the secrets it held were still her own,
and no one suspected a thing.

She recognized the servant, a woman named Daphne. She was
deaf, and didn't speak unless she had to. Lucy must have been lost in
her thoughts for quite some time.

"Is something wrong?" she asked, careful to twist her head fully so
Daphne could read her lips clearly.

Daphne hesitated. Lucy's heart sank; judging by the look on her
face, something was very wrong indeed.

"I'll help you get dressed," Daphne said at last. "The king has
summoned you."

Lucy knew she was in trouble the moment she walked in and saw
Romero waiting for her.

He was dressed more formally than he had been when she'd seen
him last, his coat buttoned up to his chin and his gilded sword
dangling at his hip. Not as he would dress to attend a ball or a formal
meeting, but the way he would dress to greet a visitor, perhaps a
wealthy merchant or a nobleman's wife. He stood behind a chair,
which he pulled out for her, making an elegant gesture with one arm.

She stepped away from the kingsguard who escorted her and sat down.

"Your Majesty," she said, and she could hear her voice quiver.

Romero smiled at her. "Lucy." She jumped a little to hear his voice say her name. "Thank you for joining me."

A servant came forward with a pitcher of wine. Romero waved her away and poured it himself, filling two silver goblets with the bright golden liquid. He offered one to Lucy, and she took it, knowing it was likely the last bit of sweetness she would find for a long time. She could see her fate as clear as day, and knew she was all too likely to end up in a prison cell before the sun set.

The Divinæ made their own wine, with the exception of a small section of the wine cellar filled with rarer vintages given as gifts over the years. But those had always been reserved for the Highest and the eldest of the Sisters. Lucy had never tried anything truly special—until now. The sweet white wine, fragrant and strong, was almost persuasion enough to change her mind on the spot. She clutched the cup with both hands, wishing she had the strength to push it away. That had likely been his plan all along: to give her a taste of luxury in her private suite before he snatched it all back. He'd even sent dresses like the beautiful one she wore now, a welcome change from the drab, filthy robe she'd worn for months on end.

"Our conversation the other day was interrupted," he said. He had not touched his own wine. She might have feared that hers was poisoned—if there had been any purpose to him doing so. He could do anything he wanted to her, and no one in this room or in the world around it would lift a finger to stop him. "Of course, after traveling for so long, you needed a bit of rest. But I'm pleased that we have a chance to continue now."

Lucy watched the sunlight cast sparkling golden motes across the surface of her wine. *Just ask it,* she thought. *Just get it over with.*

When she didn't speak, he continued. "It occurred to me," he said, "that we must reevaluate our positions, you and I, if we aim to understand one another a bit better. True, I am a king, and you come from a...different sort of background. But you are a Divina. And that makes you very powerful indeed."

He seemed to want her to respond, so she nodded. "I know the

Divinæ were considered very highly by the crown before you banished them."

If he regretted that decision, he didn't show it in the slightest. He gestured to another servant, who slid a tray of cakes and tarts between them.

"They were. And they still could be. Perhaps I was too hasty in banishing the Divinæ outright. Perhaps the kings before me were wise to have a Divina at their sides."

Lucy waited, sensing that there was more. Romero poured more wine into their cups, though she'd barely drunk from hers.

"I know you're young and not high in the order. But you have the same abilities as any other Divina, do you not? I can't imagine what it must be like. These gifts must seem like a burden to you at times. As if you've lived a hundred lives before this one." He swirled his wine absently in his goblet, though his eyes never left hers. "And knowing the future, even just glimpses...how can a person even live that way? I don't know how you aren't paralyzed with all the possibilities. And I'm sure it's thankless, as well. No one is ever grateful to the bearer of bad news."

He took a sip of wine, and she was grateful for the moment's respite. It took everything in her to remember that he was just telling her what he thought she wanted to hear. That he didn't actually feel the sympathy and understanding he conveyed. He was charming her, that was all.

But he was very, very charming.

"And the Divinæ don't seem to appreciate you either, do they? They just kidnapped you to possess you, because they think everyone with your abilities belongs to them. They'll say it was for your own good, but it wasn't. It was for theirs. And for what? So you could be their errand girl, or their glorified servant? With abilities like yours, you should be able to do whatever you like."

She closed her fingers around a handful of her dress under the table.

He doesn't know. He can't possibly know. How would he know?

No. He was guessing.

Accurately.

The king continued as if nothing were amiss.

"There are so few of you as well—and your abilities are unique, to say the least. I imagine if given the chance, every one of you could become a powerful and influential member of her community on her own." His gaze drifted lazily to the window, but she knew he was tracking her every movement out of the corner of his eye. "Perhaps I could work with the Divinæ again and make that happen. Perhaps I should reach out to them and try to restore things to how they were—or something better." He looked down at his wine, swirled it idly, took a sip. "Rafael had an interesting plan for a public place of learning, backed with gold from the crown. The Divinæ could benefit nicely from an influx of gold and a place to interact with the community, instead of scurrying around in the shadows like rats. That sort of behavior is demeaning to women of your influence. Don't you think?"

He paused, clearly waiting for an answer. But she didn't know what answer he wanted. She didn't know why he was saying this at all. To manipulate her, certainly—but to what end? After a moment's consideration, she risked a hesitant nod.

His pleasant smile reappeared. "Yes, of course. And won't that be a magnificent accolade for you, being the one who arranged for it all to happen? That is, if you care for such things. I would understand completely if the approval of the Divinæ doesn't matter to you anymore. They must have upset you if you ran from them, and they've made no attempt to get you back....Do you even *want* to go back?"

"Of course," said Lucy, struggling to keep her voice steady.

He nodded, as if this was the answer he had expected. "It's remarkably admirable to feel loyalty to them even now. While I don't understand, I commend you for your dedication." He paused for a beat, his fingers tracing the edge of his goblet. "It's not as if anyone would blame you for wanting a different life."

She lowered her eyes to her hands, trying hard to block out his words. But it was no use. They wriggled into her head like earwigs, latching on, refusing to let go.

She'd seen a touch of the king's violent temper—but that was not, she realized, what made him truly dangerous. He kept that hidden and secret, a tool that he could pull out when all other strategies had failed. No—*this* was how he had gained his power, how he had kept it for so long. Honeyed words, flattery, bribery, and a knack for reading minds that nearly rivaled her own abilities. He charmed the unwary with his courtly manners and his undeniable good looks until he got what he wanted—or sussed out enough sensitive information to sour his bribes into threats.

"As lovely a woman as you are—if you'll pardon me saying so—with talents such as yours, you could have any life you dreamed. You'd only need a bit of gold...and a good relationship with the crown never hurt. You could do anything you wanted, anything at all. You could have the kind of power and freedom that most women couldn't even imagine."

She could see it in his mind as he pictured it. He knew what a life of wealth and influence was like, what it felt like to gain that power. To discover how many things the peasantry took as a matter of course could disappear with a snap of the fingers. To speak and watch those words mold the world like wet clay, shaping it to her desires....

Stop talking, she begged him silently, squeezing her eyes shut. *Stop talking, stop talking, stop talking.*

He paused again, watching her. She didn't trust herself to speak.

After a minute of silence, he refilled her wine again.

"So, Lucy. What did you dream your life would be before you joined the Divinæ? Did you ever dream of traveling the world and experiencing all it has to offer? Meeting every fascinating person in the Peninsula? The food, the wine, the music, the dancing....Did you ever want that life for yourself? Or did you have something different in mind?"

He paused to take another sip of wine. But this time, his eyes bored into hers, and he let the silence linger. He wanted an answer.

Lucy took a deep breath, her eyes still fixed on her hands.

"I'm afraid I would only waste your time if I expounded on what I want, Your Majesty," she said quietly. "It's meaningless if I can give you nothing in return."

"Nothing?" He laughed aloud. "I've seen your talents at work. To say they are impressive is an understatement. They're *formidable.* We could do a lot for each other, you and I."

She risked a glance upward. His entire demeanor seemed relaxed and pleasant—but she knew it wouldn't remain that way if she refused him. He'd turn ugly very quickly.

Goddess, but she wished she didn't have to.

It took all her courage to speak up.

"Your Majesty...I know what you want from me," she said. "I know what you're going to ask...."

"Do you?" His smile never wavered. "How could you? I don't even know myself."

"Yes, you do," she said, speaking to the table in front of her. "You're debating if you should ask me about this person you're convinced is behind all the unrest in Bermeia—but you don't need me for that. You already know who he is, and you don't care *where* he is. Because he'll be irrelevant if I...if I can find...."

She trailed off—but Romero was watching her. Waiting. She swallowed.

"I'm sorry, Your Majesty. I'm afraid it is impossible."

"Impossible? I think not." He didn't even take a moment to consider the idea. "Not for a woman with your abilities."

"But it *is*." She straightened her back, folded her hands in her lap, and looked him straight in the eye. If she was going to do the thing, she may as well do it properly.

This was, however, a mistake. His expression was so calm, so friendly, so disarming, that for a moment she wondered if she'd been wrong about him. If everything she'd learned about him had been a lie. Every horrible thing she knew he'd done seemed like a dream of a dream, distant and irrelevant.

Goddess above. Was she going mad?

It took her a moment to gather her thoughts again. "Do you like to look at the stars, Your Majesty?" she asked him. She was suddenly and overwhelmingly grateful that she had known beforehand what he would ask, that she had had time to think through her answer and rehearse her response.

"I should think everyone does, when they are able," he replied.

"Of course. Well, a star is nothing more than a tiny pinprick of light. Quite simple, really. But there are countless thousands of them —millions, even. One could spend a lifetime counting them through a spyglass and still never reach the end of them. And those are only the ones that we see. There are many others that are too dim to shine among the rest. And in a few weeks, the skies will shift, and even more stars will appear.

"People are the same to us. When we look at them from afar, we see everyone alive, and many who are dead. We could focus on any of them, explore the twists and turns and choices and possibilities of each in the present moment, and with their past behind them. *And* their future. When a person's made their choices, the other doors all close behind them—but when those choices are in the future, there are hundreds of thousands. All the things that could happen if the right conditions are met branch out like a tree until a person comes along and chooses their path. New choices are created every instant, for every person on this earth. It can be...overwhelming."

Romero listened closely, frowning a little as he did. When she paused, he nodded slowly, taking a deep draught from his goblet. His eyes followed the waterfall of gold that flowed from jug to cup as he poured himself another.

"I'm afraid that I don't understand your point," he finally said.

"There is a young boy," Lucy told him, "who might die today, in just a few minutes, right here in the lower city. He is two or three, a darling little child, and he likes chickens. He likes to chase them, catch them, and pet them like cats. Some of them tolerate this, but some of them don't, and when they run from him, he runs after them. He has been warned many times not to chase them into the street, but he is very young, and he is not yet able to focus on his task and his surroundings simultaneously. Right now, he is playing with the chickens. In a few minutes, if he chooses the spotted one instead of the white one, he will chase it out onto the street and be struck by a runaway cart."

She looked up at Romero, but he merely blinked, a little confused but waiting patiently for her conclusion. She should not have been surprised. She doubted that the man even knew how to feel the shock and sadness and dismay and injustice and frustration that any normal human being felt at the idea of a small child's death.

"But that cart will only lose control," she continued, "if the owner slips on an oily patch of stone. And the oil will only be there if the blacksmith's apprentice trips and stubs his toe while carrying the barrel to the forge. And he will only do that if he is late and in a hurry, which will only happen if he runs into the girl he likes on his way to the well and gathers the courage to speak to her, which, on most days, he cannot. And she will only be there if...." She trailed off, shaking her head. "You get the idea. And as time passes, the possibilities narrow down, and I can start to see his future clearly. By now, the oil has already been spilled, but the cart hasn't yet slipped on it. He could still easily live or die—but if any one of those things had not happened, there would be no question. If any of these events had changed, then that little boy would live to see tomorrow. And who knows what he could become?

"And that is true for...*everyone*. Every living person, and there are as many as stars in the sky. I could choose any of them and tell a story just like this one, with all its different endings. But finding one in particular, with no guidance? It would be like choosing one of the stars without knowing where to start looking or what you're looking for or even if it exists."

"That isn't impossible," Romero said quietly.

"Perhaps not. But it is extremely difficult, and has a very low chance of success. I would be working utterly blind. So, you see my dilemma."

"Not completely blind," he pointed out. "You aren't starting with nothing, Lucy. I am not quite certain what you need, but whatever it is, you have it. You're sitting in the castle where he was born. You know his name, his parent's names, his entire family tree. You'll even have items that he touched."

She shook her head. "Those things don't help me. Those are all things I could find out if I knew where he was, or what he looks like, or what he might be doing. But it doesn't work the other way. It's not as if he's going about announcing who he is. It's possible he doesn't even know. Children don't form stable memories until they're four or five years of age. And if he can't remember any connection to the information I have, then even if I do stumble across him, he won't know anything that could tell me so."

Romero switched tactics without hesitation. "Then you can find his mother. That would be just as useful. He'll return here with her—"

"She doesn't know where he is."

Romero stiffened, leaning forward. "How do you know that? You've seen her?"

"No. But...." She chose her next words with great care. "This is a woman known to every royal and noble in the Peninsula by face and name, and by reputation to many of the common folk as well. A former queen. She can't pass through this world unnoticed. I don't know where she is exactly, but I do know that everywhere she goes, she searches for her son." And Goddess, she could feel the woman's pain from here, even after so long. "If she'd found him, she'd stop looking."

"It could be a trick," Romero pointed out, but he didn't seem convinced. "She and that brother of hers—but fine. Let's focus on what you have available to you here."

"That's indicative of the larger problem, I'm afraid. He *was* here. He was known to be here. But the connection between where he was and where he is now simply isn't there. No one knows what happened to him."

"Yes, I am aware." It took work to keep his voice under control; she could hear the strain. "I lost the trail years ago. But I'm not a *Divina*. Surely you can see what happened the night he disappeared if you—"

"I *have* seen it."

Romero gripped the edge of the table so hard that his fingers turned white. He spoke softly, barely above a whisper. "And?"

She looked him straight in the eyes. She couldn't deny the terror she felt watching his cold gaze fix on her. But the fear itself caused her no harm. *It must be done, so do it. And if you're afraid, do it afraid.*

"The queen fled the castle," she said. "In the company of several guards, with her son in her arms, in the middle of a stormy night. She knew the storm would slow your men down when you sent them to find her. But she and her companions knew there would be soldiers waiting at the gates, keeping a lookout for a woman with a child. So they split up. Serena left the city on her own while some of her companions took the child, to smuggle him out on a ship. But your men caught up with them. There was a fight...." She closed her eyes, focusing. "The man with the baby...he hides the child, then joins the fight. But then he falls. He dies. Only two men are left alive—the queen's men. They're searching, but they don't know where the child is hidden. And even when they find the hiding place, the baby is gone. He crawled away...."

She opened her eyes again. Romero stared at her, clearly shaken.

"But—you *saw* him! He was right there!"

"He was. But he was a baby," said Lucy. "They don't form memories. When Serena's men lost track of him, so did I. Finding him now, seventeen years later, would be like finding a grain of salt in the ocean sands. And that's if he still lives."

Romero's lips were pressed in a thin line, his nostrils flared. "So that's it, then," he said. "You refuse to do it."

"I...I'm afraid I *can't.*"

"I see."

There was a long, horrible pause. Then Romero drained his goblet in one long gulp and rose to his feet. His eyes were already looking past her, through her.

"Then we have nothing left to discuss."

And he turned his back on her and walked away.

Lucy looked up to the ceiling, praying silently to the Goddess for strength. She had a choice before her now, one that she'd known she'd have to make, one that she'd desperately hoped she wouldn't have to. If she was of no use to Romero, then he would kill her. It was as simple as that. But if she did as he asked....

Save the prince. Save the secrets of the Divinæ. Save her own skin. There was no way to do it all.

"But I could try," she said.

Romero paused with his hand on the latch. Waiting.

"I doubt I can find him before he comes of age." She averted her eyes, twisting the fabric of her borrowed dress between her hands beneath the table. "Perhaps I won't even find him during your lifetime. But I can try."

He was watching her, but she didn't dare look up. She hardly dared to breathe. She didn't need her gift to sense what he was thinking, which options he was weighing.

"So then," he said at last, "I suppose we're right back where we started."

"A-are we?" she stammered down at her hands.

He sighed—but he turned around, at least. Considering it. Considering her.

"I won't force you to do it, girl," he told her. "I can't. But I can offer you motivation. Find him, and I'll ask nothing more of you. I'll give you anything that is within my power to give you and send you on your way."

"And...and if I don't?"

Lucy looked up—and regretted it instantly. The look on his face turned her blood to ice. It was a stony mask with just the barest hint of contempt, the eyes blank and cold. The face of a man who would order her dead and watch it done without so much as blinking.

"Then he'll find me," he said. A short, harsh laugh escaped him, but it didn't reach his eyes. "And then what will I need you for?"

She swallowed. So there it was. Her voice broke as she finally gave in.

"I'll try."

"Excellent." Suddenly he was all charm again, all business, his expression arranging into something pleasantly neutral as if he'd never threatened her at all. "I greatly appreciate your efforts, Lucy. What do you require to begin?"

"Well...." She was tempted to ask for a large open field, a crystal ball, a dozen human sacrifices, and a vial of his blood, just to see what would happen. But she was afraid he might actually do it. "Is there anyone who knew the prince well? A servant who cared for him, perhaps?"

"Of course there is. I'm right here."

She winced. "Um—you?"

"Who else? He was my nephew. I was there when he was born, I lived here while he was a baby. What is it you need?"

"I...um...." She hadn't expected him to volunteer himself. She didn't particularly want to speak with him or be around him.

But no—this was a good thing. A chance to probe for further information. To lay the groundwork for her larger purpose. She steeled herself, straightened her back.

"Sit down, please," she said, gesturing to the table. "And give me your hands."

He did as she asked without question. He held out his hands, and she took them in hers, closing her eyes.

The Divinæ had taught her this. When people like her were viewed as envoys of the Goddess, mystical and powerful beings with unknowable power, a little bit of mystique went a long way. She didn't need to touch him anymore than she needed to dim the lights or wait for a thunderstorm. She didn't need to speak in tongues, either, but she whispered a mantra in Ancient Lyric anyway to help her focus.

"Soihlasich an durchad, glan a céo, fosgail ad shuleàn, noch an fachad léo. Siohlasich an durchad..."

But all she needed was to see what was already around her. Romero Sangor's hands were warm and smooth, but she felt rough calluses on his fingers. They were from hunting and swordplay, two crafts he had honed to a sharp point over the years, but they were fading from lack of practice. The ring on his hand was heavy, and she felt a permanent indent in his finger from it. It couldn't be comfortable to wear so much. What if it provided some sort of comfort to him, a tangible symbol that he was king? All his talk about power... was he afraid to let it go?

"...glan a céo..."

Focus.

She could glimpse inside his head, just a little. A near-unsettling calm, born from the confidence that she couldn't hurt him, was spoiled just a little from the anticipation of what she might find. And dread—he wanted to find the prince, but he was afraid of what would happen next. Something to do with Serena, and with the former king...Rel, Romero called him, Rafael....

"...fosgail ad shuleàn..."

Oh, but there was something lurking there, all right—something that he didn't want to think about. He was pushing a different memory to the forefront. A stormy night on horseback, galloping through the streets at breakneck speeds, ordering his men to all corners of the city. To find the prince, who—

"...noch an fachad léo..."

He wasn't concentrating hard enough. The memory slid into another just beneath the surface: another stormy night, only days earlier, watching a little family play on the rug. It was a room in the castle, without a doubt, but not one she had seen before. A Savillan woman and an Alronelinian man, both dressed in fine clothing, chased a crawling baby on hands and knees. The former king and queen, and the baby prince. She heard their laughter, and she felt pain —not theirs, but his, Romero's, squashed down deep so he'd never have to face it. Someone else lurked nearby—someone familiar, someone hated. Who?

"Soihlasich an durchad…"

Another memory leaked in through the windows, soaking the carpet like water from the raging storm, darkening and warping the little family. Waiting, tense and anxious, in that same room, watching the king pace back and forth, avoiding the eyes of that same lurking man half-hidden in the corner. Silently worrying for hours on end that she would die, knowing the other two were worrying about exactly the same thing. The dread when the king was summoned. The relief at hearing the sharp, squealing cry of a newborn from the other room….

"…glan a céo…"

Further. His darkest day, though the sun was shining and music was playing. A wedding. The queen standing before a crowd, so beautiful she took his breath away. The king—his brother Rafael—claiming the crown, then the woman, that were his by right. Sneaking off to his rooms, blind drunk, sobbing, knowing that she was bedding another man.

"…fosgail ad shuleàn…"

The stormy night again, the horse and the dark city. Freezing rain pouring in sheets down his back. A long, miserable, bitter night—and at the end of it, he was left with nothing. Serena had escaped. That man who lurked in the shadows had disappeared—

Sergio, that's his name. But who is he?

—and so had the child. But he had a plan. She saw a building in the lower city, something to do with her own kind, the Divinæ —saw him giving swift orders, sending men galloping away…to find the prince…the prince…who—

"…noch an fach—"

And then another memory reared, striking her like a physical blow. She tensed as it crashed over her, drowning her, screaming like the winds of the storm in her ears. The building again, the darkness and dust inside, a soldier pointing him into a room. Walking in and finding nothing but a crib—and inside, a baby boy. The baby recognized him and sat up, crying, reaching up for him, hungry and soiled and frightened. The crying twisted into Romero's brain like a corkscrew, and rage flared within him, bright and violent—

And then he staggered back from the crib. Blood was everywhere —staining the blanket in the crib, coating his hands, dripping onto the floor. Someone was speaking, but he couldn't understand them. His eyes were fixed on the little body in the crib, lying very still. He could remember the feeling of bones snapping beneath his fingers, remember seeing the life leaving the bright brown eyes—

"NO!"

Lucy snatched her hands back and recoiled, stumbling over the chair, knocking it over as she scrambled to her feet. Her ribs were closing in on her lungs and strangling the breath from her. She stared in horror at Romero. The blood on his hands, there had been so much blood, and she had *touched* them, how was it possible that it hadn't stained her own skin? She scrubbed her fingers against her dress and backed away, fighting the urge to be sick.

"You monster!" she screamed at him. "It was a *baby,* just a *baby,* how *could* you? How *could* you?! You're twisted, you're *evil,* you—"

In a sudden surge of power Romero jumped to his feet, sending the table tumbling to the floor, wine and tarts and silver flying everywhere. She flinched at the crash and backed away, tripping over her own feet, clumsy in their borrowed slippers. But then she hit the wall, and there was nowhere else to go.

In two quick strides he crossed the room, and she found herself pinned against the wall.

"I told you," he said, his voice dangerously soft, "to *find him.*"

"I did," she whimpered. She struggled, but his grip was too strong, and his entire weight pinned her to the stone. "I saw you kill him."

The rage bled from his face. She felt his grip slacken, saw his eyes widen. His voice was a hoarse croak.

"I did?"

"What are you—? What are you *talking* about? I *saw* you, And I saw—the blood—"

"No—no." He backed away from her. One hand rose to brush distractedly through his hair, and he turned away, shaking his head. "No—I didn't. I don't—I don't remember, I—that was a dream!" He rounded on her, his face twisted in rage, and lashed out with one arm. A vase on the sideboard shattered as the whole thing toppled to the ground. "That was a *dream!* Damn you, girl, can't you tell the difference? Who gave you permission to dig around in my skull? How *dare* you? I should have you strung up as an example to the other witches, I ought to flay your skin off your back myself!"

"I'm sorry," she sobbed. "I'm sorry—ow!"

He grabbed her wrist and twisted it, forcing her onto her toes. Blinding pain shot up her arm as he yanked her close.

"*Find him,*" he hissed in her ear. "*Before* he comes of age. Or your precious Divinæ will never find all the little pieces of *you.*"

And he shoved her away, letting go. She lost her balance and tumbled to the floor. Pain blossomed from her shoulder, blinding her, and she gasped for breath between the wrenching sobs forcing their way out of her.

"Get her out of my sight." Romero's voice seemed to echo from a fast distance, dim and muted beneath the whining in her ears. "And keep her there until she has something to tell me."

But then she heard his footsteps retreating and heard the door slam. He was gone.

Someone rushed over, and she flinched as they reached for her—but it wasn't Romero. It was his attendant. Maximilian.

"It's all right—it's all right," he murmured as he helped her to her feet. "Are you hurt?"

"M-my arm—"

"Don't try to move it. Sit here—just there—good. I'll fetch something to drink, wait here."

She let him steer her to the other side of the room and sit her on a different chair, one that had not been overturned in the altercation. She didn't move her arm—but her other hand gripped her shoulder so hard that her fingers tingled. She couldn't make herself let go. Some primal part of her was convinced that the arm would fall off if she did.

She stared at the soiled rug, at the scattered cakes and the wine-stained cloth on the upturned table. She was trembling, but she couldn't stop. She couldn't block the sight of his face from her mind, so close to hers and twisted in fury, or his shouting voice—or the memory she'd dredged up.

A dream, he'd said. Could that be true? He certainly believed it to be. Her mind raced as it tried to make sense of it all. That building—she recognized it. It had once been a hospital for the Divinæ, a place where sick people could stay and be healed. But she'd heard years ago, before she'd even joined them, that the Divinæ had been forced out so it could be turned into an orphanage. No one was quite sure what that meant exactly, but the rumor was that bad children were sent there, branded like criminals and locked up for the rest of their lives.

He'd set up the orphanage like a spider laying a web, a repository for stray children that might stumble across the missing prince. And when they'd found him, he'd gone to the orphanage and killed him.

Or—had he?

What she'd seen had been intense, charged with emotion, heightened by fear—but it hadn't made sense. If Romero had murdered a child and then walked out of the orphanage with blood on his hands, wouldn't someone have seen him? How could the rumors not have spread after such an event? And wouldn't Romero himself have known he'd done it? Why would he ask her to look for the prince if he knew he was dead?

And so much about the vision had been...*off*. Who had been speaking to him? What had they been saying? She could have sworn it was a woman's voice. And that horrible feeling of bones crushing under his fingers—he only remembered the feeling of it. He didn't remember *doing* it. There was no memory of what he'd done at all, only the aftermath.

A dream, he'd said. She wasn't sure about that—but whatever it was, he was working hard to suppress it. She hadn't sensed much in the way of guilt, but the memory certainly caused him distress.

What had happened?

And where was the prince?

By the time Maximilian returned, Lucy had pulled herself together a little bit. She accepted with gratitude a sip of strong liquor before sipping at the punch he'd brought for her. He tied a sash to her wrist and around her neck in a makeshift sling, then summoned Daphne to bring her back to her rooms. She had the feeling he'd done this many times before.

Once in her rooms, Lucy let Daphne undress her and tie her arm in a proper sling. She was left in just her chemise on the window seat, pressing a cold compress to her shoulder. Her window looked out onto a short stretch of scrubby grass that dropped off abruptly into the sea. She shivered as the cool breeze snaked under her chemise, but stayed where she was.

So Romero wanted to use her gifts to find the prince. The Highest had expected as much when they had sent her to intersect Auna. She'd been instructed to keep this from happening at any cost —because whatever Romero would do with the only person alive who could challenge his power, it would not be pleasant. If he got his hands on the boy, those hands would immediately wrap around his throat.

But the Divinæ didn't know where the prince was, either.

She'd planned to feign ignorance, to pretend that finding the prince was impossible. But faced with that decision—with the threat of imprisonment and death waiting to drop like a headsman's ax— she'd made a different choice. To play along.

To use the resources and gold Romero had hinted at.

To find the prince for herself.

That, she was certain, was the only way to keep him out of Romero's hands until he could take his throne.

And this was a clue. These memories of Romero's—especially the last one. If it had any basis in reality at all, that meant that Romero was the last person to see the prince and know who he was. He was the last stable link in a chain she meant to follow right to the boy's feet. She had to find out what happened. She had to know more.

The pain in her shoulder was terrible—it was almost certainly sprained or torn—but she could handle it. Romero's was not the first tender ego that she'd had to tiptoe around.

She'd swallowed her fear today. Found her courage and stared down a king, lied to his face, defied him, denied him—even shouted at him. The pain was nothing compared to the exhilaration it brought.

I did that.

I really did that.

And if she'd done it once, she could do it again.

She traced the diamonds embedded in her collarbones with her fingertips as she looked up at the stars.

Keep praying for me, Sisters. I think it's working.

R ose had never slept in a real bed before.

That can't be right, she kept thinking as she sat at the edge of the bed in the room that was, supposedly, hers. *There's gotta be once.*

But no matter how hard she racked her brain, she could not conjure a memory of a real bed. Not even a mattress, really. She'd slept on a lot of surfaces—and on a lot of objects—but none of them were quite this large and this soft. The flour sacks might have been close— or the hay pile.

This mattress had hay in it, she guessed. But wrapped in linen like this, it was far less likely to poke her in odd places. Still, she couldn't bring herself to lie down on it. It might be *too* soft. What if it turned *her* soft? What if she couldn't wake up if someone attacked her? Or what if she got too used to it and could never sleep on a floor again?

She cast an uneasy glance at the open door. The night-shrouded garden waited just out of reach beyond the balustrade, unnaturally dark and still to eyes accustomed to a restless city.

Truthfully, the bed and windows were the least of her worries. This room *had* to be a trap. She'd checked, and Dominic was right: the door latch didn't lock. The door opened inward, so she could always barricade it, or break the latch like Liam had. But then she'd be trapped in a smallish room not much larger than her cell had been, and what good did *that* do her? The big window opened out onto a steep drop, so that was only an option if she wanted to break all her bones on the cliffside before falling into the ocean. And the other window—

She froze, frowning at that patch of wall. She'd half-glanced that way and thought it was a window—but into *what?* She could see straight through the murky glass into another room just like her own. But how was that possible?

And someone was there. She could see someone lurking just out of sight, could make out the hem of a skirt and a scuffed brown boot.

She jumped up—then paused.

The stranger's skirt was made from olive green wool, and the cut of it seemed very familiar to her. Was that—?

It *was.*

It was *her.*

She nearly laughed aloud with relief. A *mirror.* Somehow, the orphans had gotten hold of a mirror. It sat abandoned in the corner, waist-high and absurdly ornate.

She stepped toward it. The ghostly reflection mimicked her every move as she approached the dappled surface and sank, slowly, to her knees. She recognized the hair, the dress, the glimmer of gold around her neck.

That's me, she thought. *That's* me.

The girl in the mirror looked younger than eighteen—which Rose nearly was. She had skin lightly tanned from the spring sunlight, a spattering of freckles, and a button nose. She was just as skinny as the orphans that she'd thought looked half-starved, with a gaunt cast to her eyes and cheekbones and collarbones jumping out of her skin like concealed weapons. Her hair was a cascade of messy curls around her shoulders in red and copper and orange and gold.

Her first reaction was shock. She'd known these things about herself, objectively: that she had no figure to speak of, that her hair was reddish (or had been last she'd checked), that she had freckles. But *seeing* it—seeing *herself*—

A shiver zipped through her from head to toe, and her stomach swooped. She couldn't put a name to the feeling swelling inside of her and trying to burst free of her chest, but it felt the same as looking at the stars.

She leaned forward, mouth open in amazement, and gingerly

touched the surface of the mirror. She jumped a little, startled by how cold it was, but then reached out and touched the freckles on her reflected cheeks.

I have green eyes, she thought. She'd never known that.

On a sudden and irresistible whim, she tugged the laces free on her dress. She wriggled out of it and the chemise and left them in a heap on the floor, kneeling in front of the mirror. Her hair fell over her shoulder, and she brushed it out of the way, inspecting every inch of her bare skin.

This girl is me.

Her reflection wasn't perfect. She didn't have a pretty face or silky hair like Artemis, and her bony figure would never rival Artemis's curves. And unlike Alysia, she didn't look prettier when she smiled. Her front teeth turned in slightly, and her smile looked more like a grimace. Her skin was far from flawless, and she found more than a few scars from injuries she'd forgotten about. Underneath the bloodied linen still knotted around her arm, there would probably soon be another.

But they were hers. All *hers.*

A soft noise from the corridor made her jump. The door was closed, but she took no chances. She dressed again, too hastily, getting herself tangled up in the laces. When she'd at last tugged it all into place, she paused, listening hard. Then, when she didn't hear anything, she opened the door and peeked out. The corridor was deserted.

She must have imagined the sound—but her nerves were still on edge. The night was too quiet, too still, and the shadows were too deep. She tried to shut the door and sit on the bed again, calm herself down, but her skin crawled until she wanted to scream. She threw open the door again just so she could breathe.

There was no way she could sleep in that room. She stormed out into the corridor—then stopped. Bit her lip. Looked around.

Where the hell could she *go?*

She couldn't leave. Half the place was rigged with traps, and the other half was full of people who wanted her dead. Locking herself in her room was probably the only way to keep herself safe while she slept—but she couldn't do it. The orphans had lured her in there with the promise of a soft bed, but who knew what they would do when she was asleep? At the end of the day, the room was just a fancier cell.

She finally hauled the mirror across the rug and propped it up, where it would be visible even from outside. Then she settled herself against the balustrade outside, her back to a pillar, with the blanket from the bed wrapped around her. From there she could look out onto the garden below. It was too dark to see much, but in the morning, she wanted to find a way down there and see it all. The faint chittering of insects filled the still air. It was nothing like the murmur of distant voices and the clatter of wheels on stone and the occasional roar of laughter or song from a tavern and the cries of gulls and the hiss of wind through narrow crevices between the buildings—but it would do.

She made herself comfortable, but she didn't try and sleep. She didn't even close her eyes. She listened to the noises of the dark garden and looked into the mirror.

That was the first shock, but not the last. It had been a long time since she'd taken a good look at her own body. It had changed since then, grown in ways she had never dreamed it could. She'd been so busy just surviving that she'd given no thought at all to growing up; in her mind, she still looked exactly the same as she'd always pictured. And yet, in the blink of an eye, her body had grown into someone she didn't recognize.

The girl in the mirror was skinny, and had her share of scars, but she didn't belong on the streets. Her dress was too neat, her hair and skin too clean. Gone was the specter who'd haunted the streets, scrounging for scraps in midden heaps and jumping at every sound like a feral cat. This girl looked like someone with a home, with parents, with somewhere to go and someone waiting for her there. This girl looked like someone who'd be missed.

This girl looked...loved.

It was just an illusion—but it made her wonder. She'd told herself, every time she dreamed of a life like that, that she'd regret it, that it would make her soft. But the girl in the mirror didn't *look* soft. She looked fierce and strong and disturbingly feminine, with hair that spilled like fire down her back.

Fire burned in her eyes, too. She'd seen it burn. She'd felt it rise in her, felt it flare and burn—and she'd felt it flicker and die in the cell. But it wasn't gone. It had come back stronger than ever.

The girl in the mirror had battled dozens of people who'd wanted to hurt her—and she'd won. That was a fact, and her scars would prove it. There was no fear in that girl.

This girl is me.

She reached up and held the pendant of her necklace in her hand. The edges of the petals dug into her palm as she squeezed it tight.

Fire, she thought. *Never fear.*

Fire. Never fear.

Fire. Never fear.

Fire....

When Dominic returned to the kitchen, the other three—Kayo, Artemis, and Alysia—were sitting at the table and passing around a bottle of wine. He took his spot between Kayo and Artemis, wrapping his arm around Artemis's waist and kissing her cheek.

"Kids all right?" Kayo tried to sound casual as he looked away from them, but not hard enough. Dominic snatched the bottle of wine out of his hand and took a deep drink.

"Took ages to get the baby down," he grumbled when he finally came up for air. "Goddess, I'm beat."

"What were you up to all day?" Artemis asked him.

"Nothin' much. Went down to the lower city, hauled some cargo for this guy who didn't ask a lotta questions—oh. Here." He dug into his pocket and slapped a few cuprums onto the table.

"That's great!" said Alysia with an enthusiasm that such a small amount didn't really deserve. *Bless her,* he thought fondly as he watched her count the coins with a fingertip before sweeping them off the table and into her pocket.

"Oh, and I ran into Rose skulking around," he added.

He expected Kayo to raise a fuss about this, but he merely snorted and took the wine back. "Yeah, she made the rounds," he confirmed. "Snooped the whole place out by the looks of it."

"You followed her?" said Artemis, raising an eyebrow.

"*Of course* I followed her," Kayo snapped. "Have all of you gone mad? Did you forget how *dangerous* she is?"

"Dangerous," Dominic scoffed. "She's six stone soaking wet—"

"She knows *everything about us.* And she also *hates us.* Remember?" He pointed angrily to his face—his split lip, his bruised nose and jaw. Dominic had to choke back a laugh.

"It's not funny!"

"Not to you." He snickered and reached for the wine bottle, which Kayo snatched away. "Just to me."

"No, it isn't!" Alysia protested.

But Artemis was laughing too. "Sorry, but you deserved it," she informed Kayo, with the vicious and pitiless honesty that Dominic so loved. "Why couldn't you just leave her alone?"

"I—she—if she hadn't been *threatening* us all the damn time—"

"Kayo, just let it go," Dominic advised him. He'd learned ages ago that once the two women teamed up on something, the battle was lost. "You're not going to win this one."

"I'm not trying to *win!*" Kayo had the same look on his face that he'd had so often as a kid, when he'd been bullied or punished unfairly and he couldn't decide whether to hit someone or burst into tears. "I'm just—she's dangerous, you didn't see her—"

"I saw plenty." Dominic scratched nonchalantly at his scalp until Artemis pulled his hand away. "When you were passed out she tore us a new one, it was terrifying."

"She tried to kill me with *shears!* She's unhinged! We can't trust her around the *kids*—"

"She seems way more scared of the kids than they are of her, if you ask me," Artemis said drily.

"They *are* a lot to handle all at once," Alysia reasoned, pausing to take a very long pull on the wine bottle. "They leave me shattered just about every day. All of this must be so overwhelming for her."

"You're feeling *sorry* for her?" Kayo demanded, his voice rising uncontrollably. "She's *killed* people! More than one! She told me herself!"

This didn't get the reaction he seemed to be expecting. Artemis and Dominic looked at each other for a moment before Artemis rested her head on his shoulder. Alysia grimaced, but set the wine bottle down onto the table with a firm *clack* and turned to Kayo with a look that said he was about to get a good scolding.

"Artemis and I," she informed Kayo, "found Rose to be perfectly pleasant, once she got comfortable around us. She just didn't know how to act around people. We're guessing she hasn't been around them very much. You didn't see her when we were helping her get washed up—she's been on the streets for a *long* time."

"I don't think she's *ever* had a home," Artemis said bluntly. "She didn't even know her real name. She's been on the streets her whole life."

"But—that's not possible," Kayo said, distracted. "The soldiers would've found her. Or Liam. Or *us.*"

"Maybe not," said Artemis. "Not in the upper city. We don't tend to hang about, do we?"

"No, but—the orphanage—"

"She was terrified of the orphanage," Alysia said. "I could tell when she asked about it. She probably did all she could to avoid it."

"Like *killing people?*"

Dominic knew that Kayo wasn't going to let that go, so he decided to intervene. "You don't live that kinda life without teaching a few crooks a lesson," he said, shaking his head. "Not all on your own."

"And not as a woman," Artemis added, and he tilted his head to her in agreement. "Look, it's not ideal, Kayo, but she's here now, so you two are going to have to find some way to get along. It's not like she's mad at you for nothing. You *did* trick her into coming here—"

"I didn't—"

"I know, I know—you didn't mean to. But you still *did.* If you'd been honest with her, *and* us, this would all be going much differently."

"Yeah," said Kayo bitterly. "Because that's something I do all the time, right? Trick girls into coming here?"

"I wouldn't say *trick,*" Dominic chimed in. "But just a few weeks ago you were trying to get us to let that other girl stay...."

"*Shut up!*"

The wine bottle tumbled through the air past Dominic's head and shattered against the wall. Everyone sat up, their arms falling slowly from over their heads, and stared in shock at the red wine trickling down the stones. Then they turned to Kayo. He sat frozen, his arm still out, his face pale. But when they all turned to him, he grew defensive.

"It's not the same!" he yelled at Dominic. "It isn't the same at all, you know it isn't!"

"Yeah," Dominic sighed. "I know."

Once Kayo stopped shouting, the room became very quiet. The silence seemed to weigh on him too, and he dropped his arms on the table and buried his head in them. Under his arm, Dominic saw him staring into the embers in the hearth with an odd expression on his face. It wasn't anger; it wasn't sadness. To Dominic, it looked like pain.

"I'm sorry," Dominic told him. "Really."

Kayo didn't answer. The fire seemed to dance in his honey-brown eyes as they stared at something far beyond the walls.

Silence fell; Alysia and Artemis were looking at each other, having one of those silent conversations that women were so good at. Finally, Alysia reached over and touched his arm. "Kayo, I think Rose deserves another chance," she said gently. "She was just scared and confused, just like we were, especially with everybody threatening her. And she's been on her own for a long time. You know what it's like out there...."

"Yeah," said Kayo heavily. His eyes squeezed shut for a moment, his brow furrowed against the firelight. "I know."

"Plus, she's cute," Dominic added, nudging Kayo with his elbow. "You could do worse."

Kayo lifted his head just high enough to give Dominic a glare that could melt metal. "Are you out of your damn mind?" he demanded.

"I'm just *saying*—"

"What the fuck makes you think I'd go anywhere *near* her?"

"I mean, beggars can't be choosy, mate—"

Kayo jumped to his feet, his expression hardening into an aggressive mask. "Fuck you," he spat. Then he turned and stormed out.

"Wait a minute—where're you going?" Alysia said desperately.

"Out."

"Kayo—"

"Just leave me alone."

The door slammed with a bang that made them all wince. Alysia sank slowly back down to her place by the fire, looking so weary and sad and lost that Artemis reached over and put an arm around her shoulders. The two women looked up at Dominic with their incredulous, skeptical, annoyingly superior expressions mirrored on each other's faces.

"Nicely handled, Dominic," Artemis told him, her voice dripping with sarcasm.

Dominic sighed and stood up, heading over to the wall to clean up the glass. "Well," he said. "At least he's talking to us again."

"Rose?"

She jolted awake with a start.

It was so dark—had she fallen asleep? She straightened up and looked around. Her eyes found the blanket that had slid off of her, then a pair of boots, and up, up, up, to the face of the person standing over her.

Kayo.

She jumped again and scrambled to her feet. One hand fumbled under her skirt for her knife—but Kayo was already backing away, hands raised.

"Sorry—I didn't mean to scare you."

She just glared at him, fighting the fog of sleep. A quick flick of her eyes confirmed that they were alone in the corridor, and he had her backed into the balustrade. She should have been scared—but this early in the morning, all she could manage was annoyance.

"What d'you want?" she snapped at him.

"I just—are you okay?" he asked her. His brow was furrowed, his eyes studying her intensely. He almost seemed...worried.

"What do *you* care?"

"You were sleeping out *here*," he pointed out, as if it should be obvious. "I didn't know if—look, it doesn't matter. If you're all right—"

"What, are you mad I didn't sleep in my pretty new cell?" she snarled.

He didn't take the bait. He just raised his eyebrows. "Is something wrong with it? What happened to your arm?"

She glanced down at the fabric still knotted around her arm. Then she stared at him again. Against all rationality, he seemed...sincere. If she hadn't known better, she might have believed he cared. After a moment's pause, in which she considered all the possible angles of deception, she finally told the truth. "Don't like being inside. It's— like a trap. The door—forget it." She cut herself off, reminding herself, sharply, that he didn't care.

"Yeah," he said, nodding. "The rooms are a little small. And the doors don't lock."

Dominic had framed this as a positive, because they couldn't lock her in—but it also meant she couldn't lock them out. Kayo almost seemed to understand her anxiety about it.

Almost.

"That's good," she retorted. "I'd hate to be *locked in,* that would be just *awful,* wouldn't it?"

He had the grace, at least, to look ashamed of himself. He reached into his pocket, and Rose tensed—but when he withdrew his hand, he was only holding a key. He held it out to her.

"Here," he said. "Take it."

She frowned at the key, then up at him. "What?"

"This key opens every lock in the place," he said. "At least all the ones we know about. You can have it, if you want."

"Why do you *have that?*" she demanded. Had he been looking around for her, just waiting to catch her off guard and lock her up again?

But he just shrugged. "I thought...I thought you'd want to have it. Maybe it would make you feel better."

He offered it again. This time, she snatched it out of his hand. She didn't want to touch him, but her fingers brushed his; his skin burned like fire, and she jerked her hand away.

"And in the morning, I could show you around," he said. "If you want."

He had the air of someone spitting out the words before he lost his nerve. One hand, she noticed, was crossed over the other, playing with one of the beaded bracelets. They were new, she thought—the string wasn't charred black, and there was no sign of where she'd cut them—but they looked more or less the same.

And then the meaning of his words finally sank in. "You wanna—what?"

"I'd like to show you around the place." He gestured vaguely to the shrine around them. "Honestly, I'm not trying to trick you, I just thought you'd want to see it. It's really something special. And—" He took a deep breath, then barreled on, his eyes fixed somewhere near her shoulder. "And I'm sorry. I just wanted you to—to know that. I'm sorry for—everything. All of it. And if you're going to stay here, I thought maybe we could start over fresh. What do you say?"

He reached out, offering her his hand.

She stared at him in utter disbelief. It was a long moment before she could find her tongue.

"No!"

And she shoved him away with all her might. He stumbled back a step, his expression frozen in shock.

"Are you *insane?!*" she shrieked at him. "After all you *did?*"

"I-I didn't—I said I was sorry...."

"I don't *care* how sorry you are!" She shoved him again for good measure; he did not stumble this time, but still he remained as utterly motionless as if he were carved out of stone. Furious, frustrated by his stillness, longing to hurt him, she flung the key at him. A rush of vicious satisfaction pulsed through her as she saw it bounce off his face, saw him wince. "You locked me in a *cell!* You left me there to *die!* I nearly *starved* to death! An' after I *saved your life!* Look what you did to me!" She brandished her fingers at him, showing him her broken fingernails, the blisters and bruises and cuts on her palms that she had obtained while trying to force her way out of her cell. "So you can *forget* it! You jus' stay away from me, I will *never* forgive you, don't you *ever* even *look* at me, *ever!*"

He said nothing, did nothing. He just stood there, stunned.

She was so disgusted with him that she could barely even look at him. She stormed past him, into her room, and slammed the door, leaving him alone in the corridor.

．　．　．

Of course, that left her trapped in her room with no way out—unless she wanted to climb out the window. She leaned against the door and waited, listening. What if he didn't go? What if he stayed outside, waiting for her—or tried to break in?

But after a moment or two, she heard his footsteps retreat.

She sighed in relief, sinking onto the bed. It was so soft that she fell sideways before she could help herself. She was so tired, and her whole body hurt from sleeping against the balustrade. She snuggled into the mattress, finding the pillow, already drifting off as she rested her cheek on it.

Dried grain, she thought drowsily as she heard the insides of the pillow shift. *No...wouldn't be food. Maybe—*

But she was asleep before she could finish the thought.

When Rose next opened her eyes, she had to stare at the room in front of her, blinking, for a long time before she realized where she was. The room looked so different in the sunlight. It fell in thick, gold slices across the bed, striping the faded rug and the old wood until it all looked bright and new.

Orphans. Orphan shrine. Right, she thought. And then: *Dinner.* She needed to find out what time it was and make sure she didn't miss it. She tried to sit up—

—but couldn't.

Her head had scarcely lifted from the pillow when a wave of nausea crashed into her and flattened her back on the mattress. She squeezed her eyes shut and swallowed, waiting for the world to stop spinning.

It didn't.

She tried to lift her arms—to clutch at her stomach, to push herself up, *something.* But they were too heavy. Her left arm slid across her hip and fell limp to the mattress, but her right didn't move at all. It just hurt—burned—throbbed so hard that she whimpered. She looked down, panting, and saw the makeshift bandage she'd tied on her forearm. It had slipped, and underneath—

No, no, no, no....

It took everything she had to lift the leaden weight that was her left arm and feel around for the bandage. She was panting by the time she found it. The knot proved too difficult to remove, so she grabbed the edge and jerked it loose—and cried out in pain. The bandage was glued to her swollen skin with blood and yellowish ooze. The dark, angry edges of the cut stood out sharp against the bright red swelling and the blood.

As the cut burned, the rest of her body went cold. She stared at the cut in horror, biting back a scream.

No no no no no no—

She had to get up. Had to fix this. Had to....

But her body would not obey her. Her limbs were too heavy, her neck too weak to lift her head. She tried to roll over, but all she managed to do was slip off the pillow and make her entire abdomen throb. She whimpered.

Help, she thought. *Help me—help—*

But even if she could have shouted, who would come? Who would care? Her cries would only attract cutpurses and sadists like an animal's yelps lured in hungry predators. And no healer in the city would take her, not looking like—but of course she didn't look like that anymore, she—if she convinced them she came from a family with money, maybe they—

But first she had to get out of the orphan's hideout.

And she couldn't even get out of this bed.

A sob bubbled in her throat. She practically choked trying to force it down.

Get up, you useless lump, she scolded herself. *Move it! Hurry up, or you'll have to saw your arm off yourself!*

Oh Goddess, they were going to cut her arm off.

The visceral terror gave her enough strength to push herself over, let one leg fall to the floor, and—

The bed slid out from underneath her. She hit the rug with a squeak and a thud as her entire body throbbed. Even when she stopped moving, the room spun.

Not good. This was not good.

The rug was warm, but she was so cold. The bed blocked the

sunlight from falling on her. And her blanket was gone—out in the corridor, she realized.

A spasm of pain made her curl up like a dying insect, fighting not to retch. When, at last, it was over, she sagged back onto the rug. Tears spilled from her eyes. She didn't have the strength to wipe them away.

I'm going to die, she thought, more in disbelief than terror. *I'm going to die here.*

The door seemed so far away. Chills and heat crawled over her body side-by-side, and she started to shiver.

No. No, I won't—I can't. I have to get up.

Her whole body throbbed. Just trying to move brought dark spots and blinding stars dancing before her eyes.

Just a few more minutes....

She heard the knocks on the door for a long time before she realized what they were. But they meant nothing to her, and she dismissed them as a dream. The voice, too.

"Rose?" it was saying. "Are you all right? I heard—I thought I heard—" A pause that felt like an eternity. Then more knocking. "Rose! I'm just trying to make sure you're not *dead,* you don't have to *talk* to me. Rose? If you don't answer, I'm coming in—I mean it, I will—"

The latch clicked. She heard a thump. Then the scrape of wood on stone.

Monsters, she thought deliriously, and her stomach gave another sickening lurch. Giant, hulking monsters that reeked of liquor and sweat and smoke. *I blocked the door but they always get in, I can't ever keep them out, it never stops—*

Someone was muttering curses behind the door. Then, after another deafening scrape, the room flooded with light.

"*Rose!*"

The monsters were closing in on her. Leaning over her. Smelling for blood.

"*Shit*—Dominic!" a scuffle, a thump, and then, louder: "DOMIN-*IC!*"

"Whaaat?"

"Go get Lis, hurry! Tell her to bring the bandages and things!"

"What happened? Are you—?"

"It's Rose, she's hurt—just *go!*"

Footsteps in the corridor, quick and heavy. Then they faded, leaving only her heartbeat in her ears.

Someone sighed.

"Oh, Rose...."

She knew that voice—not by the way it sounded, she could barely hear that, but by the surge of annoyance it summoned. She opened her eyes and confirmed that Kayo, of all people, was inspecting the cut on her arm.

"Go 'way," she rasped.

He ignored her. "What'd you *do* to yourself?" he asked her. "Goddess, that's nasty. Did you—?"

His fingers brushed her skin. Her entire body recoiled, and she snatched her arm back as nausea choked her again.

"*Don't touch me!*" she yelled.

Kayo jumped back as if she'd stung him, swearing. "Sorry—I'm sorry—Goddess—"

She fell back to the rug with a sob. She couldn't speak. The pain was like a searing white light before her eyes, blinding her of all reason and thought.

"What happened?" Kayo asked her. His voice was soft and gentle, feather-light under the roar of her heartbeat.

"The—found a—" The words weren't coming out right. She swallowed and tried again—but the sight of her own arm distracted her. She took a deep breath. "You—you gotta—" She reached out blindly with her left hand and found fabric; she clenched it in her fist. "Cut it off," she ordered him. "You gotta cut—before it—"

"I'm not going to cut it off," he reassured her.

She shook her head. He didn't understand. "No, it'll spread, it'll *spread*, you gotta—" Her voice rasped and burned, and she had to stop to heave a painful cough. But this was important. "I don't wanna die...just do it, do it now...."

"How about we try something that *doesn't* leave you maimed?"

The words, the sarcasm, that was like him—but his tone was different. He was speaking in a low, soft voice, as if soothing a frightened animal. It terrified her. Why was he so calm? Was it because he was watching her die, because he knew she'd be out of the way soon?

"Go ahead," she snapped at him, then winced as pain lanced up her arm again. "Get that big sword—just do it fast—"

"Rose, stop it. I'm not chopping off your arm."

"Then gimme a knife." She let her hand fall, feeling at what she thought was his shirt, searching for the knife she knew he kept at his belt. "Bigger one—mine's too small—"

"I don't even *have* a knife."

"*Liar.* You just want me to *die*—"

She swung her fist blindly in his direction and was rewarded with a sharp yell.

"Ow! *Damn* it, would you *please* stop hitting me?"

She didn't have the strength to hit him again anyways. "Coward," she choked out. "Can't even kill me when I'm—you're g-gonna jus' sit there an'—"

She wasn't making sense anymore. Kayo just sighed.

"It's too late—" She stopped and swallowed again. She would not, could not cry. Not now. Not in front of *him*. "It'll spread, I can't fix it, it's too late...."

"Rose, listen to me," he said softly. "Alysia knows how to fix this, she's done it a thousand times. All we have to do is get the swelling down, she's got something to put on it—"

"No! Don't *pour* stuff in it, have you—have ya lost yer—"

"Rose, please. We know what we're doing, we're not going to make it worse. She'll probably just put some vinegar on it, and then wash it and ban—"

"Nooo! No, not *water,* you can't—"

"*Clean* water. We have plenty of it, remember? If nothing else, it'll cool you down. Are you hot?"

"Freezing. It's cold...."

"Okay—hold on. Just hold on—"

He left—but before she'd even realized it, before she had time to wonder if he would ever be back, he was blocking the light once again. A blanket settled on her, a comforting weight. Her shivering stopped at once.

"You're going to be fine, I promise. I'm going to touch you, okay?"

"No—don't—"

"I just want to look at the cut. I'm not going to hurt you. Is that all right?"

She couldn't find her voice, couldn't tell him to stop. And then his fingers touched her arm. They were cool and feather-light, and though she flinched, it didn't hurt.

"Goddess. You're burning up...."

He lifted her wrist, slowly and carefully, and turned her arm toward the light.

"Did you fight a lion while we weren't looking?"

"Traps," she choked out. Now she remembered—the kitchen, the darkness, the trap. "You t-trapped the place. So I can't leave."

She felt his hand tense against her wrist. "What did you say? Did you say *traps?*"

"Woulda killed me," she muttered. "C-coward. Can't just...kill me outright...."

"Ah, *shit,*" Kayo groaned. He lowered her arm gingerly to the rug. "I'm so sorry, I would've warned you if—I-I thought we disarmed them all. And blocked all the ways down there. I don't know how you got in, but—"

"Huh?"

"The traps. *We* didn't put them there—well, Liam did. To keep people out, to protect us. We got scared that one of the kids would wander into one, so we disarmed them after he—" He stopped. Then he said, again, "I'm so sorry."

"Liam did...?"

"Yeah. He was a little...paranoid. Which one was it?"

"It was a...like a log that swung in...."

He winced. "Damn. You got lucky. You should take up dice. If you don't get lockjaw after this, I mean. Not that anyone would mind...."

"Shut up," she mumbled. "It's *your* fault if I die."

"Yeah," he sighed. "I know. But you're not going to. Lis knows what she's doing."

"Jus' let me leave," she said hoarsely. She tried to lift her head, opening her eyes. "Let me go. An' I'll—I'll find a healer—"

"No one's stopping you."

"Liar," she said. "I heard you. You an'—an' Dominic." She swallowed—it hurt—and let her head fall again. "You're gonna shoot me if I leave. You weren't ever gonna let me go."

Kayo sat back on his heels, brushing his hair back from his face. He was silent for what felt like hours. And then he said the last thing she'd expected.

"No one showed you the door?"

She blinked at him. "Huh?"

"The *door*. That goes to the street. I thought for sure Lis would've showed it to you."

"There's...a door?"

"Of course there is. What, you think the only way in is through the sewers?"

She couldn't lift her head, so she shifted and rolled, twisting her neck at an odd angle, so she could fix him with a flat glare.

"You're lyin'."

"Uh...no," he said, as if he had to stop and think about it. "No, there's definitely a door. Try not to die, and I'll show it to you. And— if we weren't...I-I'd...if Lis can't fix this, I'll take you to a healer, all right? I swear. I just—they don't, um—like—people like me—much. So if we can...."

She frowned at him. "Y'mean you'd...let me...?"

He nodded. He wasn't looking at her; he was twisting a bracelet around and around his wrist. "I don't know what you told them. My brother and sisters, I mean. But they don't think you'd really sell us out. It's just—just me you have a problem with. And they want you to stay. We haven't been watching the doors, Rose—well, I have. But only because I—I thought, if you left—maybe I could convince you to take it out on me, and not them." He turned to look at the other side of her room—but spotted the mirror and quickly turned away again. "But the others think we should trust you, and...well, you haven't left yet. I thought you knew about the door, though."

She didn't know what to make of this, didn't know how to translate the look on his face. He almost looked as if...he *meant* it. But that wasn't possible.

Pain lanced up her arm again. She flinched, but bit back her cry of pain. She would not show weakness. Not in front of *him*.

"It's okay," Kayo reassured her. "You're going to be all right. Lis'll be here in a minute."

But Rose shook her head. The wound was too big, too deep. "She can't fix this...she can't...."

"Sure she can. She's done it before."

"You're jus' sayin' that...." Her chest felt so heavy when she tried to speak; the effort left her breathless. "It's bad...."

Kayo sighed, his mouth twisting. Then he said, "Let me show you something."

He twisted around and lifted his shirt, exposing his back and side. Rose squinted—and then sucked in a breath. Scars slashed across his back, white and pinkish against the golden brown of his skin. The largest of them was a pinkish burn that clawed its way up his side, vanishing beneath his clothes on both ends. She recognized the ropy slashes across his shoulders as whip scars—dozens of them.

"Whoa," she said with reverence.

"Yeah." His mouth twisted bitterly as he let his shirt fall. "I've had a lot worse than this, and Lis got me through okay. You have nothing to worry about, I promise. Just relax."

So many scars....She closed her eyes and settled back against the rug. Despite her own better judgment, she believed him. People could lie, but scars didn't.

"That from the orphanage?" she asked him.

"...yeah," he admitted, looking away. "Mostly. By the way, when did you—um, how long have you been—on your own?" He chose these final words with great care. When she didn't answer, he rambled on: "I just wonder because we—well, it depends on the timing, but we should've run into you at *some* point. Were you always in the upper city? ...Rose?"

His voice was quite soothing—not very deep for a man, but she liked it. Even when it sounded strangely flat and distant, or when the whining in her ears wiped away half of his words.

"*Rose!*"

"Ouch!" She snapped awake as he pinched the skin on her uninjured arm. "Don't *touch* me, go *away*—"

"Not happening, princess. Rise and shine."

"I w's jus' *sleepin'*...."

"Well, sorry, Your Royal Highness, but if you go to sleep, you might not wake back up. So cut it the fuck out." He seemed angry—irrationally so, in her opinion. She grumbled wordlessly, wishing she had the strength to hit him again.

"C'mon," he encouraged her. "Talk to me. Tell me about your family."

"What family?" she mumbled into her arms.

"You must've had *someone*. Right?"

"No."

A pause. And then he said, "...really? No one?"

As soon as she heard that, she knew Sara had been right. He *did* feel sorry for her.

She didn't blame him. She was feeling pretty sorry for herself.

She shook her head—then winced as the effort made her brain throb against her skull. "No...just a...o-ow, *ow*...."

"You're all right. Here—I'll hold your hand, you can squeeze it if you're hurting—if you want?"

She just groaned. Her good hand curled into a claw as a fresh pain burned through her arm, scratching at the rug—until his fingers twined through hers. A jolt of pain lanced up the arm resting on the floor, and she squeezed his hand. The pain did not disappear, but it helped considerably.

"Just a...what?" he asked, gently. "A friend? A cousin?"

She closed her eyes. His hand was so warm that she couldn't bring herself to let go, or tell him off. Instead, she said, "I had...a nana. A grandma. For a bit. I think. I 'member she was real old...."

"How old were you when...?"

"Dunno." She coughed again, swallowing with a painful effort. "Maybe four? Five? I don't 'member much. I just 'member one day someone knocked, an' she got real scared...she hid me behind some stuff under the bed....An' then people came in, an' searched everywhere, there was a lotta noise...."

Kayo swore softly; she could tell by his tone that he knew what had happened already.

"...an' when it was quiet, I went out, an'...an' she wasn't movin'. I waited and waited for her to wake up, but she didn't. I got hungry, so I went an' found somebody we knew, they gave me food, someone else let me sleep on the rug, but then...after a while nobody would talk to me no more, they kept threatenin' to call the soldiers on me, so...."

"Is that when you left for the upper city?"

"Nuh-uh. Met some people...we'd meet up an'...share stuff...."

"Rose, don't fall asleep. C'mon."

She blinked up at him dazedly; she could not remember what they were doing. But when she looked at him, she felt, for some reason, vaguely surprised, almost impressed. It took her a minute to remember why. The scars. "You got whipped," she said.

"Yeah. I know," he said curtly. "I was there."

"Why?"

"Why do you care?"

He seemed to regret the words the instant he spat them out; the response seemed reflexive, uncontrollable.

"I don't," she said, closing her eyes again. "Jus' wanna know where I can get some a' those scars. They make y'look tough."

A laugh burst out of him, and it seemed to startle him as much as it startled her. "Oh, that's fine then," he choked out, his shoulders shaking. "Completely worth it."

"Mm-hmm," she said, and he chuckled again. But then his smile faded.

"I know you think we're all criminals," he said. "I know that's what they say about us. But it's not true. We were kids. Just—kids. And the place was run by soldiers. You know what they're like."

"Yeah," she said, because she did. "But if they whipped you—"

"They just did it because I was too slow." He reached over his own shoulder, feeling at the scars on his back. "Or I didn't listen. We were locked up—I couldn't 've caused trouble even if I wanted to." His eyes strayed toward the door as he rubbed the back of his neck, focused on the empty air. "Liam always said it was lucky that the place burned down. *Lucky.* Can you imagine? Like the fire that killed half of us was a blessing. But—sometimes—I think he was right. Even when the soldiers were hunting for us, setting dogs on us, trying to kill us—even starving and freezing and hiding—at least we weren't prisoners anymore."

Rose nodded—then stopped, because it hurt too much. "You can go anywhere in the lower city," she murmured. "An' steal *anythin'*, break into *anywhere*—you can have weapons, you can defend your-self, you can hurt people before *they* hurt *you*. You can breathe the sea air. Can't leave Bermeia, but...." She coughed, grimaced, and started again. "But I'd take it over a cage any day."

"Yeah." His voice was soft. "Me, too."

Silence fell between them. Rose would have been happy to close her eyes and sleep—but another horrible throbbing pain clamped down on every muscle in her body. She winced and squeezed Kayo's hand so hard she surely must have hurt him, but he didn't complain.

"You're all right," he said quietly. "Talk to me. Tell me what happened when we met."

"You *still* don't r'member?"

"I don't think that's how memory works," he said, but she could hear amusement in his voice. "No. I really don't. What happened?"

"How should *I* know?"

"Don't tell me *you* don't remember."

"I ain't got a clue what you was doin' with half a hundred soldiers on your ass. All I know is I let you drag me down into the sewers. Never doin' *that* again...."

"Aw, why not? It turned out so well."

She pressed her lips together to stop herself from smiling. "If I'd known the Beggar's King was here, though...."

She waited, but Kayo didn't say anything else. So she persisted. "You said he was your brother."

"He was," said Kayo. His eyes had found the mirror in the corner.

"But everyone else—they're not *really* your brothers 'n sisters—are they?"

"Of course they're my real siblings," he said quietly. "Blood doesn't matter—it's who's there for you, who cares about you."

"Blood's *all* that matters," she protested. "That's why people love *their* kids, an' nobody else's." If it wasn't blood, if it wasn't simply due to the whims of fate and biology, then it was a choice. And if it was a choice, she'd have to sit there and think, really think, about why no one had chosen *her*. And she wasn't about to do *that*. "If you had *real* brothers 'n sisters—"

"Dominic *did*. He had a brother. And—maybe it isn't the same. I don't know. But it's as close as any of us will ever get. We grew up together, we look out for each other, and I'd trust any one of them with my life. That's better than a lot of families get. And Lis—Alysia —she's been more than a sister to me. We might be related somehow, I don't know—but she didn't know that. She didn't remember *anything* when we came to the orphanage. But she remembered me." A note of pride crept into his voice. "Nobody there had time for a baby—if not for her I would've been completely on my own. But she took care of me. And when someone taught her numbers and letters, since she was too fragile for the other work, she taught me. I owe her *everything*. If that's not what a family is, then—"

"Kayo? Kayo!"

Footsteps in the corridor. Kayo hastily snatched his hand away and, with nowhere else to put it, stuffed it into his pocket. Rose hadn't realized he was still holding her hand until he let it go.

"In here!" he called.

A pair of battered leather shoes appeared in the doorway. Rose looked up to see Alysia standing there, pink-faced and out of breath.

"Kayo? What—oh, Goddess! What *happened?*"

"She's got a cut on her arm that looks infected, I found her on the floor."

He kept talking as Alysia knelt beside her, a basket of supplies in hand, but Rose wasn't listening. Alysia was feeling at her face, lifting her arm and turning it over. Rose tried to push her away, but she wasn't strong enough.

"Oh, you poor thing, you're burning up—Kayo, go boil some water, will you? And fetch some cold water too, we need to get her to drink."

"I've got a pitcher in my room, I'll grab it—"

"Ow!" Rose flinched as Alysia touched the edges of the cut. "Get *off!* Stop—touchin'—you bloody—"

"Watch out," Kayo said as he reappeared, a ceramic pitcher in one hand and a cup in the other. "She hits." And he caught Rose's eye and flashed her a grin. He set the pitcher on her bedside table, but placed the cup on the floor, in easy reach.

"Don't worry," he said in an undertone. "You'll be okay."

She could smell him—the soap on his clothes, and something else, something warmer and spicier that lingered on his skin.

"Kayo—"

"I'm going, I'm going."

Rose watched him walk to the door, scoop his abandoned boot off the floor, and lace it tightly up to his knee. Then he vanished.

"Owww!" Her arm jerked involuntarily as Alysia poured something on the cut that burned. "Fuck, shit, *ouch!*"

"Come on, Rose," Alysia huffed. "I know it hurts, but is the language really necessary?"

Rose sighed and let her head fall back, closing her eyes against the sun.

A letter came by pigeon in the night. A tiny scroll, bearing a black wax seal. When Romero tilted it toward the fire, he saw no sigil, no markings whatsoever. But when he unfurled the scroll, he recognized the handwriting. It was the lazy, looping scrawl of Eduardo Allesino, king of Savilla.

And it only bore two lines, written plainly in Courman to be sure he understood them.

> *Do your worst.*
> *If you dare.*

As Romero grew older, his weddings grew shorter, and that was just the way he liked it. He could not bear the pageantry anymore: sweating beneath a dozen layers of heavy clothes, waiting starving and exhausted for some woman that he barely liked to totter her way down an aisle, his thoughts drifting as the old man babbled on about the Goddess and commitment for an hour or two. He would rather have slit his own throat than suffer through that again.

It was the same old man today, the same ballroom, the same golden light from the setting sun draped over him and the woman at his side. But today, he delivered his speech to an empty room. There were no guests in attendance, no one to witness but a handful of servants that waited in a nervous cluster in a distant corner. The doors and windows had been thrown open. His eyes drifted to the fluttering drapes and beyond them, into the summer gardens, and wondered if the scent of jasmine came from them or from Auna.

She looked beautiful in her golden dress, beautiful in the way that only young women were, slender and doe-eyed and innocent. A tiara borrowed from the castle's collection sparkled in her hair. It didn't matter what she wore—for an affair like this, she was barely required to be present at all—but he'd given in to all of her requests. The old man had decided wisely to save his grand speech for a proper audience and had delivered a truncated version of the dusty old words. *Bound in the eyes of the Goddess, loyalty and faith, naught but death can part thee.* He wasn't enjoying himself as much as Auna, but it was almost bearable.

The letter was an unfortunate setback. But he had expected it, planned for it. It had been his idea to marry Auna, and he certainly wouldn't mind bedding her. And then it couldn't be reversed. They were married, and he could apply that leverage in all sorts of ways. Everything was going according to plan.

So why couldn't he shake Serena from his mind?

She and Auna didn't look much alike—Auna had too much Courman and Alronelinian blood for that. But every time he looked at her, he saw Serena on her wedding day. A little older, a little taller, and so beautiful that his gut had twisted every time he looked her way. Just the sight of her had been like strong liquor, filling his gut with heat and muddling his thoughts.

If the Divina were here now, he had no doubt that she could see it in his mind. The royal wedding ceremony had been woven into Rafael and Serena's dual coronation. Serena had scandalized the stuffy old nobles with her dress, sewn in the Sangor colors of crimson and gold but cut in a very Savillan fashion, with bare shoulders and a silhouette that accentuated every curve. Her hair had cascaded loose over her shoulders, held back from her face with a gold-and-ruby comb. She had held herself so perfectly, bent her head to accept her crown so gracefully, that Romero had thought her born to be a queen.

Naught but death can part thee, the Divina had said then. But when death had come for Rafael, Serena had remained faithful to him. She would rather have worn mourning colors all her life, slept alone in a cold bed, and let her son grow up without a father rather than loosen the iron principles that bound her to a rotting corpse.

Or perhaps it was just him that she didn't want.

When the ceremony was done, the final words echoed in an eerie silence, with no applause or music to break it. Then, after a lengthy and awkward pause, the bells had started to ring. Auna took him by the hand and led him straight out into the garden. A little table awaited them, set for two and overlooking the vibrant flowers. As soon as he sat beside her, two servants appeared out of nowhere and plied them with fruit, bread, and cheese, as well as sweet yellow wine. One of Auna's hands closed around his fingers under the table as her other hand lifted her goblet.

"And now, amore, you are mine," she said, and the hint of wickedness in her smile made his stomach clench in a way that was not unpleasant. He smiled, raised his own cup, and drained it in one swallow.

Why didn't all men have multiple wives? It seemed the only practical solution. The main problem with royal marriages seemed to be strategic: one could only select a single spouse, and so one had to compete for the best ones, had to choose carefully from the options that were available. Marrying the wrong woman meant that even if the right one came along later, one was stuck. But he hadn't wanted to give up his claim to the Courman throne, hadn't wanted to bother with having Marisa killed—and hadn't wanted to say no to Corrine while she held a knife to his throat. So instead of choosing, he'd had them both. And now he could add a third, and reap the benefits thereof. Why should a king, of all people, have to limit himself?

Auna chattered away happily as the sun set and the moon rose—about the ceremony, about her new chambers and her new servants, about how she was adjusting to a new castle and a new climate. Romero wasn't paying much attention until the servants came again, this time setting a candelabra between them to illuminate the next course. Fish, he guessed by the smell, served with sauce and fish eggs—or so he thought. But when sweetness burst in his mouth at the first bite, he realized what the little red orbs really were. The seeds of a pomegranate, a rare fruit that grew only on Khal Aleen and the western coast of Riazli. Rumored to aid in fertility—and heighten lust.

He looked back to Auna and saw a crafty glint in her eyes. He realized abruptly that she'd barely touched her wine, even after insisting on pouring him glass after glass—and that her hand had found his knee under the table. She leaned forward, and that hand slid a little higher.

"My darling," she said, "we must talk about our future."

Their future? He had assumed she was plying him with wine and aphrodisiacs to be sure he consummated the marriage, so there was no backing out later. What future did she see for them beyond that? "I'd like nothing better," he said.

She beamed at him as, with a graceful movement, she scooped up pomegranate seeds and dropped them casually in her wine. "I've been wondering," she said as she swirled her goblet, "what I shall do as your queen. I know you have your other wives, and they do a great deal for you. But surely there is something left for me."

He stopped himself from wincing just in time. He had hoped his other wives wouldn't come up tonight. "You were born to be a queen, Auna," he told her, hoping a bit of flattery would soothe her jealousy before the questions and demands began. "I am sure you will do beautifully, no matter what you choose."

Her spoon dipped again, but this time, the shiny red seeds tumbled into his glass. She smiled as he took an obedient sip. He knew what she was doing, and he doubted it would work—he'd had pomegranate before and felt nothing—but he would take any help he could get.

"Hmm...yes," she mused. "It is a great responsibility, being a queen. I know that Queen Marisa is a valuable resource for you in your control of Courma and Lyrma—she all but rules in your stead there. And Queen Corrine is your spymaster, of course—"

Romero choked on his wine. "My *what?* I don't—"

"It's all right, amore," she spoke over him with a careless wave of her hand. "I know all about it. And you're clever to have her—my father has struggled every day since he lost his own. She's quite valuable. I would never think to take her place. But I believe there is something only I can do for you, my husband."

"Oh?"

Her hand squeezed his thigh under the table. And then she said the last thing he expected.

"I can give you Savilla."

Romero slowly lowered his cup. Auna's smile was pleasant, but her eyes were sharp and cold as they bored into his. It gave him the oddest feeling—as if he were staring down a snake.

"I...don't understand," he said slowly.

"Of course you do," she practically purred. "You have such a brilliant mind, Romero. I knew when you invited me here that you saw the possibilities. If you married me, you'd have a claim to the throne of Savilla. And now, what is there to stop you from taking it? My father? He's a coward and a fool. But you, my love—you've claimed half the Peninsula as your own already. Savilla is the key to conquering the rest."

He stared at her. A brilliant mind? Him? He was not the one who had seen straight through every plan and cut to the heart of it all with a handful of words. Did she know his courtship of her had been a ruse? Did she know he'd tried to hold her hostage? He didn't know—and he was suddenly terrified to find out.

He chose his words with great care. "My darling, I could never do that to your father. Why would you want him to lose his throne?"

Her smile tightened into something like a grimace, stark and ugly on her pretty face. "I don't much care if he loses his head," she spat. "Nor my brothers. They're the real threat, not him—but with my help, you can kill them all."

Good Goddess. He could feel his heart pounding, the adrenaline sizzling in his veins. "Auna, you don't think that's why I married you, do you? I would never dream of using you like—"

"Of course you would." Her words were soft and soothing, honey sweet. "And that is why I love you, my silly husband. Because you will use any means you must to claim what is rightfully yours. Since the moment I met you, I dreamed I would one day stand at your side as you surpass the Conqueror himself. History will remember you as a grand emperor, and I want to be your empress." She leaned in closer. "Use me, my husband. Use me however you must. A tool in the hands of a master must be happy, don't you think? To be *worked* by those hands to create such *beautiful* things, until one is left *broken* and *shattered,* pounded flat, hollowed out....*Dia mi,* what an honor it would be, to be used to create such *greatness....*"

Her voice was lowering, throaty and husky now, thrumming richly with each word she emphasized oh-so-carefully. He knew exactly what she was doing—but it was working. Every fiber of his being was honed in on the hand creeping up his thigh.

"I know you want Savilla," she said. "I know you want to claim her for yourself. Let me help you, amore. Please."

He could barely string a coherent sentence together. "How... would that work?"

"Oh, it's simple, my love. A few letters to my father, a few soldiers sent to Arrow's Pass...a few old friends sent to Aldaeza...and a little help from our new Divina friend wouldn't go amiss...."

She leaned in even closer, her body pressing against his arm. She craned her neck to whisper in his ear.

"And you'll need an heir, of course."

His skin tingled as a burning heat washed over him. His clothes felt suddenly too tight, too close. "An heir?"

"But of course. Surely you want an heir, il mio amore? With an heir, your rule would never be questioned. Your line will rule forever. Oh, but those *other* queens—I understand why you did not want an heir from *them.* It is a rare woman that can give you a future king." Her fingers strayed around the edges of where he most desperately wanted them to go, hovering just close enough to make his head spin. "A woman you can trust. A woman of royal blood and superior breeding. A *true* queen."

Her lips brushed the shell of his ear.

"Use me, my love. Let me give you *everything.*"

He jumped to his feet so quickly he knocked the chair over.

Auna rose too. Romero had just enough sense left to offer her his arm.

"Perhaps," he said, his voice ragged around the edges, "we should discuss this further in my chambers."

Auna's little smirk made his insides clench with excitement. She moved so serenely back into the castle, with such poise—and far, far too slowly. She was a proper lady, of course she was, and it was their wedding night. She'd want to do the thing properly, in his bed—

Her nails raked lightly against his sleeve, sending goosebumps up his arm.

Her room. It was closer.

They barely made it there before she whirled around. Her body pressed his against the door of her bedchamber. She stood on tiptoe to kiss him, grabbing two handfuls of his doublet, and he was lost.

Maybe she *had* drugged him. But he didn't care. He hadn't felt so reckless and free in a long time. He'd take Savilla, why not? It would be oh so easy—and perhaps he'd take Kedarth next, or Kypris, or Yazmin, or even Khal Aleen. Who could stop him? He dared them all to try, even the Goddess herself.

Nothing could stop him. He was invincible. He'd claim the whole world just as he'd claimed the throne, and Serena—

Serena—

When he came to his senses, she was whispering in his ear in Savillan, tangled around him and holding him as if she would never let him go. The words drifted around him, floating through his brain—just nonsense, platitudes, saying something just to say something. He whispered back against her neck, but he was barely even listening to himself. Everything in him was focused on the touch of her skin, the sound of her heart.

Then she laughed in Auna's voice, and he nearly jumped out of his skin. Auna. It was Auna. And every whisper of *amore, caro, tesoro* was just another way to manipulate him.

Somehow, he managed to extract himself from her. But then what? There was the usual routine: dressing, tying up bodice laces, looking for shoes, saying all the right things to soften the blow when he finally left. Getting rid of a woman afterward was always the difficult part—but tonight, he couldn't, and that was even worse. It took all of his strength to lie still beside her, all of his patience to listen to her contented babbling, all of his wits to find the right thing to say in reply while somehow convincing her to stop talking and go to sleep.

But all the while, he couldn't shake Serena from his mind.

He stared up at the peach-colored hangings around Auna's bed as she curled up against him and drifted off, and he remembered a different wedding altogether—not the big, formal affair of Rafael and Serena's coronation, but the ceremony he'd witnessed the night before it. Somehow, Serena had talked Rafael into a Savillan ceremony— something *very* Savillan, utterly untouched by the influence of the Conqueror and the rest of the Peninsula. As soon as he saw the two of them sink to their knees, facing each other and clasping hands in simple white clothing, he knew that he was witnessing something no noble or royal in Savilla would be caught dead participating in.

There were only five of them there: the couple, the Savillan Divina presiding, his witness, and hers. Romero had stood silently next to Serena's brother and watched, torn between bewilderment and irritation. Back then, it had meant nothing. Just a silly game the two were playing—as their entire courtship had been, in his opinion. Even when they'd invited him and her brother up to the King's Tower to celebrate, he'd laughed and drank and toasted the two of them with a smile on his face. It wasn't *real*. They were just toying with him, testing him.

But then the two of them had slipped into the bedchamber. Alone.

With her brother there, Romero couldn't do anything to stop it. He had to paste on a smile and tear himself away, walk back to his own rooms, when every part of him wanted to run back and tear Rafael away from her. He went to bed, but he lay awake then, just as he did now, eyes open, imagining what the two of them were doing behind that closed door until he nearly made himself sick. She'd betrayed him. She'd chosen another man right in front of him, and now she was bedding that other man without even the courtesy of trying to conceal it. And he could do nothing but lay there, cuckolded, alone.

The ceremony the next day had felt like a knife to the heart: a final, public admission of the affair that had left him shoved back into the shadows. But looking back, he realized that hadn't mattered at all. It was only a funeral for something that had shriveled and died the moment the Divina had bound their hands together with rope. He should have seen it then—in the flutter of nervous laughter in their voices as they'd declared their love for each other, in the way they could not stop smiling at each other, in the way they had forgotten that everyone else in the world existed. He should have torn them apart then, sent the Divina away and tossed the rope into the fire and challenged Rafael to a duel for Serena's hand and slapped some sense into her for choosing the wrong man after he won.

But the worst part was, he knew it wouldn't have made a difference.

Serena had made a mistake, but he could forgive her for that. He could overlook that she'd been with another man, that she'd had his child. If she'd just come back....

Auna was curled up against him, asleep. He extracted himself from her with difficulty and escaped her rooms without being spotted. Maximilian wasn't far—he never was—and it took only a few brief words to send him off into the night. Then Romero made his way slowly back to his own rooms. The castle was dark and quiet, and though the day had been warm, a damp chill followed him through the corridors.

He was still drunk, or else Auna really *had* drugged him, and it hadn't quite worn off. And though he tried—good Goddess, did he try—he couldn't shake Serena from his mind. Her body sliding against his in the dark. Her voice whispering into his ear, sweet nothings that switched to utter filth and right back again. Her neck under his lips as he whispered back everything he'd longed to say to her since she'd left. What could he even say? Where to begin? There were no words—he'd simply have to show her.

He slipped into the map room on the way back, fumbled in the darkness for the decanter of brandy he knew his servants wouldn't dare to water down. It burned like fire on the way down, but he poured himself two more. Only then could he finally summon the courage to make his way back to his bedchamber. He paused for a long moment with his hand on the latch, then took a deep breath and went in.

Angela was waiting by the window. He wasn't sure what he'd expected, but it wasn't this. She wore nothing but a chemise of thin white silk that shone in the moonlight, hugging every curve of her body. Her hair was loose and wild over her shoulders. She had her back to him, gazing out at the moonlit gardens. At the sound of the door closing, however, she turned, one hand brushing her hair over her shoulder.

Her eyes shone like pools of ink. He could see the outline of her breasts clearly beneath the thin shift, the bold protrusion of her nipples. Suddenly, he couldn't breathe. He wanted to stand there for the rest of his life and stare at her, live and breathe only the sight of her—but it wasn't enough. It was like staring out over a vast lake as he died of thirst. He wanted to drink her in, all of her, fill himself to bursting with the taste and feel and sight of her, consume her until there was nothing left of either of them.

He couldn't speak. All he could do was hold out his hand. And to his amazement, she came to him. The bewitching lines of her body beneath the silk chemise taunted him with every step she took.

She smiled as she took his hand. His heart jumped to his throat and throbbed there, hurting when he swallowed. He thought she might speak—he wanted her to speak—he was terrified that she might speak.

Instead, she pressed her body against his.

A dam within him broke then, and as the heat and fire flooded him, he let himself do exactly what he longed to do. He pulled her close and kissed her. When her lips parted, he poured all that he was into the kiss, tracing his tongue across her lower lip as one hand slid down her back and the other tangled in her hair. She threw her arms around his neck and dug her nails into the back of his shirt. He laughed aloud as she clawed it over his head, paused just long enough to help her throw it aside before he threw himself at her again. This was just as he'd imagined it, just as wild, just as intense. He'd always known she'd be just as fiery in his arms as she was in public, that she'd take what she needed without hesitation, show him exactly what she wanted. Like making love in a whirlwind or a stormy sea, hanging on for dear life by his fingertips.

She was practically tearing his clothes off. Could it be possible that she wanted him just as much as he wanted her? He had never dared to dream of such bliss, but here she was in his arms, stroking his bare chest, sliding his breeches down his hips. Then she broke away and stepped back. He nearly yanked her right back—but then he saw her slip the silk chemise off her shoulders. It rippled to the floor to collapse into a shimmering pool at her feet.

Her body was just as beautiful as he'd always imagined. He lunged for her with a groan and pressed her against him. A quick struggle with his clothes, and he was naked too, and the feel of her bare skin was bliss. He grabbed her by the waist and swung her onto the bed. He leaned in, climbing on top of her, pressing her down into the mattress. But she wrapped a leg around him and shoved him over, and he lost their little wrestling match before he even knew it had begun. He couldn't find it in himself to care. Not when she was straddling him, pinning him down, leaning in to kiss him in a confusion of black curls and warm skin and gasping breath....

A flash of white teeth, bared in a mischievous grin. No. Not mischief—

Triumph.

A flash of silver in her hand.

A sting against his ribs.

Something as cold as ice plunged into his skin, spreading from his heart, sending shivers through his limbs as the heat was sucked from his body. He tried to breathe, but his lungs were frozen, heavy as lead in his chest. He clutched at his heart, and his fingernails scrabbled at a stream of blood pouring over his skin.

Angela vanished. His head fell to the side, and he saw her as if through a spyglass, from a great distance, as she pulled her chemise back on. As she came toward him again, bloodied steel flashing in her hand. His knife—the one he kept under his pillow.

She hissed something in Savillan, but his drowning brain could not translate it. Then she raised the knife again.

Something in him knew to move—how? Where? He didn't know. He slipped and plummeted through space, blacking out, still falling even as he felt the cold stone floor against his back. It took everything in him to breathe—to cough as his lungs burned—to suck in air past the blood dribbling from his lips.

Angela's bare feet appeared in front of him. Fear jolted his belly as he saw her raise the knife again, but he couldn't move. A blur of brown skin, a glint as the knife caught the moonlight.

The sound of wood smashing against stone. Shouting men. A woman's scream. A meaty thud.

Darkness swept in, wrapping around him like a blanket. Blessed darkness, soft and sweet, like sleep at the end of a long day. He fought it, struggled, lost ground bit by bit.

He blinked, and the simple action seemed to take hours. When his eyes opened again, he saw someone kneeling over him. A woman's sweet voice was singing—flat, without passion, but well-trained.

> *A hundred thousand stars above*
> *Fade and glow, fade and glow...*

No, he thought desperately. *No, don't.*

> *A hundred thousand tiny lights*
> *That point me where I need to go....*

Don't sing. I'm not dead yet. Don't sing.

> *Over mountains, through the snow,*
> *From treach'rous paths to the roads I know*
> *Yet the one bright star that leads to home*

He didn't have the strength to keep fighting.
He couldn't remember why he'd been fighting at all.

> *When it fades*
> *When it fades*
> *Where am I to go...?*

He let go, and the darkness took him.

The bells woke her sometime in the afternoon. Alysia must have come in to air out the room: the window was wide open, and Rose could hear the castle bells ringing in the distance. Normally, they only chimed the hour, but today they were...enthusiastic. She lay in bed with her eyes closed, stretching under the blankets, and listened. The belltower had at least three bells in it, by the sound of it, but likely five or six. If she could hear them this far away, they were probably bigger than she was.

She thought eventually they would stop—but they didn't. It was close to sunset by the time she finally rose, wrestling her way out of the tangle of blankets—had they *multiplied* somehow?—and the bells were still going. She sat at the edge of the bed in her chemise, rubbing the sleep out of her eyes. Was something going on, or did this happen all the time, and only people in the shrine got to hear it?

Maybe she'd slept the day away—twice in a row—but she'd never felt better. Two days in bed had made her good as new—that, and the disgusting tea Alysia had forced down her throat. Alysia had given her a new bandage, too, soaked in something cool and soothing. Kayo had been right: she knew what she was doing.

There wasn't much to do, but she dressed herself anyway, laced up her boots and tied back her hair. She thought maybe she'd poke around a little more before dinner and find that door Kayo had mentioned. And if she felt like slipping out and never coming back, well—someone else could have her share.

As she stood up, something on the bedside table caught her eye. It took her a moment to place it: it was a key. Not just any key, *the* key, the one that opened all the doors in the place.

How was this here? She thought she'd left it firmly lodged in Kayo's forehead. Had he come in here while she slept? She cast an uneasy glance at the tangle of blankets on the bed. What else had he left behind? And more importantly, what had he *taken?*

She stepped out into the corridor. Soft orangish light flooded the place, and the sound of the bells drifted down from the broken ceiling, echoing faintly. She took a deep breath and turned her face to the sun. After being cooped up in her room for so long, the fresh green scent floating up from the garden was intoxicating.

She glanced around—and froze. From the corridor, she could see a sliver of Kayo's room. And his boots were sticking over the edge of the mattress.

If she snuck away, perhaps he wouldn't hear her. But something about that didn't feel right. Something in his room looked wrong— what was it? She crept a bit closer. He was lounging on his bed, reading a book. And—

She realized, suddenly, that the blankets on his bed were gone. That's why it looked so strange.

Suddenly, the extra tangle of blankets on her bed made sense.

She tried to back away quietly, but—

"Rose?"

She backed into the railing and tried to look innocent as Kayo came out. His hair was damp and shining, falling in slight waves over one shoulder. The marks from the beating she'd given him, she noted with disappointment, were almost gone.

"What?" she challenged him.

But he just smiled at her. "Are you feeling better?"

"Um...yeah."

"Good." And he seemed like he really meant it. He reached up to tie back his hair. "You picked the perfect time to get sick. Artemis brought home a dress she had to finish, and she made everybody help. I don't think I'll ever get the feeling back in my hand."

He gave it a little wave. It did look a bit red.

"Doesn't matter," she said, shrugging. "I can't sew."

"Oh, she would've made you help somehow. She tried to drag the kids into it too. But—you know. They can't."

She didn't know—and he was distracting her. His fingers were combing through his hair as he smoothed it back and tied it in place. It was hard enough to concentrate without him moving so much....

"Did you put a blanket on my bed?" she blurted out.

His smile melted away, and his hands fell. "Yeah," he said. "You were shivering."

She tensed. "So you were *spyin'* on me?"

"I checked on you, yeah." He just shrugged. He didn't look nearly as sorry as he should have. "Lis asked me to. She was worried—I mean, we all were. That fever could have killed you."

She didn't know how to respond to that. She didn't know what to say to him at all. Where did they stand now? Did they like her or hate her? Were they going to kill her, or leave her alone? And what about *him?* She backed away from him, shaking her head.

"Right—well, you can have it back," she said. She strode into her room and bundled up the brown blanket on top. It might be useful later, having an extra blanket, but she refused to be indebted to him. Goddess only knew what he thought he'd get in return.

She marched back out and shoved the blanket into his bewildered arms. "Here," she said. "Now *stay outta my room.*"

"Um...thanks." He dumped the blanket unceremoniously on the floor. As if she were dirty, as if he didn't want to get her filth on him. She would have kicked him—but then he grinned.

"Can I show you something?"

Rose started, eyeing him suspiciously. She was already calculating how fast and how high she'd have to kick to hit him somewhere that really hurt. "Huh?"

"Come with me. I have something you'll like to see."

On the streets, that would've been enough. He would've been doubled over on the ground in a heartbeat, with her knife jabbed through his neck if he hadn't gone down easily....But she didn't have her knife. She felt for it, subtly, but it wasn't tied at her hip as it should have been. Had Alysia taken it? Or Kayo?

It suddenly struck her how very alone she was, how isolated from everyone else. It was just her and Kayo. And she still wasn't well. If she called for help, who would even come?

"Please?" he said with what he must have thought was a winning smile. "I want to try and—and make it up to you. For everything. That's all."

"Yeah," she muttered under her breath as she took a step back. "I bet ya do...."

"You know your necklace?"

Rose stiffened, her hand flying unconsciously to her throat. "What about it?" she said, endowing every syllable with icy contempt.

"Have you ever seen one? A real one?"

"What?"

"A rose. The flower. Have you ever seen one?"

"I...no...."

"Do you want to?"

She stared at him. He met her eyes with a little smirk, as if he knew he had her cornered. That look alone should have earned him a broken nose.

She could feel her chest tightened. This was a trap—but if she followed him, she bought herself some time to flee. And if she defied him, he'd attack.

Fire. Never fear.

Men like him couldn't scare her anymore.

She straightened her back and spat her challenge in his face. "You touch me *or* my necklace and I'll put you in the *ground*, you got it? I ain't goin' *nowhere* with you, *ever!* Don't you even *talk* t' me ever again!"

He backed up half a step under the force of her tirade, flinching as if she'd hit him. "I just—"

"You jus' what? Y' think a key an' a blanket 'll make up for what you *did to me?* You wanna make up for it, go jump off a fucking cliff!"

He swallowed, his face paling. "Are—you sure?" he stammered.

"Do you want me t' say it again in Lyric?" she shot back, with all the scorn he deserved.

He sighed. To her amazement, she could see him wilting like a dying plant, shrinking away as he brushed his hair back from his face.

"I was afraid you'd say that," he sighed. And then he patted the balustrade. "This high enough?"

"It—what?"

"It's not a cliff, but if I jumped from here—is that high enough?"

"You—"

He was climbing up on the balustrade. He hauled himself up and just stood there, watching her, his arms outstretched.

"Should I jump, then?" he said.

Anger surged in her belly again. He thought he could make her feel guilty enough to let it go? He thought he could threaten her, blackmail her?

"Go ahead," she snapped at him.

His arms dropped. *He's not going to do it,* she thought with grim triumph. *He's too much of a coward. I called his bluff, and he—*

Then Kayo fell.

Rose heard herself scream as she ran to the balustrade. She thought she saw his outline tumble in midair—but then she lost sight of him.

A soft thump.

A horrible silence.

She clung to the balustrade and leaned as far out as she dared. He *couldn't* be hurt—what would the others say? They'd think she pushed him, they'd never believe her. He'd be happy to blame her—if he lived. And if he didn't....

She'd already half-made plans to flee the shrine when he walked back out into the open, beaming up at her.

"What the *hell?*" she shrieked.

"I jumped off," he called up to her. "So we're even, right?"

"*I'm going to kill you!*" she shouted back at him.

"Have to come get me first." He smirked, touching his fingers to his forehead in a sailor's salute. "Now who's the coward?"

She knew he was baiting her—but she didn't care. If he'd done it, so could she. It must have been a soft landing. She swung a leg over the balustrade, her heart pounding in her ears.

"Rose, what—?"

It didn't look that far. All she had to do was drop—now, here, before she lost her nerve.

"Rose! Rose, *don't!*"

She let go.

The half-second of empty air felt like an eternity—but the end would be worse, she was sure of it. She braced herself for the impact, for the crunch of broken bones, for horrible pain—

Her boots landed with a thump on damp soil. One of them sank into the dirt; the other slid out from underneath her. She staggered, throwing her arms out to catch her balance—and Kayo caught her.

He set her back on her feet before she could protest. She looked up at him, shoving stray curls out of her face, and started laughing. The terror melted off his face at once.

"Why would you *do that?*" he demanded—but he was laughing too. "Are you *insane?*"

"Are *you?! You* did it *first!*"

"I do that all the *time,* Liam taught me how to land, you can't just *jump off* something—"

"You called me a coward! You told me to do it!"

"I didn't think you actually *would!*"

She shoved him—but she was still laughing so hard she couldn't breathe. And looking up at him, at the huge grin spread across his face, just made her laugh even harder.

"Are you all right?" he asked her. "You didn't get hurt, did you?"

"Nuh-uh." She shook her head, still giggling. "What *is* all this?"

"Um...the compost heap," he said, rubbing the back of his neck with a sheepish smile. "I knew it'd be a soft landing, so—"

"You *tricked* me!"

"Hey, you said to jump, you didn't say I had to break my legs—"

"Well, *now* I am, go back up and do it again—"

But they were both laughing as he led the way down the earthen hill, littered with pungent and unidentifiable bits of detritus, and onto a gravel-strewn path. The path wound upward through a mound of rocks mingling with stone bricks that had fallen from up above. She climbed up one of them, staring open-mouthed at the garden around her.

"Wow," she whispered.

It wasn't large—but it was just large enough, and the vegetation high enough, that she almost believed they'd left the shrine behind.

Somehow, impossibly, a verdant paradise had sprung up in the ruins of the courtyard. Water the color of green glass cut through on a bed of rocks, the little stream ending in a small pond full of fish. And everywhere she looked, she saw flowers.

"How is this *here?*" she asked Kayo, who stood just out of arm's reach with his hands in his pockets, watching with unmistakable pride.

"I think the Divinæ put it here. At least some of it. When we got here, it looked just like this. Do you see the water lilies?"

"The what?"

"Look over here, floating in the water—"

"Wow!"

The pond was a miracle of its own: it had green algae crawling along the banks like a living rug, and as she approached, a frog hopped into the water. Something moved in the depths, and Rose shrank back with a yelp. But Kayo just laughed.

"It's just a fish. See?"

The fish in question swam just under the surface. She caught a glimpse of bright orange scales before it dove into the lily pads and vanished.

"Are there more?"

"A few. Not many."

"Enough for a good meal, though, huh," she said, sticking her arms out to keep her balance as she walked across the rocks.

"It's not worth it. This whole place is—it's just better left alone. We'd only mess it up, we don't know the first thing about plants."

"Sure you do," she said, and pointed to one of them. "What's that?"

"Um...a bush?"

"See?" she said, and grinned at him as she hopped down. "You know a *little.*"

He laughed. "C'mon," he said. "I want to show you the rest."

And for once she had no qualms at all about following him. The stream was so tiny that they could have stepped across it, but there was still a little wooden bridge to cross that made a satisfying sort of thump as their boots landed on it.

They stepped into the shade of a tree, and Rose spun in place, her head leaning all the way back, as she tried to see all the way to the top.

"It's so *tall!*"

"It's actually small for a tree."

"*This* is small?!"

"They have some that are so wide you could build a house inside them. And they're taller than the castle."

"You're lyin'."

"I'm not—some of these trees live for hundreds of years, and they just grow bigger and bigger all the time. There's a tree in Myvanwy that big—or there was, anyway."

"In—where?"

"The Isles of Myvanwy? In Courma? It's where the Conqueror was born. Anapoline was there before it burned down."

"Anapoline?" At last, she ripped her eyes from the tree. "How d'you know?"

"It's in one of my books."

She frowned at him. "Like the story about it?"

"Yeah, I read all about it."

"But—books don't have *stories,*" she protested. "They just have numbers and—I dunno—boring people sayin' boring stuff."

"They have nothing *but* stories," he said. He was smiling, clearly amused, but somehow she wasn't offended. "Can you read?"

"No...?"

"Oh. Well. If you like stories, you should learn. All the best ones are in books."

She scoffed. "Right, I'll just *learn to read,*" she said scornfully. "'Sides, they can't be *that* great. They wouldn't have The Gold Dragon, or Kip and Esther—"

"Sure they do. *And* Heidi of Sigilline."

"*Heidi?* The whole thing?"

"The whole thing."

Despite herself, Rose was impressed. All the more reason to snatch one of his books when he wasn't looking. She couldn't read it, but if she could sell it, she'd be rich enough to pay someone to read it *for* her.

"Oh—here," he said suddenly, pointing. "This way—this is the best part."

She'd forgotten that he'd mentioned her necklace, but as soon as she saw the flowers sprouting from the bush, she realized what they were. They bloomed in the shape of the one that hung around her neck, the petals shaped the same way. She gasped and ran forward.

Roses.

"Careful...." Kayo stood beside her, his voice soft. "There are thorns."

"Oh, yeah...wow," she whispered. "*Wow.*"

Each one was so delicate and fine that a master craftsman couldn't have made it—and yet the dirt below her feet had made dozens of them. And the smell of them—it was as warm as bread, as fruity as cherry pie, as rich as deep red wine, yet somehow it did not smell of food at all. She wanted to breathe in that smell until it flowed inside her like ale and filled her to the brim.

"I didn't think they were *real.*" She was afraid to speak too loudly, in case the beautiful dream around her cracked and shattered. "Not anymore."

"They're real. They're still around all over the place—just not in Alronelin. This one's from Savilla."

"It is?"

"Sure." Kayo reached out and lifted a crimson flower. "It's called a tesora. It's Savillan, it means 'treasure', but I think it's referring to the wine with the same name. And this one over here, see the little pink ones? They're called southern mountain roses. They grow wild all over the mountains. And over here, the ones on the vines...."

"They're *huge!*"

"Mm-hm. Lean in and smell them—see? It's a different smell than the other ones, it's lighter, kind of spicy almost. It's called a white oceanspray. It's supposed to smell like sea air, I don't know about that...."

"Which one—Kayo, look—" She fumbled with her necklace, pulling the pendant free of her dress and holding it up to show him. "What kind is this one, what d'you think?"

Kayo looked at her oddly for a moment, smiling a bit, his eyes warm and shining, his cheeks flushed. She felt herself blushing as well

—but no, she realized, he was looking at the necklace, not at her. He touched it gently at the bottom with one finger to stop it spinning.

"I know what this is." He took her hand and led her further down the path. "Come see."

The sunset brushed golden fingers across the last small clump of roses. She was not sure if it was a vine or a bush; its stem was sturdy and wooden, but it clung onto the trunk of the tree and spread violently in all directions, its thorns digging into the bark. Kayo separated one of the roses near eye level gently from the rest and showed her the fanning array of blade-shaped petals—deep crimson with a bright orange-pink center and a reddish-orange fringe bordering each petal.

"This is called a firerose," he told her. "And *this* is what your necklace is, I'm sure of it."

"Really? Mine isn't—it doesn't have all those colors...."

"Have you ever held it up to a light?"

"Huh? Umm, not...not in a while...."

Rose tugged the chain over her hair and wrapped it around her wrist, holding the medallion up to the sun. The light shot through the rose and refracted a thousand times within the glass, glowing reddish and, when it turned slightly to the side, brilliant yellowish-white. The gold gleamed a bright, vibrant orange.

"Goddess..." she breathed.

"It's beautiful," Kayo agreed. "I really love these roses. They don't really have a smell, they choke everything else around them, these vines can even split rocks apart—and half the time the flowers don't even bother to bloom. But they're not interested in being pretty. They're survivors. Once they take root, they'll grow like mad, and they'll outlast everything else. Give them enough time, and they'll tear down stone walls. They're...I don't know." He shrugged. "I just like them."

"Yeah...." She slid her necklace back over her head and stepped closer to the flowers, tracing the petals of one with her finger. "Me, too."

The world had been dirty and ugly and bloody for so long. Her life had felt fragile in the worst way—not fragile like glass, but fragile like an eggshell, because ultimately, it was worthless. The world itself seemed determined to snuff her out like a candle. And if it had, nobody would have cared.

But this place...these people...there was something about the way they'd burrowed into these ruins and made it into a home. Something about the place itself, with its delicate arches and colored glass and hidden garden. It was almost like magic—like a secret world, hidden away. And here, now, were the roses. Kayo thought they weren't interested in being beautiful? But they were—that was *all* they were. They only *existed* to be beautiful, and they were beautiful just for existing.

Being here, now, hearing the bells and smelling the tesoras and seeing the fireroses and feeling the sun on her skin—wearing the clean dress and the clean skin of another girl—it was like living another person's life. A life that she could never have, could never earn, could never deserve....

A life she wanted so badly it hurt.

She couldn't have put a single fragment of these thoughts to words—but she had to fight back sudden tears.

"You know," said Kayo suddenly, "you're really lucky."

She quickly wiped her eyes with the heel of her hand while he was looking away. "Huh?"

"These roses are probably the last roses left in Alronelin. And when they're gone....That's it." His voice fell so low she could barely hear it as he leaned against the tree. "They'll probably never come back."

"Why not?" She knew he was probably right, but something in his voice made her hackles rise, made her want to fight. "They made it here in the first place, and the sickness is gone now—"

"There never was a sickness."

She straightened up and looked at him, frowning. He was craning his neck, looking up at the foliage as it waved in a gentle breeze they could not feel, but his mouth was twisting into an angry snarl.

"They weren't sick," he repeated. "Sangor had them all destroyed. Pulled up from the roots."

"Sangor? You mean—the king?"

Kayo snorted. "In a manner of speaking. He certainly calls himself one."

"Well...he's got a crown," Rose said slowly. She was starting to think that something was...*wrong* with Kayo, that he'd been possessed by something when she had looked away. He'd turned stony and cold in the span of a heartbeat, and his bright smile had gone, replaced by an angry mask of a face that looked as if it had never smiled at all. "So he can call himself whatever he wants...right?"

"It's not the crown," he snapped. "It's the gold. He's got enough to do whatever he wants. No one will stop him. No one cares, not as long as they get their piece of it. Now the roses are gone, and the weeds and thorns are all that's left." He scowled into the darkness behind her. Rose backed up a step; she'd never seen that expression without being on the receiving end of it, and she never wanted to see it again.

"Why'd he want to get rid of 'em?" she asked, trying her best to sound casual. It wasn't too late to run away from him...but she had to be careful. Remembering the effortless way that he'd leapt from the balustrade—that he'd flown through the air and climbed sheer walls—made her blood run cold. If she meant to outrun him, she'd need a good head start.

Kayo shrugged. His expression didn't soften at all. "I heard a lot of reasons. That they were making people sick, or he was allergic, or they were the symbol of Courma and we were at war with them. It doesn't matter. People like him don't need a reason to go around destroying things that make people happy. They just do it because they can. They can do whatever they want. Treat us like criminals, like less than nothing. And they won't lose a bit of sleep over it."

It was almost funny—but she had no desire to laugh. Because he was right. Anyone with power would happily destroy all that was good and pure in the world, anything they didn't want for themselves. Not just kings and nobles, but the physically powerful, the manipulative and selfish people of the world, the brutal and stupid. Everyone was out there searching for someone they could overpower, and when they found them, they did exactly that.

After a long pause, Kayo said quietly, "D'you hear them?"

She paused, listening. "The bells?"

He nodded. "They're celebrating at the castle. Because the king's getting married. *Again.*"

"Wh—to *who?* What happened to his other ones?"

"Oh, they're fine. He just decided he needs a *third* wife. And so there's a grand party going on up at the castle, paid for with gold he stole from his people, from all of us, while we sit here and worry about starving to death."

Rose wanted to scoff at this—he of all people had no room to talk about letting other people starve—but Kayo's temper was clearly building, and she didn't want to agitate him further.

"Well—it ain't for long," she reminded him. "The prince'll be back soon, and then—"

"He's not coming back, Rose," Kayo cut across her. "He's dead."

"No he isn't!" she protested. "*You* don't know! He's *hidin'*, that's all, 'cause he's not old enough to be king."

"Don't be ridiculous."

"I'm not! But he comes of age this summer—same day as me," she added proudly.

Startled out of his temper, Kayo raised an eyebrow at her, the corner of his mouth lifting slightly. "You don't know your name, but you know when you were born?"

"Well...no," she admitted—how had he known she didn't know her real name? Hadn't he been the one who insisted it was "Rose" even when she said otherwise? "I picked my own. The same day as the prince's."

"That's a good one," said Kayo, nodding. "Because everyone's already celebrating."

"Exactly!" She suspected that he might be making fun of her, but if it stopped him from being angry...."There's music an' food everywhere already, an' nobody cares if I'm there too, it's real fun. And *this* one's going to be the best one, because we're turning eighteen!"

"Well, enjoy it," said Kayo, his smile fading. "Once people realize he's dead, they won't celebrate it anymore."

"He's *not* dead," she said hotly. "He'll be back, you'll see—"

"And so what if he *does* come back?" he retorted. "*Nothing* will change, not for people like us. You're just swapping out one rich, spoiled prick for another."

"You don't *know* that!"

"I'm sure of it. If there was ever a king who was halfway decent, he'd never get anything done. The nobles wouldn't let him. All they do is use people and hoard gold—and Sangor's the worst of them. He couldn't fuck things up more if he *tried*."

He was getting angry again. Rose stepped out of arm's reach as casually as she could, trying to make the movement seem natural.

"Well then, that's royals, ain't it?" she said dismissively. "Ain't nothin' to do about it. So ain't nothin' to lose if the prince takes over —right?"

Kayo didn't answer right away. He reached up and plucked a leaf off of the tree, then started to shred it into smaller and smaller pieces. His eyes were focused on the empty air in front of the leaf, his mind clearly elsewhere.

Finally, so quietly she barely heard him, he said, "It won't bring my brother back."

Her breath caught. "You mean—Liam?"

He nodded.

His brother. The Beggar's King. Her heart clenched, and the pain was almost real. She was almost angry with herself, in retrospect, for letting herself hope things would change when she'd heard of everything he'd done...or that he'd somehow survive the pyre.

She should have known better. Kayo was right: for people like them, nothing ever changed.

"I wish I coulda met him," she murmured.

He didn't speak. He just nodded. She looked around.

"Never woulda thought *this* was his hideout, though."

That forced a dry chuckle out of him. "You don't know the half of it. Without Liam...I mean, he helped us with all of it. Everything we have here is because of him."

Rose leaned against the tree beside him, tucking her hair behind her ears. "He was *amazin',*" she sighed. "I don't care if half the stories was made up, he was still—I mean, I couldn't believe anyone could stand up t' the soldiers like that. It made me think, you know, if one person could do all that—then *I* didn't have to put up with it neither —and I felt safer. Like he'd protect me. An' with the way things were, before...." She tried, but she couldn't put it into words, so she fell back with a sigh and twisted her fingers into her necklace. "He was like a hero out of the stories. I always wanted t' meet him."

"He would've liked that." Kayo crossed his arms and looked up at the sky; his eyes seemed a little too bright. "That you felt safer with him around. He always—well—you wouldn't think he'd be like that, if you met him, he was a bit—a bit harsh—but when something wasn't fair, when it wasn't right, he wouldn't let it go. Once, at the orphanage—I don't know what happened exactly, I was too young, but a soldier was messing with one of the girls. Then the next day he was just—gone. And no one could ever prove it, but—"

"It was him," said Rose—she was certain of it. "Wow."

Kayo nodded. "And that wasn't even the half of it. Even before the orphanage...he didn't talk about it much, but...."

"He killed his parents," Rose said softly. "Didn't he?"

Kayo stiffened. "Rose, orphans aren't all murderous *criminals*—"

"Yeah, but they don't have parents."

"I—" But Kayo couldn't seem to find a good argument. Finally, he sighed, his shoulders slumping. "Yeah," he said. "He did. But from what he told me, they deserved it. He was just—he did what he did to protect everyone. Not just me, but all of us—and other people too, people who couldn't defend themselves. Anyone who hurt people, anyone he thought was *evil*—he wouldn't stop until he made them pay, so they couldn't hurt anyone else. Sometimes, I think...he must've thought of himself as...not a hero, exactly, but an exterminator. He'd find evil in people and—and stamp it out."

"Good," said Rose savagely. "Th' world was better for it."

"Yeah," said Kayo, but he didn't sound convinced. "If he hadn't been looking out for me, I'd be dead right now. A hundred times over. And that was just me. All the people out there...."

"Yeah. He was amazin'."

"Yeah," Kayo said softly. "He was."

They fell silent, listening to the bells. Rose watched the sunlight dappling the tree leaves for a minute, but then she glanced at Kayo. He was staring at the roses as if trying to memorize them. His hands were always moving: tugging at his shirt, brushing his hair out of his face, fiddling with the bracelets on his wrist.

Then he spoke, startling her; she quickly pretended that she hadn't been looking at him. "I don't know what to do without him."

She didn't need to ask who he meant. Something told her, too, that this was something he'd never said aloud—something he couldn't say to the others.

"I don't know, either," she said, because she didn't. No one had sung for him, but the words that they should have sung had echoed in her head for a long time. *The one bright light that leads me home, when it fades...where am I to go?*

It felt like that. Everything around her was the same, but something had vanished from the world, something important and cherished, something she'd been relying on. And she hadn't even realized it until it was gone forever.

"You're probably the only person around here who actually *liked* him," Kayo admitted. "He and Dominic *hated* each other, and Artemis didn't like him—the kids barely even noticed—I thought maybe Lis would be sad he was gone, and she was for a while, but now —It's been months, and I still—it's like a missing tooth, where you can't leave the hole alone."

She knew exactly what he meant. When she'd lost her first tooth, the one right in the front, she hadn't known it would grow back. She'd spent the next several months trying not to panic, probing the gap with her tongue and wondering what she'd done wrong, waking in a cold sweat from nightmares about all of her teeth falling out at once and choking her.

"I just feel...lost," Kayo went on, his hands making a helpless gesture. "And I feel like I failed him, like I'm still failing him, and—" He slumped against the tree with a sigh. "I never thought about what I'd do when I came of age. Now I am, and—I don't know that there's anything I *can* do. Everything I thought would happen is just...gone. It's just been weeks and weeks of trying to scrape enough food together for the kids...and I guess that's all it'll ever be...."

No—that couldn't be true. She couldn't *let* that be true. Because when she came of age in the summer, she had many, many plans for her life, and she wasn't about to let them go. "Well, *I* know what you gotta do," she told him. "You gotta get better at being the Beggar's King for a start. The real one wouldn't 'a gotten cornered like *you* did."

He blinked at her. "Huh?"

"When you nearly fell on me. You *still* don't remember that?"

"Uh...no. It's all a blur. I just remember going out with Dominic, and then—what are you talking about?"

"I *mean* you can run an' climb an' stuff, that's good," she said. "An' you can probably fight, I dunno. But I ain't even *heard* of anythin' you did—an' I mean, you people are scrapin' meals together, you really ain't even close to what 'e was. You gotta go after bigger people, like *he* did, the people who're really monsters—"

"What? No," he cut across her, holding up his hands. "I'm *not* taking Liam's place. I was never *trying* to, I just borrowed his *clothes*."

"What? But then what were you *doin'* that day?"

"I don't remember—but Dominic and I go out sometimes and see what we can find. Sometimes on the docks there's stuff sitting out, no one notices a few sacks missing. We can't risk getting in trouble—"

"Are you *kidding me?*" she demanded. "You're stealin' a couple handfuls of *grain?* That's pathetic!"

"No one's trying to make some big *statement,* Rose, we're just trying to *survive!*"

"But if *you* don't take his place, who *will?*"

"No one," Kayo snapped. "And that's how it *should* be. My family can't lose anyone else to some idiotic crusade—"

"*Idiotic?*" She was shouting now, but she didn't care. "How can you *say* that? Don't you know what he *did* for—?"

"I know what he did!" His voice was rising too. "He went and got himself *killed,* that's what he did! You didn't see him, you didn't see what they *did* to him, they *burned him alive!* Just to scare us, just to make a *point!* Because it wasn't someone *he* cared about, it wasn't some horrible thing *he* had to watch—Liam was *tortured,* there was practically nothing *left* of him, and that's what they'll do to us—to *any* of us—"

"I know," she said, and her voice trembled. "I was there. I watched it. *I know.*"

He stared at her blankly—with eyes, she couldn't help but notice, that were wet and shining. When he spoke, he sounded as if he were choking.

"You were there?"

She nodded. "Yeah—an' you know *why* they did that? Why they wanted to scare us all so bad? Because *they* were scared o' *him.* You keep sayin' one person can't change anythin', but *he* did. He changed *everythin'*. People weren't gettin' what they had comin' to 'em, so he made it happen, all those nobles an' soldiers an' crooked merchants, we *needed* him—and now *you* can do that! It could be *you!* There has to be *someone,* you at least gotta *try*—"

Kayo stood frozen as she ranted at him, his eyes wide, his expression stunned—but then he pushed her abruptly aside and strode away, shaking his head.

"Hey—hey, wait!" She grabbed at his sleeve, but he tugged her loose. "Get back here!" she yelled, running after him.

But he took off running, too—and he was faster than she was. By the time she'd found her way out of the garden, he was gone. She was left standing alone, shivering at the cold wind that snaked through the columns of the arcade, as the sun finally sank below the horizon, and the bells fell silent.

A small *plop* startled her, and she found herself bolting for the stairs before she remembered the fish and the frogs. Still, the quiet was eerie. Feeling very small among the enormous arcades, she climbed back up to her room, then down the corridor, toward the kitchen where she knew his friends would be.

Kayo had left the door to his room open, so she could see clearly that he wasn't in there. She thought he must be with the others—but he wasn't in the kitchen, or with the little kids, or in the courtyard when Alysia enlisted her help in washing all the bowls in the fountain. And when she finally returned to her room, his was still empty and dark.

It was for the best, she told herself. She didn't even know what she'd say to him. *He* was the feckless idiot that had taken the image of her hero and warped him into a weak, soft-spined coward that couldn't scare a kitten. The Beggar's King had hand-picked him to follow in his footsteps—but he didn't have it in him. She was so furious with him that she sat on her bed with the door open for a long time, waiting for him to come back so she could shout at him some more.

She was still waiting when she finally fell asleep, the big iron key still clutched in one hand.

"*It's coming.*"

Rose woke with a start and rolled over. A shadow was moving outside her open door, sliding like dark silk over the balustrade outside. She grabbed the knife under her pillow and held her breath, keeping one eye open.

The shadows concentrated into a black shape, slinking closer. She sat up—

And the cat froze in place. Rose stared at it, and it stared back, its yellow eyes glowing faintly in the darkness.

"Shoo," she hissed at it. When it didn't react in the slightest, she waved her arm at it. "Get lost or I'll cook you for dinner, fleabag!"

The cat sat down and started licking one white foot.

"Oh, sure, just make yourself comfortable," Rose snapped at it in a harsh whisper. "*Get lost!*"

She got up and stomped at the cat with her unlaced boots. Only then did it trot out of sight—but not, in her opinion, as quickly as it should have. She scoffed as she sank back down onto her bed. Even the cats around here were impudent little sneaks. The ones in the city at least had the good sense to bolt when threatened—which was a shame; cat meat wasn't bad. If the orphans really were starving, they could try setting a few traps for *them* instead of her....

"*They're coming....*"

She stiffened. This time, she knew she hadn't imagined the voice. She tiptoed to her door and listened hard, gripping her knife so tightly it hurt.

"It's coming...I can't stop it...can't stop it...."

She knew that voice—but she kept her knife in her hand as she crept forward, peeking around the open door and into Kayo's room. She could just make out the shape of him in the blankets, tossing and turning—

She nearly jumped out of her skin as he sat bolt upright.

"No!" he yelled. "No, don't touch them! *Don't touch them!*"

"What the fuck are you two *doing?*"

Rose had to stifle a cry as someone spoke up behind her—but it was just Dominic, emerging from the furthest door in just his drawers.

Kayo screamed. Rose jumped—but Dominic just shoved her unceremoniously aside. He grabbed Kayo's shoulder and shook it.

"Kayo. *Kayo.* Hey—"

"It's coming! They're coming! It's—"

"Kayo, *wake up.*"

"—it's—it's gonna—"

"*Kayo!*"

Kayo sucked in a gasping breath, looking around with half-open eyes.

"Wh—huh...?"

"It's okay. Go back to sleep."

His eyelids fluttered, then closed. "Dom?" His voice was an indistinct mumble, a far cry from the harsh clarity of his earlier shouts.

"Yeah, it's just me. Go to sleep."

"Mmkay...." And Kayo sank back onto his bed, rolled over, and fell still.

Dominic got up with a sigh and walked out past Rose, scratching his head. "You go back to sleep, too," he yawned at her.

She realized her mouth was open and closed it. "*What the hell was that?*" she demanded of Dominic's back as he walked away.

He paused, glancing over his shoulder. His eyes were heavy with sleep. "He gets nightmares," he said.

He clearly seemed to think that was a sufficient explanation. Rose ran after him before he could vanish back into his room. "*Nightmares?* That wasn't a *nightmare,* he was—*possessed!*"

"Dunno what to tell you." Dominic paused for a jaw-cracking yawn. "It happens sometimes. Got better for a while, then worse again. 'S why he can't sleep upstairs with the kids, they got enough to deal with."

She gaped at him; she didn't know what to shout at him first. "You *could have warned me!*" she finally blurted out.

"Did no one mention it?" He gave a sleepy shrug. "Guess we forgot."

"Oh, that is such *horse shit*—"

"Okay, fine. We didn't want to scare you. Happy?"

"*No!*"

"Yeah, well. Ain't any other mattresses but these, so sleep wherever you want." He paused, frowning at her. "You goin' somewhere? Why're you wearing your boots?"

"Why aren't *you* wearin' *anything?*" she retorted.

"Dom, shut the door." Artemis's voice, heavy and slurring, drifted out of the open door. "And put some clothes on."

"I'm coming," Dominic called back to her. "G'night," he added to Rose.

"Wait a min—"

But he'd already shut the door in her face. Rose was left to punch furiously at the air before stalking back to her room.

As she passed Kayo's open door, she thought she saw something moving inside. She doubled back—but then she heard a click behind her as Kayo's door shut. She retreated into her room, closing the door against more stray cats and nocturnal outbursts, and threw herself onto the bed.

Right before she fell asleep, she heard the click of the door latch again, and soft footsteps. But she was too far gone to care.

Muffled voices woke her what felt like minutes later.

Rose dragged herself up again and threw open her door with every intention of strangling every single orphan she found outside— but then she caught a few words.

"—saw fires in the lower city—"

She froze, lurking just behind the doorway, and listened hard.

"...don't mean anything," Dominic's voice said. "Could just be cookfires—"

"You think I'd wake you up for that?" That was Kayo's voice, angry—and scared. "Something's going on, I know there is, I could hear alarm bells and shouting—"

"Whatever it is, we'll hear about it tomorrow."

"And by then it'll be over, the soldiers might have killed half the people there—"

"Sounds like something we should run *away* from, Kayo."

"No, we *have* to go. *Now*. If you'd just—"

"What's the damn rush?"

"Just trust me, we have to go—people need help—kids. There'll be kids caught up in this, they'll need us—"

"We can't *afford* any more kids, Kayo. If we bring home any more we'll all starve to death."

"We can't just leave them on their own—"

"Yeah, we can. They're probably better off that way. There's food out there—which *we* don't have."

"We could steal something tonight. The soldiers will be too busy to stop us."

"Why are you so desperate to stick yourself into that mess?"

"Just go with me, Dom. Please."

"No."

Silence. Rose kept expecting a door to shut, or footsteps to retreat, but nothing happened. Then:

"I'll go myself."

"Kayo, *don't*—"

"I can't just sit here."

"Kayo, you *can't*." Artemis's voice was chiming in now. "What are we going to do if something happens to you?"

"I'm going. I'll try and be back by morning."

"You can't go *alone!*"

"Don't have much of a choice, do I?"

"Just don't go at all!"

"I—I just—

"Kayo, I know you want to help, but there ain't anything you can do, you'd just be stirrin' up trouble and riskin'—"

"Fine," Kayo snapped.

"I just don't want you to—"

"I heard you. Forget it."

"Kayo...."

Footsteps. Rose risked a glance and saw Kayo slam the door of his room. Dominic stood out in the corridor for a second or two, then quietly disappeared inside his own room.

That seemed to settle the matter—but something told Rose that wasn't the end of it. When she lay back down, she found herself looking out the window, watching the clouds pass over the moon. It was nearly full. She wondered if perhaps the chaos in the lower city was some sort of crime spree. They always waited until the moon was bright before picking over the docks and warehouses and stealing anything that wasn't locked up or nailed down.

Or maybe it was a riot.

That did it: there was no way she could sleep now. She sat up and laced her boots a little more tightly. She'd go up to the tower and take a look—she'd be able to see what was happening from there.

She was tying the pocket Alysia had given her to her waist under her dress when she heard a door open. Footsteps, so soft she could barely hear them. She unlatched her door with great care and peeked out. The corridor was deserted—but Kayo's door was open. And when she took a look, she found his bed empty.

She ran on tiptoe down the corridor and turned the corner just in time to see a shadow retreating. She followed it all the way to the courtyard, then hung back, watching as Kayo walked into the moonlight. He veered straight into the kitchen, but she could see him in there through the open door, rummaging around. He came out a moment later with a sword strapped to his back and a coil of rope over his shoulder. She watched, bewildered, as he tied a crude noose with one end and threw it over a stone arc near the fountain. He gave it a tug, then, clearly satisfied with it, kicked the whole coil into the hole in the fountain.

She nearly groaned aloud as she watched him disappear. She'd thought he'd go out the door, the one he'd said someone would show her. But the sewers? What was the point of going in there? Was there a way through them into the lower city?

She reminded herself firmly that it didn't matter. Kayo was gone, and nobody knew he was gone—which meant she could pillage his room and steal anything of value. She could find a hiding spot for it all, the books especially, and then when she left, she could retrieve them and sell them. That was the sensible thing to do. The only practical course of action.

So why was every nerve in her body screaming for her to go after him?

Later, she would tell herself that she'd never get away with stealing Kayo's things. She'd insist, in her own head, that she saw an opportunity to get out and took it. She wasn't worried at all about what was happening in the lower city, or what would happen to Kayo—*especially* not him.

But in that moment, all she did was stop wrestling with her gut and follow it instead. She hurried back to the corridor, but paused in front of Dominic's door. Then she debated internally with herself for a full-half minute before she realized that she was wasting precious time and finally forced herself to knock.

She heard a groan from inside. Then Dominic grumbled, "What?"

"Uh...Dominic? I, um...I saw Kayo run off, I just thought—"

"*What?!*"

Dominic jerked the door open. Rose, averting her eyes, saw Artemis behind him, still fast asleep.

"Where'd Kayo go?" he demanded.

She pointed. "Down into the water. I ain't sure what he—"

"*Damn it!*" Dominic growled, and slammed the door in her face. Rose stood there, blinking, and listened to him rummaging around his room. He and Artemis spoke quietly, but she couldn't make out the words.

She backed away from the door, but she didn't leave. After about a minute, the door opened again, and Dominic burst out, now fully dressed. He almost didn't notice her.

"Oh—hey, thanks for letting me know," he said as he strung his bow and slung it over his shoulder. "Tell Lis where I went, will you?"

"What? No, I'm comin' with you!"

Dominic stared at her—but Rose was just as surprised as he was to hear the words come out. *Was* she going? She couldn't think of one reason why she should—but she also couldn't stand the thought of staying behind.

"You *want* to come?" he asked her, and for some reason he cast a nervous glance back at Artemis.

"Yeah. I'm comin'."

She expected Dominic to try and talk her out of it—but he just nodded. "Then let's move."

And he set off. She ran after him, silently wondering what the hell had come over her.

Dominic, too, ducked into the kitchen on the way to the fountain. He emerged with a little glass lantern, the candle inside already lit.

"Here—hold this," he said, and handed it to her before bending to lace up his boots properly.

"Kayo didn't bring one o' these."

"Might not need it. I dunno. My eyes ain't as good as his." He straightened up and checked the knot that Kayo had tied with a sharp tug. "Want to go first? Or should I?"

"Um—I will. I guess."

"Then c'mon, we gotta move fast."

He was right—but Rose still had to bully herself relentlessly as she tied up her skirt before she could force herself to hold onto the rope. She slid down cautiously, bracing her feet against the stone, the lantern looped over one wrist.

"Just walk down backward," Dominic called down to her. "Yeah —just like that."

If he cut the rope, she wouldn't fall far, and there'd be a bit of water to soften her landing. But that wasn't much consolation. She looked down, regretted it, closed her eyes, realized that was much worse, and finally trained her eyes on the stone below her boots. The stone was a little slippery, but the rope held, and before she knew it, the wall gave way, and she was dangling over the water. She slid down the rest of the way and landed with a loud splash.

"I'm down!" she called up.

Dominic's silhouette appeared overhead a moment later. She backed up and watched him lower himself down with much more confidence than she'd felt, landing with barely a ripple.

"Let's go," he said, and took the lantern from her as he led the way.

If the point of using the sewers was to be discreet, Dominic certainly hadn't gotten the message. His splashing footsteps echoed loudly off the raw stone, and he didn't bother to keep his voice down as he muttered to himself in what sounded like Lyric. She tied her skirt up and followed him at a safe distance. In the pitch-black darkness, the lantern in his hand shone so brightly that she could have spotted it a league away.

The smell of the sewers hit her well before the little stream joined the larger flow of water. She was suddenly immensely grateful that Alysia had sewn the sleeves back onto her chemise: it gave her something to press over her nose. She hesitated at the edge of the faster, fouler water, but Dominic trudged forward without fear, so she steeled herself and followed. To her relief, her boots kept her feet snug and dry even in the ankle-deep sludge.

She kept her eyes up—on Dominic and the light, not on the water rushing past her.

I'm not afraid, she told herself. *Fire, never fear. I'm not afraid of anything anymore.* And the more she repeated, the more she almost believed herself.

But when their passage met another, larger and fouler and moving fast enough that little white caps of foam glowed in the candlelight, a little sound escaped her. Dominic looked back.

"You okay?" he asked her.

"Yeah—fine—"

"You sure? I know you don't like water or whatever—"

"Nobody likes *sewer water*," she snapped.

"True—but it ain't like we're gonna drown. We're okay."

"Yeah, sure, *you'd* think that," she grumbled, half to herself. "*You* ain't the half-wit who followed a stranger underground...."

He scoffed. "I'm not gonna do anythin' t' you."

"Yeah, right." She kept her eyes on her boots, walking carefully so she didn't slip. "You said like five times you'd shoot me if I left."

"That was *ages* ago."

She glared at him, but he couldn't see it. "So you *wouldn't* shoot me now."

"Nah. I mean—if it's between you an' my family, I'm pickin' my family. But, you know."

"Oh, really?" Rose said, as scathingly as she could muster.

"Ha! Don't act like *you* wouldn't stab me in the back as soon as look at me."

"I ain't done it yet, have I?"

"Only 'cause it won't help you any."

He had a point, but she refused to admit it. "Ain't nothin' changed since the last time you people said you were gonna shoot me."

"Sure it has. Or, well—" He shrugged. "Maybe not. But you ain't done anythin' to deserve it yet. It ain't hard. Just don't threaten me or anyone I care about, an' we're good."

She hugged herself, rubbing her arms to stave off the chill. "What's he doin', anyway?" she asked Dominic.

"Who, Kayo?" He shrugged, shaking his head. "Not a clue. Was hopin' you knew."

"Nuh uh." What was *she* doing? Whatever this was, Kayo and Dominic didn't want or need her. She should have just stayed in bed.

But what if Kayo went to do something exciting? Something like the Beggar's King would do? Maybe Liam had set out just like this on the night he'd gone to murder the king. The idea of Kayo doing anything like that was laughable...but she still remembered clearly the way Kayo had looked flying through the air. The way she'd felt —the flickering hope that maybe the Beggar's King might still be alive.

"You ever find out what happened?" she asked Dominic.

"Hmm?"

"That day when—when I met Kayo. Did he ever say what happened?"

He shook his head. "Nah. Earliest he can remember is when we was lookin' around at the docks. That was *way* before the ship."

"The what?"

"Oh—you didn't know about the ship he blew up?"

"He *what?!*"

"Yeah, I can't believe he don't remember that. You'd think that'd stand out."

"How the hell did he *blow up a ship?* What happened?"

"Oh, Goddess, it's a *long* story."

"Tell me!"

"All right, all right. So—we needed food, right?" That was all the prompting he'd needed to launch into the full story, his voice echoing along the tunnel. "So we were checking out some of the warehouses by the dock, and we got up on the roof to see what we could see. Then there's this ship that comes floating in, all suspicious, lights out an' all, and soon as they moor, they drag out this woman who's just *screamin'* her head off—"

"Who?"

"I think she was the captain? I told Kayo we should hang back, but he went without me to go see, so I followed him down and we were eavesdropping, right, and two *more* women come off the boat, and one of 'em's got guards with her, and she's given' orders left and right—turns out she's the *Savillan princess.*"

"*No.*"

"I swear to the Goddess, that's what they said—and I mean, she just married the king, so she's *here*—"

"What was she doin' on some busted old tub?"

"Not a clue. Best I can tell, she commandeered some ship in Savilla and made 'em take her here. It was all *real* suspicious—the women with her were prisoners or somethin', and they had more on the ship. An' so Kayo hears *that* an' just takes off."

"Takes off *where?*"

"To go on the damn ship and rescue 'em, I guess."

"He *what?!* Weren't there *guards?*"

"More'n a few." Dominic shook his head. "I don't know what he was thinking, couldn't talk him out of it—then he ain't in there five minutes before the damn thing explodes."

"The *ship?!*"

"Yep. Big explosion blows out the side, and the whole thing starts burning. Draws people toward us like flies to shit. 'Course, I think Kayo's blown himself up too—but then he runs out onto the deck with a bunch of Savillan sailors. The rest of 'em jump off, but then one a them starts *kissin'* him—"

"*What?*" yelped Rose, her voice hollow and loud over the rushing water. "*Why?!*"

"If you ask Liam, it happens all the time," said Dominic with a shrug. "He'd rescue women and they'd throw themselves at him, they'd be so grateful." He snorted. "So he said. Anyway, then she jumps in the water too—"

"Was she pretty, at least?"

"How the hell should I know? I barely even know what *you* look like."

"Oh." Why did she care, anyway? What was wrong with her? She was just caught up in the drama, that was all—and she was starved for entertainment.

She realized suddenly that she was walking beside Dominic and not behind him, easily within arm's reach. She didn't bother moving.

"So then—?"

"So, I think Kayo's going to jump in the water behind them, because that's what makes sense if he doesn't want to *die,* but he doesn't. He stands his ground. Whole flood of soldiers comin' toward him. So I back him of, o' course, I shoot as many as I can—"

"Oh, so *them* you can see?"

"Kinda," he said. "I just track the movement. Ain't like I gotta read."

"And that works for you? Somehow?"

Dominic chuckled. "Wanna try me?

"Kinda, yeah."

"Let's not," he said, and his lopsided grin glinted in the faint light. "But yeah—works good enough so far. Worked all right then. But I didn't know what he was doin'—but then he kept lookin' back, and I realized he was stalling so they could get away. So I switch up, grab someone's lantern and start makin' fire arrows, tryin' ta make the ship burn in the right spots—I think it slowed 'em down a little."

"And then what?"

"Kayo finally jumped off, but then he got right back on the docks and started runnin'. I think he was still buyin' those prisoners time, looked like one of them was hurt, that seems like the sort of stupid thing he'd do. I tried to follow on the roofs and cover him, but I couldn't keep up. So I went home. I was hopin' I'd see him there, but —you know the rest better'n I do. How far'd he get?"

"You know that fountain in the upper city with all the horses?"

"I think so?"

"He was a couple levels above that."

"Damn. He got *far*."

"Yeah," said Rose. She couldn't deny that she was impressed. "Don't even know how he got through the gates. He was climbin' an' swingin' around like—I don't even know what. I thought—"

She broke off. But Dominic was looking at her expectantly, so she looked away, shrugging. "I thought he was the real thing."

"Well, he did *learn* from the real thing," Dominic pointed out. "Liam was always good at that shit. I think it's 'cause he didn't give a fuck if he lived or died."

"What's that got to do with anything?" said Rose, annoyed.

"You can probably jump a lot further if you ain't worried about hittin' the ground. I dunno. I'd never do all that—Arty needs me."

"'Arty'?" she sniggered.

"Uh, yeah? The beautiful woman who puts up with too much of my shit as is? And *yours,* I might add." She rolled her eyes. "So how'd he hit his head?" Dominic asked her.

"Oh—it was my hidin' spot. It used t' be a—a blacksmith's, I think. He fell through th' roof. I think he hit his head that way, there was a lotta junk in there."

Dominic winced. "How'd he slip the soldiers?"

"I, uh—I hid him. They got mixed up an' thought he ran off."

Dominic didn't reply. She glanced up at him and saw him staring at her, eyebrows raised.

"Whoa," he said at last.

"I mean—yeah, it was stupid of them—"

"No, you," he said. She couldn't puzzle out what his expression was supposed to mean. "You really *did* save his life."

She scoffed, crossing her arms and rubbing them with her hands. "Yeah, right."

Again, Dominic didn't say anything. He seemed to be waiting for her to speak—but what could she say? She wasn't about to admit how stupid she'd been. How she'd let a pair of sweet brown eyes and a bright smile trick her into following a total stranger into the sewers.

She'd done it again tonight, too. What was *wrong* with her?

"Well," Dominic said at last. "If no one else told you...thank you."

She shot a sideways look at him, frowning. But he seemed to be sincere. "You're—*thankin'* me?"

"Well, yeah. Kayo's family. And if you hadn't done that...." A troubled look flitted across his face, but he just shrugged. "That's it. He'd be gone."

"The soldiers would've *arrested* 'im, not *killed* 'im. Probably."

"That's about a thousand times worse," Dominic pointed out.

He was right. Still—she didn't like the way he was looking at her. She scoffed. "Well, I ain't doin' it again, so."

"Then why'd you come with us?"

She glanced up at him again. She couldn't tell if he was making fun of her or not. "What, and miss another Savillan princess hostage rescue?" she said. "You're dreamin'."

Dominic's laugh reverberated up and down the stone tunnel. They'd traveled a fair distance already, she was glad to see, and abandoned the shallow water for the uneven stone path. The tunnel had widened, and they passed more of the buried ruins of the ancient city, little empty houses staring at them with their dark shutterless windows. It made her skin crawl. The Goddess only knew what—or who—could be lurking in there unseen.

"You ain't got any clue why he'd do this, do you?" Dominic asked her suddenly.

"Huh?" She blinked up at him—Goddess, he was tall—but it took her a moment to understand. "Oh, Kayo? Nuh-uh."

Dominic sighed and ran his fingers through hair that wasn't there, as if he'd forgotten how short it was. "Damn it," he muttered. "I just —I'm worried about him. This ain't like him."

"It isn't?" She snorted. "It's stupid as hell, seems like 'im t' me."

Dominic scowled, glancing at her out of the corner of his eye. "Oh, don't start with that again."

"Start with what again?" she said scathingly. "How he kidnapped me and locked me up?"

"Yes, *that.* Believe it or not, you got off lucky."

Rose gaped at him, stunned by the sheer audacity. "...you wanna run that by me again?" she snarled.

"You did," he insisted. If Liam'd been alive he would've killed you the second you set foot in there. An' he'd never've lost any sleep over it."

"I shoulda never been there at all!" she said indignantly.

"He was just tryna *help*, Rose. If he could remember he'd tell you the same thing. He wanted t' *help you.* Anyone with eyes could see y' needed it, for the Goddess' sake, all of us felt—all of us—"

He stammered and trailed off, wincing. But Rose knew exactly what he'd been about to say. She could read it on his face.

"*You* felt sorry for me?" she demanded. "*All o' you* felt sorry for me? You're fuckin' *orphans,* you horse's ass—"

"Hey, now—"

"You think I *wanted* t' be locked up with all o' you?" She was yelling now, but she had no intention of lowering her voice. "You think you're *better*'n me, you think you know what's *best* for me? I didn't need *you,* I didn't need *any* o' you!"

Dominic snorted. "Yeah, okay."

She punched at him, but he stumbled back, dodging it.

"Hey, stop it!"

"I *don't!*" she yelled. "My *whole life* I took care o' myself, I never needed no one else! Sure, it was a-a rough week, but I didn't need his stupid help, I woulda been *fine!*"

"No, you would've been *alive*," Dominic pointed out. "Not the same thing."

"Don't you *dare*—"

"Rose, just shut up," Dominic cut across her, coming to a halt. "Okay?"

She whirled around to face him. For a moment she was so furious that she actually was incapable of speech. But Dominic seemed just as angry as she was.

"Look—*they* don't get it, Arty and Kayo and them, they always had *someone*—they don't know what it's like to wake up and—and have *no one*. But *I do*. And it's *awful*. I *wasn't* fine. *You* weren't fine. We're barely fine *now*. You just...don't know what you're missin'."

"Oh, and you do?" she snarled.

"Yeah," he shot back. "I *do*. Do whatever you want, but if I was in your shoes, I'd be fuckin' thankin' Kayo for draggin' my ass off the streets. So what if he felt sorry for you? You *needed* someone to feel sorry for you. You think anyone else in this city gives a fuck about you? You think they feel *anything* for you? *Grow up.*"

Her stomach twisted with a sinking suspicion that he was right—and a horrible fear that he was. Because if he was right...if these were the only people who had cared about her, ever, in her whole life....

She slammed her fist into his shoulder as hard as she could. He winced and slapped his hand over the spot.

"Ow!" he yelled. "What the hell was that for?!"

"*You* grow up," she grumbled, marching past him. "Stupid flea-bitten son of a whore—"

"I am, actually," he said, massaging his arm as he followed her. "*Son of a whore* is practically tattooed on my face, I've been very open about that."

That startled a laugh out of her. "Shut up."

He just shrugged. "I'm sorry. Really. It's just—I've known Kayo a long time. He'd never hurt you. Or *anyone*."

"Yeah, okay," she muttered. She still couldn't reconcile the Kayo she knew now, the Kayo Dominic knew, with the one who'd slammed the door on her in her cell. The one who wouldn't listen to a word she said, who snarled and shouted at her, who hadn't cared if she'd starved to death. "Said no one'd even notice if he killed me, but sure, he's a nice guy...."

Dominic winced. He scratched at his jaw, where stubble was beginning to darken his skin. "He's not usually like that. He's just been...you know. All over the place. Since...since Liam died. But I don't know what to—I-I just can't say anything right about it, he just yells at me when I try." He grimaced.. "Guess he doesn't wanna hear that he was better off...."

"Yeah, he should just get over it, *I guess*," Rose snarled, sarcasm dripping from every word. "Wouldn't want 'im to get *hysterical* about it."

Dominic snorted. "He should. Liam was a *prick.*"

"Hey!"

"What? *You* didn't know 'im. Coulda been a prick for all you know."

"Well what'd *you* ever do for anyone?" she shot back.

Dominic shrugged again. "I mean, don't get me wrong, I—it's not like I miss him, but the way he died...it was hard to watch. It still —" He broke off, shaking his head. "But it's different with Kayo. They were close. And—well, he had a funny way o' showin' it, but Liam really cared about him. I think. He was hard on' im, but Kayo don't know any different."

"What makes *you* such an expert?"

"I dunno, I had a loving family? And a soul?"

"Well now *you're* being a prick."

"Trust me," he snickered. "I'm *really* not." But his laugh broke off abruptly. Perhaps the sound echoing off the stone had reminded him where he was, or perhaps he realized that he was making fun of a dead man. He rubbed the back of his neck. "Look, I—I know it's hard, losin' him like that, even for us it was hard. It's not like I don't understand—"

"Neither does *he*," Rose pointed out, her voice hardening.

Dominic frowned at her. "Huh?"

"An' you *definitely* don't! *Neither* o' you understand! He's dead for *two seconds* an' you two go around dressin' up like 'im? Pretendin' to *be* 'im?"

"That's exactly what he would've wanted us to—"

"But you don't even have the stones to *do it right!*" She swiped her hands angrily through the air as the words poured out of her. What was she doing, insulting a man this much bigger than her while he had her alone in the sewers? She couldn't make herself stop. "You just, what, steal a coupla sacks o' grain an' call it a day? The Beggar's King was a *hero*. He *meant* somethin', and *you people*—"

Dominic snorted. Rose whipped her head around, glaring at him.

"Don't you even *start!*"

"Rose, your *hero* is someone who went around killin' people he didn't like."

She bristled. "Well, no one else was gonna make 'em pay for what they did!"

"He wasn't doin' it for you, Rose. He wasn't doin' it for anyone but himself."

"So? He was—when he was around—" She couldn't even begin to explain. "When I heard o' the stuff he did—" She threw her hands up in frustration. "I never thought *anythin'* would get better. But then he *made* it better. The soldiers were scared o' him, I could tell—"

"Yeah, and they were *way worse* because of it."

"Because he was *doin' somethin'!* Even the king was scared o' him! And all the other people, they were startin' to fight back, and I thought they—it felt like—like it wasn't just me anymore. Like...."

"Like you were a part of something bigger," Dominic said quietly. "Something that mattered."

She had to stop herself from kicking him in the shin. "If you get it, why're you bein' such a *prick?*"

Dominic opened his mouth, then closed it again. Finally, he said, "You're right. Sorry." He shrugged. "I just—if you knew him, I don't think you'd admire him so much anymore."

Then why was he so hell-bent on ruining this for her? "That's true about *everybody,*" she said peevishly.

"...huh. Good point."

The paths were joining now instead of separating. The tunnel wasn't widening, but the water was getting deeper. They had to be close, now. All of this had to flow out into the ocean somewhere.

That gave her pause. The only way out of Bermeia aside from the bridge was by water. The harbor was out of the question—but the soldiers couldn't guard the whole ocean. The orphan's shrine was right next to the open sea, nowhere near the docks—and the soldiers that guarded it. If she could find an exit that way....

She'd steal a boat. Or she'd have to swim for it. But she'd focus on that part later.

Were they going to follow the water until it ended? She felt a sudden flutter of excitement crawl up her belly. Maybe none of this would matter after all. Maybe she'd finally find her way out of this damned city tonight, and the orphans could just—

Dominic stopped dead. "*No,*" he groaned. "He *wouldn't.*"

"What?"

He pointed at a smaller tunnel up ahead, emptying into theirs. Rose didn't understand—it looked just like any other that they had passed.

"See in the mud?" he told her. "Tracks. That's gotta be him. But why *here?*"

"What are you talking about?"

"Just—c'mon." Dominic swerved to the right and followed the tunnel, wading upstream through a river of what appeared to be—but definitely wasn't—mud. "He's gone mad. He's gone completely mad...."

"What the hell's your problem?" she demanded. But Dominic just waved an impatient hand in her direction.

"Not now. Just—c'mon."

And he started muttering to himself in Lyric again. They followed the tunnel up a gentle slope as it began to shrink around them, the water drying to a thin trickle, but Rose could see nothing at all up ahead.

The path branched without warning, and Dominic stopped dead.

To the right, the tunnel ended in the source of the water, which dripped from a rounded hole in the ceiling. Through it, she could see the night sky and the glow of torches, could hear footsteps and voices and the distant sounds of loud, shouting voices that floated across the entire lower city after dark, as she recalled. Though they sounded different than she remembered.

To the left, a dry dirt tunnel carved an uneven path into darkness.

"No," Dominic groaned. "No, no, *no,* he *wouldn't—*"

"*What?!*" Rose demanded, exasperated. Dominic finally deigned to pay her the slightest bit of attention.

"*That,*" he said, pointing out the hole. "Kayo went that way, the grate's missin'. But *why?* What the hell is he *doing* here?"

"In—the sewers?"

"In Fishgut Alley," he told her.

Rose physically recoiled from the hole, putting Dominic between her and it. "Fishgut Alley," she repeated flatly.

"Or—maybe the orphanage," he corrected, biting his lip as he tried to get a glimpse through the hole. "But he wouldn't go back there, none of us would. So what's he *doin'* here?"

"Can I borrow that?" Rose said, reaching for the lantern. Dominic barely seemed to notice as she plucked it out of his grasp. "Well," she said. "'Bye."

"Wh—hey, wait a damn minute—"

"I ain't goin' to Fishgut Alley! At *night! You're* the one who's gone mad."

"You said you wanted to come with me to find Kayo!"

"Yeah, well—"

But she stopped. She'd spotted something odd in the opposite tunnel. Her stomach lurched as she raised the lantern—but it was just a pile of rocks.

No—not rocks. Embers. That much was obvious from the ashes they were buried in and the smoke that had stained the stone black overhead.

"Rose...."

"Did he—build a fire?" she asked, bemused. But no—it was cold. It had burned itself out ages ago. So then, who—and why?

"Rose!" Dominic said sharply. "Get out of there!"

Rose jumped and turned—but then she did a double take. There were dark stains in the dirt, and judging by the location, and the pattern....

"*Rose!*" Dominic snarled.

His voice shattered her focus. She whirled around on her heel, glaring at him. "Who the *fuck* d'you think you're talkin' to?" she demanded.

"Just—get *out* of there, it's a dead end," he insisted, waving her toward him. He was clearly trying to keep his voice steady, but every move he made was stiff and frantic. "Leave the lantern, just *come on, we gotta go find Kayo before he gets himself in trouble. Please.*"

She had the feeling that he was less desperate to find Kayo than he was to get out of the sewers. But she couldn't deny that she felt the same way. Something about the tunnel made her skin crawl. She cast one last look at the dark stains, then dropped the lantern and left.

Dominic was practically vibrating with anxiety as she stopped below the hole and looked up. The surface was close enough that she could have shoved her arm through it to the elbow—but that didn't mean she had the strength to pull herself up.

She wasn't going to anyway. She was not going into Fishgut Alley. That was that. She'd stand watch or something, wait for Dominic to get back with Kayo. She wasn't afraid. This had nothing to do with being afraid. It was just common sense. Even people in Fishgut Alley didn't want to be in Fishgut Alley.

"Here—I'll give you a hand," said Dominic. He laced his fingers together and crouched down. He was clearly distracted, his eyes straying from the hole in the ceiling to the dark tunnel they'd left behind, but when she placed her grimy boot in his hands, he lifted her up without complaint. And then she found herself clambering out of the hole and pulling herself up onto her feet, far closer to Fishgut Alley than she'd ever wanted to be.

Right away, she realized that something was wrong.

She hadn't been back to the lower city in years—but when she'd lived there, she'd seen it in every state. Happy, grieving, angry, fearful. Each part of this city had almost its own soul, and its emotions ebbed and flowed and changed.

Tonight, she recognized its mood. It was more a feeling than anything, an anxiety taking root deep in her chest. But she could see the thicker smoke clogging the air in every direction—seen only on icy winter nights, when every house had a fire going—and she could hear the city's voice. Yelling, but not the happy drunken kind typical of this time of night, interspersed with laughter and off-key singing, or the hawking of hundreds of merchants vying for attention during the day. The sort of yelling that mingled with crying and wailing and miserable groaning.

The foul smell in the air told her exactly why.

Blackwater.

Another outbreak. In Fishgut Alley.

She could not think of a worse time and place to be. Even if it started raining, it would be an improvement. At least the fresh water would wash away the sickness.

She looked around as Dominic followed, his height and his thick arms serving him well. He straightened up and dusted the mud off of himself. The grate that usually covered the hole sat nearby, and he kicked it mostly back into place without looking down, frowning at the street around them.

"Dunno where in Fishgut he'd go," he muttered, half to himself. "Is he here to gamble or something? Gotta be a million places for that around here...so where...?"

Were they that close to it? She didn't even know this street. She'd made a habit of staying far away from Fishgut Alley for most of her life, so that meant that she was closer to it now than she'd been in a long time. She'd only been there once, but she remembered it vividly: ramshackle huts thrown together from debris and sailcloth, drunks roaming the streets and picking fights, ragged-looking salacious girls— emphasis on the *girls*—tar addicts sprawled out against the walls and staring blankly into space, debris and rotten food and broken glass everywhere. Sharp, sly gazes had followed her everywhere she'd went, sizing her up, estimating her price and worth in gold, wondering how they could use her.

She would never stray too close to Fishgut Alley again, and that was that. It was simple common sense.

"You sure it ain't for—you know—" She lowered her voice. "'Cause of Liam?"

"Huh?" He half-turned her way, still distracted. "What's that got to do with anything?"

She raised her eyebrows. "The Butcher of Fishgut Alley?"

"I—" Dominic tensed, and his eyes snapped to hers, focusing fully for the first time as he scowled. "How the hell did you know about that?"

"Because I'm not stupid," she scoffed. "Maybe that's where he went?"

"No...no—if anything, that'd keep him further away." With one last suspicious look, he turned away from her, looking around for signs. "But then, why...?"

"Where's the orphanage?" Rose asked him.

Dominic pointed vaguely in a different direction. "That way—but he ain't there. C'mon, Rose, if he's in Fishgut we gotta drag 'im out, ain't no good can come outta that place—"

"What makes you so sure he ain't there?"

"You kiddin'? I'm s'prised he came *this* close. None of us—*Rose!*"

But she headed in the direction he'd pointed, ignoring his insistent hissing of her name. If it was between the orphanage and Fishgut Alley, the two places she'd loathed the most, she'd pick the one that was burned to ashes. And the sooner they got this over with, the sooner they could leave, and be far away from blackwater and the corpses it left.

She wasn't afraid. She just wasn't stupid.

"Rose—"

Dominic grabbed at her skirt. Rose whirled around, fists raised.

"Don't *touch me*," she growled.

"I know, sorry, but you're going the wrong way—"

"Well, I'm not goin' to Fishgut Alley!" she snapped at him.

"Keep your *voice down*—I *told* you, Kayo wouldn't *be* there—"

"You said he wouldn't be in Fishgut Alley, either!"

"He wouldn't, but *especially* not the orphanage—"

"Why not? It *burned down*. Ain't nothin' there anymore."

"That's not—"

Then Dominic swore, and Rose looked up. A dark shape broke off from a nearby roof, dark against the night sky. She nearly screamed —but then it hissed at them in Kayo's voice.

"What are you two *doing?*"

"What are *you* doing?" Dominic shot back. "Get *down* here!"

Kayo slid down the straw thatch and landed on the street in a neat crouch. His angry glare passed right over Rose before landing on Dominic.

"You brought *her?*" he said, and there was no mistaking the anger and contempt in his voice.

"*Hey!*"

"What the hell are you doing here, Kayo?" Dominic demanded. "Have you lost your mind?"

"I already *told* you, it's not *my* fault you didn't want to come—"

"No, you didn't," Dominic cut across him. "What's *wrong* with you? You shouldn't be anywhere *near* here!"

"Just go home," Kayo snapped. His hands were dirty; he kept rubbing them on his breeches, trying to get them clean. "You didn't wanna come, so I'll handle it myself."

"Handle *what?*"

"Forget it. Just forget it—and what are *you* doing here?" he added, rounding on Rose.

She stiffened, her mouth twisting into a sneer. "I guess *leaving,*" she said as scathingly as she could muster. And she stepped right past him and headed down the street.

"Wait a min—Rose, *wait,*" Dominic called after her. "I *wanted* her to come."

"For the Goddess's sake, *why?*"

Dominic just shrugged. "Seems like she knows what she's about."

"So do we," Kayo shot back. "We don't *need her.*"

Rose laughed aloud at that. The two boys looked up at her, Kayo glaring, Dominic merely glancing her way before turning back to Kayo.

"Liam would've brought her along."

In the space of a moment, Kayo went from tense and angry to practically spitting fire. "Oh, don't you fucking *start* with that—"

"We need all the help we can get, okay?"

"Do we? Just *look at her!*"

"Look at yourself!" Rose shot back, but neither of them were listening.

"She looks fine to me—"

"We're *trying* not to be *noticed.*"

"So what?"

"What d'you mean, *noticed?*" Rose demanded. "Lotsa people have red hair!"

"Your hair is red?" Dominic said blankly.

This bizarre response threw her, and when she opened her mouth, nothing came out. Kayo threw up his hands.

"You're *wearing your hair down,*" he groaned. "You can't *do* that."

"What—?"

"Ohhh," Dominic said, wincing. "Shit. Yeah."

"What are you *talkin' about?*" Rose snapped.

"Women wear their hair *up,*" Kayo explained, clearly at the edge of his patience. "In braids, in twists. The only women who wear it down are—"

"Oh." Rose saw Dominic make an expression that perfectly mirrored her own embarrassment. "I forgot."

Kayo stared at her. "You *forgot.*"

"Yes, I forgot," Rose snapped at him. "It ain't ever been a fuckin' issue before now, you horse's ass, but I can *put it up* if you're gonna be—"

"Sorry, sorry," Kayo said quickly, holding up his hands in surrender. "You can do whatever you want, I know, it's just—"

"I'll put it back," Rose scoffed, rolling her eyes. She reached up and tried to wrestle her curls into a braid—she could only hope that by the end of it, she'd figure out a way to tie it off. "It ain't *that* big a deal, you *babies....*"

"Well, between that and my old boots," Kayo pointed out, raising his eyebrows. "At least your dress has sleeves again."

"Hmph," Rose said with a disdainful sniff. "If I don't run into no more *traps....*"

"Here," Kayo cut across her. He stepped behind her, and she flinched—but his hands just brushed against her hair.

"No, no," Dominic said quickly as she tried to step away. "Let him do it. He's better at it."

She hated the idea of turning her back to Kayo and letting him touch any part of her, including her hair, but she took a deep breath and stood still. The last thing she wanted this close to Fishgut Alley was to be mistaken for a salacious girl. When her hair had been matted and tangled and dirty it hadn't mattered if she'd had it up or down, but she was old enough and clean enough now that people would start to look for it. Unmarried women wore their hair in a braid. Married women wore it up and covered. Those were the rules. Only loose and unrespectable women wore their hair down because it tempted men too much.

Kayo was right.

But she was still going to punch him if he pulled her hair.

"I hate this," she muttered. "It's so *stupid*."

"It is," Kayo agreed, to her surprise. "It shouldn't be anyone else's business what you look like." His voice was low and soft, coming from somewhere just behind her ear. Whatever he was doing, she barely even felt his gentle fingers in her hair. "Just think of it as a disguise, I guess."

A disguise. She liked the way that sounded. Come to think, she'd been wearing a disguise anyway to fit in with the orphans, keeping clean and wearing the borrowed dress. This wasn't so different.

"And you'll need your hair out of your face," Kayo added, his voice dropping even lower. "But listen...." His fingers paused ever so briefly. "Hanging around us is dangerous. You should know that."

"I can take care of myself."

"I know," said Kayo, surprising her yet again. "It's not that. I just...I need to know that you'll have our back if we've got yours."

She almost twisted around, but caught herself just in time. Her hands, half-lifted to yank him away if he pulled too hard, slowly fell.

He was talking about trust. About trusting *him*. Both of them. And by the sound of it, despite it all, he already trusted her.

"...yeah," she said at last. "I got your back." At least while they were far away from Fishgut Alley. If they strayed in that direction, they were on their own.

"Good. You've got a knife, right?"

"Yeah." How had he known that? "Well—a small one, I mean."

"You can borrow one of mine. Here." And he paused briefly to tug the knife out of his boot. She felt him press it into her hand and grabbed it on instinct. "Can you run in those boots?"

"I—yeah. If I gotta." She lifted her foot to tuck the knife into her own boot, and tug on the laces a little for good measure.

"All right. Just...be careful. Here...."

His arm extended past her shoulder, his hand held out to her. For a moment, she couldn't figure out what he wanted. But then he said, "I can't untie the knot on the yarn. Do you mind?"

His sleeve was too short. Where it hiked up his arm, she could see the brightly colored bracelets climbing up his wrist, five or six of them in all.

There had to be another way to tie off a braid—a loose thread, maybe, or he could just tie it in a knot. But she reached out and untied one of the bracelets anyway. The string was definitely new; she could easily pick it apart with her fingernails.

Her fingers brushed his skin. Underneath, she felt hard muscle—and scar tissue. At least one of the scars ran the length of his forearm, a puckered line paler than the rest of the skin. It vanished into a purplish burn scar just like the one on his side, disappearing under his shirt.

"Just don't lose it," he said. "Or steal it."

She tensed a little—but then she realized he was teasing. "Who'd want to steal a bunch of string?" she sniffed.

"They're good luck charms," he told her. "The kids made them for me."

She managed at last to get the bracelet loose. "Good luck? You?" She dropped it into his waiting hand, then held still as he tied it into her hair. "I think you need your money back."

That made him laugh as he stepped away. "Just think how bad it'd be without them."

But as he looked around, his smile faded. His eyes fixed on a point in the distance. Then, quietly, he said, "I really think you both should go home."

"Not until you tell me what the hell is going on," Dominic growled. Rose jumped; she'd half-forgotten that he was there.

Kayo winced. For some reason, he glanced at Rose. Then he turned back to Dominic.

"I just need to...see something, real quick," he said. "Around the ashpile."

"The what?" Rose asked them.

"He means the orphanage—Kayo, *why?*" Dominic demanded. "There's *nothing there.*"

"*And* it's cursed," Rose chimed in.

She expected them to ignore her—Goddess knew they'd done enough of that—but instead, they both turned to look at her.

"Cursed," Dominic repeated flatly.

"Well, not—not a *curse,* probably," Rose quickly explained. "I think it's mostly the smell—you know, the kind that makes you sick."

Kayo snorted. "Pretty sure the whole lower city smells like that."

"Nuh-uh, I heard it was *awful,*" Rose insisted. "Like something rotting. But—"

The two boys' eyes widened. Kayo's face paled, and Dominic looked at him, frowning, then back at Rose. The look on their faces brought a sick feeling coiling in her gut.

"What?" she demanded.

Kayo and Dominic shared a look that she didn't understand. Then, his voice tense and strained, Kayo said, "Can I talk to you?"

Rose watched as the two of them moved just out of earshot and stopped, heads bent toward each other. They were arguing, but she couldn't make out the words.

There was nothing to worry about. Smells didn't bring *curses.* Maybe sickness, but it didn't matter, because nothing was there. The orphans had set the fire and then fled. Simple as that. Curses weren't real.

She leaned against the wall and waited, fiddling with the end of her braid. The old yarn had been a faded grayish color that could have once been anything, but now it was a dull yellowish-white. The little beads tied at intervals were still shiny and bright. Whichever kid made it had no future as a whitesmith. Still, it was...sweet. He might have said it like a joke, but she thought he might really believe that they were good luck charms. He certainly hadn't taken them off in a long time....

"*What?!*" Dominic yelled.

Rose jumped and looked up, reaching for her knife—but Dominic and Kayo were still talking. Dominic was much more invested in the conversation now, leaning in, his brow furrowed in clear disbelief.

"That's not *possible!*" he said loudly—then, with an effort, brought his voice back down. Once again, she couldn't make out their words—until his next outburst, anyway.

"*Sara?!*"

Kayo hastily explained something, gesturing with both hands. Whatever had upset him before, it still did—and now Dominic was upset, too.

What was going *on*?

She didn't have to wait long to find out. Dominic shook his head as Kayo spoke, in denial, in anguish—and then he broke away, storming off. Kayo ran after him.

"Come on," Dominic barked at Rose, and then they were both gone.

Rose scrambled to follow them. They were headed away from Fishgut Alley, at least—but what the hell was their problem? And what was the rush?

She turned the corner—and came face-to-face with what remained of the orphanage.

It had been six years since the fire—she remembered it too vividly to forget. Six years, and yet the wreckage still remained. A beam or two still stretched high overhead, marking where the tallest floor had once been, and the skeletal ghost of the former walls stood around it. But most of it had caved inward, forming a tangled, twisted pile of rubble. Whitewash and straw had been blown and washed away by the elements, but charred wood and stone were left behind.

Even after six years, the place still reeked of smoke.

Cursed, she thought, suddenly and violently. She felt immediately ridiculous, but she could not shake the sick feeling in the pit of her stomach. Cursed by spirits no one laid to rest—

No. they'd never found any orphans at all. Dead or alive. Nobody died. She'd heard that a thousand times.

It couldn't be cursed. Curses weren't real.

Dominic ran straight for the rubble, ducking under a blackened beam and weaving his way through. Kayo followed on his heels.

"What are you *doing?*" Rose demanded. She didn't want to raise her voice too loudly, but she was genuinely concerned that they'd lost their minds. The whole thing looked ready to collapse if one of them looked at it sideways. "Dominic! *Kayo!* Get out of there!"

But they weren't listening. She could see them through the beams, picking over the rubble, searching at their feet for something.

She skirted around the rubble until she could see them more clearly. They'd found a flatter space, stone and twisted metal instead of wood, and they were digging. She stopped where she was, terrified of coming closer.

"What the hell are you two doing?" she hissed.

They didn't even glance her way.

"It was further over," Dominic was saying.

"Are you sure?"

"Pretty sure—it's not like we did a damn good job of it, it shouldn't be this hard to see—"

They'd forgotten that she even existed. She could only watch in utter confusion as they tossed aside loose rocks and boards and the sort of spikes used on metal fenceposts, trying so hard to keep their panic contained that she could feel it at a distance.

"Kayo, no one's touched this stuff, no one's been here—"

"You *sure* you checked the other side?"

"I did, ask Rose, no one's been down there either."

"I just—I have to make sure—"

"Why?" Dominic snapped. "Because of one bad dream? Or because an eight-year-old told you?"

"You know she's never wrong," Kayo snapped back. "And I just...I just...."

"*Here!*"

Dominic had found it. He and Kayo dug frantically through the rubble, all pretense of calm forgotten. Rose balanced on a heap of stone and craned her neck to see, holding her breath.

But when they sat back, breathing sighs of relief, all she could see was stone.

"Thank the Goddess," Kayo said shakily, brushing his hair back from his face. Dominic whispered a stream of Lyric that sounded like a prayer.

"What is that? What's going on?" Rose demanded.

They looked up at her as if they'd forgotten who she was. "N-Nothing," Kayo stammered. "It's all fine."

"We just had to check," Dominic agreed. "Um, check something. But—"

Something was odd about the circle they'd cleared. The cobblestones were just like the ones on the street, and indeed the ones at the edge of the cleared spot, but—something was off. They were a different color…or the mortar between them was. And the stones looked ready to cave in at the slightest touch. Dominic and Kayo, she noticed, were giving it a wide berth.

"…what's under there?" she asked them.

"Under wh—?"

"What the hell did someone seal up in there?" Her voice was harsh, but she couldn't soften it, not with raw terror rising to fill her chest.

"Nothing—"

"Don't give me that shit! What is it?"

They glanced at each other again. Then Kayo slumped, his hands falling into his lap. They were dirty again—covered with ash. How long had he been digging before they showed up?

When he didn't answer, Dominic did. "It's just a drain," he told her. "See?" And he brushed aside a few stones and splinters to show her an old, dented sewer grate. "It used to be under the orphanage, but the rubble plugged it up, that's all." He stood up. "We gotta move. Kayo, help me—"

Kayo seemed to understand. To Rose's bemusement, they started pulling the rubble back over the discolored spot.

"But—what's—aren't you gonna—?"

They ignored her completely.

Dominic kicked a pile of rocks and spilled them over the rest of the rubble, and Kayo dragged a beam on top of them, and then they were climbing out of the rubble and back onto the street.

Rose followed them, hastening to keep up. Dominic kept looking back—but not at her. The last thing on their minds was making sure she kept up. They just wanted to get as far away as possible.

The back of her neck prickled. She couldn't say she disagreed.

She broke into a run to catch up with Kayo.

"What's in the hole?" she demanded.

"Nothing."

But she distinctly saw him flinch.

"You're both liars," she snapped. "If you think—"

"Listen, Rose—you should go," he said over his shoulder.

For a moment, she wasn't sure she'd heard him correctly. "*What?*"

"You should leave. I'll talk to the others, they'll be fine with it. Dominic'll walk you back if you're worried you'll get lost."

"I won't—wait, you mean leave the—your—*hideout?*"

"It's not like you wanted to stay anyway," he said curtly. "So go. It's for the best."

"You can't just—"

"He's right," Dominic chimed in.

Rose couldn't believe her ears. "You *said you wanted me to come!*"

"That was before. We're busy tonight. You can go back to ours if you want to, but we need to—"

"That's horse shit!" Rose said furiously. "You've both lost your minds!"

"Do whatever you want," Kayo said, shrugging—but his voice was harsh and cold. "Just do it somewhere *else.*"

She'd had enough. She ran the last few steps and grabbed him by the wrist.

"Hey—!"

"What the hell's going on?" she demanded.

"It's none of your business," he retorted, shaking her loose. "What do you care anyways? I thought you *wanted* to leave."

"I ain't goin' anywhere just 'cause a couple of *boys* tell me to!" She whipped her head around to snarl at Dominic as she said this, and he winced and kept his distance.

"Well, we're not waiting up for you, so—"

"You said we'd watch each other's backs!"

"We changed our minds."

"Because of whatever's in that hole, right? There's *somethin'* in there, I *know* it—"

"You *can't know it!*" His hands swiped through the air in an anxious, angry motion. "Don't you get it? The less you know about us, the better. What the hell are we supposed to do if you run off and tell everyone everything?"

"Hey, I didn't ask to be dragged into this! *Any* o' this!"

"Yes, you did," Dominic pointed out. She glared at him again, but he didn't budge. "Tonight, you *did.* You wanted to come. But I didn't know it would be this—this dangerous. Just go home. Please."

She sized them both up, eyes narrowed. Whatever was buried

under the orphanage, it had changed their whole demeanor. It had to
be something big.

"I'm *not goin'*," she told them. "An' if you try an' leave me behind,
I'll just follow you."

"Rose—" Dominic began, but Kayo threw up his hands.

"There's no time for this. Come if you want, just—*hurry.*"

"*Where?*" Dominic demanded, exasperated.

Kayo paced back and forth, shaking his head. "Can't. I just need
to find—somewhere people would be. Somewhere they'd all gather."
He brushed his hair angrily out of his eyes. "Damn it, I wish the
Divinæ were still around...."

"What the hell *for?*"

"It's not—I—" He paused close to Dominic, lowering his voice.
"I just want to find a healer and—and ask them about—last rites.
Things like that. But we've got to go soon, it—"

"Kayo. *Kayo.*"

He had already turned around. He half-turned back, barely even
looking at Dominic. "What?"

"We should go back," he said firmly. "*Now.* It ain't safe here."

"It's never safe for us," he said with a dismissive wave of his hand.

"No—he means the *blackwater,*" Rose snapped. Good Goddess,
how dense could they *be?* "Didn't you *notice?*"

"What? No, I—"

He looked around. They both did. And she knew that suddenly
they were seeing and hearing and smelling exactly what she had: the
thick haze of smoke, the revolting odors, the yelling, the crying.

"Shit," said Dominic.

Kayo shook his head. "We'll be fine."

He set off. Dominic and Rose followed him, both protesting.

"Wait a minute—"

"Would you just slow down and—"

"We have to *go.*"

"Wait a damn *minute,*" Rose demanded. "Where the hell 're you
goin'?"

"I don't—I don't know yet. Just—" He gestured vaguely onward.

"Well—*why?*"

"Later."

"Why can't you just tell me what—"

"*Later,*" he repeated, turning to look at her. "I can't talk about this here. I'll tell you later. Okay?"

The look on his face shut her up at once. He clearly meant to be stern, but she could see none of that in his face. No more of the harsh, cold anger.

Just pain.

She swallowed what she was about to say and nodded. The tension in his face eased ever so slightly, and he set off again. She and Dominic followed.

What the hell did they have hidden? Her imagination ran wild trying to puzzle it out. Before, she'd thought they must have hidden some sort of treasure under there, or a secret passage, or something of the sort. Something they'd found and hidden away while they'd lived there.

But after seeing the look on Kayo's face, she was scared it was something far worse. A hidden torture chamber, or a demon, or—

Not scared. I'm not scared.

And she almost believed it.

But then they turned into the main street.

It was the middle of the night, but the street was cluttered with huddled bodies. She could see them in the light of at least a dozen different cookfires, slumped against the walls or curled up in the dirt. Some of them groaned and whimpered, but most of them didn't move, didn't even look up as they picked their way past. Rose said a silent prayer of thanks for her boots every time they splashed in a puddle of foul-smelling water, the contents of which she preferred not to guess.

Kayo kept going, but she could see him hesitate every so often, his determination flagging, before he shook himself and started up again. She couldn't imagine what his problem was. It was taking all her self-control not to burst into a run. Blackwater outbreaks had been a chronic problem in the lower city her whole life, but she'd been in the upper city for years now. Outbreaks simply did not happen there—and all she wanted was to run right back and leave all this behind.

Kayo kept looking into the cookpots, like he expected to find something in there other than brownish water, and frowning at the fires. These people would likely get in trouble for setting them if soldiers came about, but from what she could see, they were past caring. It looked as if they were burning their clothes and furniture in place of coal and wood, anything and everything that they could.

When Kayo saw her looking at him, eyebrows raised, he paused until she caught up. "What are they boiling?" he asked her in an undertone as he walked beside her. "Is that just water?"

"Uh...yeah. You boil water t' get the miasma out," she told him, making no effort to hide her contempt. What the hell was in those books he read? Wasn't he meant to be clever?

"Miasma?" By the skeptical look on his face, he felt the same way about her. She rolled her eyes.

"The *blackwater*. The stuff that makes you sick. You boil the water, it leaves."

"It doesn't *look* any cleaner."

"That's just mud and stuff, you can't get that out, not without cheesecloth or something, but it won't hurt you—didn't you *live here?* How do you not know this?"

"It's not like anyone taught us this stuff," he retorted. "We couldn't make fires, we'd get caught."

"So what'd *you* do to clean your water, then?"

"Nothing. We just got sick with everyone else."

"Blackwater can *kill* you."

"Yeah. It *did*."

"Oh."

That shut her up. There were so many orphans at the shrine that she found it hard to imagine that there might once have been more of them. She looked around.

"You all were...around here?" she asked him.

He nodded. "Yeah. Wherever we could hide."

She couldn't even imagine where that would be. All she could see were little houses, most of them just two rooms stacked on top of each other, and the sealed-up windows and doors of shops. There were plenty of places to hide if one was a rat—and she saw several of those—but a human? A group of humans? It seemed impossible. She started to ask, but Kayo had already moved on.

The street split. He veered left, heading for a little square. A well with its roof broken off took up the center, with two exhausted-looking women pulling up bucket after bucket of water. As she watched, one of them hauled a full bucket over to the communal ovens, where a small crowd of people were gathering to use them, shoving their way closer. Pots and bowls and the like were scattered everywhere, discarded after their owners had found leaks or holes or had simply realized they were too large to fit into the oven. As they passed, voices rose angrily from somewhere near the ovens, and Rose winced as a fight broke out. Kayo hesitated, looking back, but she shook her head.

"Don't. It ain't worth it."

He didn't seem to believe her, but he listened—perhaps because Dominic wasn't even glancing their way. He, at least, seemed to have some sense.

They turned down another street, this one so crowded that they had to pick their way through with great care. They weren't the only ones shoving through; others passed in both directions with their heads down, eyes averted from the people huddled against the walls, most of them hauling water or holding empty buckets. Tensions were high; several people shouldered her out of the way as she walked along, and more than one of them spat curses at her as they walked away. She muttered her own curses right back, unbothered, and stuck her foot out to trip one of them. The noise his buckets made when they crashed to the ground was deeply satisfying.

Up ahead, Kayo stopped in his tracks. Then he backed up, cursing, and pressed against the wall.

"Soldiers!" he hissed to Dominic.

Rose had to press close to Kayo so she could peek around the corner, gripping the wall just by his waist. She was so close she could hear him breathing.

Two soldiers were walking down the narrow street—and everyone in sight was fighting to get out of their way. Anyone who was too slow got a steel-toed boot or the butt of a spear for their troubles. The street clogged in seconds with people trying to shove their way through, darting into any side street or doorway that they could find.

But not everyone was quick enough to escape.

"Move it!" one soldier snarled at a man who was stirring feebly, only able to push himself up onto his elbows. "Hey, move it along! Out o' the street!"

But the man was too weak to move. He tried—and then fell back, panting.

"I said *get lost!*"

When the man still didn't move, the soldier stomped on him. Rose winced at the nasty crunching sound it made.

"Anyone else wanna get smart?" the soldier shouted to the retreating crowd.

"Kayo, let's go," Dominic hissed. "We gotta get outta here."

Rose could not agree more. They had to run—if the soldiers got too close, if they saw her—

She looked around—but they were stuck. There was nowhere to go but directly in their path.

"*Kayo.*"

"Kayo, we gotta go," Rose insisted, and she hated how high and tense her voice sounded, but she couldn't make it stop. "We gotta move—"

A woman shepherding her sickly, wobbly-legged children tried to run, but a soldier caught her by the arm. She screamed and struggled, but he just laughed in her face.

"Where you goin', darlin'? Me an' the boys are bored, come an' keep us company...."

Her blood turned to ice. Cold sweat broke out on her palms, and she clenched her skirt to stop them shaking. She pressed against the wall, shut her eyes—but she could still hear.

"Lemme go! Lemme go, please!"

"C'mon, don't be like that—eh, boys?"

The soldiers were jeering, and the woman's screams only seemed to egg them on. She couldn't be here for this. They had to move, they had to go—

"*Kayo!*" Dominic said in a sharp whisper. "*Move!*"

But Kayo stood frozen, his eyes on the soldiers. "We can't just—"

"It'll be us next! Don't do anything stupid!"

He was doing it, he was talking Kayo down—Rose could see him wavering.

And to her surprise, she didn't want him to.

Do something, she begged him silently. *Don't just stand there, don't run, DO SOMETHING!*

But he wasn't going to.

She'd have to do it herself.

Terror electrified her every nerve, erased all rational thought. Later, she'd wonder if that was what possessed her to do the bravest, stupidest, most reckless thing she'd ever done.

She stepped out into the open.

"HEY!"

The soldiers, still wrestling with the struggling woman, looked up. Their eyes were like blades, pinning her to the spot—and yet she heard herself shout at them as if possessed by some sort of demon.

"You fuckers so pathetic you gotta *force* women to hang around you?" she challenged them.

The woman wrenched free and took off. The soldiers cursed and lunged at her—but Rose distracted them again.

"Let 'er go," she said with a derisive laugh. "You always judge women for how easy they can get away from you? Have some pride, you fuckin'—"

The soldiers started for her. Rose turned on her heel and took off running back the way they'd come.

Then someone stepped in front of her, blocking her path.

N*o*, Rose thought, looking around wildly. *No. No—*
The soldier towered over her in a studded leather jerkin, wielding a spear in both hands. She stumbled back, tripping over her too-big boots.

The walls were high and smooth, with not a single rat-hole to hide in between this soldier and the other two. She was trapped.

"Wait—"

She had a vague impression of someone coming up behind her—and then Kayo was stepping in front of her, shoving her firmly behind him.

"She didn't mean it," he said quickly, raising his hands in surrender. "We're sorry, we'll take her home, just don't hurt her—"

The soldier swung the spear around, pointing it at Kayo's nose.

"Drop your weapons," he snarled. "*Now.*"

"No, wait," Dominic protested from somewhere behind her. "We're allowed to have these, we're of age, we weren't—"

"*Now!*" he shouted, and Rose saw Kayo jump. "Or you'll die where you stand!"

Rose saw Kayo's eyes flick in Dominic's direction. But there was nothing in his eyes but fear. They had no plan at all.

Don't do it, she screamed inside her head. *Don't do it, fight them, can't you see they're gonna kill us all?*

But instead, Kayo slid his sword off his back.

"Okay—okay," he said. "We will. Just—just don't—"

The soldier slammed the butt of the spear into Kayo's stomach.

Rose let out a strangled cry as she watched Kayo stumble back with a grunt of pain. He doubled over, gasping for breath.

"We're not fighting, we're doing what you say," Dominic said loudly, throwing down his bow. "See? Just—just let us go, we're sorry, we swear we'll just go home—"

One of the other soldiers grabbed Kayo's sword from the ground and slid it from its sheath. Then he snorted and tossed it aside. "Trash," he said scornfully to his companions. "Probably stole it."

"Definitely stole the necklace."

Necklace? Rose's stomach twisted as she realized they meant her. "I didn't *steal it—!*"

Without even glancing in her direction, the soldier's hand lashed out, and it cracked against her face. The world spun into darkness, the taste of blood filling her mouth.

Someone grabbed her—holding her up, their grip strong but careful.

"Just give it to them," Dominic's voice whispered in her ear. "Rose, just give it to them, it isn't worth it, maybe they'll go away—"

"Hey—hey!" Kayo stepped forward, hands raised in supplication. "That's *enough,* all she did was mouth off, don't—"

Dominic shouted a warning, but too late: the shaft of the spear was already whipping through the air, hissing in the instant before it hit Kayo in the face. He staggered, and the soldier planted a steel-toed boot in his chest and sent him sprawling.

"No—no, no, no—"

Kayo rolled over, pushed himself up—but another soldier planted a boot on his back, pressing him against the ground until he groaned.

"Wait—just *wait—*"

"Think there's a bounty for Savillan boys," one of the soldiers commented. "Eh?"

"No, it ain't for Savillans, it's for orphans," another said.

The tall one looked them up and down, a nasty sneer curling underneath his beard. "Orphans, huh?"

"No, we're not orphans," Dominic said swiftly. "We're not, I swear, I'll prove it—"

"No, *don't!*" Rose cried, and she flinched as Dominic pulled his shirt down, revealing—

Nothing.

She stared at him. She'd seen his orphan's mark several times, including earlier tonight, but all she saw was smooth skin. What kind of trick...?

Kayo made a horrible gasping sound. She looked and saw him struggling weakly in the dirt.

"Can't breathe," she heard him rasp. "I...I can't...."

"I'm not an orphan either, we're not orphans!" she yelled. "Just get *off* him, you're gonna *kill* him, look—"

And she shoved up her sleeve—but it was too tight, and got caught at the elbow. She struggled with it, yanking, ready to claw out the seams if it meant getting out of this alive—

"What about that one?" said one of the soldiers, aiming a kick at Kayo's thigh.

"Got yer knife?"

"*No—*"

The soldier lifted his boot off Kayo's back at last, but Kayo barely had time to suck in a breath before he was dragged to his feet. One soldier twisted his arm behind his back and grabbed his hair; another one raised the knife.

Fight, damn it, fight, do something, ANYTHING—

The soldier flipped the knife in his hand and stabbed downward. He ripped through cloth and skin and muscle as if gutting a carcass, ignoring the horrible scream that ripped from Kayo's throat, the way he writhed and thrashed—the other soldier tightened his grip in his hair, forcing his head back and his face to the sky, and surely the whole city had to hear him howling in pain, surely—

She prayed silently that somehow, Kayo had used the same magic that Dominic had, erasing his mark from view. Just for a minute—a few seconds—

But the tip of the knife flipped the fabric aside, red stains spreading fast over the undyed wool, and there it was, plain as day.

"Well, well," the soldier said softly. "Look what we got here."

He looked up at the others. "Let's take 'em all," he said. "All three. Bound to be a good bounty for that."

"No—wait—" Blood was pouring from the wound like wine from an overturned bottle, and Kayo's chest was heaving, his face twisted in pain—but still, he tried to break free. His body twisted in the soldier's grip—

And the tall one slammed the shaft of his spear into his ribs. Rose distinctly heard something crack.

"Stop it—!"

But the soldier struck him again—and again—and again. The soldier holding him shoved him away, and Rose's heart cried out in silent desperation as Kayo collapsed onto the ground. He tried to rise—

And the soldier brought the shaft of the spear down on his back. He kept hitting him, beating him mercilessly across his back and head and shoulders and anywhere he could reach, and he wouldn't stop. She tried to close her eyes, to block it out, but she couldn't erase the sound each blow made as it hit, or the soldier's raucous laughter, or the horrible cries of pain....

Dominic stood frozen in horror. He wasn't going to do anything. He couldn't. The soldiers were going to beat him to death right in front of them both, and all they could do was watch.

No.

Suddenly she could hear nothing else over the blood pounding in her ears. Fury rose within her like an inferno, burning hot and bright through every limb until every fiber of every muscle was aflame.

Fire, not fear.

She wasn't afraid of them.

She wasn't afraid of anything anymore.

She reached into her skirt and whipped out her little knife.

The soldiers had barely glanced at her except to rake their eyes over her, judging how attractive she was and how easy to subdue she would be like they were assessing a piece of meat. They were too busy slowly murdering Kayo to pay her any attention. When she finally struck, they never saw it coming.

They never did when she aimed for the eyes.

The first soldier's laugh cut off with a roar as she buried the knife in his back. He staggered, and she whipped her hand across his face, clawing mercilessly at his eyes. He howled and collapsed, his hands flying up to his face. The knife was wrenched out of her grasp, but she dropped to her hands and knees, reaching for the bow.

"*Rose!*"

The warning came too late. A hand grabbed her arm, dragging her up. She threw herself down to the ground—startling the soldier, who hadn't expected it—and when he came with her, she reared up with all her strength. The back of her head exploded in pain as it cracked against his face—but judging by his yell, it hurt far worse for him.

She wrenched free and landed on one knee. The bow was still strung, the quiver close at hand—a bloody miracle. She'd never touched a bow in her life, but when another soldier charged toward her, she raised it and fired blindly. The vibration rattled her teeth in her skull, the string whipping a line of fire across her forearm, and she didn't, couldn't, aim—but the arrow still sank obligingly into the soldier's thigh. He fell back shrieking into the dirt.

That was when Dominic fell on top of him, elbow first.

Someone grabbed her wrist.

The touch of rough fingers on her skin clenched every muscle in her body. Terror roiled low in her gut, and she lashed out without thinking, whacking flesh with the end of the bow. The hand let go—but then another grabbed her braid, winding it around his fist. She screamed and started clawing at everything she could reach, raking her fingernails against his skin as she scrabbled for purchase. She found his mouth and wrenched it open, found his eyes and dug her fingers in—

He bit her, and she wrenched her hand free—but then she started kicking. One foot found something soft, and the soldier groaned—but his grip didn't loosen.

She felt something scrape her foot inside her boot.

Kayo's knife.

With the soldier's hand still tangled in her hair, she had to kick up her heel to reach it. She grabbed it, slid it free, and started stabbing.

It caught something—but when she jerked, it came out easily. His hand let go as he shrieked, taking her hair with it as the braid unraveled, but she wrenched her head free and whipped around. She stabbed again without bothering to look where, then tore the knife free and started slashing, at his face, at his throat, at his arms as they rose to protect himself.

He fell, but she didn't stop. She kept slashing, snarling with rage, until his arms finally fell. One hand brushed against her, and as her entire being recoiled, she yelled and plunged the knife straight through his leather jerkin, all the way up to the hilt.

With a choking sound, the man went still.

Rose stumbled to her feet and whirled around, ready to fight—but the other two soldiers were down. As she watched, Dominic extracted himself from the still body of a soldier, grabbed the blood-smeared shaft of a fallen spear, and slammed the point straight into his throat. The soldier convulsed, gurgling, and then went limp.

Dominic didn't waste time catching his breath. He flung the spear aside and fell to his knees, kneeling over Kayo—who lay in a pool of blood, as still and pale as any of the soldiers.

"Kayo—*Kayo*—"

His hands hovered in the air. He was afraid to touch him. Rose would have been, too. The back of his shirt was ripped to pieces, gashes and welts covered every inch of skin they could see, and there was blood *everywhere*—staining the entire right sleeve of his shirt, gluing pieces of it to his back, sticking his hair to his cheek, soaking the dirt underneath him.

"Kayo...Goddess, Kayo, please...."

Dominic hesitated, then brushed the back of his fingers gently against Kayo's cheek. And the look on his face....Kayo had called them brothers, but Dominic never had, and Rose suddenly realized why.

"Kayo...."

Kayo groaned and stirred.

"Dom...?"

Relief flooded through Rose's stomach, turning her limbs to water, loosening the iron bands of fear around her chest. She crouched beside him as Dominic helped him up, supporting his uninjured arm.

"Ow...." Kayo winced, his breath catching. "What...what happened...?"

"It's okay—it's okay, you're fine," Dominic assured him. "Tian ban'Diie, ciuán dic crúdagh—everything's okay, you're going to be fine, Kayo, I swear. Can you move? Can you get up?"

"Yeah...think so...."

Slowly, painfully, they helped Kayo to his feet. By the time they hauled him up, he was panting, his chest heaving, his eyes open but unfocused. A cut above his eye was bleeding, and the spear shaft had left a nasty welt on his cheek. Dominic kept whispering to himself in Lyric; Rose caught the Goddess's name more than once.

"You get the other one?" Rose asked him.

"Huh?"

Rose pointed to the soldier who still had Kayo's knife stuck in his back. Dominic shook his head.

"Just leave 'im, it doesn't—"

But Rose left Kayo in Dominic's grip and crept over, stepping as quietly as she could. She grabbed a fallen spear and used it to poke the soldier's chest. It didn't move; neither did any other part of him.

"Oh," muttered Dominic. "I guess he *is* dead..."

Rose raised the spear and plunged it through the soldier's eye. He thrashed once, shrieked horribly—and then fell still.

"Yep, he's dead," she said. The spear made a disgusting sound as it wrenched free.

She turned to the boys and found them both staring at her.

"Damn," said Dominic weakly. "That was cold."

"You...killed them," Kayo rasped. He looked around slowly, his eyes falling on all three bodies. "You killed them all...."

Rose snorted and tossed the spear aside. "Idiots," she said scathingly. Even she didn't know if she meant the soldiers, or the two boys.

"What—the *hell?*" Kayo demanded. He swayed like a drunk, and every word clearly cost him, but she could see his expression change—twisting in anger instead of pain. "You *killed them?* You can't—you can't just—"

"Kayo, don't," Dominic said quickly. "Thank the Goddess she did, that was—we was almost—oh, fuck." He looked around desperately, pushing his fingers through his hair. The street was empty—but it wouldn't be for long. "Okay. Okay. We made it. Um. But now—okay—"

"For fuck's sake, spit it out, Dominic!" Rose snapped.

"I'm sorry, okay?" he shot back. "I don't know what to do! If people know we did this—w-we gotta do something—"

"Yeah—*for once!*" Rose said furiously. "You just *stood* there, *groveling,* you were just gonna let them *kill us,* what is *wrong* with you?"

"They're—they were *soldiers*," he stammered. "We can't fight *soldiers*—"

"It's that or we fucking *die!*"

"We were outnumbered—"

"No we weren't! It was three to three!"

"Yeah, well, I didn't *count* you, I'm *sorry,* I didn't know you would *claw a man's eyes out*—"

"Well, that's your problem," she fumed. "They die just like anyone else."

"Well, now there's gonna be *hundreds* of them on our arse, that's why I didn't wanna *fight* 'em, there'll be more any second—"

"So hide the bodies," Rose snapped.

Dominic tried to let go of Kayo—but he stumbled immediately, his legs almost collapsing. "Ah, shit—uh—" He looked around again, then made a decision. "Rose, you gotta take Kayo home. I'll clean this up and—and be right behind you."

"Wh—*me?*"

"Just *do* it before he *bleeds* to death! *Please,* Rose!" And when he turned and looked at her, she could see his raw terror, see how close he was to falling apart. "I'm trusting you—*please.*"

That stopped her short. No one had ever said they'd trusted her before. And now, tonight, both of them had put their faith in her.

"...fine," she said. "C'mon, Kayo. Let's move."

They were two streets away before Kayo finally found breath enough to speak.

"Wait..." he mumbled. "Dom is..."

"He's comin'," Rose said curtly. "C'mon, you big lump—"

She hoped he was. She hoped desperately that Dominic knew what he was doing. And that he'd grab her knife.

To his credit, Kayo tried his best to stumble along at the pace she set. But his toes kept catching in the dirt, and his legs wobbled.

"C'mon, *c'mon,*" she grumbled. "Goddess, would you *move?*"

"I'm *trying,*" he snapped—he had the strength to be angry, at least. "*Ow,* that *hurts*—"

"Shut up, you baby. You're lucky it ain't worse."

"I'm lucky you didn't *stab my eyes out,*" he retorted. "What the *fuck was that?*"

"That was me *savin'* your ass. You're *welcome.*"

"You want me to *thank* you? You *killed three people!*"

She scoffed. "Soldiers ain't people."

"Yes, Rose! They are!" He wrenched away and pried himself free, one hand gripping his injured arm below the cut so hard his fingernails dug into his own skin. His legs shook, but they held. "They're *people!* If you hadn't *mouthed off* to them, everyone would still be alive!"

"Didn't you see what they were gonna do to that woman? Don't you *care?* They deserved what they got just for *that—*"

"No! They don't! It's not for us to decide if people die for shit they haven't even done yet!"

"Oh, fucking *men,* I swear to the Goddess I'm gonna—"

"I just mean—we're—we're not judges, we're not—"

"They're *soldiers,* Kayo! The judges just do whatever they say! They can do whatever the hell they want!"

"You didn't have to *kill them,* you could've just—just knocked them out, or—"

"That shit only works in plays an' stories! *Knock 'em out,* have you lost your *mind?* They were gonna *kill you*! An' you two weren't gonna do a damn thing about it!"

"At least then there'd only be one body, not three," he snapped.

"You dragged me into this fuckin' mess, this's *your fault,* an' if I gotta kill people to get myself out of it, I'm damn sure—"

"Who'd you kill?"

"Huh?"

His face was bloodless, but when his eyes locked on her, they were perfectly clear—and burning with anger. "Who *else* have you killed?"

She bristled. "It's none o' your *business—*"

"Yes. It *is.* I'm not letting you back home if your idea of justice is killing anyone who—"

"What's buried in the hole?"

This time, it was his turn to be taken aback. "What?"

"What did you bury under the orphanage?"

She didn't think it was possible for his face to turn paler, but she was wrong. "I—nothing—"

"You said you'd tell me later. It's later."

"Not—not now—"

His whole body was shaking. He could barely stand. She let out a groan of frustration.

"Just let me take you home, you idiot, I promised Dominic I wouldn't let you die—"

She reached for his arm, but he jerked away.

"I can walk," he said irritably. "I don't need a wet nurse."

"Oh, don't you?" she scoffed as he turned away from her and started down the street at a pace she knew he couldn't sustain. He was limping badly, and she could hear him struggling to breathe. She followed just behind him, making sure he didn't stumble.

When at last they reached the entrance to the sewers, Rose reached down and hauled the grate out of the way. When she looked up, she saw him staring in the direction of the orphanage.

"I'll go down first, then help you," she said.

He didn't speak. He just nodded.

It took him a long time to ease himself into the hole. Rose had to brace her arms against his chest, slowing his fall, and even then, he hit the ground hard. She grabbed his shoulders to steady him, but regretted it instantly. Not because of the sharp breath she heard him suck through his teeth, but because she felt blood dripping thickly over her hand.

"C'mere, let me tie that up or—or something—Kayo?"

But he was already wandering down the passage, splashing clumsily through the mud. And then he veered into the tunnel Dominic had warned her away from.

"Kayo, what are you—?"

The lantern was still there, and still burning. Kayo didn't seem to need it. He walked right past it and vanished into the darkness. Rose snatched it and followed behind him.

"Kayo—"

It was a dead end, she saw—but Kayo didn't stop until he stood right in front of the stone wall at the end. And then he just stood there and stared at it.

"*Kayo,*" she said, exasperated. "Can we move?" Goosebumps crawled up her arms and across the back of her neck. She wasn't afraid —or at least, she wasn't prepared to admit that she was—but she didn't like this place. She wasn't sure if it was colder than the rest of the tunnel, or if it just made her skin crawl.

And she could smell something—faint, but revolting. Something worse than sewage. The wall was badly made...she could see holes between the stones, more than enough for something to seep out....

She realized suddenly where they were. This tunnel crossed the street above at an angle—and led right to the orphanage.

"Kayo," she said, and she hated how high her voice climbed. "What's—*in there?*"

He reached out with his bloodied hand, touching the stone with something almost like reverence.

"It's a crypt," he whispered.

"A—what?" she stammered. "For—who?"

"For the kids who died in the fire."

She opened her mouth, then closed it again, searching for the words. But all she could think to say was, "I don't understand...."

"We buried them there. Here." His head sank, resting against the stone. "After the fire. And I—I worried we—didn't do it right. And their spirits weren't at rest...and that's why I was having nightmares about them...."

No—nightmares sounded more than appropriate. This tunnel alone—

"Wait, that's not—*no*," she protested. "No, there can't be. I—I heard a thousand times all the orphans escaped, they never found any bodies—"

"We didn't want them to." He squeezed his eyes shut against the memory. "*Liam* didn't want them to. He said we had to get them all before people came near the place—before it even cooled down. I kept burning my hands, digging through it." He spread one of his hands, staring down at his palm. "We hid down here for —for ages, right here—but when we left we sealed them all in. Liam said it was so we could put them to rest—because no one else would do it properly. But sometimes I think it was just out of spite...so they'd never know how many of us died, they'd think we all escaped...."

She tried to swallow, but her mouth was dry. A sick feeling, cold and clammy, spread along her skin, brushing across her like the breath of some giant, foul beast. She wanted to stumble back—to run—but her feet were glued to the ground. "And how...how many of you...?"

It took him a moment to reply, and when he finally did, his voice was just a whisper.

"Thirteen."

"*Thirteen?*" she practically yelped, her voice growing louder while his grew softer. "You buried *thirteen kids* under there?"

"...no," he murmured. "Thirteen *left*. We...buried forty-three."

She stared at him, praying that he would correct himself. That he would say he was joking, messing with her—something. *Anything.*

He just looked away.

She was going to be sick.

"So it is cursed. It *is* cursed...."

"No," Kayo said, shaking his head. "It's not. As long as—I mean, I wanted to find a healer and check, make sure we did it properly. That we buried them the right way. So they shouldn't—"

"The right way? *They're in a sewer under a bunch of rubble!*" she hissed—but she regretted it immediately. Not because she was wrong, but because of the way Kayo flinched.

"It was the best we could do, okay? It was—we didn't have anywhere else, we didn't have a choice, we couldn't just *leave them there,* so we sealed it up—"

"Not very *well!*" she snapped. "Oh, Goddess, the *smell*, no *wonder* people think it's cursed—"

He winced. "We did all we could—"

"Forty-three! Goddess *above*—" She started pacing, hardly even realizing what she was doing. Thirteen was horrifying enough. *One* was horrifying enough. Forty-three was—a *nightmare.* Enough to curse the entire lower city. It was a miracle he hadn't had *more* bad dreams about it.

Forty-three dead children.

Right in front of her.

"So you just—just—they're not in a—"

"No one's messed with them," Kayo said, a bit defensively. "It's been years, and they've been left alone—"

"In the middle of a city! People *live* there—oh Goddess, the *water,* what if it—"

"It wasn't that," Kayo said quickly. "Blackwater was a problem before then, we didn't cause this—"

"Well, it can't have *helped!*" It was all she could do not to shout at him. "An' it ain't even *marked,* they're just *sittin'* there, all o' you— you—"

But she trailed off. She'd just looked up at his face—and seen him swipe at his eyes with his sleeve.

"...Kayo?" she said weakly.

"I'm—I'm sorry." He sniffed and wiped at his eyes again. This time, she saw the tears shining in his eyes in the candlelight before he blinked them away. "I'm sorry...I just...."

She could see blood dripping down his hand. They had to get out of here. She had to get them home.

"Kayo—let's go," she pleaded. "Let's just go home—they're fine, okay? They're fine...."

But he wasn't listening. He rested his forehead against the stones, closing his eyes.

"I'm sorry," he said again—but she knew he wasn't talking to her. "I did the...the best I...."

He pried his left hand from his right and touched the stone. His fingers left a streak of blood.

"Kayo—Goddess, Kayo, you need to get home, we have to get back—"

He brushed his fingers across the stone again—he was doing it on purpose. Painting with his blood.

"Kayo, *stop it*—"

His arm was trembling, but he finished the shape—a flower with five petals.

When his hand finally fell, he still didn't move. She grabbed his wrist and pulled.

"Okay, you—that's done—now come *on,* please just come on—"

And finally, to her eternal gratitude, he let her pull her away. She dragged him stumbling through the dirt and back into the faint light from the street.

"Goddess, you're covered in blood—just let me—"

Just like she had with her own injured arm, she ripped off the sleeve of her chemise and slid it over her hand. She added the other one too, for good measure, and tied them together before winding them around Kayo's arm just above the cut. She wrapped it as tightly as she could, then tied several knots in a row. Kayo winced and grimaced but didn't complain.

The moment she let him go, she saw his hand rise to grip his arm again. He didn't even seem to know he was doing it; his face was still twisted in pain. And the blood—how could someone lose that much and still be conscious? Did it look worse than it was, or was he about to drop dead in front of her?

She had to get him home.

"Come on," she whispered. "Just...come on."

She set off—her back turned to the crypt, past the remnants of the cold fire where the orphans had huddled years ago. Kayo walked along beside her, slowly but steadily, his eyes on the ground in front of them. His labored breaths were loud in her ear, and his other arm dangled, limp, without so much as a finger twitching.

"You okay?" she whispered. "Is your arm...?"

"I—I can't move it," he said hoarsely. "I can't feel my hand. That's...is that...?"

It certainly wasn't *good,* but she wasn't about to tell him that. "It's fine," she said with as much cheerfulness as she could muster. "It ain't that bad. Worst comes to worst, y' can just attach something fun to the stump."

That made him laugh—an unsteady, shuddering sort of laugh. "Good thing it's my off hand...."

"Your—what?"

"I use my left hand for...everything." He winced and gasped, his steps fumbling—but whatever it was, it passed quickly. "The orphanage hated it. Thought all the stuff I made would be worth less. But my right hand just...can't do it."

"Oh. Huh." It stood to reason that half of people would use their right hand, and half their left. She'd never given it any thought. "Well, good. You can tie a sword to this one or somethin' and you'll never miss it."

"Right...."

The sewers were worse than ever—knowing blackwater had broken out again, dragging someone through the sludge instead of picking her way carefully past it. But the smell of rot was like a living creature behind her, reaching after her as she retreated, its eyes on her back.

"Kayo...," she said slowly. "What'd you draw on the wall?"

"A starflower."

"A—what?"

"Starflowers. They're not real—or not anymore. The Goddess's flower. I...I just want...I-I don't want them to be...disturbed."

"*Disturbed?* What the hell does *that* mean?"

He was silent for a moment, and she wondered if he was thinking —or just deciding whether or not he could trust her. "I had this... dream," he finally admitted. "This terrible dream that—that some-thing happened to them. I came here and they were just—gone. Dug up. And they weren't at rest anymore. And then Sara said—she said it was real, it wasn't just a dream. And she's *never* wrong. So I had to...I had to make sure that...."

Her stomach lurched as she heard his breath hitch. If he started crying again...

"Sorry," she said quickly. "I'm sorry I brought it up—"

"No—it's okay. I'm...relieved. Beyond relieved." He took a deep, shuddering breath, and she felt his weight shift as he leaned on her a little more. "That they're...okay. Resting. You don't know what I...." He trailed off, shaking his head. "It's always been a—a weight on me. What we did. We—we couldn't do anything else, but...there were just...no good options. And it's all...it's all my fault...."

"*Your* fault? *Why?*"

He shook his head. "I don't know what I could've done. What else I could've done. If I could've stopped it...."

"Stopped...what?"

"The fire," he whispered.

She waited—but he didn't say anything else. She didn't know if he could.

"What...happened?" she asked, cautiously. "When it burned down...?"

He didn't reply. She was starting to think he never would when he finally whispered the answer.

"It wasn't an accident."

She thought at first she must have misunderstood. "Wh-what? No —no one would—that's not—"

He stumbled, lurching forward. She tried to catch him, but she was too slow, and he landed on his hand and his knees. Rose heard him hiss in pain, saw him struggle to push himself back up.

"Here, lemme help—"

"I'm fine," he muttered. But he didn't push her away when she took his arm, and she felt him lean against her as he stood. Reddish scrapes were starting to bleed on his palm. "Just tripped...."

But she could see the strain as he got moving again, and hear his labored breathing. She wondered if that cracking sound when the soldier hit him had been one of his ribs.

"You know somethin'?" she commented, more to keep him talking than anything else. "You sure know how t' take an ass-kickin'."

He smiled faintly. "Talent of mine."

"Good thing, too. Never met anyone as good at gettin' into stupid fights."

"Yeah, I've heard that," he said wearily. "Liam said it all the time."

"Did 'e?"

"Mm-hmm. Once, when we were out on the streets, when...when things were bad, I told him I was scared. And he didn't even stop to think, he just said, 'I'll tell you exactly how you're gonna die. One day you're gonna piss off the wrong person, and they're gonna run you through. See? Nothing to worry about.'"

He seemed to think this was funny. Rose might have, too, if she hadn't seen for herself that Liam had been absolutely right.

While she was trying to think of a response, Kayo doubled over. Rose reached out, ready to catch him, but he hadn't tripped. He was clutching at his arm, breathing hard, his face screwed up.

"You all right?'

"Yeah—yeah, just—"

"Y' want some water? We got plenty."

Kayo made a wheezing, breathless sound that might have been a laugh.

"I'm—I'm fine," he insisted, and straightened up—though his hand kept clutching his arm. "I mean—we've done this before, right? I just...don't remember."

"...yeah," she said. "I guess so...."

He nodded as he stumbled along. How much farther was it? How much farther could he make it?

Come to think, she had no idea where they were going. She could only hope he did.

Goddess above, it IS the same as last time.

"You still can't remember that day, huh?" she asked him.

"Not really how memory works," he pointed out. "Last thing I remember is—is me and Dominic scouting by the docks. Next thing I knew, I woke up at home."

It annoyed her irrationally that he still couldn't remember everything he'd done. How was he supposed to feel properly guilty about it all if he didn't even remember?

"What happened?" he asked her. "Will—will you tell me?"

"Tell you—what?"

"Everything." He grimaced, his breath faltering as another wave of pain hit. "I don't like having holes in my head, and Dominic only knew part of it. Please?"

The *please* startled her, and she frowned at him. It occurred to her that he probably didn't care about what had happened. He just wanted her to talk to him so he could stay awake.

Just as he'd done for her when she was sick.

She sighed. "Okay," she began, "so the sun was just comin' up...."

And slowly, she told him the story. All of it—Kayo wanted every detail. He kept asking for her thoughts, her analysis, her opinions, what she'd noticed and felt. So she told him everything, even the parts where she'd been terrified. They strolled along like lovers in a garden along the river of sewage, and Rose almost laughed at how ridiculous her life had become, how much had changed. She kept pausing to look at him, to ask him if he needed to rest—and finding him in a sort of trance, hanging onto her every word with his gaze fixed on her face, his legs moving almost independently of his will.

By the time she finished, they were nearly back. But Kayo was slowing. The final path climbed uphill, with loose rocks and scree, and it was giving him hell. He kept stumbling, then pretending he'd done it on purpose, reaching down into the water under their feet—clean and clear now—and taking a drink. Rose did the same, to flush any trace of blackwater out of her system, but she knew he was lying to her.

When he fell again, he couldn't seem to push himself back up. She bent down and pried his hand off of his arm—it was digging in so tightly his fingers had no color left, and she wasn't sure he could have let go if he tried. Then she slung it over her shoulders and helped him up. He kept insisting he didn't need it, but she could feel how much he was leaning on her.

"...thank you," he said quietly.

"I'm just tryin' ta move this along, I ain't got all night—"

"No, for—everything. You saved my life. Twice, now. And tonight...." His head sank, and she could feel him putting more and more of his weight on her as they walked along. "You were so brave. And the way you fought, I've never—I mean—weren't you scared?"

"No," she sniffed. "I ain't scared of *anything*."

"Because you aren't a coward," he mumbled. "Like me...I just froze...I was scared to fight them because—because I can't—I didn't want to kill—them. Anyone."

She walked along with him in silence for a moment, thinking this over. "This whole time you've been actin' like the Beggar's King, you've never killed *anybody?*"

"I don't think so. Not on purpose. I...I don't want to. I can't. You and Liam and Dominic are just braver than me, it's so easy for you, but I...I just...."

"It ain't easy," Rose said quietly. "It ain't easy for anyone."

He didn't answer. She thought about telling him about the men she'd killed, about how she still saw their dead bodies as much as their living faces in her nightmares, about how guilty and sick she'd felt over what she'd done for ages even knowing they'd given her no choice. But then he'd want to know what they did. So she pushed it all down, and all she said was, "I don't think you're a coward. I just hope—if ever comes to it, and you gotta make that choice—you do what you gotta do."

He nodded. They were getting close now. She could see light up ahead—the shrine.

"Two minutes," she promised him. "Two minutes, an' then you can go collapse anywhere you want, okay? We just gotta—"

"Did they deserve it?"

"...what?"

His eyes were closed. It was taking everything in him to keep going, she could see that clearly on his face. When he spoke, his voice was just a murmur.

"The people you killed...did they deserve it?"

Her stomach tied itself into knots. It was all coming up—the memories, the terror, the sick feeling low in her gut, like a warning that it was happening again—but she pushed it all down. And all she said was, "Yeah. They did. Both of 'em. People get what's comin' to 'em in the end, an'—an' that's what they got."

To her surprise, Kayo nodded. "Okay," he said, and that was that.

She raised her eyebrows. "Okay?"

"If you say they deserve it, I trust you. I know you're not just some—murderer. You wouldn't do something like that...for no reason...."

"Hey. Don't quit on me." She gave him a little shake. "We're almost there."

"Almost there," he repeated, slurring like a sleepwalker. "Almost home."

Rose looked up at the waterfall—and beyond it, above it, to the courtyard that surrounded it.

"Yeah," she muttered, her gut twisting. "Almost home."

He drifted in a pale twilight, floating peacefully, painlessly, through sunlit clouds. Every now and then, he blinked, and his bedchamber appeared before him, swimming in sunlight, in moonlight, in total darkness. Then another blink, and he was floating again among clouds stained pink and gold and blue.

Then, after what felt like weeks, Romero opened his eyes.

He was back.

Reality had become fluid, boundless, tethered only thinly to who and where he was—but then the pain snuck in, a drop of ink slowly spreading to darken the world around him. By the time he realized what it was, it had become a horrible, throbbing, burning pressure on the right side of his chest, as if the blade that had pierced him still weighed heavily on the wound. He groaned, raising a leaden hand to his leaden head.

"I told you."

He let his head fall to the side, struggled to focus. A blonde woman sat with her legs crossed in a chair near the bed, a heavy book balanced on her lap. He blinked, and she grew sharper: bare feet, loose hair over one shoulder, an ill-fitting blue riding dress laced up a well-fed frame.

She looked up at him, her eyes icy, her mouth tight. It took him a moment to recognize the captive Divina. Lucy.

"I told you that you'd want me around if you punctured a lung."

He tried to speak, but the effort made him cough, sending agony lancing through him like a red-hot poker. He groaned and sank back against the pillow.

"You...knew this would...?"

"Not until it was too late to stop it. But these armored buffoons would never have let me warn you anyways." She lifted her foot, showing him the manacle that bound her ankle to the leg of the chair. "Even if I'd wanted to."

"You—were you trying to—t-to get me *killed?*"

She gave a soft scoff deep in her throat. "If I'd wanted you dead," she said softly, "I would have just let you choke on your own blood." She turned back to her book. "Not that you wouldn't deserve it...."

"What...why...?" It cost him a great effort to drag the words out, and his mind kept drifting, but he had to know. "Why—s-save me?"

She watched him for a moment, her expression inscrutable. Then she sighed, shaking her head.

"I don't know," she said. Then she added, almost to herself, "Perhaps I shouldn't have."

The way she talked was odd, somehow, in a way that he could not at first identify—and then he realized it. She was reading, enunciating, speaking clearly and eloquently. She was educated. Part of him remembered, sleepily, that an educated woman was dangerous, and reminded him of all the women who gave him trouble—Marisa, Corrine, Auna, Serena, and too many others to count. Too many women who didn't know their place. But if one of the books she'd read had helped Lucy save his life, he found he didn't mind as much.

He took a breath—or tried. His lung seemed to catch, refusing to inflate. "Can y-you—c-can—"

She sighed and stood up, navigating her way carefully to the bedside table while trying not to trip over her chains. She picked up a small green bottle from the table and held it in front of him, her face twisted in clear contempt.

"Do you know what this is?"

He could guess. No wonder he had been floating for so long. She pulled out the cork and stepped closer.

"You need to sleep until you're healed. Stop panicking, you can breathe just fine...."

She trickled a few drops of the green elixir into his mouth. It tasted strongly of licorice. He swallowed, feeling the numbing effects seeping instantly into his throat. Her eyes were cold, and for a moment, he worried that she was going to poison him.

"I *should* poison you," she said coldly. Had he spoken aloud—or had she read his mind? "But what are the odds of me making it out alive if I did?"

His head drifted sideways, sinking deeper into the pillow. "Bloody woman," he mumbled, his eyes drifting closed. "Should lock her...in the Pit...watch her starve...."

He felt a slight pressure against the bed as the Divina girl leaned against the mattress. "You know," she told him, "I would've thought you were more clever than this." Her voice seemed to drift down to him from a great height. "What were you thinking? It was your *wedding night.* What were you doing forcing yourself on a woman who didn't want you when you should have been in bed with your inappropriately young new wife?"

It was growing difficult to focus on what she was saying. "Not her," he mumbled. "Serena."

A moment of silence. Then the girl sighed.

"It wasn't Serena," she said quietly.

"But Serena isn't *here.*"

His voice broke. It should have been humiliating, but he was too far gone to care. The words seemed to be drifting out of him like smoke, of their own accord, out of his control entirely.

"You're in love with her, aren't you?"

"Always." He didn't even have to pause to think. "I have always loved her. But why...why couldn't she ever...see that? Why did she keep chasing Rel? Just because he would be king...."

"She loved him," the girl said simply. "And she didn't love you."

The mere thought of it was agony. A pain so huge he couldn't wrap his head around it. "But—she—she...."

The girl rested her head in her hand, her elbow resting on the bedside table. She had bags under her eyes. How long had he been out?

"You want to know why I saved you?" she said at last.

He didn't answer. He couldn't. But she told him anyway.

"When I first met you, and I saw that vision—about how you

came to live at the castle. I'd always thought you were a fosterling or some such, that's what all the rumors said. I never imagined the truth. What those soldiers did to your mother and father...and to *you*....It was sickening. I'd say it was monstrous, but...well. Humans are more than capable of doing such horrible things without help. To call it monstrous is an insult to monsters."

What was she...? His stomach twisted as he remembered. She knew. She knew everything.

"I saw it all," she continued, relentless. "I wish I hadn't, but I did. I know you remember it. I know it still hurts. And it's foolish, I know it is, but...I thought maybe, you do all you do because you're in pain, and you don't know any other way to be. I thought maybe you were worth saving. Maybe you just need a little grace."

"Grace...?"

"Forgiveness. Mercy. From the Goddess and from each other. Maybe the Goddess thought you deserved it, too, and that's why she compelled me to help you. Even though my shoulder still hurts."

"...grace." He couldn't wrap his head around the concept. He was floating far above the pain now, soft and warm and peaceful. Grace. It sounded nice. "...because..."

"But mostly I saved you because you're my best chance of finding the prince. There's something in that head of yours that I still need."

"Head...?"

"Don't worry. You won't remember any of this. All you have to do is lay there and talk." She shook out her sleeves, wincing a little as it jostled her shoulder, and raised her hands. "Now. Let's get to work."

R ose watched Alysia hold the needle out with a pair of tongs. As it dulled from white-hot to cherry-red and back to gray, she used the pliers in her other hand to bend the whole thing into a half-circle like a fishhook.

Kayo, slumped against the wall next to her, watched with clear apprehension. A sheen of sweat coated the sickly pallor on his face, and dried blood was smeared all over his bare chest. The makeshift bandage Rose had tied on his arm was already soaked, and a steady stream still leaked out from under his fingers. "Lis," he said weakly, "I don't..."

She shoved a corked flask into his lap. "Drink up," she advised him.

Kayo didn't have to be told twice. He ripped the cork out with his teeth and drank deeply. Rose caught a whiff even from a distance: whatever it was, it was definitely stronger than wine.

By the time Alysia had the needle threaded and ready, he'd drained the whole flask. Rose didn't blame him.

"Wait—Lis—"

"Bite down on this," she told him, and held out a scrap of leather. He did as she said, screwing his eyes shut. "And move your hand."

His left hand spread on his thigh and dug in until his fingers and fingernails turned white.

Rose cringed as the needle dug into his skin. Alysia was quick and efficient—she had clearly done this several times before—and under her guidance, the needle dove in and out of flesh like a dolphin through the waves. But Kayo's whole body tensed with every stitch, and a small, involuntary sound escaped his throat, muffled by the leather between his teeth.

Rose lost count of how many stitches she gave him—nearly a dozen, she thought—before she was satisfied. When she snipped the thread on the last stitch, she immediately poured clear liquid from a large bottle over the wound. Kayo winced and groaned, then sank back, spitting out the pockmarked leather.

"Thanks, Lissy," he said weakly, watching her mop dried blood from the wound before wrapping it in a clean bandage.

"Don't," she advised him. "I'm still mad."

"Sorry," he told her, his eyes drifting shut.

Alysia gave him a look—but not an angry one. Something soft and sad and pained, as if she hated to see him in that state and wished she could make it all go away. The sort of look his own mother might have given him, if he'd had one.

But then she rounded on Rose.

"And *you*," she snapped. "Like we don't have enough work to do without putting new sleeves on your chemise *again?*"

"I was just stoppin' him *bleedin' to death*," Rose said peevishly.

She scoffed. "Easy for you to say—*you're* not the one who has to sew it. And I'm *not* scrubbing those spots out of your dress." She started gathering things up and throwing them back into the basket. "From now on, those clothes are the only ones you're getting. And if you want it cleaned, or sleeves sewed on it, you can just do it yourself!"

And she heaved the basket on her hip and stormed away.

"You're welcome, too," Rose muttered after her. "Goddess, you people...."

She'd had to climb the rope herself and yell for Alysia until she came running. Then it had taken both of them—and all their strength—to haul Kayo up. By the time they had, he was barely conscious. Rose had hastily explained that they'd gotten into a fight with soldiers, but that had only made Alysia more upset, even after she'd explained that they were all dead. Somehow, she'd come out of it convinced that Kayo had done something incredibly stupid—which he had, but Rose didn't know how *she* knew. Apparently Artemis had found her after they left and told her everything, and that couldn't have helped.

She glanced at Kayo. In the light of the rising sun, he looked worse than ever. It had been a long night for her, but far worse for him. She wouldn't have been surprised if he fell asleep right there and then.

But he was awake. She could see a faint glimmer as his eyes opened halfway, then drifted shut.

She swung herself off the edge of the fountain and walked over. He didn't open his eyes as she paused beside him.

"Go away," he grumbled.

She ignored him. Without his shirt, she could see clearly all the wounds he'd gathered tonight—the bruises like ink blots, slowly spreading and darkening over his entire chest, the welts from the spear shaft, the distinctively shaped wound common to the lower city that the soldier's boots left behind. And underneath them, she could see all the scars he always kept hidden.

The largest was the purplish burn scar on his neck—but she'd had no idea how large it really was. It spread across his shoulder and all the way down his side to his hip, a parallel tendril snaking down the underside of his arm. But there were many others: deformed ridges of skin, white lines and blotches, little dots from stitches. She couldn't even imagine how many times he'd been beaten bloody or whipped raw.

Distorted white lines traced an unsteady path along the side of his hand. With a jolt, she realized that those must have been from burning the skin off his palms as he dug through the rubble.

Kayo spoke without opening his eyes. "Either go away or hand me a shirt," he said irritably.

"Can't," she said sweetly. "Dunno where they are."

"Fine. Then take off yours."

"You think I *like* lookin' at you?" she snickered. "You look like meat gone bad."

She *did* like looking at him, though. She liked scars—but only if she didn't think too much about how he'd gotten them. About how it had felt tonight, watching the soldiers hurt him, certain that he was going to die.

It surprised her how much she hadn't wanted that to happen.

"Thank you so much," he said, his voice dripping with sarcasm. "I'll get right on that. I just have bigger problems right now."

"Oh, I'll say. But it ain't yer arm. It's all in yer head."

"Goddess, your *accent*," he groaned. "And I thought Dominic was bad...."

She scoffed. "Oh, please. I ain't half as bad as him." She sat next to him, stretching out her legs and sinking back against the wall. "Least I don't start goin' off in Lyric."

He grumbled, too tired to be truly annoyed. "I guess it wouldn't be properly humiliating without you here. You've got a knack for showing up when I'm at my worst."

"Oh, you don't even *remember* yer worst," Rose said cheerfully. "'F *this* 's botherin' you I'll tell you all 'bout it."

He didn't say anything. His eyes were closed again. She felt a little guilty—had she made him feel bad?—before she realized how ridiculous that was.

"'S fine," she told him. "You've seen me in bad shape too."

He nodded without opening his eyes. "Not your fault. Cuts get infected, things happen...."

But she hadn't meant that. Well, not *just* that. She'd meant when she'd first arrived here, caked in dirt and dressed in rags. Her hair had been so filthy, she hadn't even known what color it was. And she'd called all of them every horrible name she could think of. They'd deserved it, but she still didn't like the idea of that version of her living in their heads.

She watched the growing sunlight, the color of butter and just as soft, creep its way up the walls.

"What a fucking night," Kayo muttered.

That startled a laugh out of her. "Tell me 'bout it. I think Lis is gonna murder you."

He grimaced. "If I turn up dead, she's your first suspect."

"I'll bring her flowers," Rose joked. But she sobered at a sudden thought. "Hey, you didn't tell her where you went tonight. Does she—?"

"She knows," said Kayo hastily. "Artemis too, they were there. But —I didn't tell her about all this. Tonight, I mean. I...I didn't want to worry her."

She just nodded. She had a thousand questions, but she wanted answers to none of them. Not with his burn scars staring her in the face.

"Guess we're never listenin' to Sara again," she commented, but Kayo shook his head.

"No, I—I think I just—don't know what she means. Maybe she doesn't even know what she means. I still need to find a healer. Or I have to find something—a book, or something—and make sure we did it all properly. And then—"

"Can I get some help here?"

Dominic's voice rang out from the sewers. Kayo tried to rise, but fell back, and when Artemis darted out of the kitchen and ran past him, he gave up. They watched as Artemis helped Dominic and his armful of weapons up, then swung her arms around his neck and covered him in kisses before he bent his face to hers. Rose looked away as they kissed, uncomfortable, but looking at Kayo was somehow even worse.

Finally Dominic broke loose and walked over to Kayo, flinging his arms out in triumph. "You're alive!"

"Yeah," said Kayo with a weak smile. He held out his good hand, and Dominic clasped his arm.

"Got all our weapons," he told them both, collapsing on the ground across from them. "Including one of our kitchen knives for some reason." He looked pointedly at Rose, who shrugged and bit back a smirk. "And I hid the bodies, I found some blankets and stuff and put 'em under, no one'll look twice at them until after the outbreak when they start collectin' bodies an' Goddess only knows when that's gonna be. No one raised the alarm so—we're in the clear." He glanced at the flask at Kayo's side. "Got any left?"

"No. Sorry."

Dominic just shrugged. She'd never seen someone so cheerful about hiding bodies and watching his best friend beaten within an inch of his life. "Well then, I'm gonna go find some dreamweed and not share it with *you*. And wash. Ugh. Glad you're okay," he added as he stood. "Oh—and I found this."

He dug something out of his pocket and held it out to Kayo. It was his bracelet. Rose felt at her hair and realized it had come out of its braid a long time ago.

"Oh, shit—sorry, Kayo, I didn't—"

"It's okay. Thanks," he added to Dominic, and plucked the string of yarn delicately out of his hand.

"Must be good luck after all," said Dominic, grinning. "'Night." And he clapped Kayo on the shoulder—gently, though Kayo still winced—and left.

"I—I really am sorry," Rose stammered. "I told you I wouldn't lose it—"

"You didn't. It came back." He held it out to her. "Put it back for me?"

She was happy to oblige. She tried very hard not to glance at the scars winding up his arm as she looped the bracelet over his wrist and tied it. She only knew one knot, but she tied that one three times, just to be safe.

The other bracelets were caked in blood now; this one alone shone clean. She hoped it came out in the wash.

When she sat back, he let his arm fall. "Thanks," he said, and he closed his eyes again. "And—I'm sorry."

She stared at him, blinking. "Huh?"

"For tonight. For everything." He grimaced, and his hand clenched around his arm again, his knees pulling up to his chest. "Dragging you here at all. And how we've treated you. And making you follow all our rules and stay locked up here and everything when you were...were probably just as happy how you were. I really am just —so, so sorry...." He sighed. His head fell back, and he opened his eyes and stared up at the sky. "Dominic was wrong. Tonight was my fault. I was the only reason you were there at all. I dragged us all down that street, and I just—froze. I don't know why I didn't just...*leave*...."

"*I* do," she said bluntly. "Because you wanted to *help*."

He grimaced. "Yeah, but...I can't. I couldn't. I just made everything worse—"

"Y'know," she spoke over him, losing patience. "It'd be one thing if you didn't even *wanna* be like the Beggar's King, if you were just usin' his clothes like you say you are. I *hate* it, but at least you're bein' honest. But this is such *horse shit*."

"What are you—?"

"You *want to be him,*" she said. "You *want* to help people. An' it's killin' you that you don't know how. Am I right?"

For a moment, he looked like he wanted to protest. And suddenly she doubted herself. She'd thought she was right, but—

"Yeah," he said at last. "Yeah—I do. But I *can't.* My family—"

"Your *family'll* be better off," she told him. "If the Beggar's King'd been around tonight, none of this would've happened. We wouldn't've all almost *died.*"

"That's not—"

"Yes it is. The soldiers were scared o' him—only thing I've ever seen them scared of at all. When he was around, they watched their backs."

"They were even *worse.* They were suspicious of everyone, they were jumpy—"

"They were scared," she said savagely. "An' they should've been. The Beggar's King was the only one who ever went after 'em. Without 'im they just—do what they want. You saw 'em. Dominic was practically kissin' their asses, an' it didn't make a difference—nobody did anythin' at all to them tonight, an' they still nearly killed you. If that ain't evil, I don't know what is. An' they ain't got *anyone* to stop 'em, Kayo."

"Maybe, but—Rose, I can't *do* that, I can't do anything *like* that, Liam was—you don't know what he was like, Rose. He was a-a—"

"A what?" she challenged him.

He winced. "He didn't—I mean, for the Goddess's sake, he killed his own *parents*—"

She snorted. "*That* ain't fair. They kinda had it comin', don'tcha think?"

"I don't—" He stopped, turning to stare at her. "How do *you* know?"

"That he was the Fishgut Butcher? I'm not *stupid.*"

"What? No, he—" He started to laugh at the absurdity of it. But then she saw it hit him—and saw the color drain from his face. "H-he wouldn't—no, he wouldn't have—"

"Did you...not know that?" Rose asked him, feeling as if she was missing something.

Kayo shook his head. "No. What—*happened?* I never heard the details...."

Rose sighed.

"Okay—look. I'm gonna tell you 'bout it—an' then we're both gonna shut the hell up about it, forever. Okay?"

"Okay...." He looked faintly sick already. She clenched her jaw. It was about to get a lot worse.

"So, in Fishgut Alley, years ago—there was this place." She watched him out of the corner of her eyes, gauging his reaction. "It was like a...a drug den. A tar den. And a brothel. Both. But they didn't—they used—kids."

She glanced at him, and saw a look in his eyes, sick and haunted. He looked as if he didn't trust himself to speak without being violently ill. She knew the feeling.

"An' the way they ran the place—they *owned* the kids, they bought 'em—"

"Rose, I—I don't want to hear—"

"Well, I didn't wanna live it," she snapped. "I was scared t' *death* of that place, an' it wasn't the only one—I heard all these horrible stories, that they'd take kids off the street—that they didn't care *where* they came from, that this place even used their *own* kids."

Kayo sat up slowly. He was finally seeing where this was going.

"When I was real little, 'fore I was even on the streets, it burned down. An' I got the whole story eventually. An' they said—a buncha kids came out when it started burnin', but none o' the addicts, or the people who owned it. They said a kid came out covered in blood. An' when they went in there later there were—all the addicts had been killed, an' the two people who owned it, they'd been tortured. An' everyone thought the kid, *their* kid, musta done it. An' everyone knew his name...."

"No," Kayo croaked. "*No.* You're not telling me...."

She nodded. "William Adeney, they said it was. I never forgot."

Kayo just stared at her. Then his gaze dropped down to his lap, to his hands—one limp, one clenched.

"He never told me that," he whispered. "I never—he said they were horrible, but I never—"

"Why would he? Stuff like that—it's best left buried," she

muttered, looking away. "But when he died...I heard 'is name, an' I knew it was the same person. Made sense. That's what he did. He—I mean, you all act like it's a surprise, that he weren't right in the head, but I knew. No one woulda been, after that. He was messed up—but he was still doin' right by people. He was still a good person—"

"A *good person?*" Kayo choked. "Rose, he *killed* people. *Tortured* them—and those weren't the only ones—"

"I know—but they deserved it," she retorted. "You look at me an' tell me they didn't."

"I—"

He tried to protest—but he couldn't. He looked away, nodding, and when he spoke, his voice simmered with anger. "They did. If anyone deserved it...it was them."

"Some people do," Rose agreed. "People like that—someone's gotta give 'em what they have comin' to 'em. It's justice. An' it's a warnin'. To others, to-to stop 'em. To make 'em scared. Like they do us."

He drew his knees up to his chest, wrapping his good arm around them, burying his face until she could only see his eyes.

He took a deep breath. "Thank you," he said. "For telling me. I can't believe I...I never knew that...."

"I know. But—what he did *helped* people," Rose told him. "He *was* a good person. An'—an' you could help people too. If you wanted...you saw how things are, an' they're only gonna get worse...."

"I know," he said quietly. "I just don't know if...if it's worth it."

"It's not." He frowned at her, but she just shrugged. "It ain't like it's *easy.* People are horrible. You find the biggest piece o' shit in the world, you can bet he's got gold an' pretty women on his arm an' all that. I mean, look at the king—if what everyone says about 'im is true, that's proof enough. Bein' selfish makes you rich, gets you what you want. But...bein' decent...it's like tryna clean those sewers. You can't do it without gettin' covered in shit. An' eventually it weighs you down, it poisons you—so the people who do it...like the Beggar's King—people who do what needs to be done, an' let it destroy 'em... they're heroes," she said frankly. "They're the only ones who are."

He frowned down at his boots. "You're not really selling it, to be honest...."

"Bein' a good person gets you nothin'," Rose informed him. "You can be happy, or you can be good, but you can't be both. But you already know that. You already are. It's your whole damn problem."

"I—what? No, I—"

"*You're* the one who took in all these damn kids," she cut across him. "You an' Liam both—don't tell me it was all o' you, 'cause ain't nobody else around here bringin' 'em home. An' it's—I mean, they got a home, they got food, they're safe. No one's hittin' 'em or sellin' 'em to a damn *brothel*. They won't ever know what it was like, growin' up how I did, or you did. It's...." She shook her head; she couldn't find the words. "If I'd heard about this place before I came here, I wouldn't've believed it. That you did all this, an' you treat 'em okay, an' you don't get anythin' out of it. But it's the truth. It's—amazing."

He just shook his head. He didn't want to believe it. She gave it one last try.

"Listen—you're *already* killin' yourself tryin' ta be a good person. Tryna be *like Liam*. I mean, you blew up a *princess's ship*—"

"She wasn't *on* it—"

"—an' you dress up like him, an'—an' I don't get why you're tryin' ta pretend like it ain't what you wanna do! Like you don't wanna do even more! I think Liam would've *wanted* you to. An' I saw what you tried to do tonight. I think that's why he taught you how to fight—not just so you could defend yourself, but so you could do this."

"No—he never wanted me to come with him, he never let me—"

"Well, you could be good at it," she told him. "If you just—just *wanted* to, you could take his place. *Somebody* has to. Otherwise things 'll just get worse an' worse...."

He didn't say anything. He didn't even look at her.

Well—she'd tried. But she hardly blamed him for not wanting to get himself killed over people who'd never thank him for it. Some other fool would have to rise up and—

"How do I do it?"

"Wh-what?"

"If I wanted to—to fix things," Kayo said, fixing her with a deep, probing look that put her nerves on edge, "where would I even start?"

"But—*why?*" It was all she could think to say.

He shrugged, then winced. "So I can sleep at night."

She had no idea how to respond to that; it was completely nonsensical. "So...?"

"I have to do—*something. Anything.* So—will you help me?"

"You're askin'—*me?*"

He shrugged. "Who else? Look what you did tonight—in a *dress.* With just a *knife.* You know everything Liam's done, and—and you know what he meant to people. You could—I don't know. I don't even know where to start. But I want to do what he did. I want to help the lower city, I want to make people feel safe. If I'm going to be the Beggar's King, I want to be good at it."

He looked at her, and Rose was shocked to see the sincerity in his eyes, shining like polished brass where the light hit them. Sincerity, and determination.

She actually believed him.

Actually trusted him.

What a fucking night, indeed.

"Yeah," she said, and a slow smile crept across her face. "I think I can help you with that. But first," she added on a sudden whim, "you gotta do somethin' for me."

To be continued...

GLOSSARY

Please see https://theorphanscode.com/the-world/ for more information, including a character list.

- ALRONELIN (al-ROWN-eh-lin): The largest country in the Peninsula. The city of Bermeia is its capital. Current sovereign: King Romero Sangor.
- ALYSIA (uh-LEE-see-ah): one of the orphans. After being kicked by a horse, she barely remembers anything, so she's not sure that's really her name, but it sounds right. Ish.
- ANGELA (AHN-ghell-uh, but it's a Savillan GH, so a soft G): captain of the *Illuminatori*, the ship that Auna Allesino hired to bring her to Bermeia.
- ARTEMIS D'LAURENT (ARR-teh-miss duh-lorr-ENT): one of the orphans.
- AUNA ALLESINO (AWN-uh owl-eh-SEEN-oh): daughter of Eduardo Allesino, the current king of Savilla, and Romero Sangor's fiancée.
- BERMEIA (BURR-may-uh): the capital city of Alronelin, and once the seat of the Conqueror's empire. It was a city-state for hundreds of years and still retains a lot of political independence as well as unique cultural traits.

- CONQUEROR: Jon the Conqueror is a historical figure who lived roughly 800 years before the current era. He and his army conquered the entire Peninsula, ending with Bermeia, and forever changed the cultural dynamic. It's rumored that a full quarter of the current population are his descendants.
- CORRINE (core-IN): the wife of King Romero Sangor's second marriage, which is concurrent with the first. Royalty can do whatever they want.
- COURMA (CORE-ma): A country known for being the birthplace of the Conqueror. It is comprised mostly of islands and sits at the northernmost tip of the Peninsula. Current sovereign: King Romero Sangor, with Queen Marisa Eorhan Sangor as his proxy.
- DIVINA (dih-VEEN-ah): a member of a religious order of women who are healers, scholars, and prophetesses. They are currently exiled from Alronelin and discriminated against heavily in Courma and Lyrma, but hold high esteem in Savilla, Kedarth, and Kypris. Plural: Divinae (dih-VIN-yay or dih-vin-YAY).
- DOMINIC (DOM-in-ick): One of the orphans.
- KAYO (KAY-oh or KAI-oh, depending on who you ask): one of the orphans. Alysia was in charge of naming him and she's only about 80% sure that she got it right.
- KEDARTH (KEH-darth): A country in the northern Peninsula next to Kypris and stuck between Courma and Alronelin, who have fought over it for centuries.
- KHAL ALEEN (CALL uh-LEEN): an island nation between the Peninsula and Riazli, known for its active volcano.
- KYPRIS (KAI-priss): A country in the northern Peninsula next to Kedarth and stuck between Savilla and Alronelin, who have fought over it for centuries.
- LIAM ADENEY (LEE-um ADD-uh-nee): the real name of the Beggar's King, the vigilante who has been terrorizing Bermeia. Also the real name of the Butcher of

Fishgut Alley, or simply the Fishgut Butcher. He's been busy.

- LUCY (LOO-see): A Divina who ran away only to be captured by Auna Allesino and, ultimately, Romero Sangor.
- LYRMA (LEER-ma): A country between Alronelin and Courma that historically both countries have had trouble sharing. Current sovereign: King Romero Sangor, with Queen Marisa Eorhan Sangor as his proxy, treating it as an extension of Courma.
- MARISA (muh-RISS-uh): Marisa Saoirse Éorahn Sangor, the wife of King Romero Sangor's first marriage, which did not in fact end when he married for the second time. She was the princess of Courma before Romero killed the men in her family and took power.
- RIAZLI (ree-AZ-lee): The continent south of the Peninsula. The Riazli Empire has controlled a large portion of it for several hundred years.
- RAFAEL SANGOR (rah-fai-ELL SAYN-gore): the former king of Alronelin and Romero Sangor's brother.
- ROMERO SANGOR (row-MARE-oh SAYN-gore): the current king of Alronelin and ruler of Courma, Lyrma, and the "Greater Peninsula", which is what he calls his empire. Rumored to have joined the royal family as a bastard or fosterling and to have gained the crown under fishy circumstances.
- ROSE (ROWS): the name given quite late in life to a street urchin with a rose necklace and a bad attitude.
- SAVILLA (suh-VEE-ya): The second-largest country in the Peninsula. The Conqueror's rule over it was not as solid as other nations, so there's a powerful cultural divide between Savilla and the rest of the Peninsula to this day, and a historic clash between the Conqueror's cultural influence and the indigenous culture. They're known for being progressive, liberal, and hot-blooded. Current sovereign: King Eduardo Allesino.

- SERENA SANGOR D'COLLINE (suh-REEN-uh SAYN-gore di-call-EEN-ay): wife of the former king, Rafael, and mother to the current heir to the throne. Both she and her son are missing.
- YAZMIN: a small country nestled in the mountains between Savilla and Alronelin. It's only easily accessible from one small port, so it's been taken over by the Riazli Empire until recently. Current sovereign: Marchesa Lorelai Fubali.

TRANSLATIONS

The Peninsula is home to many cultures and languages, and Bermeia, as a port city, is exposed to them all. The characters in the book may not understand what the others are saying, but you, the reader, can.

SAVILLAN

- Amore [love]
- Il mio amore [my love]
- Basti [enough]
- caro/a [dear/darling]
- tesoro/a [treasure]
- Spute ancira sul su punte e te scappo la lingua, curvetza [Spit on this bridge again and I'll tear out your tongue, pig]
- *Il regalo de fiore* [The prince of ? (doesn't translate well)]
- Amica, esso amica, [friend, I am friend]
- ei–sta–bena? [you are–you stay–good?]
- È muerta, Dia mi, è muerta, Antonio è muerta, puertaci furi di qua, piacere–[He's dead, my Goddess, he's dead, Antonio is dead, get us out of here, please–]
- Ch'esa? [who are you?]
- No importi, [not important (incorrect, gibberish)]
- È muerta! [he's dead]

- Mueva [move]
- Che? [what?]
- andiano [let's go]
- si [yes]
- sinnora, va, piacere va [ma'am, go, it pleases if you go (incorrect, but he is doing his best)]
- sinnorina [miss]
- grazia [thank you]
- Me aieta! [help me!]

LYRIC

- N'am bei nan skei, m'leihaan eisbahn cruaidh...[If wishes were fishes, we'd all have full bellies]
- Tian ban'Diie, ciuán dic crúdagh [thank the goddess, holy fucking shit]
- Tà sinn uihe arahn aité. [we're all headed to the same place]

ANCIENT LYRIC

- Soihlasich an durchad, glan a céo, fosgail ad shuleàn, noch an fachad léo. Siohlasich an durchad.... [light the darkness, clear the mist, open my eyes, reveal the unseen]"

Afterword

I have people to thank, but first, a quick note about the book.

The Orphan's Code series is based off of early Renaissance Europe - before colonialism, but after those damn shoes. I just can't with the shoes, you guys, I can't. History fans will know.

Alronelin is based off of France and Germany, Courma is based off of Scotland and Ireland, and Savilla is a blend of Italy, Spain, and Mexico. There's a thick coat of English all over everything because that's the language I do all my research in, and most of the literature about France tends to be in French, et cetera. And yes, I know that's going to make some people so mad, the French and Germans especially, but you guys only hate each other because you're right next to each other, you have a lot more in common than you think, I swear.

There's a lot of info to be found about the world of The Orphan's Code series at the website, www.theorphanscode.com. I highly recommend that if you want some background info or history! It's interesting stuff! And I simply do not have the room here!

There is also a list of anachronisms on the website. In the 19 years I worked on this book, I did a lot of research. A. Lot. Plus I put my castle guy on it. So it's all accurate, except for deliberate deviations and adjustments. (Oh, and the artwork is non-canonical. Sorry. Sometimes aesthetic and my lack of skill > accuracy.)

It's my pet peeve in movies and books when a character gets whacked on the head and is fine. Or they're spitting up blood and somehow recover. No! If you are rendered unconscious by a blow to the head, that's a concussion and it's very serious! If you spit up blood or cough up blood that means there's an injury in your stomach, lungs, or esophagus, and that is very bad! I didn't flunk out of med school to stand for this in my own book! So medical accuracy is important to me. There's already been two major concussions in this first book (well, one concussion and one TBI) and they were not shrugged off. All the bummers of being in a human body are going to play a role, sorry in advance.

Alronelin, and Bermeia, are exactly as diverse as any city would have been. People have always been roughly 10% gay, 1% trans/intersex, 1% autistic, and 10-15% disabled (with 15% ish of those people disabled from birth and a significant chunk disabled due to age). Whether or not they hid it or denied it is cultural, but they were still there. If you have any doubts about that, I encourage you to research queer history. Furthermore, immigrants and travelers from different countries have always been a thing. It isn't inaccurate at all for Bermeia to have such huge populations of immigrants or mixed-race people like Dominic and Kayo.

It is important to note, however, that just because these things existed doesn't mean they have words for them. Some readers really enjoy having modern-day labels in fantasy so there is no ambiguity, but so many of these labels are brand-new and would not have existed for these characters. Part of their struggle has a lot to do with the lack of labels, and instead of "cheating" and giving them words they didn't have, I decided to lean into the struggle, because it reflects my own. Knowing you're different without knowing what to call it or how to define it is its own particular kind of dilemma, and worth exploring. But as of book one, I can tell you for a fact that Rose and Kayo are both autistic, Kayo has depression, anxiety, and PTSD, Rose has cPTSD, and Dominic is both colorblind and legally blind. The characters are still figuring out their sexuality, so that'll be a surprise. There are probably a lot of other autistic characters that I just don't realize I wrote as autistic, and there will be a lot of characters coming with a lot of labels that I can clarify later on.

And lastly, I am always down to talk about this series. It's basically my life. No one ever hesitate to hit me up. That's basically the only part about social media that I've ever liked.

Frankly, if anyone ends up reading this, I will be surprised. I can't believe this is all happening, I keep expecting the universe to pull out the rug from under me like it usually does. But I look around, and my life is–perfect. A publisher is actually encouraging me to write a long book series (terrible idea, I have so much to write!). We moved to the EU (lifelong dream) and now we're German! I have the best little family in the world and a beautiful apartment that no one wanted because it's up six flights of stairs and who even cares if I have asthma it has a beautiful attic and I love it. I have amazing friends and amazing readers. I have meds that actually make me feel like a human. It's surreal! I'm sure I'll be super grateful once I actually believe that this is my life. I keep getting grouchy or depressed or annoyed or whatever like usual and then I'm like, wait what the hell are you doing, brain, we are HAPPY get with the PROGRAM!!! Depression is weird.

I'm torn between excitement and joy and terror (I am absolutely scared to death of saying the wrong thing, I'm autistic, I do it all the time, I can't not do it, but people are not always nice about it and it is making me so anxious) and also being so mad that it took this long and was this hard (although to be fair, I had to write this version for all this to happen and I wasn't able to before, I guess it's about as useful as being mad at my son for staying in the full 42 weeks, sometimes you just gotta let stuff be born on its own time)(except for my son, he got evicted). So so so many things went wrong that weren't supposed to, so many things fell through that were supposed to work. I used to be so frustrated and so jealous but I should've just taken my own advice. Keep at it! Write for you, not for others! There's room for all our stories, each in its own time! It's hard to swallow though. Maybe I'll have more advice when I'm finally convinced that this is actually happening. But for now, all I can say is: if it takes you less than 19 years, you're doing amazing sweetie. And the time will pass anyway.

And if you're the sort of person who just likes to read, and doesn't want to write at all...you got off lucky...but also, what do you do with your free time??? And free RAM??? Other stuff??? That doesn't seem right.

This is where I thank everyone. So here it is: thank you, thank you, thank you. To everyone who supported me, even the ones who just picked up a book and read it without caring what it was. To all the people who messaged me or left reviews and told me that they loved my book. To Brigid Kemmerer, Helen Hoang, and CG Drews, who probably didn't even know how much they helped me. And to my biggest supporters in this endeavor–Abby, Stella, Irem, Joanne, Steph (hi Oliver!), Elora, Lauren, Kevin–you are the best people in the world. And I hope you never, ever, in your entire life, feel worthless or useless or unloved or like you don't have a place in this world, because you made my dream come true. That was you. And it wouldn't have happened without your love and support.

Thank you to Tanya and the amazing team at Oliver Heber and my amazing agent, who all took over work that I would have otherwise had to do myself and are doing a way better job of it. Thank you to Kim, my editor, who really, really believed in me and is the best editor anyone could ask for. This Afterword was written without her help, so you can just imagine how much work she's put into this to make it great. LOT of semicolons murdered in the process of creating this book. Thanks to Sally, who is another subjunctive girlie and therefore immediately one of my favorite people. Thanks to Katherine - I did the illustrations, but she and Hilary did all the real hard work in making the interior. Thank you to Emerence Walraven, who helped me with the blurb (and saved me from a fate worse than death: writing it myself). Thank you to my father-in-law Joe, who not only read the book against all advice, but also did the photography for the original covers.

And my son. Who's the reason I do everything that I do *except* this. This is all for me. But he's my little buddy and he loves me unconditionally and he gives me ten thousand kisses a day. And I hope one day he reads this book (but not until he is much much much older) and forgives me for giving him less attention while I wrote it.

About C.R.R. Hillin

C.R.R. Hillin (she/they) is from Beaumont, Texas and Austin, Texas, but now lives in Bavaria, Germany, where she pretends she isn't three alligators in a trench coat. Originally pursuing a career in medicine, she took a detour into childcare and social work, got kicked out of therapist school, taught science and ELAR, and then ditched all of that to pick up graphic design and disability/queer advocacy. As a proud AuDHD she picks up skills and hobbies all over the place, usually book-related, and is now proficient at digital art, cover design, graphic design, audio and video editing, video game writing, languages (Spanish, Italian, German, French), Tae Kwon Do, and a dozen different softwares as well as writing. Her toxic trait is painstakingly researching any and all things pre-1600 A.D instead of working and then ditching it all to write fanfic instead. She's destined to die petting something she shouldn't. Probably a polar bear, but her husband's cat Weasel is definitely plotting something.